I0535669

BROKEN LIGHTNING
LEGEND OF THE QI SYMBOL

Also by Jonathan V. Cann

Brokən Lightning
legend of the qi symbol

Jonathan V. Cann

Hushed Forest Entertainment
New York

Broken Lightning
Legend of the Qi Symbol

Copyright © 2013 Jonathan V. Cann
All Rights Reserved

This book is a work of fiction. Names, characters, places, and incidents are
the products of the author's imagination or are used fictitiously, and any
resemblance to actual persons, living or dead, events or locales
is entirely coincidental.

ISBN-13: 978-0-9894852-3-4

First Edition

Cover: Paint and etching on copper plate
by Christopher Curry John O'Connell

For Bard, and Bardians everywhere.

Acknowledgements

First and foremost, I thank my editor, Elizabeth Smith, and my cover artist, Chris O'Connell. Whether it was asking tough, smart questions about the technicalities of Linking power, or coming up with a truly brilliant abstract representation of the story's central themes and concepts, they each played a key role in constructing the final product you see here, and I couldn't be more grateful. Thanks also to Steven Tong, who contributed the beautiful Chinese calligraphy seen on the act title pages.

Thank you to Professors Li-Hua Ying, Peter Sourian, and Robert Culp for their many words of wisdom, and for their patience and generosity in dedicating so much time to me and my story. Thank you also to all the other professors who worked closely with me or played important roles during my time at Bard, including but not limited to Bruce, Brad, Rebecca and Kristen. All of you opened up a whole new world for me, and helped make me the person and the writer I am today.

Special thanks are in order for my family and friends, for their support as well as for all the good times and good stories. My mom, dad, and sister, my grandmother and my aunt, Ed and Andi, Ace, James, and more of you than I can name have all had a positive impact on my life in one way or another, especially those of you who were willing to read and talk with me about my writing, and those who made me smile for any reason at all. I count myself truly fortunate to have you all as part of my life.

And, finally, thank *you*, whoever you are, for picking up this book and giving me a chance to entertain you. I hope you'll find it worth your while.

"The Perfect Man has no self; the Holy Man has no merit; the Sage has no fame."
— Chuang Tzu

ACT I

三个自我

THE THREE SELVES

"How's it going up there, Kurt?"

"I've almost got it, Mr. Barret. Don't worry, it wasn't too serious."

"Good. That means it probably won't cost me…the school much, correct?"

"Nobody's gonna break your bank, sir. Look, I'd better get back to it now, though. I'll run down to the office and talk with you about the bill after I'm done."

"Very well. Carry on."

Kurt Ciardi was often on the grounds of Lowval Community College, but he was no student. That life wouldn't have fit him as a twentysomething any more than it had as a teenager. What he was, above all else, was a man with a talent for conducting electricity, and so it fell on him to repair clocks as a representative of Lowval Electric, while rooms full of students and administrators hummed around him indifferently. This profession had been more or less thrust upon him at his grandfather's insistence, but still, he had no complaints.

Kurt was another ten minutes into the job, nearing its end, when a man wearing almost perfectly ironed Dockers, a blue, collared shirt, and a brown tweed jacket came to a stop beside his chair. He looked up, smiled, and waved.

"'Afternoon, Mr. Ciardi," he said.

"Call me Kurt, Blue, I'm not a teacher. What's up?" asked Kurt, without looking away from his work.

"I let my class go early. We weren't really getting anywhere…nobody did any of the reading I assigned for today. Just a heads up, though—in five more minutes, this hallway's going to be crawling with people."

"Not my problem," Kurt said. "The kids are your headache."

"Yes, well…." Blue cleared his throat. "Anyway, how's Lowval Electric treating you? I guess Mr. Garrison hasn't promoted you yet, if you're still hanging around here."

"I got the promotion two months ago. Just a title, is all."

"Hey! Well, that's great. I'm glad they didn't move you to a desk job. I enjoy our little talks—nearly a hundred professors on the faculty, counting visiting nobodies like me, and I still say you're the sanest one around here."

"Whatever, Blue."

At twenty-two years old, Aaron Bluefield was the youngest professor ever to land a job teaching literature at Lowval Community, mostly because he was too young for more prestigious schools to consider anything other than a risky hire. Ever since he'd arrived, he'd struck up conversations with Kurt whenever the electrician came to fix a problem at the school, which was surprisingly often. For his part, Kurt had been a detached witness as the arrogant, fading students of the college continued to eat Blue alive in class. It was a wonder the man still had himself convinced he was teaching.

Crkkk! Tzzzt!

"Whoa!" Blue jumped back and lost his professional demeanor for a moment when the clock shot out a brief waterfall of sparks. Kurt didn't even flinch to avoid it, let alone act surprised.

"Don't worry, I got it," he said.

"Yes…of course you do, I trust you." Blue took a deep breath and exhaled. "I'll never understand how you can be so comfortable getting shocked. No matter how much reading I do on electronics, I still can't seem to program my VCR, let alone reach into it with my bare hands."

"This school's a freakin' firetrap, Blue. Wiring's practically bare. I'm used to getting current in my hands, coming here." Kurt shrugged. "'Sides, I've been working with this stuff all my life. It's just never bothered me, getting shocked.

"Riiiiight. There we go." Kurt cracked a half smile as he always did when he got the stubborn inner workings of Lowval Community to obey him. He snapped the face of the clock back where it belonged and watched as the hands started to move. The time was several hours off, but he couldn't do anything about that—the computer in the main office would reset things eventually.

"So you've been readin' stuff about electrical work?" Kurt asked as he stepped down off his chair. "You want my job or something? You seem pretty happy as a teacher, not that I understand why. Freakin' college kids…."

"Oh, no! Nothing like that. I *am* quite content with my current job. It's just…well, you know that I like to read everything I can get my hands on. Whenever you have lunch with me, I can barely even keep you awake if I start talking about my books! Speaking of which, I skipped lunch today, so even though it's late, I'll buy you a sandwich if you've got time to stick around."

But Kurt had barely put his tools away when he felt a vibration at his waist and heard four beeps go off in pairs of two. He reached down and unclipped his pager from his belt, read the tiny screen, and furrowed his brow. He wouldn't have the luxury of falling asleep in front of Blue today.

"Another emergency call? I must be the only one working this week." Kurt shoved the chair off to the side, out of the way of the impending traffic. "Do me a favor, Blue? Run down to the office and tell Barret I'll mail him the bill. I wanna get this other job done before quitting time."

"I'd be glad to. Oh! And here…." Blue grabbed the electrician just before he would've walked away and thrust an envelope into his hands. "This is for you—I'm glad I got to see you in time! Tomorrow night, I'm going to be having a small dinner party and get-together at my apartment in Hightop; directions and everything are in there. Well, it's not so much a party as it is an excuse to surround myself with people and make it less obvious that there's only one lady I really want to speak to…but I digress. I'd be very happy if you would come, you…being my only local friend and all."

"I'll think about it. You know stuff like this isn't really my thing," said Kurt. He stuffed the invitation into his left pocket.

"Yes, I know. Nevertheless, I thought it would be friendly of me to ask. If you find yourself bored and wanting to get out of your house tomorrow night, just know that you're welcome."

"Sure…uh, thanks. I gotta go now, Blue. Take it easy."

"You as well, Mr.…Kurt."

Blue stood in place for a moment and watched Kurt rush to the nearest exit. Soon, though, the bells rang, and the professor was lost in a sea of chattering youth.

*   *   *

Kurt went straight from the college to his next pressing job, after checking with the boss to get the address and details. Some elderly man had tried turning on one too many appliances at once or something, and now none of them would work. It was probably just a tripped circuit breaker, as simple to fix as flipping a switch in the basement back and forth, but for some reason, the man had insisted on getting help from Lowval Electric. What was more, even though Kurt didn't recognize the client's name, he had apparently asked for Kurt specifically. Mr. Garrison had said that he must be getting a good reputation, which was good for the company, and that he had to keep it up. Kurt would do what he was told.

It was a strange house on the outskirts of town, and despite having lived nearby all his life, Kurt had never noticed this particular property. The gravel driveway took a steep dive away from the road, and the house sat at the bottom of a grassy depression, carved out over centuries by a small stream. The water had been rerouted through a stone-bottomed path, which directed the flow into a little waterwheel, into and out of an ornamental pond, then all the way around the house and back into the wilderness. The building itself was cream colored, with a black roof made from half-cylinder shingles, which curled up in triangular points at its four corners. The windows and front door were made of a light-colored wood; there was no doorbell, so Kurt had to knock gently.

No answer. He knocked again, a little less gently this time.

"Mr. Song?" he called, hoping the man was near the front of the house. "Mr. Song! It's Kurt Ciardi from Lowval Electric!"

Kurt continued knocking for another minute or two, intermittently, and then he tried the knob. It was locked. Annoyed, he turned to walk back to his van, get his phone, and call the boss, but was immediately startled—there was an elderly Chinese man blocking his path. From the look of his posture, he'd been standing behind Kurt the whole time, watching him try the door with no success.

"You assume I would be in the house, because that is what you are used to, and also because that is where you will do the work that I called you to do," said the man. "I prefer to be outdoors, however. It is much purer here…I feel closer to the Earth."

"Uhh…all right, Mr. Song. But would you please let me in now?" asked Kurt as politely as he could, forcing professionalism over his bemusement. "You can stay out here while I do the job, if you want. All you have to do is show me where it is."

"Very well. You are committed to your trade, and I respect that." The man walked up the front stairs and opened the door; he turned and smiled at Kurt, beckoning him to follow. "And please, if you must be formal, call me Laoshi."

The house was unlit, but not dark. The décor inside was a lot less Asian than the exterior, Kurt noticed, as if Mr. Song had remodeled only the portion of his home that a casual passerby might see. The one exception was a room they passed on the way down the hall—it was closed off by double doors, which, like the walls immediately around them, appeared to be made of thin, white paper.

The breaker box was in the garage, which connected to the back of the house. Kurt knew the problem was there, so he put on blinders and got right to work. It turned out to be a more complicated job than he'd predicted—some of the wiring behind the box's faceplate was dislodged, and some of it had burned out completely, showing evidence of a fairly serious power surge. Kurt became even more focused, not even looking down at the pockets of his tool belt as he reached for new wire, solder, cutters, pliers, and all the other things he would need to get the job done. At any given time, he would barely be aware of which was in his hand—all of them were the same, extensions of his person and his mind. He had been doing this practically since infancy, and was no stranger to the technique, which he had learned to improvise to a great degree.

He lost track of time as he repaired and rerouted wires, picturing in his mind a living river of power that bent at his command, but all was said and done in about forty minutes. He snapped the faceplate back on the breaker box and flipped the master switch, smiling with satisfaction as a light bulb behind him projected his shadow onto the wall.

Only once he turned around again did he notice that Mr. Song had stayed in place, watching him.

"All done, sir," Kurt said, a bit unnerved but still sticking to his script. "I'll have my supervisor mail you an invoice, all right? I'm not exactly sure what to charge you for this job, but I'll put in a good word for a fair price."

"It is more art than vocation to you, is it not?" asked Mr. Song, as if he hadn't been paying attention. "You have an…affinity with the force of electricity. It is as if you feel what it feels, know what it knows, and wish to give it what it needs and desires. This is why you are a master of your trade, just as Cook Ting was the master of butchering an ox. Do you know that this is why I requested your aid in my home this day?"

"Well…um…thank you, Mr. Song—"

"Laoshi, please, young man."

"Right. Thank you…Loww-shirr," said Kurt. "Listen, it's my quitting time now, so I'd like to go home if there's nothing else important."

"Permit me one question first," said Laoshi, raising his palm. "Are you a man who believes in fate—that all of our actions and their consequences are preordained from life until death, from the beginning until the end of the world?"

"Uh…I don't see how this is—"

"Give an old man his amusement, if you would be so kind."

"Well, fine then. No. I don't believe in fate," scoffed Kurt. "The only person living my life is me. I make my own choices."

"Ah! But this is not so, is it? You let those around you guide your choices, whether or not you wish to be subordinate. Otherwise, you would not have your job, would not live in concert with your fellow man, and would certainly not have come here to see me.

"In one sense, your approach is to be admired—in the Chinese tradition, the sage knows his place, and he is at peace letting the world ebb and flow around him without allowing it to affect him or throw him off. This is the greatest harmony one can achieve, but you are not yet a sage, because although you let the world ebb and flow around you, you do not have a sense of your place in it. It is as if you stand in the middle of a great stream, but do not grasp that it is your perch upon a rock that keeps you from being carried off."

"Look, I—"

"Hold on a minute, my good man. How is it that the rock saves you, even though you do not know it? It is because it knows you. Just because you have not recognized your place in the world does not mean that it does not recognize you. This is why your mind and hands are at home among wires, connectors, and the power of electricity, like the lightning that falls from the sky. This is why when you are thrown into the stream but do not struggle against it, you drift to the rock nonetheless. You need only look down at your feet and see what saves you, and you will know it as well as it has known you all along."

"Huh." Kurt couldn't help but laugh a little. "Guess you believe in fate, then."

Laoshi smiled. "No. I do not believe in predetermination any more than you do, Kurt. However, I do believe that certain actions beget certain consequences, and vice versa. Because of the way things are, certain other things are bound to be. A man can avoid these things by force of will, but he will be less whole for doing so. We all know what we must do, lest our hold on the rock begin to slip. Remember, the true sage knows his place, and thus comes to find it."

"Okay, old man. It's been fun, but it's already five-fifteen and I don't work for free. So I'll see ya next time you have a power surge, all right?"

Kurt closed up his tool belt and walked around Laoshi toward the door. As he went by, though, the aged man reached out and grabbed his right hand. Kurt felt a sudden jolt of horror, but before he could react enough to pull away, Laoshi had examined his palm with intense eyes, then released him with a little pat.

"Do you know, Western culture is quite fond of giving names to everything…to bathe all in light and leave no shadows to trace the contours and shapes of things. I, however, see the things I encounter through the points of the Way—the yin, the yang, and the other, which is the yin and yang turning in harmony. Westerners call the three selves in all men the id —the man who desires to be happy; the superego—the man who desires to be virtuous; and the ego—the interaction of the two which makes a man a man," said Laoshi. "From the vantage point of the yin, you cannot see the yang, and vice versa. But from the vantage point of the other, the ego—the true self—the yin and the yang need have no difference."

"Whatever. We'll bill you."

Kurt stormed through the hallway, out the front door, and back up the hill to his van. He was done being delayed. He made himself laugh again and shook his head. He'd visited some weird customers over the years, but Mr. Song was the first one he would actually have called insane. Kurt hoped someone else would be available to take the next job at this house.

*   *   *

"Kurt, is that you?"

"Yeah. Hi, Grandma." Kurt came into the kitchen and hung his black jacket across the back of the nearest chair. His grandmother was working over the stove, preparing a dinner of pasta and homemade tomato sauce. She turned around to give her grandson a quick smile, and he walked over to lay a hand on her shoulder in kind.

"Papa's out back, chopping up another limb off the old maple tree." Grandma sighed. "I swear, he's gonna make himself even older from all this work he's been doing. I almost wish the tree would run outta limbs, just so no more would fall!"

"Another one blew down in the storm last night, I guess?" asked Kurt. He craned his neck around to the window and caught sight of Grandpa wiping his brow in the back of the yard. "I'd say we have too many storms, not too many limbs. And these have gotta be strong storms to knock down branches that thick."

"Maybe you should go talk to Papa. He could use some help anyway, but now he thinks that every one of these limbs has been hit by lightning. He says he's starting to notice that the tree is burned where they fell from."

"Huh. This I gotta see. Don't worry, I'll make sure we're both back in time for dinner."

"Ten minutes! Whether the wood is chopped or not!" Grandma insisted, mainly for Grandpa's benefit, Kurt knew.

Kurt heard the screen door squeak and crash shut behind him, but by then, he was already halfway across the yard. He followed the old stone path to its end and continued to the farthest point on his family's property, where the fence disappeared into the trunk of a massive, old, and stately maple tree at the edge of the wilderness. The tree was beginning to look rather bare now, and Kurt's grandfather was correct—it was also charred at every place from which a limb had fallen. Kurt heard the *thock...thock... thock* of the axe grow louder as he approached, and when he walked up, Grandpa used his arrival as an excuse to take another break. He was showing great fatigue, but the limb on the ground appeared almost as complete as it might have looked on the tree, despite his efforts.

"We're gonna need another garbage can, Kurt," he said with a chuckle, gesturing toward a brown tub that was already almost full of scraps.

"Maybe we should save some for firewood," Kurt said. "So...lightning, huh?"

"You can see the burns right in front of you," said Grandpa. "I tell you, Kurt, I've never seen anything like it. Four storms in a week, every other night. Gone by morning like they were never there—not even rain on the ground. Just another branch to chop up every time."

"And another hernia for you, if you keep trying to do it all by yourself while I'm at work. Look at how little you got done on this one, you're so tired from the last three." Kurt took the axe and buried its head in the remaining wood. "Come on inside and eat dinner. I'll help you finish up after."

"Yer a good boy, Kurt." Grandpa patted him on the back. "So, how was work today? You said you were going over to the school again."

"It was just another broken clock. Didn't take long. After that, I fixed a breaker box for a crazy old man who went on about fate and…rocks in rivers, or something."

"Ehh ehh ehh!" laughed Grandpa. "That's the way it is, Kurt. There's a lotta nuts out there…look at me, how I'm getting senile in my old age. Was the guy from Lowval?"

"Yeah, his name was Song. He lives in a weird Chinese house on the west side."

"Huh. Never heard of him…."

The conversation continued into and through dinner, changing shape, topic, and speaker dozens of times during its lifespan. Before long, the plates were cleared, the wood was chopped, the sun had set, and it was time to head upstairs to bed.

*   *   *

Kurt could always tell when he was halfway between waking and sleeping. Snatches of conversations from throughout the day—moments spent with his grandparents, Mr. Song, and Blue—replayed themselves persistently in his mind, interspersed and out of order. The chatter denied him rest. The more tired he became, the more his imagination bled into his thoughts, conjuring for him a slideshow of how the old maple tree might have looked as it was struck over and over again by lightning without a rainstorm.

And then, he felt a pull against his hand, a sensation both real and unreal. It was like a muscle ache he couldn't rub out, a tug coming from within, as though a ghostly presence had taken hold of his palm through the meat itself. Something was pooling there, trying to break free—he knew it on a primal level. And then, suddenly, he found himself standing dockside in a city he'd never seen before.

It was a majestic place, taller than it was wide, shinier and colored differently than any city he knew. The buildings looked as if they were carved from smooth stone—glassy, golden and purple. Kurt realized he must be on a boat, and then his view began to pull back, although he didn't feel the waves rocking him. The boat moved into the ocean behind him at a delicate speed, but almost before Kurt knew it, he was far enough away to see that the city was rested on an island, with only water visible in all directions. There was, however, a plume of black smoke drifting over the horizon—perhaps that marked the mainland. Whatever fire was fueling it must have been fantastically huge.

Kurt perceived that the city was changing, fading from him. He tried to describe it to himself—it was sinking, burning, collapsing, exploding— but he felt frustratingly unable to strike to the heart of the matter. Then, all at once, he was inside the city somewhere, watching a woman in a lavender gown and cap weep from despair, rage, or maybe both; Kurt wasn't sure. He saw on her breast a necklace, from which there hung a white stone no bigger than a battery, and inside the stone was inscribed a symbol that burned itself into his memory. The woman turned to face a man made of the same black smoke that still poured over the horizon; Kurt saw that he had red eyes, but otherwise no face or body. His ethereal form was a shape and nothing more.

He had it: death. That was the word for what he was witnessing. This city and its inhabitants were dying.

With that realization, Kurt felt a will, a need gathering itself within him, and at last, he gave in to the pressure persisting upon his hand. He raised his palm high, eager for relief, and saw the skies above him darken. He wasn't scared—this seemed to be a benign sort of darkness, unlike the smoke, the red-eyed man, the death.

He felt something flash up through him and then out from his palm, bringing with it a visceral rush he couldn't have described if he tried. The clouds reacted to his call and swirled like instruments in a conductor's orchestra, and a kite-shaped symbol appeared on his hand, glowing golden in a manner that made it seem almost to be floating above his skin. Kurt knew, however, that it was a part of him, and as twin points of yellow-white light chased each other around the symbol's edge with rapidly-increasing speed, he saw a network of intricate lines flash into being at its center.

Lightning struck.

Then Kurt awoke. His eyes clung to the ceiling, the details of his room acute as he reeled from what he'd just experienced. His breathing was the only sound in the house. Something compelled him to turn toward the window—he was just able to make out a pulsing red glow near the back of the yard. It took him a few moments to figure it out, but the old tree had been hit again.

Ohhh. That's what it was. The storm was getting to me. Kurt leaned against his headboard and laughed quietly. *Geez, I thought lightning was never supposed to strike twice. We're almost up to half a dozen here!*

But then he realized he'd been scratching at his hand: it felt itchy from an unfamiliar irritant. Abruptly tense, he raised his palm to his eyes and gasped away the last of his lingering sleep. Although the dream had faded into memory, the kite-shaped symbol was still there, and although its circling lights and flashing had lessened in speed, its golden glow was as bright as ever in the waking world.

*   *   *

Morning came. Kurt forced his eyelids open millimeter by painful millimeter, unsure when he had passed out again. The last thing he remembered was a moment right around dawn, when fear, denial, and exhaustion had combined to blur the line between reality and his troubled dreams. The light coming from his palm had seemed like a hallucination, a trick of his tired mind, too terrifying to actually exist. He'd become unsure that he'd ever woken up completely. He must have clenched his fist, talked himself into doubting what he'd seen, and shivered his way back to sleep.

Thankfully, it was Saturday, the beginning of a weekend off from work —Kurt turned to his clock and saw, with a start, that it was almost 12:30. The process of sitting up, leaving bed, and walking to the bathroom was agonizingly slow. His eyes wouldn't focus. As he brushed his teeth, shaved, and washed his face, the only task that received his full attention was keeping his right hand closed.

But a dread curiosity was building in him—he knew that he couldn't avoid looking forever. His movements slowed and then stopped, the hissing of the running water echoing off the walls into his ears. Kurt took a deep breath, opened his palm, and turned it toward his face.

The symbol was still there.

It wasn't glowing anymore. As a result, most of the intricacies within it were invisible; Kurt thought, through the leaden feeling that had settled in once he was sure the symbol was real, that they might have just been the natural creases of his skin illuminated. The main, kitelike outline of the mark had turned from the brilliant yellow it had been the night before to a dull bronze. It looked like a burn scar, except that it wasn't raised quite enough above the surrounding flesh, nor did it have the proper texture.

In my dream, it made lightning come toward me, Kurt remembered.

More guarded than afraid now, Kurt resumed his morning routine and finished washing his face. He let the water keep running afterward, cascading over his hands like a river kissed the rocks. He watched the swirls and drops play on the symbol, marveling that he felt no disturbance from it at all, neither pain nor pleasure, nor even an itch anymore.

I was on the ocean...there was an island sinking...why didn't I feel the boat moving?

Suddenly, the symbol lit up. Kurt cried out and jumped away from the sink—he'd felt it again, that buzzing sensation from the dream, amiable perhaps, but still an intrusion upon his body. An instant later, he was being sprayed directly in the face with water from the tap, and even though he kept backing up, he couldn't seem to escape it.

"Aaaaaahh! Stop, stop!" he shouted, as if the water would obey him. He couldn't think, his attention divided between trying to block the stream and shaking his right hand in an attempt to make the odd feeling and the strange light go away. Finally, with a loud swear, he was forced to give up for the moment and raise both hands in front of his face so he could hold off the water enough to open his eyes.

He felt his chest tighten. The water was bending out of the faucet into the air, flying in an impossible, arcing trail that ended by impacting the glowing symbol, spraying droplets everywhere. That was why Kurt had been getting sprayed more while he was flailing about—the stream had been following his hand.

Puk puk puk! There was a knock at the door.

"Kurt? Is that you? Everything okay?"

"Yeah, Grandpa! I just cut myself shaving and—now I spilled water on the floor! I'll clean it up!"

Kurt wasn't usually a liar. It wasn't something that came naturally to him, but desperate times, he supposed, created unusual necessities. Lying was hardly the strangest of things in that bathroom, and Kurt's mind was only half on the story he fabricated as he spoke it, so its urgent detachment helped make it sound more convincing.

"Okay! Let me know if you need any help!"

Kurt was sure his grandfather could hear his nervous panting right through the door, over the sound of the rushing water still spraying from the flume that connected his palm to the faucet. For all he knew, his panic was loud enough to be picked up from across the house—it certainly felt strong enough. Now there was even a new dimension of fear: if he couldn't stop this and get out of the bathroom soon, his grandparents would get suspicious.

And then they'd find out. And then he didn't know what would happen next.

Grandma and Grandpa'll have a heart attack if they see this! It'll kill them! And what if it kills me?! *What if they have to take me to the hospital and cut off my hand?! No, I can't let this happen, I've gotta make it stop! Please stop! Please, please stop! Please, God, let it—*

The power of will, apparently, prevailed. The water spout broke up and splatted to the floor. Kurt couldn't move at first, for fear that he'd accidentally start it up again. Slowly and carefully, he turned his hand around to examine the symbol—it was still there, but its flashing had slowed down. The faucet was still running, but only because Kurt hadn't shut it; he stepped over to the sink and did just that, afraid to press his luck.

I gotta clean this! he realized. *There's water on the ceiling! They'll know something's up if they see that! But I'm waiting too long, they'll come up here again looking for me if I don't get downstairs—daah, but I gotta hide this thing first!*

Kurt leaned down and grabbed some toilet paper, wrapping it around his hand like a bandage until the symbol was obscured completely. He'd already said that he'd cut himself shaving: he could specify that he'd actually cut his hand while picking up his razor after dropping it. The lies were piling up, but he told himself it would be better for his grandparents this way.

By the time that train of thought had played out, Kurt was already downstairs and halfway to the kitchen, where he smelled pancakes. He'd shut the bathroom door behind him, hoping that his grandparents would stay out until he had a chance to excuse himself and return to clean up the mess.

To Kurt's surprise, he found his grandmother helping his grandfather put on his jacket. She was already dressed—they were going out.

"Good morning, Kurt!" Grandma greeted him. Then she laughed, and corrected herself. "Or maybe I should say good afternoon! How come you slept so late? You haven't been in bed past twelve since you were a teenager!"

"Uh, I guess I just had a rough night. Storm woke me!" Another lie. "Where are you guys going?"

"She's—"

"I'm taking Papa out to see a movie, so he won't break his back chopping wood all day. Another limb fell off that tree last night, Kurt!" said Grandma. "I'm starting to think there's a lightning rod in there!"

Kurt stiffened. *In my dream, it made lightning come toward me…!*

"Besides, it's been too long since we've gone to an afternoon show," Grandma finished.

"I'm deciding what movie we see! She already agreed to it!" Grandpa insisted.

"I know, honey." Grandma leaned toward Kurt and stage-whispered, "You know how he is. He always wants it his own way, and since I'm making him go in the first place, I had to promise to let him pick the movie."

"You heard it! Kurt, you're my witness!"

"Go warm up the car if you wanna pick the movie so bad! We're gonna get there and everything will have already started!" Grandma gave Grandpa a light shove to get him moving down the hallway. "I saved some pancakes from breakfast, Kurt. They're on the stove, under the tin foil on that plate there."

"Thanks…." Kurt felt a pang of remorse for his lying. "You're too good to me, Grandma. You too, Grandpa. You treat me like I'm still your little kid, even though I'm working and—"

"What's this? This isn't like you, Kurt! You don't have to pretend to be all gushy just 'cause I saved you breakfast!" Grandma came over and pinched his cheek. "Yer a good boy. You don't have to prove it to me. Been years since I hadda tell you that!"

Kurt made himself smile. "Thanks."

"I'm gonna pee before we head out," said Grandpa. "Nana, you go wait in the car. My keys are on the hook."

Kurt felt his face twitch. *No! Don't use the bathroom!*

Fortunately, since he was already in his coat, Grandpa had no reason to go back upstairs—he used the downstairs bathroom instead. Kurt still couldn't relax, though. He started unwrapping the pancakes even though he didn't feel hungry, just so he wouldn't be standing around looking nervous. As it turned out, the only other words that passed between grandson and grandparents were brief goodbyes, yelled across the house from kitchen to foyer.

Kurt crashed into the nearest of the kitchen chairs as soon as he heard the front door close and lock. The waterlogged mess in the bathroom hadn't been discovered. It was incredible luck that his grandparents were going to a matinee: after the lies he'd told, Kurt almost felt guilty for catching a break. But this was his chance to examine what was happening to him in greater detail, figure it out, and find a way to take care of it without worrying anyone.

He ripped the toilet paper off his palm and exposed the symbol again. When he thought about it, his grandparents hadn't even noticed the bandage.

The symbol had stopped flashing completely now, and was back to the scarlike appearance it had borne when he first saw it that morning. He remembered how thinking about it, focusing on it, had seemed to awaken it, but no matter how anxious he felt, he was at a loss to turn away.

I've never heard of anything like this before…it's like magic. Is it magic? he wondered. *Why does it bring things toward me? Am I making it happen somehow…?*

And the symbol lit up again.

"No!" Kurt shouted; he threw his arm away from his body, and turned his head in the other direction. "Nononononono stop! Stop! Stop stop stop!"

He felt that strange humming sensation again. Suddenly, his mind was split into two warring halves: on the one hand, he was scared of this phenomenon and knew he had to get rid of it before anything bad happened, but on the other hand, something about it felt good. He found himself beginning to enjoy the warmth coursing through his body, and a part of him started tentatively reaching into it, curious to explore, understand, discover….

The feeling became stronger, reacting to his interest, and Kurt pulled away like he'd just touched a hot stove.

"Stop! Stop stop STOP!"

Once again, his willpower and his fear were stronger. The glow died down, and this time, Kurt shoved his whole arm back through his sleeve and into his shirt. There would be no more exploration, no more curiosity, and most importantly, no more destruction.

But I have to find out what it is! How else am I gonna get rid of it?!

The emergency room was out of the question: if something was terminally wrong with him, Kurt didn't really want to know, and besides, if he went to the hospital in a small, rural town like Lowval, his grandparents would certainly find out. He briefly thought of looking up a diagnosis online with the computer in the living room, but without knowing what the symbol actually was, he'd have no idea what words to use to search for it.

Kurt felt alone for the first time in his life—he needed help and companionship, things he'd never particularly wanted or sought before. But now he knew that the only way to put this to rest was for someone to tell him that everything would be okay, someone smart enough to figure out exactly what this symbol was but trustworthy enough to keep it a secret.

He jumped up from the table and ran down to the laundry room to dig through the pockets of the pants he'd been wearing the previous day.

*   *   *

"This is a nasty burn scar. Or…." Aaron Bluefield paused; he let go of Kurt's hand and looked the man in the eye. "What is this, anyway? How did you do this to yourself?"

"I was hopin' you could tell me! You're smart—you're a professor teaching kids who're only a year or two younger than you, and you're always telling me you read a lot…." Kurt's face scrunched up. "It was there when I woke up this morning. I had a dream about it…it made lightning come toward me. And then this morning, it made water come toward me. You ever read about anything like that, Blue?"

"Huh. Well…." Blue stood up. He'd found Kurt sitting on a fallen tree limb in the Ciardis' backyard and was tired of crouching in the dirt.

"I'm flattered you would come to me for help, Kurt, I really am! But I've never seen an injury of this type before. It looks like a scar, but it isn't…." Blue shrugged. "I'm sorry, but I'm at a loss."

"Great."

"Well, let's not give up altogether!" Blue added quickly. He didn't want to paint a hopeless landscape for one of his only friends, especially when that friend was looking so distraught. "My interest is piqued, and like you said, I always enjoy expanding my knowledge. Just because I don't know something doesn't mean that I can't. Maybe we can figure it out together! Tell me everything you do know, for starters."

"I already did." Kurt sounded annoyed. "I had a dream last night. There was a city on an island and it sank. Then I saw this thing on my hand and it was glowing, and it made lightning come toward me. Then this morning, it was still there, and it made water come toward me in the bathroom. It lights up if I think about it too much, so I'd better stop."

"It…lights up?" Blue knelt back down on the ground and reached for Kurt's hand. Kurt put up a fight at first but then surrendered.

"What do you mean it made lightning come toward you? Or water? I mean, obviously, strange things can occur in dreams, but in the bathroom this morning?"

Kurt said nothing.

"Can you make it happen again? Maybe then I'll understand," said Blue.

"No. We're lucky it hasn't happened with me talking about it!"

"Kurt. If you want me to help figure this out, I need to see it." No answer; Blue pressed the matter. "Listen, as a student and as a professor, I'm willing to believe in a lot of things. I've read about strange phenomena from all over the world. But if you expect me to believe that your palm lights up when you think about it, then draws the elements in toward you, I'm going to have to see—"

"Fine!"

Kurt jerked his hand out of Blue's grasp and pointed it at his face instead.

"Here!"

Without really knowing what he was doing, Kurt let go of his inhibitions and willed the exact opposite of what he'd been praying for and holding in all day. He told the symbol to light up, and when he felt that pleasing warmth run through him, he reveled in it. It was as if he were truly experiencing it for the first time, in all its mysterious glory. It seemed to flash out from somewhere in his torso, his core, spreading in an instant to every corner of his body, then arcing back in and centering on his hand.

Perhaps because he pushed the phenomenon out of him this time, the symbol didn't just light up—it flashed to attention with a brilliant burst that set the spinning lights and flickers in motion with gusto. There was a sound like a metallic, echoing whisper.

Blue fell over backwards at the sight, but he was off the ground and on his feet immediately. He froze for a moment in an awestruck stare, then dove back toward Kurt and grabbed his hand again, bringing the symbol in close.

"Incredible!" he said.

"Ha! Well, I'm glad you think it's exciting. For all I know, I'm gonna die!" said Kurt. Blue was deaf to him for the moment; the symbol was all he could think about. He watched its pattern closely, observing every change in state that the lights cycled through. The flashes seemed to occur whenever the two points of light that ran around the outline of the symbol returned to their starting positions at its top and bottom, meaning that the faster they moved, the more often the flashes occurred.

"You say it draws elements in your direction?" he eventually asked again.

"Elements? When did I say that?"

"Well, natural elements, I mean…I've heard lightning and water referred to in that way. May I see that as well?"

"Aaawww, no! When that happened before, it took the whole time I waited for you to get here to clean up the bathroom! And I'm pretty sure it's my fault that lightning keeps hitting this tree here. The last thing I want is to—"

And then, the sky turned dark. The clouds rolled in quickly, like sand pouring over glass. The wind picked up, and the air around Kurt and Blue became stormy. Blue glanced at the symbol: its activity had increased again. After that, he stared upward as if he were seeing God.

"Hey! Knock that off!" Kurt had turned his hand around and was yelling at the symbol. "I did not ask you to do that! No more lightning! No more water spouts! All I wanna see out here is air and trees!"

He paused and looked up at Blue. "Wait, is air an element?"

As soon as Kurt had that thought, the winds swirling around him coalesced, and seemed to pour directly from the sky into his hand. The force of the concentrated gale knocked him backwards off the log and pinned him to the dirt. Only his palm was still raised, both shielding him from the winds and continuing to provoke their attack.

"It's true…!" Blue cupped his hands around his mouth and shouted, "Kurt! To what degree can you control it?!"

"What do you mean?!" Kurt called back, his voice muffled.

"Does it just draw elements toward you, or can you control them in other ways? Can you make the wind blow in a different direction so it helps you stand instead of pushing you down?!"

The wind changed; Blue presumed that Kurt had willed it so. Sure enough, his friend rocketed back to a stand as if he'd been violently pushed. In fact, he kept right on moving forward until he slammed face first into the ground on the other side of the log. After that, the wind died down. Blue looked up and saw that the clouds were parting, albeit more slowly than they had arrived. It seemed like this task was taking more effort.

"Shutting it off is the hardest part," Kurt confirmed, rolling over on his back and rubbing his aching nose. "That's why I didn't wanna turn it on the first place!"

"But you just proved that you *can* control it! Kurt, that emblem on your palm doesn't just draw the elements toward you—it allows you to direct them!" Blue said, breathless with excitement.

"So? No matter what it does, I didn't ask for it! And look how hard I have to try to stop it—no! Nonono, I'm not thinking about it anymore!" Kurt willed himself.

"My point is, Kurt, whether or not you 'asked' for this, I think you can safely stop seeing it as a threat to your well-being. You've been granted superhuman powers! I'd call that beneficial," said Blue.

"Who cares?!" Kurt exploded. He stood up and stuck his hand into his pocket, so he could take his mind off it a little. "All I wanna know is where the hell it came from, what it's doing to me, and maybe how to get rid of it!"

Blue couldn't help but smile. "'Maybe?'"

"Look! The point is that I can *not* let my grandparents find out about this. I called you over because I wanted to make it go away before they have a chance to, but you don't know any more about what this is than I do!"

"Not yet, but we're on a roll so far. We've already figured out that you can control these powers, at least to some degree. I mean, we'll have to experiment more with that later, but for the time being, let's concentrate on the 'how.' May I see your hand again?"

Kurt extended his arm; Blue grasped his wrist and guided Kurt into turning the symbol several different ways.

"Hmmm…it's really quite complicated once it's lit up," he remarked. "It reminds me of some Celtic markings I've read about—they're called runes…but then again, what we're seeing might just be the way the basic symbol is lighting up the rest of your hand. The emblem itself I almost want to say looks Asian…it reminds me of the roofs of some Japanese houses…but I've studied a number of Asian languages, and this doesn't look like a character that belongs with any of them—"

"Whoa, whoa. Hold up." A dark look came over Kurt. "You said Asian, right?"

"Yes. Why?"

Kurt yanked his hand away and stalked across the yard. "Go start your car, Blue. I'll be right back, as soon as I find a glove to wear over this hand!"

*   *   *

Birds took off out of the trees around Mr. Song's house as the pounding echoed through the small depression of land. Kurt was relentless: he punched at the front door with both hands, then switched to kicking when they started to ache. When he tired of kicking, he punched some more.

"Kurt, he's clearly not home," said Blue.

"Yes, he is! He doesn't even have a car, so where would he go? He's just hiding 'cause he knows I figured him out!" Kurt continued his barrage. "Open up, old man!"

"Just because I said your rune looks Asian doesn't mean that this customer of yours has anything to do with it," Blue said for what felt like the fiftieth time. "You told me that you thought he was crazy at first. Maybe he *is* just crazy, and it's only a coincidence."

"You don't sound sure of that at all!" growled Kurt. "Admit it, it makes too much sense! He was talking about me having a knack for electricity, like lightning, and how my fate would find me or something. He did this and he's gonna undo it!"

"Not if he won't even see us."

"He doesn't get to not see me!" Kurt stopped pounding momentarily. He looked around the garden and spied a large, decorative lump of granite at one end of the flower bed. "Hey, Blue! Is that rock an element?"

"Um…well, earth is an element, so I suppose that counts—"

"Great!" Kurt actually grinned as he tore off the black glove that had been obscuring his palm and activated his symbol again. "I hope he's had his fun screwing with me, 'cause I'm about to use his rune to smash open his front door!"

Now that Kurt knew he was in control, he assumed he'd be able to latch on to the rock and hurl it easily. Sure enough, as soon as he willed it, the rock began to glow a pale yellow, and it levitated about an inch off the ground. But that was as far as it went. It continued hovering laboredly, shaking as if it were having a hard time holding this admittedly unnatural position.

Blue was puzzled. He looked at Kurt and found his friend straining and sweating as if he were trying to bench-press a great weight.

"Maybe you oughta back off, Kurt."

"This is…stupid! I…changed…the sky this morning…without even meaning to!" grunted Kurt. He was unwilling to give up, but the rock was barely moving; it would never have the speed to break down a door. "I could lift this rock with my…hands if I wanted to! So…why is it…so hard to—"

"Stop!"

Startled, Kurt dropped the rock. Mr. Song had come around the side of the house from the backyard, just as he'd done the day before. Blue was afraid, at first, that he and Kurt were about to be accused of vandalism, and rightfully so, but then he saw that the man's expression was concerned, not angry.

"You are not ready to control something so large in your weakest element," he said to Kurt. "The path to self-realization is not so long as some would tell you, but it is not traveled overnight in any case. You might do yourself more harm than good by overreaching in this early stage."

The surprise wore off. Ignoring Blue's shouts, Kurt charged forward and grabbed the old man by his shirt, lifting him onto his tiptoes. He brought their faces close and glared into Mr. Song's eyes, then pushed him back a little so he would have room to shove his rune between them.

"What the hell did you do to me?!" he demanded, his voice louder than it had ever been in his life.

"I did nothing," Mr. Song responded, calm as ever. "I merely pointed out to you those things which I knew to be true. However, I could sense last night that the time for you to manifest was not very far in the future."

"Manifest?! What does that mean? You'd better start giving me some answers, Laoshi!"

"Laoshi?" Blue was surprised. "Kurt, have you studied under this man?"

"No! What the hell made you think that?"

"Well, I learned a little Chinese when I was in college…and 'Laoshi' means 'teacher'!"

"Ha! I already told you, this guy's just one of my crackpot customers!" Kurt spat. "Laoshi is just what he said to call him!"

"It is good that I have patience," Mr. Song spoke up. He was still calm, but now he sounded authoritative as well. "One of us must, if anything is to be learned today."

Kurt turned back to him, but paused. He studied the man's face carefully, but could find no way to read what he was thinking. Gradually, and still restraining massive rage, Kurt released Laoshi and took a step back.

"I am willing to be your teacher in this. I always have been," said Laoshi.

"Does that mean you'll tell me what I wanna know?" asked Kurt, still on-guard.

"I will tell you all that I can. Some things in this life are not so simple—again, you are accustomed to the Western idea that all can be expressed in words." Laoshi turned and walked past Kurt and Blue to his front door. "All I can teach you are facts—the truth about your situation, and the goal which will arise for you as a natural result of that situation. The shape and truth of that goal, and the nature of the path taken to reach it, you will decide for yourself, in your own time. I cannot choose your future for you, nor would I."

Laoshi opened the door and went inside. He didn't gesture or say anything more, yet his movements were so deliberate that he drew his guests in behind him.

He brought them to the paper door Kurt had passed in the hallway the day before. Inside was a tearoom with a wooden floor; a tiny, low coffee table sat on a small rug at the room's center. There was a hot plate in the far corner, on a wooden stand—apparently, Laoshi had a teapot ready in advance.

Long scrolls filled with Chinese characters adorned the walls, one in the middle of each of the four. As Kurt sat down beside Blue and edged up to the table, he got the disturbing feeling that the scrolls were staring at him, and at his rune.

"I must say, I'm quite eager to hear your explanation, now that it seems you actually have one," said Blue, breaking the silence. "Kurt's… transformation, I guess I should call it, is extraordinary! If you are responsible for it, I want to know about it inside and out, just as much as Kurt does."

"There's no way you're as 'eager' to hear this as I am." Kurt was still just barely holding himself in check. "Right—Laoshi, this is Blue, he's a professor. Don't hold anything back from me just 'cause he's here. I don't care what he knows."

"Aaron Bluefield." Blue extended his hand upward as Laoshi came over with the tea tray. "Despite the odd circumstances, it's a pleasure to meet you."

"And a curiosity, I gather, for one who seeks knowledge as you do." Laoshi put the tray down and shook Blue's hand. "Your friend is very polite, Kurt, and it is a good thing that you have brought him. I will hold nothing back from him."

"Good," said Kurt.

"However!" Laoshi paused to pour out three cups of tea, then took a drink from his own. "He is incorrect. As I said, I could tell when I met you that your time to manifest was approaching…I knew even sooner, to tell the truth. It is why I made certain to meet you and begin to prepare you in advance. But the power you see flowing through your body and out your hand is yours, and has been since your birth."

Laoshi stared hard into Kurt's perplexed eyes. "Through your fear, I am certain you have still experienced happiness as a result of this power. It may have been new and unexpected, and your unwillingness to accept it may have prevented you from having full control over when the flow stopped and started, thus unsettling you even more. But your power brings with it a good feeling, which entices you in spite of these fears. Am I wrong?"

"No," Kurt admitted, after a brief pause during which he could feel Blue's gaze on him. "You're right…yeah…but why is that?"

Laoshi took his seat then, and his eyes drifted downward as he continued sipping his tea. Blue had tried it and found it to be not half-bad; it was a Chinese blend that had sort of a calming flavor. Kurt was too preoccupied to try any, and his grew cold while Laoshi continued.

"You are what I would call, in my language, *qi ren*, literally 'qi person' in yours. Qi is the energy of life—of the soul if this description suits you better—and to feel this energy rushing through your body and out your hand, which is the point at which qi can be made to exit the body, is a profoundly pleasurable experience. All living things possess qi, but clearly not all can do what you have done today...at least not yet."

Another drink.

"I have heard a different translation of *qi ren* into English—this word is *Linker*. I use it because it seems as accurate a description of the... mechanical truth of your power as English is likely to give you. A mechanical approach is the only understanding of Linking that your brain is likely to accept from an outside source such as myself. So I will use it to open the gate, that one day you may reach true understanding on your own, from the inside out.

"The world has energy, the same as any of the living things that inhabit it, but its character is expressed differently. The rocks on the ground, the water in the streams, the wind that moves the clouds...everything you see around you is an expression of the qi of the world, just as your hands, eyes, and motions express the qi within you."

He drank again. Kurt was grateful for the pause; he had been feeling the concepts Laoshi spoke of begin to escape him. This was his chance to catch up.

"Remember what I told you about the yin, the yang, and the other. There are seven Linking elements, and six of them are pairs of... complementary forces, as the yin and yang. These are water and fire, wind and void, lightning and earth. The first of the elements in each pair are the Light elements; the second are the Dark elements. All are expressions of the world's qi. *Qi ren* such as yourself can manipulate the elements with... individually varying degrees of ease and...magnitude, by putting some of their own qi into the world and accepting some of its qi in return."

"Forging a link," said Blue. He smiled hungrily. "Fascinating...!"

"Hang on, I just remembered something," Kurt said. He was considerably calmer now, and had been studying his rune for the last few minutes. "Yesterday, you said it wasn't a coincidence that I became an electrician even though I never really tried to be anything. Does that have something to do with me being a...Linker?" He still wasn't quite used to the word.

"You are thinking with…totality. This is good." Laoshi nodded. "Every *qi ren* naturally has one dominant element. For you, it is lightning. Your command of it is almost effortless, and I would venture to guess that your job is largely mental, even largely artistic, from your point of view, as I told you yesterday."

"I never really thought about it before…." But Kurt knew that Laoshi was right again.

"Lightning is the rock in the stream—that which knew you even before you knew it. Despite this, any *qi ren* may become at least somewhat proficient with all of the elements. For you, whose dominant element is one of Light, the other Light elements will come easier and more completely than the Dark elements. Earth, the element opposed to lightning, will always be your weakest—this is why I cautioned you against overstraining outside my home today."

"Laoshi, you spoke of a seventh element. What is that?" asked Blue.

"Ah—just as the other six elements are the yin and yang, so the seventh is the other. The seventh element is qi itself, which is not only the bridge that connects Earth to man and man to Earth, and therefore the meeting point of the *qi ren* and the element he Links to, but is also the Spirit of the *qi ren*. Qi is the energy that connects body and soul, and which also embodies the soul. It is the other in the sense that it is the ego, the person born from id and superego, desire and duty. Qi represents the yin and yang turning together at the highest level, in all their many forms."

"Slow down for a second! None of this answers the most important question!" Kurt held his rune up in the air again. "Maybe everyone has qi, but why am I the only one with a rune on my hand that lets me actually do all this stuff?! Why am I the only Linker?"

"You aren't," replied Laoshi.

"What?" Blue's curiosity was suddenly overwhelmed by shock.

Laoshi finished off his tea and set the cup aside.

"The world is falling out of balance, and has been for some time," he said, his gaze fixed down on the table. "Because it desires to remain in balance, the world reaches out in its hour of need. Remember, just as you can put some of your qi into the world, so that you may Link with it, it can give some of its qi to you. You are unusually strong in your ability to Link…the strongest, in fact. So it is you the world has reached out to, and thus the ability for you to trade qi with it has been opened."

"You have got to be kidding!" Kurt sprang up from his seat. "You're saying that there's something…world-endingly bad happening right now, and I'm the one who has to save the world?"

Laoshi stood as well and began to clear the table. "The balance must be restored."

"What?! What are you saying I actually have to do?!"

"I cannot answer that. I do not know. All that I am certain of is that the world does not come out of balance on its own—that is not the Way of nature. Only men can threaten the balance, and thus only men can end the threat. The moment of greatest crisis may be some time away yet, but as the world deteriorates further, it will cry for help even more desperately, and even more Linkers will begin to manifest. Because balance is what the world wants, and also because balance is the Way in which the world conducts itself, the Linkers will always come in pairs, one of which will be strong in the Light elements, and one in the Dark elements."

Laoshi returned the tea set to its stand and turned back to Kurt with a serious look on his face. "I can guarantee you, somewhere in the world, the strongest Dark Linker manifested today, at the same time you did."

"So you're saying there's an evil me out there someplace?!" Kurt exclaimed.

"Ah…I cannot tell you how to interpret the events that will soon begin to transpire around you. But remember, from the position of the yin, the yang cannot be seen, and vice versa. Only from the position of the other do both appear as one. You, as *qi ren*, both contain and embody the other. You must learn to master this if you are ever to complete the task the world has set before you. However, this is only the truth that I know from my studies—I cannot teach you how to proceed, because that truth will be written by you."

"Congratulations, you lost me. Look, this is all too much for me anyway!" Kurt ran his hand over his forehead and back through his hair. "If you don't mind, I think I'm gonna go home and lie down now. Unless you have any more 'facts' that might help me figure out all this stuff you 'can't teach me'…."

"I will leave you with this thought—today, you already have taken a step in the right direction. Do not retreat from your instincts, but do not run toward them, either. And remember that there is more than one type of Link that can be forged. All that is required is an even trade of qi."

Laoshi smiled thoughtfully. "At one time, I had quite a collection of papers and legends that spoke of Linking from various points in history, manifesting itself in various cultures the world over. Unfortunately, I lent them to another promising student some twenty-five years ago, and have long since given up hope of seeing them again. I trust in the Way, however, to ensure that they have gone or will go where they are needed."

"Ha! You really had me going with this 'Way' stuff until you said that, 'cause if it was true, I'd have them!" Kurt rubbed his head again. "Come on, Blue, let's go. You haven't heard the last of me, though, Laoshi! I'll be back to ask you more questions whether you like it or not!"

Kurt let himself out, leading Blue along. Blue stopped just outside the tearoom door to wave goodbye, but moments later, the old man was left alone regardless. He was still smiling in that same knowing way.

"You will be all right," he said. "You already have everything you need. It is how you use it that will determine your fate, and the fate of this dying world."

ACT II

凯拉

KAYLA

She ran. Through day and night, through campus, city, suburb, and country, this was the only constant: she ran. She would stop for food or sleep periodically, but as soon as these necessities were taken care of, she'd start running again, like a race car coming out of the pit with tailpipes blazing. She was always checking back over her shoulder, looking for a pursuer that was never there.

But she ran on.

*   *   *

"Good evening, Blue! How are you?"

"I'm fine, Mr. Ciardi. Yourself?"

"Hey!" Kurt's grandfather waved a dismissive hand and insisted on taking Blue's coat. "I've told you a million times, Blue, you can go ahead and call me Grandpa. Everyone else around here does—I barely remember my real name anymore! Ehh ehh ehh!"

"I'll try and get used to that soon, I promise," said Blue.

"You've been coming here six months, and I say it every time. I'm not holding my breath." Grandpa laughed again and patted Blue on the back. "Ehhhh, I'm just kidding, Blue, you know that. Kurt's in the TV room."

"I thought so. Thanks, Mr…um, Grandpa!" tried Blue before he awkwardly slunk away down the hall, while Grandpa continued chuckling behind him.

"Hi, Blue! Dinner will be ready in a little while." Grandma was filling up her big pot with water and placing it on the stovetop.

"Oh, thank you! I brought you a loaf of bread from the bakery in Hightop." Blue detoured into the kitchen to bring it over and place it on the cutting board beside the stove. "I really do appreciate you feeding me all the time. The least I can do is contribute once in a while."

"You're sweet, Blue, but it's no trouble at all. A young man like you shouldn't starve to death just because he's living alone!" Grandma winked at Blue. "Speaking of which, how is Sarah doing? Are you still seeing her?"

"Actually, no. We broke up last week," said Blue. He shook his head, and his eyes became sad for a moment. "It just wasn't…well, see…she told me I never 'act my age,' except I think she…never mind. I'm pretty much over it now."

"Aw, I'm sorry, Blue. Why don't you go sit with Kurt and get your mind off it?"

"I think I'll do that. Thanks, Mrs. Ciardi."

The TV room was just outside the kitchen, on the other side of the hall, and its door was closed. Blue could hear the television even before he got close enough to turn the knob, so it didn't surprise him that Kurt was endangering his hearing yet again by blasting already-loud shows. He *was* surprised to see Kurt sitting on the couch against the back wall, pouring glowing electrical energy between his hands like liquid. His rune was fully lit and very visible.

"Hey," he said.

"I…geez, Kurt!" Blue jumped into the room, trying to block any view Kurt's grandmother might have been able to get from the kitchen.

"It'd be easier to close the door," said Kurt. "Never mind, I'll do it." He held up his hand, allowing the yellow energy to dissipate, and called up a powerful but localized wind that shut the door behind Blue.

"You're…getting a lot better at that. It didn't slam this time," Blue said, still recovering. "Your control is getting more and more fine. I just wish you'd be more careful, if you still plan on keeping this a secret."

"Don't sweat it. I've been Linking around the house and at work for months now, and no one's caught me." Kurt smirked. "I wasn't ever a high-profile guy, so why should Mr. Garrison notice something different about me now? Sure makes my job easier, though. I can get stuff done a whole lot faster, letting the power put itself in the right place. Half the time I don't even need to touch the wires anymore."

"So you've told me. It's really remarkable, Kurt—your whole career, you've worked by imagining that electricity bent at your will. Your subconscious was preparing you all along for the day you could actually do that!" Blue shook his head. "But I still don't see why you won't tell your grandparents."

"We've been over this, Blue."

"Those two are the nicest, calmest, gentlest people on the face of the Earth," said Blue. "I don't understand why you're shutting them out in a situation where it would be beneficial, not to mention much easier, to seek their support…."

Silence.

"Y'know what? TV's boring tonight." Kurt stood up and slipped on the single black glove he'd been using to hide his rune every day since it had appeared. If anyone had noticed, they had either kept quiet or chalked it up to a strange new fashion statement.

"Let's keep talking upstairs. I'll show you some of what I've been practicing." Kurt grinned, and whacked Blue with one of the small couch pillows he'd been leaning on. "Oughta be more fun for you like that, anyway. You get off on learning new stuff, especially if nobody else knows it yet."

"Um…right. Okay." Blue became flustered. "I wish you wouldn't put it like that."

"Ha!"

Kurt peeked into the kitchen and told his grandmother that he'd be in his room with Blue but would make sure to come back down in time for dinner. With that, the two friends disappeared upstairs; they didn't speak again until they were behind the closed and locked door.

As soon as he kicked a few articles of clothing aside to clear up the floor, Kurt removed his glove and smiled as he felt the rune flash back to life, qi gathering in his palm. The more he got used to Linking, the better it felt, and the better it felt, the more open and exploratory he was willing to be with his powers. In this manner, with the occasional encouragement from Blue, he'd been able to accept that he had a desire for the feeling, and from there, turn the desire into skill.

"Last time you were here, you were worried that I wasn't doing any practice with earth stuff, so maybe I'd stay too weak with that element," said Kurt; he smiled in such a way that Blue could tell he was hiding something. "Welp, I tried picking up some rocks and stuff outside one night when my grandparents went out, but it just got me tired real fast. Like, *really* tired, where I felt like I hadda stop Linking for a couple hours."

"Presumably, that would get better with more practice," Blue said. "You should just keep at it, whenever you have the chance. I know it's not often, since you can't really do it inside very well—"

"Or, I could try to come up with another way to use the earth element. Remember when we figured out that this—"

Water flew across the room from a full glass on Kurt's windowsill; Kurt kept it there for Linking, since water wasn't readily available indoors unless he wanted to suck it out of the pipes through the walls. He made the liquid flow through the air into the shape of a donut, which then froze solid and dropped down onto the carpet.

"—means water plus cold wind equals ice?" Kurt finished.

"Yes. There's no reason two elements can't be used together, and it was quite a revelation when we discovered that you could also control the temperature of the air you were Linking with." Blue paused. "Are you saying—?"

"I thought it might be easier if I put earth together with something else. Here, look at this."

Kurt walked to the left side of the room and moved the area rug next to his bed aside, exposing a mark beneath it. Blue was intrigued—it was an impression in the shape of the rune.

"I'm not really sure, so I wanna hear what you think, but…I think this one is earth plus wind plus void."

"Void?!" Now Blue was riveted. "I thought you were still having trouble figuring out what void is! I'm not sure I've ever even seen you use it successfully!"

"Yeah, but it got me thinking when you brought over that book about science like two weeks ago…."

"You mean the article about empty space in molecules." Blue grinned. "Kurt! Don't tell me you found a way to put my theory to the test!"

"Yup! Proved ya right, too, but you're smart, so I expected that." Kurt took a few steps away from the impression on the floor. "So you said that even solid stuff is actually mostly empty space, right? At first I thought maybe I could bring the empty space in stuff to me like the other elements and…I dunno, maybe hide in it and be invisible or something. But that didn't work. So then I thought, well maybe the empty space doesn't move, but maybe *I* can move *through* it."

"Interesting! That's really a good idea. How does it work?" Blue asked. "And what does that thing on the floor have to do with it?"

"It's a pad…I guess it's an exit, really. Here, it's probably easier for me to just show you."

Kurt raised two fingers to his forehead, and his rune flashed. In less than a second, he disappeared, fading through a gray shadow of himself almost too quickly to be seen, and then reappeared standing on the "pad." It was only a movement of several feet; he could have accomplished it just as quickly by walking. Still, the quiet whistling sound the Link made, coupled with its suddenness, got the desired reaction out of Blue—he almost fell over.

"Good lord!" He was sputtering with excitement. "That was incredible, Kurt! How far can you teleport? Can you move through solid objects?"

"Way ahead of ya. Empty space in everything, remember? There's another pad hidden in a bush out back. Go to the window." Kurt raised his fingers again and was gone. After he got over his shock, Blue charged to the other side of the room just in time to see Kurt poke his hand through a thick shrub on the far end of the yard, waving toward the house. He teleported back to the bedroom seconds later, fearful that his grandmother would see him through the kitchen window and wonder how he'd gotten outside without passing her.

"See, what I figured was that maybe I could make, like, a permanent Link with some earth that didn't need me to move anything," Kurt said. "It doesn't make me tired to have the pads around—I just let the world keep that part of my qi for a while, or whatever. But I can only manage three of them at a time. I tried to make a fourth one, and the first one disappeared. Felt it happening, too. I gotta picture the place where the pad is in my mind to go there, but I just couldn't picture four at once. Oh, and I think wind's part of this, too, because I feel like something's gotta blow me through the empty space and stuff so I can get where I'm going."

"Astonishing. It is simply astonishing that you discovered this power. I would never have thought to try warping, Kurt! And if what you're saying is true, about how you can see your path through the empty spaces in molecules, being blown toward an exit point bonded to the earth, well… you've used one of your strongest elements to bind two of your weakest! It's really an amazing accomplishment."

Blue squinted. "Where's the third pad, if you don't mind my asking?"

"Hidden under the upstairs bathroom mat. Y'know, in case I gotta go in the middle of the night and I don't feel like walking all the way down the hall." Kurt chuckled. "Grandma and Grandpa almost never use that bathroom anymore, so I don't think they'll find it by accident."

"That's…wow. That's just amazing. I can't get over it!"

They grew quiet then, out of things to say for the moment. Kurt moved the rug to re-cover the pad, then sucked some electricity out of the nearest wall socket, through the air to his hands. He began playing with it absentmindedly like he'd done in the TV room.

"So, you ever wonder why I live with my grandparents?"

"Um…." Blue was surprised at himself. "No, I guess I never gave it much thought. It just seemed to be the way things were."

"Heh. Well, it's because my parents died when I was five months old. Car accident down in New York City…they flew right off the highway into the East River along with the car that hit them. I was the only one who survived."

"Oh…Kurt, I…well, I'm not really sure what to say. I'm sorry, of course—"

"Don't be. You didn't do anything," Kurt said. "My dad didn't have any other family, but my grandparents lost their only daughter. They were real protective of me when I was a little kid…that's why I didn't do anything they didn't want me to. They made things easy for me, so I didn't really mind. But I knew if they worried even a little bit about losing me, they'd be worrying about losing the only other family they had. They never talked about my mom, and I've never even seen a picture of her, but I think that says a lot more than if they talked about her all the time."

"That's awfully astute of you."

"Huh? Eh, never mind. The point is, they'd be worried if they knew what was happening to me now, and the older they get, the more dangerous it is for them to be worrying." Kurt threw the electricity back into the wall socket.

"True enough, I suppose." Blue's mouth twisted. "That's why you haven't gone back to Laoshi all this time, isn't it? It's because you're afraid of what he might tell you you have to do to restore the balance."

"Since when was he gonna tell me anything? It's 'my future,' remember? 'Sides, I just don't like talking to that crazy old fart." Kurt moved on to practicing one of the harder Dark elements: fire. With a snap of his fingers, he could create a flame in his hand, but it was no larger than the flame of a cigarette lighter. He tried to play around with it, make it take other shapes or at least stretch itself out.

"Laoshi told me I hadda be on my own, so I'll be on my own! With you giving me ideas for new things to try, I'm getting more powers outta the rune every day. Besides, he said stuff would come to me no matter what, so I'll deal with saving the world or whatever when it's time. If he's even right about that. Just 'cause he taught us what Linking is doesn't mean he knows everything—this world-balance stuff could just be some crap from one of those legends he hasn't seen in twenty-five years. As far as I'm concerned, the rune is just something that makes my life easier until it either goes away or my job as a Linker drops into my lap."

"Look, I'm sorry…I won't ask again," said Blue. "It's your decision whether or not you tell your grandparents, regardless of your reasons. I respect that."

Kurt grunted—the flame in his hand had gotten bigger, but not by much.

"Dammit! Fire isn't getting any easier at all this week! How can I do more with earth and void than I can with fire?" Kurt gave up and shut off the flame; he got over his frustration shortly afterward and smiled at Blue again. "Hey, enough worrying about the heavy stuff, all right? I got something else to show you."

"Aha! You worked on using your qi as a separate element, didn't you?" Blue remembered suggesting as much to Kurt a few days earlier. "I'm eager to see what you've done with it, especially after the way you got creative with that teleportation trick."

"Yeah…but first, remind me again why you think it's safe to even try this? I've got something, but I haven't actually followed it through all the way yet," said Kurt. "You said something out of that religion book…."

"The Daoism text, right. Well, it says that you actually have two kinds of qi—your original qi and your body qi. Nothing about Linking should touch your original qi, which is permanent and tied to your soul, and your body qi should always regenerate, so I doubt there's any danger in trying to project it away from you. In theory, it can only make you stronger in the long run, just like the rest of your practicing."

"Okay, then…I've been trying to trap qi between my hands like this." Kurt clasped his hands together, sticking both his thumbs upward and both his pointers and middle fingers outward. It looked as if he were holding a gun. Blue began to hear a faint whine from the space between Kurt's palms —qi was indeed gathering, like a camera's flash charging up.

"See...I think...." Obviously, this was a strain for Kurt, both because it was a new experiment, and because he was still a little afraid of it. "I think that maybe...if I close my hands together all the way around...except at the base of my fingers...I can force the qi up and out through there like a bullet."

"Yikes! Well, don't point your qi gun at me!" Blue said. "Don't point it at the walls, either—we don't know anything about the physically destructive power of qi as a separate element. Here, I'll go open the window and we'll pray it's not so bright that someone notices."

"Hm. Didn't even...think of that. And Grandma's right down at the kitchen window, probably," said Kurt. He drew his qi back inside his body. "Do you think maybe we should try this another time? Maybe at your house instead?"

Blue didn't answer—he was hunched over at the window, staring out.

"Kurrrt!" he yelled, in a rising voice of alarm.

"What?" Kurt just scrunched up his face at first, but then he walked over to Blue to see what was the matter. He followed his friend's eyes and saw almost immediately. There was a girl lying in the backyard grass, not far from the scorched and nearly limbless maple. She was facedown and apparently unconscious.

"Shit! We'd better go see if she's okay!" Kurt ran to the door and pulled his glove on as he pounded down the stairs. Blue was right behind him.

"Who is she? Do you know her?" he asked.

"No, I don't think so! I don't have a clue what she'd be doing here!"

Grandma looked up when she heard Kurt and Blue charging through the hallway and into the kitchen, on their way to the back door.

"Everything okay, boys?" she asked; she knew the answer right away. "What's wrong?"

"Nothing, don't worry about it! Just gotta do something in the backyard quick!" Kurt shouted on his way past. He tried his best to sound reassuring, or at least calm, even as he felt himself failing.

It didn't take long for Kurt and Blue to reach the girl. She had blond hair that ran down a little farther than her shoulders, and looked to be no older than twenty-one. Despite their ragged and dirty appearance, her clothes had once been stylish, and she was wearing an expensive-looking red backpack with a brown leather stripe at the bottom.

"She looks like some sort of student!" Blue said.

"Well, do *you* know her?" Kurt asked as he knelt down beside her. She appeared to be in okay condition, besides being exhausted enough to pass out. He reached for her wrist to get a pulse.

"No! She doesn't go to Lowval Community, I don't think, but she looks too old for high school…God, but still so young! This is awful!"

"Don't worry, she's just tired, as far as I can tell. Maybe she's a runaway or some—"

Kurt stopped. His body became rigid.

"What? What's wrong?!" asked Blue.

"Blue…look!" Kurt held up the girl's right hand by the wrist; she had a strong pulse, but that wasn't what was important now. On her palm, plainly visible, was a rune identical to the one hiding under Kurt's glove.

Blue jerked forward. "She's a Lin—"

"Kurt! Blue!" It was Grandpa; he wasn't much for running, but he still managed to cross the yard from the back door at a brisk pace. "Nana was worried, so she sent me out here to check on you. What's going on? Who's this?"

"Nobody! Uh—I don't know, but it's okay! She just fainted, probably from being too tired or something!" Kurt was about to hide the girl's hand and her rune, but just before his grandfather got close enough to see, he felt the arm pull away from him on its own.

"She's coming around," said Blue. He knelt down and helped her into a sitting position. "Hello? Are you all right? You seem to have fainted…."

"Mmmmm…hm? I…fainted?" The girl was still very groggy. But then, all of a sudden, she snapped into awareness. "Oh, my gosh! I'm so sorry, I didn't mean to fall asleep on your property! I have to go, excuse me…."

But when she stood up, she swayed on her feet and couldn't find her balance. If Grandpa hadn't reached out to catch her, she would've fallen again.

"Whoa, hang on! You're in no condition to go anywhere right now, sweetie," he said. "Why don't you just calm down and come inside with us for a while? We're your friends…we'll call an ambulance if you need one."

"No! You—you don't understand! I can't stay in one place too long—I can't go to a hospital because they'd keep me there! I have to keep running!"

"Why? Is someone chasing you?"

The girl hesitated, but then replied, "Yes...my boy...my ex-boyfriend."

Grandpa's face darkened. "Was he hurting you? Is that why you were running from him?"

"Yes. That's why," the girl said quietly. Grandpa put his arm around her.

"Don't worry. You're safe here," he assured her. "Come inside now... we were just about to sit down to dinner. You can stay here tonight. We can call the police for you tomorrow, or whatever you want us to do to help you. What's your name, honey?"

The girl sniffed. "Kayla...thank you, sir. Thanks so much...."

"Call me Grandpa...and don't worry. I'm glad to help."

The four of them walked back across the yard and into the house, where Grandma had just finished setting the table. Kurt kept his eye on Kayla's right hand the entire time; he noticed that as soon as she got the chance, she slid it into her pocket and didn't remove it again. He glanced at Blue, who just raised his eyebrows and shrugged. Obviously, he was still too concerned for the girl's safety to be questioning the truth of her motivations.

Maybe everyone else was convinced that Kayla was earnest, but Kurt knew that she had at least one thing to hide. She was already on his bad side for worrying his family and disrupting their routine. If she went so far as to let her rune be discovered, Kurt would never forgive her, no matter how deep his curiosity was about finding a second person with the same powers as himself.

*   *   *

"Kurt, honey, would you hand me that extra pillow from next to the couch?"

"Sure, here you go," said Kurt, passing the pillow to his grandmother. They were in the TV room, continuing a long process of gathering and redistributing practically every piece of bedding in the house to make room for two overnight guests—with how late the conversation at dinner had gone, it was decided that Blue should stay, too. He'd happily accepted a place on the Ciardis' couch, curious as he was to see how this all turned out.

"Doesn't Kayla have enough pillows and blankets yet?" Kurt asked.

"Don't sound so annoyed, Kurt! She's been through a real tough time," said Grandma. "Besides, these are for Grandpa. He let Kayla borrow some of his stuff, but he needs something to sleep on, too."

"Do you need any help carrying things upstairs to your bedroom, Mrs. Ciardi?" asked Blue.

"No, that's all right, hon. Me and Grandpa are gonna go to bed now. You two can stay up if you want—just shut off the TV when you're done."

Grandma kissed Kurt's cheek, then pinched Blue's on the way out the door. The young professor blushed and said a quiet goodnight.

"I wouldn't worry too much, Kurt. She seems to be handling this stress quite well, and so does your grandfather," Blue said, once Grandma was upstairs and out of earshot.

"It's 'cause I'm not in any danger, as far as they know. They're just bein' nice. Too nice if you ask me." Kurt sat down and groped around in the couch cushions for the TV remote. "Let's just shut this off—I'll go upstairs for a while. We should give my grandparents time to fall asleep before we start asking Kayla questions."

"Maybe it should wait until tomorrow morning. We can always get her in private if we want," said Blue. "Your grandma's right—she has been through a lot."

"Oh, don't tell me you bought that story about her abusive ex-boyfriend forcing her to run away from college! By the way, a college she wouldn't even tell us the name of! And did you see the way she kept hiding her right hand all through dinner? Something's up with her, it obviously has to do with Linking, and I'm not gonna trust her until I know what it is!"

Kurt finally came up with the remote and aimed it at the TV. Blue glanced at the screen and held up his hand.

"Hey, hold on a second. Don't turn that off yet—there's something I want you to see."

It was well past eleven o'clock, and the news had just come back from a commercial break with teasers for upcoming segments. As Blue sat down beside Kurt, the voice of a female correspondent was just starting to talk over a stock footage montage that featured hypodermic needles being filled with clear liquid, medicines being made on a factory conveyor belt, and white-gloved doctors administering shots to grimacing adults.

"What are we watching?" asked Kurt.

"Shh, shh—listen," said Blue. "We're actually waiting for the next story, I think, but this is interesting, too."

"...the Sidney Grant Research Facility in Freeport, New Jersey, scientists claim to have cracked the code of biological degradation. Using a just-perfected formula that combines all-natural ingredients with small amounts of certain heavy metals, they claim to have successfully treated human cells to regenerate themselves continuously. This formula is the result of a fifty-year endeavor exploring alternatives to curing disease, as well as saving and lengthening lives.

"Tissues treated with the serum effectively cease aging, potentially nullifying the necrotic effects associated with illnesses such as cancer. While the serum does wash out of the body over time, the results of clinical trials suggest that the formula's half-life may be well over one hundred years. But will this treatment lead the human race to immortality, or is it merely a creative way to delay the inevitable? Doctor Julius Harding had more to say—"

"Oh, please! Is everyone in the world full of crap tonight?" Kurt couldn't help but laugh. "How can they even pretend they've tested something when you'd only know whether or not it worked after a hundred years? It's stupid!"

"It's been whispered about for decades," said Blue. "I mean, there's certainly a lot of testing left to be done before they can prove anything, but even if the vaccine's effects do turn out to be less potent than expected, a cellular regeneration treatment of any sort is something that half the world's population has been praying for. The implications for disease treatment and organ replacement alone are staggering."

"If it's even true," said Kurt.

"Mmm, yes—oh, here! Here's the story I was waiting for," said Blue, pointing Kurt back toward the screen. The view had returned to the newsroom for the moment, and a graphic that read "CAMPUS ABDUCTIONS" had appeared in the upper-right-hand corner of the screen, level with the anchorman's face.

"Six weeks into the crisis, there is still no word on the twenty students and three staff members who have vanished from Kline University. If anything, the rate of unexplained disappearances seems to be accelerating."

The view switched over to file footage of the school, in which a handful of students were traversing the footpaths. *"Five more undergraduates failed to report to roll call this week, following the two who disappeared just before spring break. Campus and city police are adamant that they are doing everything in their power to secure the area, as well as search for the missing persons. Still, Kline U's dean of students, Professor Warren B. Fincher, is facing mounting pressure from parents to close the school until their children's safety can be assured."*

"What, you're thinkin' Kayla's mixed up in this?" asked Kurt.

"It was the first thought I had when I saw a bedraggled college student collapsed in a strange yard. Kline University is about three hours north of here by car—if there's a kidnapper on the loose in that area, Lowval is certainly close enough to contain some sort of hideout, and I don't have to tell you that escaping from a possibly murderous criminal could easily leave someone as exhausted as Kayla was when we found her," said Blue. "The only thing I don't understand is why she would hide that from us, even if we are strangers. It seems like a failed kidnapping attempt would be much easier to discuss than domestic violence."

"See?! Something doesn't smell right," Kurt said. "I mean, even if she *is* from Kline U, what are the odds that out of all the people who got kidnapped, the one who escapes is a Linker, and she comes straight to my house?"

"I don't know, Kurt. After what I've seen coming out of your hand these past few months, I'm ready to believe almost anything." Blue smiled thoughtfully. "Actually, between the advent of Linking and now this 'immortality treatment,' the world seems to be positively filled with miracles lately."

"Ha! Except that the world is supposedly in the middle of dying, or else I wouldn't even have these powers!" Kurt shut the TV off and dropped the remote on the coffee table. "I'm goin' upstairs. You stay down here on the couch and pretend to be asleep, but don't actually fall asleep! I'll come get you in a little while, and then we'll get to the bottom of this Kayla thing."

*   *   *

She hadn't been asked to talk much at dinner, though she had volunteered the same information to Grandma Ciardi that she had to Grandpa—she was on the run from an abusive boyfriend named Eric, who went to the same college as she did. She hesitated to say precisely where, but the Ciardis had assured her they wouldn't pry. She had been a witness for the rest of the meal, and the rest of the night, as the Ciardis, their grandson, Kurt, and his friend Blue had attempted to go on as normal in spite of the strange circumstances she'd brought with her. And as the hour had grown later, she'd been taken down a hallway at the back of the house to a guest bedroom that looked like it was almost never used, beyond a closet and a locked study that, according to Grandpa, hadn't been used at all for years and years. Clearly, these people weren't accustomed to sleepovers, and she appreciated their charity even more when they gave her some of their own blankets and set her up to rest comfortably.

But two hours later, she wasn't in bed. She was stuffing her backpack with food taken from the kitchen and pulling her shoes on. She'd lost too much time already. Sleeping was out of the question, and she anticipated having to eat on the run even more than usual for the next few days.

"Goin' somewhere, Kayla?"

Kayla gasped and looked up—Kurt was in the room, leaning against the wall next to the door. In her haste, she hadn't heard him enter. Blue was right behind him, and he shut the door once he was inside, giving them privacy.

"Dammit, don't scare me like that!" She remembered the family's kindness and tried to restrain herself. "Look, Kurt, I appreciate what you're trying to do for me, but I can't stay here any longer. I can't let your grandparents call the police! Eric will find me if I don't keep moving…I've already said more than I wanted to. Please, just let me go."

"Maybe my grandparents believe that bullshit story about your ex-boyfriend, but I know there's a lot you're not telling them."

"They were polite enough not to ask too many questions I didn't want to answer," said Kayla. She zipped up her backpack and got ready to shove past Kurt, if necessary.

"But they wouldn't know to ask you about this." Kurt held up his palm and activated the rune; his qi illuminated the darkened bedroom.

Kayla didn't just stop, she recoiled so hard that she almost fell back onto the bed. For a moment, she looked as if she wasn't sure whether to hide her own hand again, scream and pretend to be frightened, or just keep running away. But her reaction betrayed her knowledge. She knew what she was looking at, and now she was just as curious as Kurt.

She pointed at the light. "You're…a Linker?"

"My grandparents don't know, and I don't want them to. But apparently, there's something I have to do with this rune, and it's supposed to come lookin' for me at some point. Now here you are. You're the first other Linker I've seen." Kurt looked at her guardedly. "I don't trust you, but I want to. Maybe you can tell me what I need to know."

"Well, she knows the word 'Linker'!" Blue was surprised. "We had to hear it from a very knowledgeable old man! How is it you found out about Linking, Kayla?"

"From Eric…Eric told me everything I know. It's not much, but…I mean, I guess I could tell you." Kayla sat down; she was still in shock. "Kurt, you're also the first other…well, you're the first other Light Linker I've seen, anyway. I'm as surprised as you are! I mean…damn, what a coincidence that I passed out in your backyard!"

"That's when I saw your rune—before you woke up," said Kurt.

"It might not be as much of a coincidence as it seems. You said it yourself, Kurt—your duty is supposed to find you. Maybe that *is* what's happening here. Or maybe Linkers just have a way of…sensing one another, heading toward one another even though they may not realize it," Blue suggested.

"Actually, I think he's right," Kayla said. "All along, I've felt like Eric was following me, and I don't think it was just in my head. I guess I was too busy trying to figure out how close he was getting to realize that I was also sensing you, Kurt."

"Wait a minute, so this Eric story is true?" Kurt walked closer to the bed and lowered his voice. Blue came over, too, but his walk was more excited—Kurt could tell right away that his friend had figured something out again, and it had him as intrigued as usual.

"You said that Kurt was the first Light Linker you've seen, which implies…Kayla, are you saying that your ex-boyfriend is a Dark Linker?"

A pause.

"Yes…." Kayla shifted in her seat, allowing Blue to sit next to her. Kurt stayed standing.

"It happened about six months ago, just after the start of the fall semester. We both go to Kline University," said Kayla. "I'm a junior there now…he's a sophomore. We'd been going out practically since he came there as a freshman. It wasn't always perfect, but I…loved him, I really did! He could be childish sometimes, but I actually kinda liked that about him…it made me feel like he needed me, appreciated me…."

"But then, one morning, he called me…he sounded so strange I came right over…and then he showed me the symbol on his hand. I mean, we didn't know what it was yet, but he already knew that it gave him weird powers, and he did a demonstration for me. He could…well, at first all he could do was dust his room. The one thing about Eric was that he was always really clean—he always needed a clean, shiny space to live in. He showed me how he could suck the dust into the air and have it disappear, like it was never there…it was like he had always known how to do it…."

"A vacuum?" Blue thought for a moment, then snapped his fingers. "Kurt! His dominant element must be void!"

"Yeah, I'm getting to that," Kayla said. "I was scared the first time I saw it, but Eric was really excited and it seemed safe, so I got used to it. We kept it a secret. At first, it didn't change much…it just gave us something new to do together. We'd go out in the woods behind campus and play around with stuff…eventually, he figured out that he could do other things besides vacuum, like light fires. I…kinda started to get excited, too, and every once in a while, Eric used his powers to play a prank on someone, like this other guy who hit on me in a really creepy way…heh, I bet he'll never set foot in the campus center post office again. Eric wanted to do good…he started calling himself 'Eric the Red, Viking Hero'…see, uh, his last name is Jaeder, which is Nordic, so he always said he was descended from Vikings, and…."

Kayla trailed off. She looked at the floor, and her mannerisms started to become more nervous; her hands wouldn't stop brushing against each other. Kurt and Blue could tell that the hard part was coming.

"But…about a month and a half ago…he changed…."

"What do you mean?" asked Blue, when Kayla didn't continue for a moment.

"There's this museum at school…a different exhibit comes through every semester. We have classes where you get to go study the things they keep there. There was this…artifact…Eric stole it. I found him with it one night, right around Valentine's Day. I was really mad at him. He'd never stolen anything before, and he was always going on about how his parents didn't want him at Kline U, how they would rather he become a doctor or something instead of an artist. I mean, did he want to give them an excuse to pull him out? And what if he got expelled?! The security cameras might've gotten him on tape—how long did he think he was gonna get away with it?! But he just held up his hand and told me it was all right, because he *had* to steal this thing.

"Well…." Kayla stopped and swallowed. "Actually…he said, '*We* had to take it. It belongs to *us*.'"

"He refers to himself as two people?" Blue asked.

"He didn't used to…he still doesn't do it all the time. When he doesn't, I almost feel like he's the same person I used to know, but I mean, still…." Kayla shook her head. "The thing he stole was a white stone hanging on a rope…he wears it like a necklace. He said he knew he had to steal it because he saw it in a dream. When he woke up, he said he could feel it drawing him to the museum, pulling him in…and he said that once he put it on, he knew it was supposed to be his all along."

"I had that same—I saw it in a dream, too!" Kurt ran his hand back through his hair; that was becoming a nervous habit. He traced two V shapes in the air with his index finger. "It has a symbol like this inside it, right?"

"Yes!" Kayla cried. "Eric said the museum called it a 'life charm,' but he knew that its real name was the Siphon Stone, and that it belonged to the ruler of a legendary island. He…he thought it spoke to him…that's how he says he found out about Linking, and it's how I know the stuff I do, too. He told me things that night, laid it all out for me, everything he thought he understood…."

Now Kurt sat down, too, against the wall opposite the bed. He looked troubled, and could barely manage to keep his voice quiet. "This is insanity! How could we both have had the same dream? How could it be real?"

"Kayla, you said Eric's rune first appeared about six months ago?" asked Blue. Kayla nodded, and then Blue turned to Kurt, a stunned expression on his face. "Kurt…that's the same time yours appeared! Maybe you and Eric had the same dream because you've been connected from the beginning. Remember, Laoshi said that Linkers always manifest in pairs!"

"You mean some spoiled college punk is the evil me?" Kurt snorted. "I'll believe a lotta crap at this point, but I'm not ready to swallow that one yet!"

"He's not evil!" Kayla sniffed; she was beginning to cry. "I…I mean, the things he's done, what he wants now…oh, God, he's not the same person he used to be, but he's not evil, God dammit!"

That was it. Kayla bowed her head into her hands and started to sob. Kurt barely knew how to deal with it—his first instinct was to get up and make sure the door was still closed, so his grandparents couldn't hear. Blue edged away from Kayla to give her some space at first, but then he had another idea and put his arm around her.

"Hey, don't cry. It's all right…you're safe with us. And…and maybe Eric isn't really evil. It sounds like the Siphon Stone has had some strange effect on him…."

"Yeah, I…I know…but there's more…."

Even Kurt was polite enough to give Kayla a few minutes of silence to find her footing again. Blue stayed with her the entire time, but eventually, she broke away and stood up. She walked over to the wall and leaned forward against it.

"I was pretty much broken up with Eric right after he showed me the Siphon Stone…it changed his powers from kind of a cool thing into a major turn-off, plus I was sure he was gonna get caught and expelled. He wasn't himself anymore. I didn't know exactly what happened, though, because he just…disappeared right after I yelled at him that night. He stopped returning my calls, he was never in his room…all my friends told me to just forget about him, and I was starting to…but then he called, four days ago. He told me to come to Rogers, that he had something to show me…."

"Rogers?" asked Kurt.

"The school science building. It's way out on the end of campus, half in the woods. I knew it was stupid, but I wanted some closure with him, so I went. I had to be sneaky about it, 'cause there's been a curfew ever since the kidnappings started…."

Kayla hesitated.

"Yes, we've heard about the situation from the news," Blue said. "I had wondered whether your running away had something to do with that, but of course now I know differently."

"Actually…." Kayla took a deep breath; she turned around to face the two men. "You're right…it does have something to do with it…see, those people weren't kidnapped. They're still at Kline, but they're…oh, God… I…."

Blue's eyes widened. "Take your time…."

"They're drained!" Kayla squeaked, her voice cracking. From then on, she spoke fast. "Eric did it! He said that's the true purpose of the Siphon

Stone—it sucks the qi right out of people! Everyone who's been missing was there at Rogers with him, and they were alive but—but they were just zombies! They stood around with their eyes and mouths open but they couldn't say or do anything! Eric said he had their qi now, and that he was gonna use it to make something called a, a Linker Weapon, and then—he said it was his destiny, that the world wanted him to do it, and that's why he got his powers in the first place!"

"Oh, my God! Zombies?!" cried Blue.

"Blue! I thought you said I couldn't run outta qi, that it…grows back or something!" Kurt said. "Shouldn't these people have gone back to normal eventually, as long as they didn't lose their original qi?"

"But what if they did?" wondered Blue. "Kurt, think about it this way —if your body qi is like the fuel for your powers, then your original qi, which remains untouched, may be the generator that makes that fuel. But if it's also some kind of conduit between body and soul, which is how Laoshi described qi, and the Siphon Stone enables Eric to drain it away…oh my gosh, Kurt, that would explain why they were zombies! Without their original qi, their souls have no connection to their bodies anymore! They're unable to use their body qi because their will has no way to reach it!"

Blue turned back to Kayla, looking horrified. "My God, Kayla! He didn't try to drain you, too, did he?"

Kayla's breathing was rapid.

"He wanted me to help him. He said the world we knew was gonna end, and he was gonna use the Linker Weapon to control it. He told me that was what was best for the Earth, that he was gonna be a hero and he wanted me to be by his side, but…God, I wouldn't have considered it for a second! I told him that what he was doing was disgusting, and he had to stop and reverse it right now, or I was going to the police! And then…."

She winced.

"Then he started talking in 'we' again. He said the police couldn't stop him, no 'mortal' could. I tried to run away, but he grabbed me…I smashed a beaker from one of the lab tables over his head, but it didn't do anything. Then he pinned me back against the wall, and then…God, then I saw the stone lighting up, and he smiled at me and whispered that everything was gonna be okay, that this was how it had to be for now, but I had to trust him 'cause he was doing the right thing…."

"Oh, Kayla!" Blue said.

"How the hell did you get out of that?" asked Kurt.

"I…I kept thinking about all the things I never got to do…I wished I had never gone to meet Eric and went swimming instead…." In spite of her red eyes and tear-dampened face, Kayla still managed to smile. "I've always loved swimming…it's my safe space. The water's always had this calming effect on me. So when Eric was about to drain me, I pictured myself surrounded by it—and then the wall behind me exploded and Eric got pushed back! It was like…a water pipe burst, and it was so powerful it knocked Eric over, but it didn't touch me. At the time, I just ran away, and I've been running ever since—I couldn't go back to my dorm or my parents' house, because Eric would know to look for me there. It wasn't until I stopped to sleep the first night that I noticed I had a symbol on my hand, too, but it was different from Eric's. He told me that there were Light Linkers and Dark Linkers, so I figured I was a Light Linker."

"And a water Linker, at that. Your will to live must've caused the pipe explosion that saved you…and because the water was charged with your qi, it probably affected Eric even if other physical attacks wouldn't!" Blue surmised. He touched Kayla's arm. "The man who taught us about Linking said that Linkers are born when the Earth reaches out to them, because the Earth is out of balance right now, and it needs the help of humans to heal itself. If you manifested right as Eric was about to drain you into the Siphon Stone, then that means the Earth helped you to escape. The Earth needs you for something, just like it needed Kurt."

Kayla smiled again. "Well, damn…that's nice to know, I guess."

"Do you know what element you use to do that invulnerability trick?" Kurt asked. "Is it void, since that's Eric's strongest element? I know I don't have it automatically, 'cause I've still cut myself and stuff at work."

"No, he made it sound like any Linker could do it. His exact words were, 'a Linker cannot be harmed by mortal means,'" said Kayla. "He was glowing when I smashed that beaker over his head, so maybe that has something to do with it."

"Huh. It's probably just qi, then." Kurt placed two fingers to his forehead again, like he'd done when he'd teleported earlier, and concentrated. There was a sound like a chime, and suddenly he was surrounded by a faint glow, the same shade of yellow as his rune. He opened his eyes and seemed startled; he kept on glowing effortlessly for a few seconds, but then shut it off again with another thought.

"Wow, that was easy," he said. "Heh. I'll have to thank Eric for that one."

"If you're lucky, you'll never meet him, and I'll never see him again!" Kayla picked up and then shouldered her backpack. "I hope you understand why I have to leave now…there's no way to stop him that I can see, and he wants me more than anyone else! I've felt him right behind me ever since I left campus, and…I just don't want to die! Hell, I don't want to give him the satisfaction of causing me to die! I-I'm sorry, but I can't stay here any longer—bye, Kurt and Blue!"

"Siddown!" For some reason, Kurt was smiling; bewildered, Kayla obeyed him. "Hey, Blue—let's say you're right, and this Eric kid is the evil me. He's out there stealing…souls, or something, so he can make a weapon to make himself king of the world. Wouldn't you say that counts as throwing the Earth out of balance?"

"I…it certainly sounds apocalyptic enough."

"Right! So maybe all I gotta do to fix the world is beat up on some college kid until he stops doing what he's doing!" Kurt laughed. "Man, it doesn't get any easier than that!"

"Well—hold on. We shouldn't assume anything, Kurt," said Blue. "After all, we don't know yet how the stone may or may not have figured into the original manifestation of Linking. All we know so far is how Eric is using it now, plus the fact that you and he apparently dreamed together."

"Come on, there's no way this is a coincidence. Linkers start showing up, Eric and I have the same dream about the stone, and now we find out that the stone is real and it's being used by Eric to zombify people. It has to be the imbalance, period, which means the only thing I have to do is get rid of it. Problem solved!"

"Don't you understand, Kurt?" Kayla said, her eyes tearing up again. "I would love nothing more than to smack Eric in the face and make him undo everything he's done. But if you or me or anyone else tries to fight him, he'll just turn us into zombies, too! And once he finishes the Linker Weapon, whatever it is…well, think about how powerful a 'Linker Weapon' could be! We don't even need to know what exactly it is or how it works to figure that out!"

"She has a point, Kurt," said Blue. "Even nuclear weapons are limited by the laws of science—they can only explode for so long, over so large a radius. A weapon powered by qi could, in theory, be limited only by the will of the user…."

"Hey, but…Laoshi said I was the strongest Light Linker, right? And if Eric manifested at the same time I did, that'd just make him the strongest

Dark Linker. So he shouldn't be any better at this than I am! No offense, Kayla, but if your powers showed up later, then it makes sense for him to be stronger than you…but at least I have you on my side, if you wanna help me. He doesn't have any other Dark Linkers with him, does he?"

"No, not as far as I know…."

"Then his only advantage is the Linker Weapon, which won't even matter if we can stop him before he finishes it! Hey, who knows? We might even be able to reverse what the stone did, and give those people their qi back!" Kurt crossed his arms, smiled and jerked his chin. "C'mon. Whaddaya say? Help me finish this guy off and fix up the world before my grandparents find out I'm a Linker. You know it'd feel good to get back at Eric."

Kayla drew her mouth into a line and sighed.

"I…I dunno…." she said. She looked up, seeming marginally less troubled now. "It is tempting, but…I still just have a hard time believing anyone could stop Eric, you included. And no offense, but I still wanna survive, which I won't if we go up against Eric and you're wrong."

"Tell ya what. You sleep on it tonight, here, where you're safe, and tomorrow I'll show you some of the stuff I can do. See if that doesn't make you feel better about teaming up with me." Kurt gave her a nod. "We'll let you go to bed now…c'mon, Blue."

"Right." Blue stood up, but he laid his hand on Kayla for one more moment. He looked down into her eyes. "If you need anything, anytime, you can come to us, no matter what decision you make. All right?"

"Sure." Kayla smiled. "Thank you."

Blue closed the door behind him softly, then followed Kurt back down the hall.

"Heh heh heh heh…."

As soon as the two of them were back in the TV room, Kurt began to chuckle. He smirked at Blue; Blue sent back a quizzical gaze.

"What?"

"You know…." Kurt winked at him and kept right on laughing.

"No, I don't know!" Blue turned red. "And I don't see how you can be so calm, or so…mirthful! All these months, you've been going out of your way to keep your grandparents from worrying about you, and now suddenly, you're so eager to go up against the most powerful Dark Linker in the world? Have you even considered the risk you'd be taking?"

"What are you talking about? You should be happy!" said Kurt. "You're the one who's been waiting to figure out about what I'm supposed to do with these powers, and as much as I hate to admit it, the old fart was right again—the job found me. Kayla's here, and she's gonna get me to Eric, then help me stop him. After that, the world's safe! We already know that he and I manifested at the same time, so we should be equals, even if he is better than Kayla. What's the problem?"

"You keep saying that, but let's be honest—we don't know anything about Eric. Any differences in the way you two have been training could create huge gaps between you. And…well, perhaps this was naïve of me, but I suppose I didn't think your mission to restore balance would involve 'fighting' a Dark Linker in the conventional sense. I had this idea that it would have more to do with manipulating nature and less to do with a physical struggle. But anyway, the fact is that we haven't really explored Linking as a combat strategy. Do you see what I'm saying, Kurt? There are more variables than you think."

"I…." Kurt rolled his eyes. "Whatever. Look, I can handle it. I'm just glad I can get this thing done without giving my grandparents a chance to find out. Kline U is far enough away that they'll never know. Besides, I still say the only thing that matters is that I have Kayla—all Eric's got is his unfinished weapon."

"If Kayla decides to help you. Whether or not she takes you to meet him, the fight could wind up being between you and Eric anyway. And I… listen, Kurt, all I'm saying is that you shouldn't just rush in without a plan. You have to be careful, for your own sake as well as Kayla's, but especially for your grandparents'. If doing that means waiting longer than one day, then so be it." Blue spread his blanket out on the couch and lay down. "Remember, no matter what else, Eric has the Siphon Stone. Think about what would happen to your grandparents if he managed to drain you. Not only would they find out you were a Linker, they'd find out they'd lost you. Just because confronting Eric might help you restore the balance doesn't mean you're incapable of failure. You've got to be careful, Kurt. That's all there is to it."

"Don't worry, I will be. I'll be too alert for him to catch me off-guard… so I better make sure I get a good night's sleep. See ya in the morning, Blue."

Kurt tiptoed upstairs, then plopped into bed. He lay there thinking until his mind exhausted itself, at which point he fell asleep in his clothes. The day had ended on a less confident note than he would've liked.

ACT III

牺牲

SACRIFICE

He could see more detail now.

Kurt couldn't tell if he was in the sky or on the balcony of the royal palace—he knew that was the purpose of the place this time. Scattered words and ideas were entering his mind as if poured directly out of someone else's.

Riktalash….

The palace was lavender in color, like most of the other buildings in the island city, and it was made of tall, pointed columns that seemed to melt into one another. The easternmost spire was topped with a golden globe in the shape of a teardrop. There was gold trim on all of the towers, in fact, stripes around their midsections or embroidery along the edges of the open windows, which were open, except for some that were draped with bead curtains.

Riktalash was still dying, still sinking into the ocean. The black smoke was still on the horizon. Kurt's point of view refused to settle—it moved back and forth between the balcony and the sky, and then between what seemed like hundreds of points within the sky.

When he finally lit on the balcony for a while, he saw the woman in the purple dress and tall purple hat once again. Her clothes seemed to be made of silk, and they dripped with beads and trinkets. It was as if she were part of the palace—her palace.

Queen….

Before, she had looked sad, but now, she looked pained. Then, she looked dead, on the floor. As she fell, Kurt noticed another difference: the necklace she'd been wearing was gone.

He saw an image of someone ripping it from her breast.

The Siphon Stone!

And then there was that man again, the man of black smoke with glowing, red eyes. Kurt could see this shade more clearly now, clearly enough to discern that the stranger had no single, well-defined identity. Sometimes he appeared to be standing alongside the queen, watching her die but doing nothing. Other times, he and the queen seemed to be the same person. Once, Kurt could've sworn that the specter took on the appearance of a man dressed similarly to the queen—maybe the king? Just as the ghost's reality refused to remain static, so did he drag all the reality around him into chaos. To look at him was to see a forest or a vast desert beyond, instead of the back of the throne room.

Drifter....

But Kurt's point of view changed again—he wasn't allowed time to comprehend the shadow-man. He was flying now, higher and higher, or perhaps the city was sinking as it had before, and he was simply hovering in place above the palace spire. Then he started moving forward, away from the city, though once again he couldn't feel anything like a plane or even the wind beneath his feet. He was heading toward the horizon, and the black smoke became thicker and thicker as he closed the distance.

For the first time, he could see the source. It wasn't the mainland or another dying city, it was a fleet of burning ships.

"Kurt!"

*   *   *

Even before the shouting woke him, Kurt knew he'd been dreaming again. But this time, something in his heart, or perhaps his hand, made it hard to tell the difference between his dream and reality. He almost didn't know which was which.

For the first instant after waking, he felt afraid.

*   *   *

"Kurt! Kurt, wake up!"

"Uuuugghhh…." Kurt rubbed his head; he could tell now that Blue was in his bedroom yelling at him.

"Kurt! Thank God!" A hand grabbed his arm, before his eyes were even fully open. "Come on, we have to get downstairs! Hurry!"

"Wha?" Kurt forced his lids up and checked his clock. 5:30 A.M. "Damn *it*! What now?!"

"It's Kayla! Hurry, we need to get outside!" Blue hesitated. "Your grandparents are already out there, Kurt!"

That got Kurt's attention. He sat up, though he was still groggy, and looked at Blue with newfound focus.

"What? What's that girl doing?" He tried to shove the covers aside; it took him a moment to realize he'd fallen asleep fully clothed and hadn't been under them to begin with. "She's not still tryin' to run away after all we talked about, is she?"

"Kurt—"

"She wakes up my grandparents in the middle of the Goddamn night just 'cause she can't be quiet about it—"

There was a flash of light out the window—it illuminated the entire bedroom for a split second. Kurt froze. It wasn't lightning, because if it was, he would've felt it, probably would've been responsible for it. Besides, it was purple, and Kurt soon realized it was flickering over and over again, patternlessly. Then, he heard the sound of someone screaming: Kayla. The house rumbled under his feet.

He felt something dark wash over him.

Kurt was off like a shot, through the door and the hallway, down the stairs so fast he almost tumbled headfirst into the front entryway. He didn't use that door, though—the disturbance was out back. Blue was arguably as motivated as Kurt, but he could still barely manage to keep up. Kurt was already around the corner and headed for the kitchen by the time he got to the stairs.

*   *   *

PKAK!

"Aieeeeeyaa!"

"Hrrrr…!" The boy brought his left hand up to his face and curled his fingers in, summoning his strength.

Kayla scrambled off the ground and tried to run. She ignored an aching arm for now and forgot all about her backpack and the few belongings it contained. The Ciardis' fence wasn't tall—she knew she could jump it if she got a good, fast start.

But the boy thrust his hand outward, palm toward Kayla, and the very ground betrayed her, rising up and knocking her back down.

"Dammit, hold still already!" he said.

"I'm warnin' you...!" Grandpa was shaking. He stepped forward in the boy's direction, armed only with an accusing index finger.

"No, don't!" Kayla shrieked, afraid to see Kurt's grandparents hurt because of her. She'd already done enough damage by bringing Linking into their view.

"Stay back!" The Dark Linker turned his palm toward the Ciardis; Grandpa flinched. "I'm not here to hurt you. I know this looks bad, but I have to stop her, for everyone's sake!"

Kayla raised her own hand and lit up her rune. It'd be okay, she told herself, as long as she was the only Linker discovered that day. Revealing herself wouldn't reveal Kurt.

There wasn't a body of water nearby, but that was the only element Kayla had any experience with, so she had to improvise. It was humid— she could draw moisture out of the air itself, or the ground. There was sure to be some well water beneath this small town. She willed the geyser, such as it was, to erupt right in front of her attacker's feet and hit him in the chin. It happened in an instant, with the force of a garden hose sprayer, before the boy could react. He staggered back, but didn't fall down.

He scowled and waved his hand—the wet dirt that Kayla's attack had produced gained a life of its own and snaked back toward her. She tried to get away again, but wasn't quick enough. The mud overtook her, covering her feet up to her ankles, then, when she fell forward, grasping at her back and wrists. In seconds, she was shackled facedown to the ground, and no matter how hard she struggled, she was trapped that way.

The boy started walking over to collect his captive, but before he got halfway there, Grandpa stepped in front of him. He now wielded the axe he'd used to chop up the fallen tree limbs.

"Don't you touch that girl!" he said.

"Papa!" cried Grandma.

"Go inside and call the police!" Grandpa told her. "I'll keep this clown from hurting her any more!"

"She's not the good guy! You're making a mistake!" The boy clenched his fist, and a faint, purple glow surrounded his body. "I can't let you get in my way. You can't even hurt me with that axe!"

Grandpa's eyes narrowed. "I can damn well try!" He reared back and prepared to bring the axe down with all his strength.

"Grandpa!" It was Kurt. He charged out the door and went straight for the intruder. "Blue, get Grandma inside! Grandpa'll be right behind you!"

"Like hell I will!" Grandpa's eyes never left Kayla's assailant. "Get everyone else in and call the police, Kurt. I got this!"

"You don't understand, he'll hurt you!"

"Better me than you, Kurt!"

Kurt was silent for a moment; he tried to speak but couldn't decide what to say. The glove on his hand practically burned his skin.

He saw movement out of the corner of his eye. The Dark Linker had raised his hand again—his rune was purple, like the rest of the energy swirling around him. It was identical to Kurt's in every other respect, except that it was on his left hand instead of his right, and the symbol was upside-down.

Kurt's decision was made for him.

"NO!"

He didn't take off his glove, but it was only on for show in the first place. Mere fabric couldn't block his qi. Instinctively, he felt himself using the shield maneuver he'd learned from Kayla. He discovered that not only did it cancel out physical attacks, it could also block Linking attacks, at least to some degree. The intruder had levitated rocks to throw at both Kurt and his grandfather, but the one on its way to Grandpa hit a translucent yellow wall and crumbled. Kurt was quick enough to dodge the one targeting his own torso.

"What the—how'd you do that?!" the boy shouted at Kayla around Grandpa.

"Herragh!" With an angry growl, Kurt tackled the Dark Linker, who was distracted enough that he never saw it coming. Both of them rolled a few yards away from Grandpa. That was all Kurt needed—he could figure the rest out later.

"Ennh!" The boy called up a column of earth that knocked Kurt backwards. It hurt: Kurt remembered all too well that earth was his weakest element, and it appeared to be one of this boy's strongest. But he recovered quickly, and took a guarded stance.

"Kurt!"

"Don't worry, I'm fine!" Kurt called to his grandmother. He thought, *Dammit...they saw his and Kayla's powers! And now here I am putting myself in danger! I have to get rid of this kid before it gets any worse!* Another thought nagged at him: how was he going to do that without using his own powers in front of his grandparents? It was either that or leave them in a more immediate danger than would come from worrying. But the worry would outlast the moment. But they would worry more *in* the moment if they thought he was vulnerable, which he wouldn't be if he used his powers.

Focus! he told himself.

He took stock of the Dark Linker. All he'd noticed up until now was the rune, but on closer inspection, this young man was quite obviously another college student like Kayla. His forest-green sweatshirt, which bore the Kline University crest, was proof enough of that. He also had that flippant, youthful style, with his gel-set black hair and baggy cargo pants, yet somehow, he looked more ready for a wake than a beer pong party. Kurt saw in his beady, blue eyes a cold seriousness built on resignation.

"You must be Eric," he said.

The boy shook his head. "N-no, I'm not Eric!"

"His name is Rick Hydrad! He's Eric's roommate!" yelled Kayla. Kurt looked over at her quickly; Blue was by her side now, trying to dig through her earthen restraints. "He must've just manifested!"

Grandpa was still fuming. "If I'd had any idea...!"

Kurt redoubled his efforts to concentrate. "Ha! So you're not even the big guy, and you think you can just barge in here and start harassing us?!" He pointed to the side with his gloved hand. "Get the hell outta my yard! Now!"

"I don't take orders from you! Especially not—wait a minute, wait a minute...!"

Hydrad closed his eyes. Perplexed, Kurt watched him even more carefully—for all he knew, this was preparation for a major attack. But then, Hydrad opened his eyes again and looked at him with something like surprise.

"That wasn't Kayla's qi shield, it was yours!" he said. "You're a Linker, too!"

Kurt tensed. *Shit.*

"And a powerful one…." Hydrad shrank back a little. "You radiate qi…like Eric…."

"Kurt?" Grandpa's shaking ceased, but only because his tremors had turned inward. Grandma looked like she was about to faint.

Kurt couldn't bear the sight of it.

"Kurt…is that true?"

"I…." Kurt couldn't lie or tell the truth. "I'm…."

Grandpa had his answer. He turned away from Kurt and walked back to Grandma. The axe fell out of his absentminded hand.

"Grandpa, wait!" Kurt shouted. "I'm fine, I'm…I'm sorry…!"

"Listen, I'll make you a deal. I won't meddle in your business if you don't meddle in mine," Hydrad said. "It's not important what you think of me—horrible things will happen if I don't get Eric what he needs, and right now, he needs Kayla!"

Kurt felt a moment of clarity as pure as ice in his veins. Now he was the one quivering. His first deliberate act was to reach over and rip the glove off his right hand. The rune was glowing more brightly than ever before, and its flashes gave off tiny sparks. The lights swirled around the symbol so fast that a crackling energy field was generated, coursing up and down Kurt's entire forearm.

"You bastard," he spat, curling his lip. "Maybe I couldn't protect them from me, but I *will* protect the people I love from you. You have three seconds to get off my grandfather's land before I tear your head off and stuff it up your arrogant frat-boy ass!"

"I can't leave without Kayla!" Kurt felt the ground shake again as Hydrad spoke. "I can control the earth. I won't let you get close enough to hit me! I don't want to fight you—please, don't make me!"

"So, your element is earth?"

Thunder rumbled in the sky. Kurt set his jaw.

"Then this should hurt!"

Blue covered his ears just in time. He glanced over and saw Grandma and Grandpa doing the same thing, as if instinct had prepared them.

KRAKOOOOOM!

The lightning bolt came, and it was bigger and louder than any natural storm could have produced. The Ciardis, Blue, and Kayla didn't even feel their hair stand up: Kurt used all the control he had to focus the electricity, making sure it would flow around his loved ones rather than through them.

Aside from that precaution, though, the act was pure catharsis, and Kurt didn't shy away from the possibilities of his power. Hydrad's scream was drowned out by the thunderclap as the bolt hit him straight on the head and drove through his whole body like a nail. The electricity hit the ground so hard that it blew a smoldering crater in the lawn and sent chunks of earth flying in all directions.

The chunks stopped and hovered in midair, never hitting the ground. One of them flew around and caught Hydrad. Undoubtedly, he was hurt, with a scorched face to prove it, but his eyes shone like those of a rabid animal about to fight its way out of a corner.

Kurt had expected more of a breather.

Hydrad's purple aura pulsed like a heartbeat, and he threw his hands out, sending the floating pieces of earth Kurt's way. Kurt put up his shield to block the first one, dodged the second, and called up some wind to try and redirect the third, but it was coming too fast and managed to clip him before he could get it completely out of the way. The fourth one hit him dead on in the face and made him stagger backwards.

There were a lot more than four, and they didn't stop coming.

"What's going on? Is Kurt fighting him?!" Kayla said; she couldn't turn her neck far enough to see while she was pinned to the ground. Blue took a brief look at Kurt and cringed.

He needs Kayla…I've got to get her out! He redoubled his efforts momentarily, but then groaned in frustration and despair. It was like scratching at stone. The dirt was too tightly packed around Kayla— otherwise, she could have just stood up and broken free on her own. He hadn't even liberated one hand, let alone her waist and legs, and if she couldn't turn around and see Hydrad, she couldn't aim at him, either.

Blue kept scraping.

Even if I had a shovel, it'd hurt her when I hit her skin— He blinked. *No! Of course, it wouldn't!*

Blue eyed the axe lying in the grass. "Kayla, turn on your invulnerable shield!"

Hydrad threw the last of the dirt clods; Kurt was starting to look ragged, his face dirty and his lip bleeding. Hydrad dropped back onto the ground and ran in for the kill. He seized Kurt's right hand, covering the rune, and his own left hand became encased with dirt drawn up off the ground and tipped with a large, pointy stone. He paused, then reared back.

"Ohhhh!"

Kurt's grandmother shrieked in horror, and Kurt's eyes went to her. She was hugging Grandpa, her face buried in his shoulder. She couldn't bear to watch her grandson getting beaten so badly.

That meant something. It either gave Kurt a new burst of strength, or else it made him realize that he wasn't getting beaten that badly after all—that it looked worse than it really was.

Kurt ignited fire in his hand. In the heat of the moment, he finally got it to form larger, more than twice the size of the lighter flame he'd been able to create until then. He burned Hydrad and forced him to let go, buying himself space to step back.

Kurt could smell ozone, and he realized that it wasn't blood in his nose —it was the charge still in the air from his first attack. He pulled it in and concentrated it around his rune, so that his entire right hand was surrounded by an orb of electricity.

He swung, but Hydrad saw the punch coming and ducked. Kurt followed up with a backhand that connected, and once he felt the tables turning, he didn't let up. He reached out, grabbed Hydrad by the collar, and kept up the assault of punches. Each hit brought forth a shower of sparks.

Hydrad only let him get away with five or six before he jerked himself free and raised another earthen wall to separate the two of them. This time, Kurt anticipated the trick, and was able to get out of the way. Hydrad kept going, making the entire spread of the ground approach Kurt like a tsunami. Rather than Link, Kurt's first impulse was to jump over it, but he could tell as soon as he was in the air that he wouldn't get enough height. And then he felt the wind swell underneath him, lifting him to safety.

Am I doing that? he wondered; it didn't feel like he was. And in fact he wasn't—Kayla was up now and helping. The first thing she'd seen fit to do was move Kurt out of harm's way. The second was to raise the wettest of the mud from her earlier fight off the ground, fashion it into a battering ram, and career it into Hydrad's body before he realized that he now had two opponents.

"Kurt!" Kayla ran over and joined her fellow Linker. Hydrad had been knocked into the bushes on the fringe of the yard, so she had a few seconds. "Are you all right?"

"I'm fine, but I'm not getting anywhere!" Kurt complained. He closed the distance between himself and Kayla and said in a low voice, "Help me get behind him. I've got an idea—"

There was a loud rumbling sound, and Hydrad came back out of the bushes. Before Kurt and Kayla's eyes, almost the entire yard began to grow miniature hills that enlarged and shrank rapidly, and in some cases broke off to form more floating platforms. One such platform plunged toward the two Light Linkers, forcing them apart as they avoided being hit.

Kurt made eye contact with Kayla, and she nodded. She continued blasting Hydrad with water, mud, and the occasional gust of wind, while Kurt concentrated on jumping from hill to hill and recapturing as much of the electricity around him as he could.

"Aaargh, dammit, Kayla!" Hydrad lost what little control he had left—the qi was pouring out of him now, making his hair stand on end. His nostrils flared and he seemed to shake along with the earth as he hurled everything he had at Kayla.

With the ground under her feet changing fastest of all, Kayla was forced to use the wind again, like she had for Kurt, and levitate a few inches in the air at all times. That made it harder for her to dodge projectiles; Hydrad clenched his teeth and sped up his assault.

Kurt was getting closer, gathering more power in his palm all the time. The waves of earth flowed away from Hydrad, but strategic jumps allowed him to clear the crests and continue making progress. One more jump and he was there, less than a foot from his target. That was when Hydrad noticed—his eyes flew open.

"No!" he yelled, throwing up the ground underneath Kurt. That was all the opening Kayla needed. Another stream of water burst from the soil into Hydrad's face, staggering him and diverting his attention, while a localized whirlwind caught Kurt and righted him. Hydrad finished his double take just in time to see four fingertips pointed directly at his face.

PSSSSHHHEEE!

The qi gun went off, dispensing a large, ovular globe of crackling, yellow energy. Kurt had mixed in all the lightning he could with the qi burst for good measure.

There was the sound and appearance of breaking glass as the glowing shield around Hydrad shattered, its shards flying several feet away before they faded into thin air. The dark rune on his hand gave forth a spurt of purple qi that came like blood from a wound, and then went dim.

The force of the blow catapulted Hydrad clear across the yard. He bounced off the ground all the way to a crashing end at the fence, then slumped down unmoving, purple energy sparking around him as if he were a machine with damaged circuitry. The shaking of the ground ceased.

"We did it…." Kayla cupped her hands over her nose and mouth. The reality of what had happened, what she'd just been doing, was catching up to her and settling in.

Kurt stood in place, examining his defeated foe from a distance. He spat in Hydrad's direction, then took down his shield.

"Kurt!" It was Blue. "Kurt, get over here, quick!"

Grandma Ciardi was leaning on Blue, looking as though she could barely stand, one step away from hyperventilation. Grandpa had sunk down onto his knees.

"God, no…!" Kurt instinctively used the wind to make his run across the yard even faster. "Grandma, Grandpa, stop! You don't have to worry, I'm fine! I was only trying to protect you—I had to!"

"Yeah…yeah…." Grandma switched from Blue's shoulder to Kurt's. "I see you, Kurt honey. I'm all right…and thank you…I was just surprised at first. It's hard…it's hard to see you like this…."

"Don't worry, I promise it's okay! Look, see?" Kurt held up his rune, which was starting to calm down now that the battle was over. "All this thing is…it's like my soul energy, it comes from inside me. There's no way it can hurt me, and that guy—"

"We know what it is."

Grandpa's shaking returned as he stood up. He was a boiling pot of rage. Kurt was startled back into the countenance of his childhood.

"You…do?"

"What I wanna know," said Grandpa, "is how you found out about that thing, and how you got it!"

Kayla wandered over, looking haunted and ambivalent. She took up residence on Blue's shoulder, now that it was free.

"How I…? I didn't ask for it or anything, it just—grew outta my hand one night!" Kurt had never prepared to discuss it. Grandma sobbed, and he hugged her. "It's…that guy, Mr. Song—Laoshi explained it to me that I was—"

"Laoshi." Grandpa grunted and ground his teeth. "That old bastard's still alive?"

"You know him?!" Another thing Kurt hadn't been prepared for was being more surprised than his grandparents. "But I told you about him that day, I remember! Why didn't you say something then?!"

"I only heard him called 'Song' once. I forgot that was his real name. But it doesn't matter!"

"Grandpa, what—"

"Put that glove back on your hand," ordered Grandpa, "and never Link again!"

Grandpa's shout echoed through the yard for a few moments afterward. There was no other sound beyond Grandma's continued sniffles. Kayla looked helplessly at Blue, who could only return the same expression. Grandpa stared hard at Kurt, waiting for obedience.

And then, the wind picked up in an unnatural way. Everyone felt from which direction it had come, and there they saw something horrifying. Hydrad was off the ground, levitating much as Kayla had earlier, glowing with an even darker version of the purple qi. He floated slowly toward the Ciardis, Blue, and Kayla. But he wasn't looking at anyone—his head was rolled limply back, and his eyes were closed.

The voice came with a deep, ghostly echo.

"Kayla…we see that you have found an ally…."

Kurt knew right away, especially because Kayla gasped and drew back, hiding partly behind Blue. Kurt looked at Blue and saw that his friend had figured it out as well. This danger put the question of what to do next on hold: Kurt might have been afraid that his power would threaten his family's well-being, but that voice represented a sure thing. Kurt forced away his daze and stepped up to Hydrad's floating body.

"Am I talkin' to Eric?" he asked in a pointed tone.

"We are Eric the Red. We speak to you now through a Link."

That's a new one, thought Kurt. He brought his rune to bear once again.

"Name's Kurt Ciardi." He raised his palm. "Let's see if you can *feel* stuff through this Link of yours, wherever you are."

"Even if you were strong enough to project more of your qi without collapsing afterwards," Eric interjected, "it would be pointless. You are hearing our voice carried on the wind toward Hydrad, nothing more."

It was then that Kurt noticed he was breathless, panting, and he felt the weight of his hand growing the longer he held it up. Reluctantly, he deactivated the rune and changed tactics.

I can't hurt him, he can't hurt me, he reasoned. *Least he's talking.*

"We could feel you in your confrontation with Hydrad from here," said Eric. "Your qi is interesting…as if it is composed of two in one…."

Grandpa tried to hide the twitching of his face.

"So I'm twice as strong as you?" Kurt made himself laugh. "Good to know. Can't say I'm surprised, though. You and I got these powers at the same time, kid. That means we're at least even. You won't be able to push me around like those people at your school."

"We look forward to draining you and exploring your qi further," said Eric.

"No!" Kayla found her voice. She approached Hydrad and stood alongside Kurt. "I'm not gonna let you drain anyone else! Kurt's right—it's two against one now. You've been…you're a monster! I can't let you keep hurting people the way you have been, and I'm tired of being afraid of you! Kurt and I are going to stop you!"

"Ha! Y'know what, Kay? *I'm* tired of people like you and 'Kurt' talking down to me!"

Kurt was puzzled. Eric's voice had completely changed; now he sounded more like the snotty college kid Kurt had been expecting. Even the echo of his speech had decreased.

"You were supposed to be the one person who believed in me, and now I gotta prove myself to you, too?! Fine! You can't stop the end of the world—that's all there is to it. You'll see that I'm right eventually!" Hydrad's body began to move, floating higher in the air, approaching the fence. "Come to Wards Island in New York City three days from now…I'll show you the truth about the Linker Weapon. If you still don't trust me after that, then I can't be held responsible!"

Hydrad's body, still unconscious, levitated over the fence, across the road, and downhill into the fields. Soon, it was just a purple speck in the distance.

"Yeah, see ya." Kayla was burning. "I'm not scared of you…powers or no, you're still just my damn whiny ex!"

"W-what do we do now?" asked Blue.

Kurt said nothing. He was staring out across the countryside, as if he were afraid the Dark Linker would return and continue attacking.

"You didn't answer me, Kurt!" said Grandpa. "You can never use Linking again! Do you understand me?"

"Grandpa, I…." Kurt felt outside his body as he heard his own words. "I didn't want you and Grandma to find out. I know how much I mean to you, and I know how much you'd worry if you thought anything might happen to me...worrying ain't good for people your age, no offense. That's why I kept it a secret all this time, so I'm sorry, really. But—"

"No buts," Grandpa insisted.

"That stupid Hydrad kid made me choose between worrying you with my powers, or letting him...kill you right in front of me! What was I supposed to do?! And now Eric knows where you live!" Kurt exclaimed. "I can't just stand by! The world is ending because of him—I have to do something! If he finishes his weapon, he could just aim it here or anywhere else he wants—"

"Better us than you!" Grandpa repeated. "Better them than you! Better anyone than you!" He scowled and seemed to trip over his words, his mouth opening only to close an instant later. "I won't let this happen again!"

"Papa, no!" said Grandma; she flew to her husband, hugging him in a way that suggested she was trying to restrain, not comfort.

But Kurt's attention was already caught. "What do you mean, 'again'?"

Grandpa was still for a moment.

"Laoshi...." His voice was trembling. "Hell...Linking already took away my only daughter...I'm not gonna let it take you, too."

With that, he spun around, broke free of Grandma's hold, and stormed back into the house. He slammed the back door behind him, and everyone also heard him slam the bedroom door a few seconds later.

Kurt looked like he'd been hit by a truck. Grandma started to cry again.

Kayla was confused. "His daughter?"

"Kurt's mother." Blue was looking down. "Kurt's mother was a Linker."

*   *   *

Blue pried his eyes open. He raised his arm to look at his watch, which, like the rest of his clothes, had stayed on his body when he'd collapsed on the TV room couch at around 6:30 in the morning. It was now a few minutes before noon, but he didn't feel very rested. He remembered flurries of thought and threads of conjecture so long and winding that they must have consumed most of the few hours he'd spent staring at the Ciardis' ceiling. All that under his belt, and he still couldn't get much further than the discovery from the backyard.

Kurt's mother was a Linker.

He heard water running in the kitchen; he opened the door and walked out. Grandma Ciardi was filling up the kettle, and Kayla was slumped over the kitchen table. Blue was relieved to see that she was still in the house.

Neither of them looked up at first. Blue went over and pulled out a chair for himself.

"Oh!" Grandma was startled by the sound. "Hey, Blue. Good morning."

"Heh. Just barely." The joke died before he could even point to his watch.

"Do you want some oatmeal? I'm making some for Kayla."

"Um." Blue stuttered. "O-only if there's enough for all three of us."

"Don't worry about me, hon. I'm not hungry, so I—"

There was a crash as Grandma lost her grip on a bowl she'd been taking out of the cupboard.

"Awwwww! We've had those bowls for twenty years!"

"Here, let me help you."

Kayla was getting up as well, but Blue stopped her. He knelt down on the floor and started to help Grandma pick up the pieces.

It was so quiet that Blue could hear the sound of footsteps overhead even before Grandma tensed up beside him. Grandpa was awake, and on his way through the upstairs hall.

*   *   *

Puk puk puk.

Kurt was sore and contorted. He'd fallen asleep on top of the covers again, this time hugging his pillow underneath his body.

Puk puk puk.

As soon as he realized that someone was knocking on his door, Kurt made a point of not saying a word. He tried to stop moving, too.

"Kurt?" It was Grandpa. "Kurt? You awake yet? Can I come in?"

Kurt hesitated. He tightened his mouth, and rolled over so that the pillow was covering his face, but then relented. "Fine. It's open."

He heard the doorknob turn and the hinges swing, and suddenly all of the frustration and confusion he'd been feeling flew away. He was back to worrying about his grandfather's welfare.

"Look, Grandpa, I'm sorry. I didn't know something like last night would happen. I never wanted to make you—"

Kurt stopped as soon as he turned far enough around to lay eyes on Grandpa. The elder Ciardi looked small and troubled; he came over and sat down on the bed beside Kurt, laying a hand on his back as if consoling a young child after a nightmare.

"Nah, Kurt. *I'm* sorry. I shouldn't have gotten mad at you like that," he said. "I know you tried to do good, Kurt. Yer a good boy…you always were."

Kurt didn't say anything.

"C'mon." Grandpa jerked his head toward the door and stood up. "Come with me. I've got something to show you."

Kurt followed his grandfather out of the bedroom, through the hall, and down the stairs. He still didn't say anything, but now it was because he wanted to listen. On the way through the living room, he heard Grandma, Blue, and Kayla moving around in the kitchen. Grandpa led Kurt into the back hallway, down toward the bedroom where Kayla had slept, but he stopped before they got there. They were in front of the door that led to his study, which was always locked and which Kurt had never been allowed to see. He'd lost interest ages ago.

Grandpa reached into his pocket, removed the key, and opened the door. It creaked from lack of use.

Kurt stepped into the room and looked around. The ceiling was full of cobwebs. The window on the far wall was the only source of light—it was dirty, and the dust motes floating through its sunbeam gave the impression that Grandpa had come in earlier to raise the shades for the first time in years. There was a strange cabinet next to Kurt, with a big, pull-front compartment on top, a shelf in the middle, and a hutch with two sliding doors at floor level. Beyond that was a desk with a black lamp turned gray, surrounded by papers. There was an armchair in the far left corner, another, taller lamp beside it, and a big, full bookshelf taking up the last considerable amount of wall space.

"Do you know what this room is, Kurt?"

"Sure. It's your study," Kurt said. He heard the uncertainty in his voice. "I always knew that, Grandpa. But you never let me in here before… why now?"

"I always told you it was my study, but that wasn't true." Grandpa opened the top drawer of the desk while he spoke. "It was your mother's."

Kurt was more than awake now. His own history was being rewritten before his eyes.

"The guest bedroom, where Kayla slept…that was hers, too. God, Kurt, if only you could've seen her…." Grandpa stopped rooting around in the drawer—he needed one hand to steady himself against the desk, and the other was pressed over his forehead and eyes. His face scrunched up, and a few small noises escaped between his lips.

Kurt became concerned again; he walked farther into the room.

"Here! Here…." Before Kurt got to him, Grandpa reached back into the drawer and thrust something out in his hand. Kurt took it: it was a photograph, taken at a picnic in his backyard.

He recognized a younger Grandma with blacker hair, and he also caught sight of Grandpa looking up into the tree in the background, the very tree Kurt had Linked half to death while his powers manifested in his sleep. The other two people on the picnic blanket, however, stood out. One was a man in a collared, short-sleeved shirt and khaki shorts, with a round head, short, stiff hair, and big glasses—he looked like a stereotypical nerd, except for the fun-loving smile on his face. He had one arm around Grandma, who returned the gesture. The other was a woman with long, brown hair and bangs that curled outward over her forehead. She wore sunglasses, but Kurt knew the look of her eyes without having to see them.

"That's her."

Grandpa inhaled then exhaled slowly.

"Her name was Anna Ciardi," he told Kurt. "She kept her last name after she married Bill, 'cause she said she was proud of her family…."

He had to stop again for a minute.

"But I swear," he laughed, "that girl was stubborn from the day she was born. She always knew what she wanted and worked her butt off 'til she got it. When Bill couldn't get up the nerve to propose to her, standing there stammering away for half the night, she said to him, 'Bill, are you asking me to marry you?' and *then* he said, 'Yes.'

"All her life, Anna had three dreams. One of them was to work for a great New York newspaper, so she got her degree in journalism, then moved to the city to start a job copy-editing. At the time, I wanted to sell this place and move down there to be closer to her, but your grandma stopped me. She said Anna needed her space.

"Anna's second dream was to have a family like ours one day. That came true a couple years outta college, when she married Bill and then had you." Grandpa examined Kurt, sad and happy at once. "You got her eyes, Kurt. Her hair, too, even though it stays in place like your dad's. Her hair was always blowing around in the wind.

"That was her third dream...really, though, it was the first one she came up with. Even when she was still in diapers, Anna wanted to fly. She'd run straight into the wind, then turn around and get it blowing on her back. She loved to stand on places high as she could go just to feel it a little stronger, get a little closer to flying for real. I tell you...I never expected that dream to come true."

"So she was a wind Linker." Kurt looked back at the picture—now it was obvious to him that Anna's palm held the same rune as his. "How come you never talked to me about her before? You avoided it whenever I asked as a kid, so I just stopped asking. I could tell you didn't wanna think about it, and I knew that I was all you had left after she...well, I...."

Grandpa squinted and then un-squinted.

"You don't know how right you are, Kurt. Guess you got her brains, too," he whispered. "Tell me something. We never talked about Anna before, but you knew what happened to her and your dad. How did you know about the car accident if I never told you? And don't say Grandma told you, because I asked her after the first time I heard you say it, years ago, and she said it wasn't her."

Kurt probed his brain—he felt it itch deep inside. If there was an answer to that question, he didn't know it.

"Well...I think I might know. Let me tell you the whole story, once and for all." Grandpa hadn't taken his hand off his forehead once, and now, the weight of his words got the better of him, and he had to sink down into the desk chair. Kurt knew better than to try and talk him out of worrying at this point. He sat on the floor and continued to listen.

"Right after she got that thing on her hand, Anna came home with Bill and showed it to us. Now, Anna was smarter than me and your Grandma put together, God bless her. We weren't gonna know what to make of the damn thing if she didn't, but then the doorbell rang and there was Song—Laoshi. He told us he didn't mean any harm, but he felt Anna's power from miles away, and he said he could tell her what it was, what it meant for her. I never liked him, but Anna saw something in his eyes, I guess...so that's how we found out about Linking, what it was called, and what Anna had to do."

Grandpa shook his head. "I always knew she was special, Kurt, but fixing the whole world was too much. I was against it from day one, but you heard what I said about her. Heart of gold and will of iron. She said it was her responsibility to the world…she believed what Laoshi said, that the Earth chose her."

"That's what he told me," Kurt said, uneasy.

"Yeah…well, it was supposed to be her, first." Grandpa paused again to rub his temples. "After that, she came up here as often as she could to practice in the backyard, where no one could see her, and she talked to Laoshi every chance she got. He'd never tell her much, said it was something she hadda figure out on her own, but she liked the old man, liked showing him her progress. I tell you, Kurt, the things she could do. She knew what was coming, and she wanted to be ready to win when the time came to meet her Dark half. I watched her every time, and it went on for so long that Grandma, Bill and me forgot when her Linking wasn't normal.

"And then there was that night…."

Grandpa stopped.

"You mean the night of the accident," said Kurt.

"There were two cars that went in the river that night, not just one. I dunno who the bastard was, but the Dark Linker who came around the same time as your mother found her before she found him. All the training in the world didn't prepare her for the guy to jump out of the shadows in the city, when she and Bill were going home from the store, with you in her arms. Knowing her, I bet she never even stopped to try and fight, 'cause you were the most important thing in her life, Kurt. More important than the whole damn world."

Kurt felt a prickling inside his nose and a burn around his eyes. He started running his hands through his hair again.

"All I know is they couldn't lose him, not even with your father driving like a bat outta hell. That damn Dark Linker wanted it too bad, but the best he could do was shove them in the East River and take himself out along with them…."

Grandpa made a sound like a weak cough, and from then on he couldn't raise his head.

"Me and Grandma were staying with Anna and Bill at the time…when we got the call, they were still trying to find her car in the water. They found his no problem…when they pulled it out I spit on it. Woulda done more if your grandma hadn't started crying so hard."

"Grandpa, I…." But Kurt couldn't find enough words to interrupt.

"I'm almost done. There's just one reason I wasn't a completely broken man that night, and you got it already." Grandpa rubbed his eyes. "While the cops were busy talking with each other and writing up the reports, me and Grandma saw a glow coming out of the water, and up you floated, right into our arms. I felt a wind blowing and then fading away, and the light went out and just…melted into you, and I knew she used all her power to keep you safe and send you to us. You were our little miracle, and you always have been."

Kurt slid his palm and fingers up his forehead slowly, until his forearm rose to block his eyes. He felt heavy, and he leaned, then fell against the part of the desk nearest him. After a moment, Grandpa laid a hand on his shoulder; they stayed like that for a few minutes, with no words.

Time slowed to a crawl. Grandpa pulled back and studied Kurt's eyes. Kurt looked timid and afraid, unsure where this was going next, but then, Grandpa smiled again.

"Whatever's left of Anna, Kurt, is in you. I always knew it," he said.

"I've tried to be a good person, I've tried to be good to you and Grandma—"

"And you have, Kurt! You're the best we could ever ask for…but I don't just mean that you look like her or act like her. You've always been your own person—it's more than that. Remember what I said, about how you knew part of the story without me telling you? When Anna passed on…she did it helping you, Linking with you. I felt it a little bit myself, when I held you that night—that's how I knew she died trying to save you from the Dark Linker, and that it was up to me and Grandma to take care of you from then on. I always thought that was how you knew, too. Whatever pieces of her survived, you got 'em, just like it oughta be. She's still your mother even now, watching over you, and I know your dad is, too, in his own way. You got her love and the memory of what she did, and that's something that'll never die in you…but I was afraid you also got her powers, and that you'd be a Linker, too, when you grew up. That's why I never talked about her with you, even when it broke my heart. I didn't want her to hear me…I didn't want your power to wake up, if you had it. I didn't want what happened to her to happen to you."

Grandpa stood up; Kurt followed his lead. Grandpa sighed.

"I'm gonna ask you one more time, Kurt. Don't do this. Nobody says you have to—I don't give a damn what Laoshi told you. The world kept on turning all these years without Anna to save it, and it can keep on turning without you risking your neck."

Kurt bit his lip. He couldn't maintain eye contact when he finally answered.

"Except…." He shook his head. "I mean, you guys come first—I never wanted to do anything that could hurt you. But if this was important to Mom…and I told Kayla we'd fight together, that I'd help her stop Eric! She was afraid to fight him alone, no matter how mad he made her when he did what he did. I told her we could stop him together. You always taught me to do the right thing—I can't just walk away after I promised Kayla, especially now that…I mean, you guys still come first! I still come first! If I —Mom wouldn't have wanted me to do anything stupid after what she went through to save me, but I don't even wanna think about what Eric could do to you guys *and* me if I just stay here! Hydrad was nobody. Eric can steal peoples' qi and turn them into zombies, and he's gonna use the qi to power some weapon that'll let him kill anyone, anywhere!

"Grandpa, I love you and Grandma, but I have to do this. Maybe there's no way I can stop you from worrying about me, but I'm starting to think…it's less likely that'll hurt you than if Eric gets his way. And if Laoshi was telling the truth, and I'm the one who's supposed to fix the world… hell, who cares about him? If Mom believed it and it was important to her, then it's important to me."

Grandpa nodded.

"Yer a good boy, Kurt." The familiar phrase had a new weight now. "You're a good son, too…your mother's son, like I always knew you would be. I love you, we all do, and we all worry about you—don't feel bad. It's our job to worry about you, and nothing you could do would ever stop us, even if you weren't a Linker. Your family can always find something to worry about…ehh ehh ehh. I'm not gonna stand in your way. It'd dishonor your mother's memory to do it."

Kurt nodded and smiled with gratitude. His nose started to burn again.

"But let's get one thing straight, Kurt—you don't have to meet this Eric kid on his terms. If he's got a weapon like you say he does, every inch you give him counts. You gotta be prepared," Grandpa insisted, "and I can help you. I watched Anna training herself all that time…me and Bill even gave her a hand, as much as we could. I don't know from Linking, I never felt what it's like, but I've got memories of what I saw, and so do you. It's all in you somewhere. Maybe I can help you get it out."

*   *   *

The TV room, the kitchen, and the downstairs bathroom became Aaron Bluefield's entire world those next two days. Similarly, the back bedroom, back bathroom, and kitchen became Kayla's. The two of them stood at the counter in the one room where their worlds intersected, watching through the window as Kurt and his grandfather worked together to harness the potential of Anna's power. Twenty-four hours had seen not only a return to a semi-normal sleep schedule, but great leaps of progress in Kurt's ability, now that he knew where to find it. No one spoke of his or Blue's working lives—it was just assumed that the circumstances called for sick days.

"That's amazing," Kayla said as Kurt warped between his trademark pads. Grandpa cast handfuls of little stones into the air, and Kurt used his teleportation skill together with a spray of electric tendrils to reduce them all to cinders before they hit the ground.

"Which?" asked Blue. "The warping, or the multiple shots?"

"Either!" exclaimed Kayla. "Damn! Kurt's really good! Maybe he's right that he'll be a match for Eric. I hope I'm gonna be able to pull my weight…this is really my problem Kurt's getting dragged into."

"Don't think like that. Kurt wants to help…and anyway, I bet you could do any of those tricks yourself. The teleportation involves combining the earth, wind, and void elements, but Kurt can probably explain it better than I can." Blue leaned closer to the window. "The multishot seems to work exactly the same way as his normal shot…I can only assume the difference is caused by the placement of his fingers."

"Huh." Kayla shrugged. "Too bad I've never fired one shot of lightning, let alone pure qi. I mean, I guess I get the theory, but I didn't have too much time to practice all the elements while I was running away."

"Well, don't be shy—I'm sure Kurt and Mr. Ciardi would be more than happy to include you," said Blue, gesturing towards the door. "I can tell you all my thoughts and theories on Linking just as I've done for Kurt, but hands-on experience is usually the best way to learn something."

"Y'know, I think I will join them. C'mon!" Kayla grabbed Blue's wrist. "Maybe you're not a Linker, but you should at least get used to moving fast if you're gonna come with us!"

Blue stammered, "Y-yes...I suppose I should!"

*   *   *

Night fell on the second day, and the backyard was still lit up by flashes of golden light. The wind picked up and died erratically. Grandpa, Kurt, and Kayla were working overtime, trying to squeeze as much benefit from the training as possible—there was a silent agreement that Eric could wait no longer, that his deadline had to be met, lest there be consequences.

Blue staggered inside, heading in the general direction of his improvised bed, and found Grandma at the window. She wore a strange, introspective smile.

"Even Anna could never do some of this stuff," she said to Blue, without looking at him. "He's better than she was...and Kayla's good, too."

"Kurt's very smart, more so than he gives himself credit for," Blue said. "He's been quite creative with combining his powers and finding new uses for the elements. I'm sure some of it is Anna's qi within him as well, like Mr. Ciardi said."

Grandma turned around.

"You're a good friend to him, Blue," she said. "I know how smart *you* must be to be a teacher so young, and you helped him figure out some of what he could do. He might not say it, but I know it means a lot to Kurt, what you did staying by his side all this time. You're family now, Blue. Thank you."

"Um...I...you're welcome, and thank *you* for your hospitality! I really appreciate it...wow, I mean...I don't know what to...we're not so—in my...well, I...." Blue walked backwards out of the kitchen, toward the TV room, as he tried to speak. He made a few, aborted attempts at waving or smiling at her. "Thanks, Grandm—Mrs. Ciar...Grandma. Good night!"

*   *   *

They had wanted to leave first thing in the morning. Kurt even packed up the Lowval Electric van and filled the gas tank the night before to save time. But with all their dallying and long goodbyes, it was mid-afternoon

by the time Kurt, Kayla, and Blue stood on the front porch of the Ciardis'
home, with Grandma and Grandpa just outside the door behind them.

Once they made it that far, they stopped moving again. A few yards
still remained between the stoop and the van.

"Be careful, Kurt," Grandpa said. "Remember, you Link right back
here the second things start lookin' ugly."

"I know, Grandpa," said Kurt. "The pad I put in the living room was
the last one I set, so I can put down two more someplace if I have to, and
that one won't disappear. I'll be right back on the couch if something goes
wrong…but that's not gonna happen."

"You be careful, too, Kayla. And especially you, Blue," added Grandpa.
"You're not a Linker like they are."

"We will," Kayla and Blue said together.

"Blue, are you sure you wanna go?" Grandma asked. "Remember what
I told you last night—we care about you, too, just like Kurt. You've already
done so much, helping him through this when he was too afraid to tell us
what was happening to him. You don't have to put yourself in danger…you
can't defend yourself like they can. We wouldn't hold it against you."

"It's all right—I have my own reasons for going. I've been intrigued by
this Linking power since the day Kurt developed it," said Blue. "Now, I'll
be able to satisfy my curiosity to the fullest. Besides, just because I'm not a
Linker doesn't mean I can't help out somehow, and I want to do whatever I
can. I'm involved now."

"Damn right you are! Go start the engine." Kurt tossed Blue the keys
to the van. "Kayla, jump in back, and stay low once we're gettin' close. Eric
doesn't know my face, but he knows yours. We've gotta try and sneak up
on him, even if he can sense us getting closer."

"Gotcha." Kayla stopped and waved to the Ciardis. "It was so nice to
meet you both! Thank you so much for letting me stay here."

"Anytime, Kayla!" said Grandma.

Kurt walked back to the door and hugged both his grandparents close.
They were reluctant to let go.

"We love you, Kurt. Make sure you come back to us, no matter what,"
said Grandpa. "That's all we care about."

"Don't worry. If this goes as well as I think it will, we'll be home by
dinnertime." Kurt stepped back and grinned, with a little nod that
suggested he'd have tipped his hat if he had one. "Be safe while I'm gone!"

"Oohhh, you just be safe, Kurt!" Grandma called after him.

As soon as Kurt was buckled in, Blue backed the van down the driveway and turned onto the road.

"You have a really nice family," said Kayla.

"Yeah. I know." Kurt leaned around his seat to face her. "Don't worry, Kay. As soon as we take care of this end-of-the-world crap, we'll get you back to yours. I promise."

The van left Lowval with the sun on its right.

ACT IV

红埃里克

ERIC THE RED

"**"Dear Grandma and Grandpa,"** said Kurt to himself, drafting an imaginary postcard. "'Hi from New York. I'm sorry, I wasn't able to save the world because I spent the whole damn night stuck in traffic.'"

The sun was just low enough to be supremely bright and annoying for the three in the van. Soon, at least, it would be lost behind the buildings of Queens and the Bronx. Thanks to heavy traffic and ubiquitous construction, it had taken hours to breach the city limits and inch through the highways that encircled Manhattan. A sweaty Blue had long since shed his tweed jacket, and now he rolled up his sleeves and loosened his tie as he merged onto a tiny bridge that led to the Triborough toll plaza. Thankfully, their exit was coming up a few yards ahead.

"You should be able to see Wards Island by now," said Kayla; she was crouched down in the back, tracing her finger over a road map. "Any sign of Eric?"

"I certainly hope he doesn't attack now, while we're still stuck in gridlock," said Blue. "We didn't think of this possibility. It leaves us completely vulnerable!"

"Chill out, Blue. If that Hydrad kid could sense Kayla well enough to follow her, then Eric knew we were getting close as soon as we hit the George Washington Bridge," Kurt said. "He wants to attack, he's gonna. Since he hasn't, that means he doesn't want to. He's probably gonna wait 'til we get to wherever we're going first."

Radio DJ Bruce Benny came on in between songs to deliver news highlights for the day. It was only supposed to take the first five minutes of the six o'clock hour, but it always felt longer.

"Hey hey there, New York, and welcome to your Frrriday afternoon! The temperature is a pleasant 58 degrees and the sky is sunny on this early spring day. If you're driving around town, watch out for the Triborough, where a stalled truck in the center lane has traffic backed up all the way to the Cross Bronx...."

"Ah, so that's what it is," muttered Blue.

"...meeting today to discuss a proposed change in Brooklyn zoning laws, and President Bush is in town, or close to it, visiting New Jersey to award a commendation to Professors Cedric Perry and Malcolm Frederick. For those of you who haven't heard, or maybe I should say those of you living in a cave, these are the wizards behind a shot that could add decades to the life expectancy of the average human, and repeated vaccinations could—"

"Dah." Kurt reached over and changed the station. "News!"

"What? That's an interesting story," said Kayla. "We've been talking about it for months at school. There's a whole class dedicated just to following the development and writing about the, like, social and environmental implications and stuff like that."

"Fascinating!" said Blue. "I'd love to be in a course like that...or teach one, I suppose. I've been keeping up with the story myself."

"Come on!" Kurt kept looking out the windows for signs of Eric—they were about halfway across the bridge now. "Even if they can prove that it works, it's not something anybody needs."

"You're joking! Who wants to die?" asked Kayla.

"Who wants to live forever?" countered Kurt. "Maybe most people don't walk around asking to die, but being immortal would probably just get really boring. 'Sides, I bet the shot doesn't save you from being killed in a plane crash or something...or from being drained, for that matter."

Kurt extended his neck to try and see around a large, white truck. The closer their exit came, the more antsy he felt.

"Kayla, you said Wards Island is small, correct?" asked Blue. "We have to find Eric before he finds us to retain our strategic advantage."

"Yeah, it's small, and we should be right over top of it." She was interrupted, jerked to the side as Blue started fighting his way across the crowded lanes to the exit. "You're right, Kurt. He should've been able to sense us from pretty far away. So how come we're this close and I can't sense him yet?"

Kurt considered that for a moment. He didn't really know what the Linker's sense felt like, though he had a notion that it was similar to the vague, twisting dread he'd felt upon waking up to Hydrad in his backyard. Still, it would've been hard for him to notice the absence of a feeling he'd never thought to look for. He shrugged and kept his eyes peeled, as if he could find the stream of ill will by sight alone.

"Maybe Eric has some way of masking his powers," Blue suggested.

"I don't think it works like that. Especially after hearing everything Laoshi told you guys, I think it's the person we'd be able to sense, not his powers," said Kayla.

"Hmm…that's an intriguing idea. What do you think, Kurt?"

No answer.

"Kurt?" Blue glanced over at him, and found that Kurt was staring right past him, out the driver's side window.

"What is it?" Kayla asked.

"Who needs Linker sense when you have a giant sign?"

Kurt pointed out the window—Blue took a moment between switching lanes to look, and Kayla craned her neck around the front seat. There was a huge, red brick building off the left side of the bridge, presumably with a foundation on Wards Island below. Daylight was fading fast, so its outside and inside lights were coming on and obscuring the façade, but a spray-painted rendition of the dark rune was still visible. It crossed many of the windows and was big enough to be seen for miles away.

"Well, that's a little obvious," said Blue. "Then again, I suppose most people aren't aware of what that symbol means. It'd probably be mistaken for an ad, or elaborate graffiti."

"It *is* graffiti," Kurt said. He laughed and shook his head. "Man, this guy is such a little kid for someone who's screwing up the whole damn world. What, did he get the idea to hide out in an abandoned building from some ninja movie?"

"I told you he was immature," Kayla said.

"There's just one thing—all the lights are coming on, and there's smoke coming out of the stacks," Blue pointed out. "That building doesn't look abandoned to me."

"Then what…?" said Kayla.

"Maybe it's a trap," said Blue. The exit for Wards Island arrived, and he hesitated, but Kurt lightly tapped the wheel to urge him back on course.

"It's all we got," he said. "If it's a trap, that just means we gotta punch through it too fast to get caught."

The exit ramp led to a toll booth, then another ramp, then a traffic light, and, finally, to the expansive parking lot and garage for personnel at the marked building. Both were filled with cars.

"Just gun it up to the front door and park there. Kayla, get ready to jump outta the back and meet me on the sidewalk—we're gonna kick the door down. All right?"

"Got it," said Kayla.

"But what if this is a diversion and Eric isn't here at all?" Blue followed Kurt's instructions even as he protested. "How are we going to explain our actions to building security, Kurt?!"

"We'll move too fast for them to get our names. It's all about movin' fast!" Kurt unbuckled his seat belt and leaned against the door.

Blue hit the brakes and sidled into the fire lane. He could barely get out quickly enough to stay a few feet behind Kurt and Kayla, who executed their plan immediately and with wind-assisted speed. Kicking down the front doors turned out to be unnecessary, since they opened inward anyway and weren't locked.

Kurt and Kayla only moved a few steps inside. Their determined charge evaporated into a dead stop just beyond the entrance.

"What the hell…?"

They were in the lobby of some kind of plant; parts of the working floors were visible through big, thick glass doors on either side. The machines were running, and people were everywhere. But the people didn't move. They stood as if locked in place, staring straight ahead. Kurt looked at the nearest man, a worker complete with hard hat and protective eyewear, and studied his vacant expression in vain. There was nothing there to answer his questions—there was nothing there at all.

Blue noticed a handful of people younger than he was, a pocket of men and women dressed in business suits, and some scattered others that also seemed out of place in the plant. He was just starting to put two and two together when Kayla shrieked.

"These are…." She raised her hands in front of her face and turned away. "The people Eric drained!"

Everyone tensed. Not only was the Siphon Stone's threat more real now, they suddenly realized that they were in a room filled with the living dead. The whole building was probably the same way.

"Oh, God…." Blue approached Kayla, sensing her discomfort.

"NO!" But Kayla ran away. At first, Blue thought he'd done something wrong, but then he realized that she was heading straight for a group of three zombies. They were clearly among the ones transported into the plant from somewhere else—a man and woman, both in their forties, and a boy in his early teens. It was an entire family, positioned together like a twisted portrait.

Blue felt his stomach churn.

"So this is how he can hang out in an occupied building," muttered Kurt. He waved his hand in front of the workman's eyes—no response. *And this must be what a living body looks like with no original qi…ugh. There'd better be a way to reverse this.*

"Kurt…." Blue got his attention and pointed to Kayla, who had fallen on her knees hugging the man, woman, and boy all at once. Her body was racked by sobs.

"Shit." Kurt didn't take long to figure it out, either. "That's her family?!"

"They must be." Blue paused and trained his ears across the room to hear what Kayla was saying between her cries. He caught fragments of phrases, many of them apologies.

"She said she couldn't go home because Eric would have known where to follow her." Blue was wringing his hands. "I suppose he must've gone there anyway."

"This is unbelievable." Kurt's rune started flashing as his anger increased. "Eric probably did it before we even met Kayla, the bastard!"

"We—should we go see if she's all right?" asked Blue.

"Yeah, we gotta stick together. This place isn't—"

"Nobody move!" said a voice from behind them.

Kurt whirled around. "Hydrad!"

The front doors had closed behind Blue, so Hydrad could only have come from farther inside the building. Still, he'd managed to get between Kurt and the exit.

"Y-you're not getting away this time!" Hydrad called across the room. He seemed to get distracted by Kayla at first, but then quickly locked his attention on Kurt. "Eric'll be here any minute!"

Blue practically ignored him—he'd dashed over to Kayla and knelt down beside her as soon as Kurt had encouraged him. He put his hand on her back and felt her lean against him.

"Even if you fixed them right now, I'd still…." Kurt fumed. "Everything you and Eric are doing—draining these people, hurting Kayla…but going after her family when she wasn't there to protect them… you don't deserve to live."

Kurt made a motion with his hand like he was pitching a baseball, and a bolt of lightning flew across the room toward Hydrad. Hydrad cried out and jumped to the side, keeping his rune up like a loaded gun.

"I tried to tell you to stay out of this!" he said. "Eric only wanted Kayla, but now he wants you, too!"

"Good!" Kurt reabsorbed the electricity. "I'm dyin' to meet him!"

Another discharge, another near miss. Hydrad's forehead was glistening with sweat.

"Would you quit shooting already?!" he said. He shook his head. "You don't get it—you're fighting for the wrong side. Eric has a plan to change the world so there'll still be something left after it ends. As long as he's in charge, no one has to die!"

Blue wrapped his arms around Kayla and edged closer to her, but now he was listening to Hydrad as well, wondering what he meant.

"HA!" Kurt was less inclined to be curious. He gestured around the room with both hands. "Whaddaya call this, kid? Or don't these people count, as far as you're concerned? When the hell did you Goddamn college kids decide you had the right—"

"When we got these!" Hydrad pointed to his rune, which flashed faster as his emotions spiked. "The normal rules don't apply anymore. We're trying to do the right thing for the greatest possible number of people. Draining some of them has to happen first!"

"No, *I'm* doing the right thing—trying to *stop* the world from ending, for everyone! That's what Linkers are for!" Kurt started charging a third shot. "All your pal's doin' is makin' it worse!"

"I know Eric. He's the smartest kid I've ever met, and the best friend I've ever had. He got picked to manage the end of the world for a reason. He sees the big picture—he knows what he's doing!"

Kurt felt his frown lines deepen. "What about Kayla? You and Eric can't justify what you did to her family. You ask me, you're just telling yourselves you've got your eyes on some 'big picture' so you don't have to admit what kinda monsters you are!"

"You really think Kayla matters against the whole world? This is bigger than any of us! And if a spoiled, judgmental…bitch like her winds up being the one to have to make a sacrifice, I'm not gonna lose any sleep over it—"

A tendril of electricity smacked him in the face.

"You're worthless," said Kurt, turning on his qi shield.

"Kurt!" Kayla jumped up and stalked toward Hydrad. Her eyes were red and her face was covered in tears, but those tears were already flying off her cheeks and gathering around her rune like the water they were.

"Let me," she said, making it more command than request.

Kurt nodded; he shut off his rune and stepped aside. "No problem."

Hydrad stood in place, panting, for one more moment. Then he struck, manipulating the island itself so that earth moved underneath the building, snapping bolts loose as he turned the metal floor plates upward. But the attack never reached Kayla, who, with a primal scream, ripped the water pipes right out of the walls and sent flumes twirling through the air toward the Dark Linker. Two impacted at different angles, knocking Hydrad first off his feet and then spinning him around. Kayla didn't stop there—the founts kept on coming, and before long, she settled into a rhythm of strikes from random angles of approach, freezing just the end of each water spout to create glacial punches.

Hydrad never got to fight back.

In the space of twenty or thirty seconds, Kayla was poised to create the biggest stream of all and surround Hydrad's entire torso with it. She kept the flow going to lift him off the floor and pin him to the highest point on the left wall, above one of the glass doors. A quick freeze of the water around him kept him hanging there while Kayla pulled the spout back, giving it the form of a cobra rearing to strike with deadly fangs. A spear of ice formed on its tip and pointed at Hydrad's chest.

Kurt was still vacillating between pride, grim resignation, and horror when Blue spoke.

"Um, Kayla—"

"Don't try to stop me, Blue!" she snapped; the force of her words nearly knocked him over. She turned back to Hydrad and sobbed even more. The ice spear bobbed back and forth, waiting for instructions.

And then, a hole broke open near the top of the wall behind Kayla. There was a sound like the wind whistling over a mountain made of crystal, and a tendril of white energy snaked across the room with immense speed. It looked like a frame of animation being painted as it moved, something that didn't belong in the real world. It struck Hydrad, causing him what looked like unspeakable agony, then lingered on him for a moment before receding through the hole it had made. Kayla jumped back in surprise, and all the water she'd been commanding rained down again, inert.

The force of the strange energy had broken the ice; with nothing left to hold him up, Hydrad tumbled to a hard landing on the floor.

"Ooooo…." Even Kurt had to cringe at the sight. He ran over to inspect the damage, but didn't deactivate his rune yet, just in case this was some kind of trick.

"You ask me, kid, you're lucky if you have a couple broken bones instead of whatever Kayla was gonna do to ya!" Kurt knelt down and turned Hydrad's head to face him, but he was met with only the same vacant stare worn by everyone else in the building.

"Kurt…that was the Siphon Stone's beam…." Kayla spoke quietly— she was shivering, hugging herself in a futile attempt to stop.

"What?!" Kurt jumped to his feet. "Blue! Did you see where it came from?"

"Through there…but…." Blue's mind was twisting even as he pointed at the plainly visible hole in the wall. All that showed through were dull magenta clouds. "There's nothing out there! And the angle is wrong—it would've had to have come from very far away, or else out of the sky!"

"So he can fly, or else he's got long-range shots. With Linking, it could be either." Kurt tried to level out his tone and stay alert. "Kayla, can you help us out here?"

"I-I…I…I don't know…." Kayla was still shell-shocked. "I only saw him use the stone once, when he tried to drain me and missed…it only went across the room then, but maybe it can go farther—"

Kurt held up his hand. "Wait. Do you feel that?"

The ground was shaking. At first it was barely noticeable, but within a few seconds, the tremors increased to near-earthquake magnitude.

"We have to get out of the building!" cried Blue. "Come on, Kayla!"

"No!" she cried, running toward her family. "I can't leave them! I won't!"

"Kay! Listen to me," said Kurt. "New York doesn't get earthquakes, so there's only one guy who can be behind this. You wanna help your family, he's the one you gotta talk to."

Kayla stood still for another moment, her arms out as if shielding her loved ones, but then she wiped her eyes and nodded.

"Right…you're right. Let's go."

Kurt took the lead, and all three of them ran toward the doors. Kayla lagged behind a little and glanced back several times; Blue stopped and waited for her at the exit.

"Are you all right?" he asked.

"What do you think?" Kayla said, her voice weak and wet.

Blue struggled with a response, but as soon as he and Kayla got outside, Kurt stole his attention without even trying. He was staring across the water, from Wards Island past the Triborough Bridge to Manhattan. His head and shoulders were leaning forward, and it seemed like he might fall.

Blue saw in his friend a man who finally believed in the apocalypse.

*   *   *

And then, it was Manhattan's turn to believe.

The pedestrians on the sidewalks had no words to describe it, let alone time to speak. Anyone on the road in a car felt it before they saw it, as the asphalt was pulled out from under them like a throw rug. All the streets on the island were reduced to their bare bones, the skeletal pipes just barely capable of holding up some of the cars, while others plunged down. The asphalt flowed to a central location in lower Manhattan, compressed to a glob the size of a golf ball. Once all the roadways had been consumed, the orb flashed with a purple light, then stretched back out and reached for the sky. Lumber and metal from construction sites, furniture from apartments, boxes from warehouses, and whole rooms from offices, pounding straight through buildings when necessary, flew to meet the rising blackness as it shot up like a hyperactive tree.

The asphalt stretched 120 stories into the air and became pulled so thin, heated so finely, that it took on the shiny appearance of purple glass. It fashioned itself into an obelisk that seemed to glow dimly. Some of the yellow from the road lines survived, and ringed around the structure just below where its point began.

The New York City skyline had gained a tower.

*   *   *

General Geoffrey Sanders had been in New York visiting one of the northeast recruitment offices when it happened. A lifetime of soldiering had taught him to act swiftly. He made calls and gathered all the officers and reserves he could find in fifteen minutes, then led them down the sidewalk in a series of green-and-brown jeeps. With all the roads gone, his convoy had to fight for space on the concrete with a veritable motorcade of police cars heading the same way. Jurisdiction would surely be argued at the site, but all Sanders cared about was containing the situation.

"Weston!" he shouted over his shoulder to a private behind him in the jeep. "You got someone on that phone yet who can tell us what the hell is goin' on?"

"Sir! Pentagon's as much in the dark as we are, sir, but they're redeploying the air force to assist us. Fighters should be circling the island within five minutes, sir," Weston answered.

"Good. Peterson, stop here! We ain't gettin' any closer in the jeeps."

Police and SWAT teams were already standing in the street, on top of the exposed pipes, when General Sanders brought his men to the front line. They were half a block from the foot of the tower, but a few soldiers were even closer, coming around from the other side to meet up with their commanding officer.

"Private!" Sanders addressed the closest of the new arrivals, who stopped and saluted. "You been on all sides 'a this thing?"

"Yes, sir!"

"And what've ya got for me?" He squinted at the man's tags—Private Kipling.

"Sir! It looks solid all around, sir! No obvious doors or windows."

"Very well, then. Good work, Kipling." Sanders moved his squinting upwards, toward the point of the obelisk. "What in the hell...?"

Fire trucks were arriving with searchlights on top, parked at an angle on the sidewalks with two wheels in the gutter. Soon, white discs probed the exterior of the tower from all sides. Sanders heard choppers above him, which were circling and adding their own lights to the upper half of the structure.

"Damn news networks," he muttered. Private Weston approached and Sanders ordered, "Get to the back and make sure someone from the police or the SWAT team is keepin' the media out of the way!"

"Yessir!" Before he left, Weston handed Sanders a portable phone. "Pentagon wants to speak to you, sir."

"Right." Sanders lifted the phone. "This is General Sanders. I am on-site at the foot of the purple tower."

"I read you, General Sanders. Delta Wing of the U.S. Air Force is in position and awaiting orders. The White House has granted you full authority to manage this crisis until further notice. I'll be patching you through to the wing commander momentarily."

"Copy that—"

"Sanders!" It was Police Commissioner Edward Needham. He strode awkwardly to the general's position, stumbling several times on the slippery pipes.

"Needham, I swear to God, this is not the time to be arguing who's in charge," said Sanders, rising to confront the red tape he'd feared. "We've got the air force on standby, and I'm about to surround this thing with all the ground troops we can pull together. Whatever's going on here needs to be nipped in the bud now!"

Needham held up his palms. "All I ask is that you wait until we can find out more about what we're up against before you open fire. There could be innocent lives at risk."

"Seems to me there could be innocent lives at risk the longer we wait to get this thing secured! You think you can put my mind at ease, go ahead."

"I said I need time to get answers, not—" Needham stopped, and did a double take at the point of the obelisk. "Hold on! There's something moving up there!"

"Kipling! Binoculars!" ordered Sanders. "Major Garamond, take the men and get this thing surrounded ay-sap! I want minimum twenty soldiers on all sides!"

"Get some lights pointed at the top!" Sanders heard Needham shout as he raised the binoculars to his eyes. Between the fire department and the news crews, he had more than enough light to guide him while he zoomed in on the disturbance. His lips pursed and then parted.

Somehow, a person was standing on the point of the tower, though his feet didn't seem to have much to hold on to. He was dressed in a black button-down shirt and pants, as if he were on his way to a job as a waiter, and he had a bright red tie that whipped around in the wind in time with his light brown hair. He held both his arms out as if he were trying to silence an auditorium.

"It's just some kid!" Sanders exclaimed.

CRUCK! The portable phone came to life. *"General Sanders, sir, this is Colonel Enrite, U.S. Air Force. We are in position and standing by, sir."*

"Copy that. Keep your distance 'til I tell you otherwise."

And then the wind picked up. Eric bent it to his whim and created tunnels for his voice, more effective than any megaphone. Sanders and Needham both heard him clear his throat.

"People of New York, and the world—my name is Eric the Red," he said. "I'm here tonight to give you an important message. The world as you know it is dying!"

"What *is* this?" Needham heard a commotion and spun around. "Keep those damn reporters back, men! This is a restricted area!"

Despite his orders, everyone in America and beyond saw the choppers' close-up shots when Eric raised his palm.

"This symbol on my hand means that I am a Linker!" he said. "I have the power to control the elements with my qi, my soul energy. I used Linking to create the building you see here, the Darklight Tower, so that I can help all of you survive the end of the world! You know where to find me now, and you have to come to me if you want your lives to be saved! With this—"

He held up the Siphon Stone for the news crews.

"I can drain your qi from your bodies! Within the stone, your spirits will be protected, and by lending me your qi, you will grant me the power to control the world's last days! All hope is not lost! I am asking for your trust—if you don't believe me, you'll die when the old world dies! But if you put your faith in me, I'll be able to save you, and we can start a new world by redefining life and death themselves!"

"Colonel Enrite, come in," said Sanders into the phone. "I have a visual on one hostile on the roof of the purple tower. Lock on target and wait for my signal."

"Copy that."

"You're going to shoot missiles at him?" asked Needham disbelievingly.

"If he's behind this thing…." Sanders shook his head. "What he's sayin' is true, that makes him the most dangerous man alive."

"We don't know—"

"Well, why don't you tell me how that tower got there, Needham?!"

"All of you have to listen for this to work—I must have total cooperation for anyone to be saved!" said Eric. "More of you will become Linkers as the apocalypse gets closer, but don't think that that means you can take matters into your own hands! As the first Linker to manifest, I am the only one with the power to protect people, and I will not tolerate any doubt that could ruin things for all of us! If anyone, and I mean anyone, tries to fight me, here's what will happen!"

Eric's palm began to glow bright purple, bright enough that everyone on the ground saw it and cried out as a collective. The Siphon Stone lit up as well, neon white.

Slowly, Eric drew his hands together. Two of the news choppers circling the tower slowed to a stop, then careened toward each other at top speed, their blades howling in a vain effort to escape. They collided in a ball of fire, and their wreckages fell, entwined, toward the foot of the tower.

"Get back! Get back!" the SWAT team shouted as fiery metal pieces rained down on the crowd. The screams were becoming a full chorus.

"My dear Lord in Heaven…." said Needham.

Sanders growled and jerked the phone back to his lips.

"Enrite! Take that bastard down!"

"Understood, sir! Delta Wing, move in and fire at will!"

The U.S. Air Force swept in as if from nowhere. Eric saw them, but if he had time to do anything about it, he didn't. The wing broke formation, and each of the three planes launched a double payload. The explosion took the entire top off the tower, creating a shower of broken purple glass and leaving the jagged ruins above in flames. Eric was lost in black smoke at the moment of impact.

"Hmpf! Excellent work, Enrite!" Sanders lowered the phone and smirked. "Scratch one terrorist."

"Mmm-hmmm." Needham shook off his stupor. "I don't envy your position, Sanders. Even with the threat he posed, the media's going to have an easy time spinning you as a killer of children."

Glass continued to fall around them.

"The hell do I care? We just saved this city from…magic genocide, or whatever the hell that was! Now, all we gotta worry about is damage control. It could take months to get the roads back…."

Sanders went on, but Needham's attention lapsed. One of the larger glass shards had slowed to a stop, hanging suspended in the air at chest level, spinning just as it had while falling. He studied it curiously.

"Needham! I asked you a question!" But then Sanders noticed it, too. "What the…?"

Needham took a few tentative steps forward and reached out his hand toward the shard. But just as he would have made contact, it shot away from him, back into the air.

All the shards of glass were doing that now, even the ones that had already hit the ground. Before Needham's and Sanders's eyes, in view of all the cameras that were still running, the top of the Darklight Tower reconstructed itself like a tape on rewind. The smoke from the blast even seemed to flow back down, dousing the very fire it had sprung from and swirling around until it dissipated, revealing Eric, glowing purple and unharmed. He sneered and laughed down at the authorities.

"Do you understand now?" he asked, blasting his voice to the entire city again. "I have the mandate of Heaven—mortal weapons cannot harm me! This proves that I am the one chosen to direct the end times!"

"Shit!" Sanders fumbled with the phone. "Enrite, Enrite! Hostile is still alive, repeat, hostile is still alive! Continue assault!"

Delta Wing made a U-turn and came back, but Eric wasn't fooling around this time. He fired a white beam from the Siphon Stone that split three ways a few feet in front of him, impacting all of the fighter cockpits at once. Drained of their qi, the pilots were no longer in control—one of the planes smashed into a high-rise apartment building, creating a gigantic fire, and another went down sideways into the street, where it lost its wings and skidded to a stop blocks away. The third was on a collision course with the tower, but Eric raised his rune and tossed the plane upward, diverting it all the way into the Hudson River.

Sanders was thunderstruck.

"Fall back!" shouted Needham. "All units, fall back!"

They never got the chance. Eric had been aware of the police, firefighters, and soldiers on the ground from the beginning, and now he turned his attention, and the Siphon Stone's beam, on them. The white split so many ways nobody could have counted them if they had time, and everyone within two blocks of the tower was drained, leaving the area deserted except for the bodies and their vacant, living eyes.

Then Eric waved his hand, opened up a hole in the roof beneath him, and glided softly down. The hole closed behind him.

*   *   *

In Lowval, Grandma leaned her head into Grandpa's chest, unable to raise it but also unable to look away from the TV screen. Grandpa had his arm around her.

While the live feed continued and the reporters kept on talking, a little window in the lower right of the screen played footage of the tower's miraculous rebirth.

God, keep him safe, Grandpa prayed.

*   *   *

All eyes were on the Darklight Tower—no one thought to look out over the water beneath the Triborough Bridge. There, Kurt and Blue rode a wave atop a platform of ice, with Kayla piloting the trip from the back. They had a front-row seat for all the explosions and sirens, which were rapidly getting closer.

"This isn't good, Kurt!" yelled Blue over the rush of water. "Despite your logic, everything we just saw indicates that Eric is far more powerful than you! Maybe we should rethink our strategy!"

"I wish you'd quit sayin' that! Only reason the cops couldn't hurt him is 'cause he's got that qi shield!" said Kurt.

"What about the Darklight Tower?" Blue had been able to hear Eric's speech as well. "You've never done anything like that!"

"I've never tried!" said Kurt. "And all it means anyway is he's better than me at the Dark elements, but I gotta be better than him at the Light elements! It all balances out like scales, right? That's what we're tryin' to do, isn't it?"

"Um, actually…." Blue broke eye contact; there was no use lowering morale. "Never mind! If he's sensed us, it's too late to run anyway!"

Kayla was silent, her distant stare focused on the point of the tower. Blue turned to her and watched for a minute. He opened his mouth and started to say something, but the ice floe shook and interrupted him before he could.

Soon, the wave hit land and washed over the gridlocked highway. It carried Kurt, Blue, and Kayla down the smaller streets of Manhattan, over the sidewalk where there was still a solid surface, and finally deposited them around the corner and a block away from the tower. Kurt had asked Kayla to stop there so he could peer in and plan an entry that would circumvent the police—Linkers were sure to be high on the most-wanted list now.

It didn't matter. They arrived right after Eric had finished draining all the authorities on the scene.

"Ugh." Kurt willed himself to look at the tower instead of the zombies. "We'd better get in there now, while we have a chance. Before Eric drains anyone else."

"Good idea, but I don't see a door," said Blue.

Kayla said, "Maybe you oughta wait out here, Blue."

"What—"

"You're the only one of us who isn't a Linker," she continued, glancing at Kurt. "Driving down was one thing. It's gonna be dangerous in there."

"Listen, you two, I came all this way to help, and I intend to do whatever I can, danger or no danger. No place is safe now," Blue said. "I'll most likely be better protected than any of the other non-Linkers in this city if I stick close to you."

"Fine. Let's just go." Kurt ran across the street and forced Kayla and Blue to keep up without further argument.

"But there's no door!" Kayla repeated.

"Screw it!" As he got close, Kurt prepared his qi gun. When he was just a few feet from the tower, he stopped, spread his feet and locked his knees to prepare for the recoil, then blew an entry hole in the exterior wall. It came out even bigger than he planned it to be—the tower's sides were deceptively, improbably thin.

They walked inside, and were greeted with what looked like an industrial cellar: bare, black and gray, with a concrete floor and stairs on the far wall, except those stairs had been ripped out of another building, and despite still being functionally positioned, they were upside-down. There were other sets of stairs, crates, pallets, and platforms running along the inside of the hollow tower as far up as the three could see, lit by small fires in places and sometimes gliding back and forth on currents of qi-assisted wind. Together, these things formed a crude, narrow walkway. It was as if Eric had prepared to entertain company, but not to make them comfortable.

"It's like a cubist Picasso," whispered Blue.

"Yeah…." Kayla said.

"Whatever. Let's get moving." Kurt stepped ahead and held out his rune. "Some of that crap looks pretty unstable. I'll go first and see if I can hold it together while we walk on it."

"No, let me," said Kayla. "You're the one who's supposed to be Eric's equal. You should save your qi for him."

Kurt agreed, and the ascent began. The path up the Darklight Tower had surprisingly good footing, even when it was made of levitating wooden crates. Kayla used the power of wind to keep a safety net in place at all times, but it proved unnecessary except as a comfort.

At first, Blue stayed back with Kurt, but all his attention was on Kayla. He puzzled over the things she'd said and done. Eventually, after looking over at Kurt and finding him completely absorbed in his examination of the tower, Blue sped up and walked next to her.

"So far, so good," Kayla said distractedly.

"I disagree," said Blue. He leaned in and whispered, "Why did you try to leave me behind? I understand that…seeing your family as they were was a shock, and I…look, I know you must be as scared as we are—"

"Did you ever stop to think…." Kayla's first words drowned out Blue's last. "That this isn't about saving the world to me? I know it has to be, I know that six billion people are more important than me and Eric, but it's…hard, Blue. It's just hard!"

"Yes, I know, I…you and Eric? What—"

"I wish I was strong enough to do this alone. Part of me…look, Eric's…he's terrible, and I know it! But I don't. And that's it. 'Cause there's also this part of me that knows Eric's a damn idiot and a baby and an angry person sometimes, but…I told you. He's not evil, I don't want him to be evil even if he is…okay, that doesn't make sense, but you heard the way he was talking! What if he really believes that he's doing good?"

"He isn't doing good," said Blue. "How can you still think—"

"I don't know! He was…." Kayla wasn't quite ready to speak, but she interrupted and then searched for her words—whatever Blue had been starting to say, she didn't want to hear it. "Eric was practically part of my family. He came home with me all the time…my parents liked him, but I'm not sure he knew that. They were really protective of me, even after I'd been dating him for a year. To do what he did to them…."

She paused to cry a little, quietly.

"I hate him," she said at last.

"I see…." Blue felt a wound opening under his words. "Of course you'd hate Eric after what he's done, but…it's still hard to hate someone you loved, even if he hurt other people you love. You want to believe there's some way that he can still be saved, some way that his actions can still be explained or excused. Well, nothing could excuse them, I suppose, but…."

He hesitated. The words strained against the back of his throat, building momentum and then finally breaking free.

"Maybe there is a way," he said. "Maybe we can reverse the draining and bring your family back, and perhaps once we understand Eric's thoughts and motivations, there'll be a way to save him as well. I listened to what he and Hydrad were saying, and things seem to be a great deal more complicated—"

"I don't think I can do this," Kayla whispered. She almost stopped walking. "I'm afraid we're gonna get up to the top and Eric will be there, and I'll see him, and even after…damn it, sometimes I think I was never his girlfriend, I was his babysitter, but I still…I don't want to kill him, Blue! He drained my family, we don't know if it can be reversed, it's…but I don't want any more death, but…."

Her voice became a tiny squeak. "What if he leaves us no choice?"

"I…."

"You said the Earth chose me to help it for a reason. I—I don't want to let my emotions make me choose not killing Eric over the whole world, or even just saving my family…dammit, why aren't I…!"

Blue struggled to formulate a response.

"Kayla…." He took a deep breath. "You're a remarkable person. You don't have murder in your heart, even if Eric does, and that's…listen, neither does Kurt, in spite of how he talks. We aren't going to kill anyone, and there's always a choice. It's okay for you to care about Eric, even if you hate him at the same time. It's okay that no matter how much he hurt you, you don't want to kill him…."

He reached out for her.

"I'm sorry, Blue, I can't think about this anymore…." she said.

Kayla pulled away and quickened her step to get back in the lead.

Stunned, Blue stood there on a floating box with his arm out until Kurt caught up and bumped into him from behind. Blue said a sheepish apology, and the hike continued in silence.

The inside of the Darklight Tower went on and on, but eventually, the three began to sense an impenetrable blackness above them. It was a ceiling—they were getting close enough now to see a last flight of stairs that disappeared into it. Kurt brought Blue forward with him to tighten up the group, then activated his rune once more.

All of them were on-guard as they approached and began to climb the last steps, leaving the hollow lower levels behind them. They were in darkness for a few minutes as the stairs wound around, and they stopped periodically for fear of ambush. Just as despair began to set in, Kayla pointed ahead. Kurt and Blue could see her hand in silhouette against the light.

They emerged in a room with a floor like a chessboard and fake, potted trees in the corners. It was deceptively, eerily normal. The walls were dark purple with gold embroidery near the ceiling, except for the wall on the left, where the tower's glass siding acted like a translucent window. New York was visible through the veil, tinted fuchsia.

"It…looks like we're about halfway up," whispered Blue. The atmosphere had hushed him; it felt like elevator music ought to be playing in the background.

"I'm in the waiting room at my dentist's office," Kurt said. Still, something about this room had the group on edge. Kurt scrutinized the mostly empty space with a growing sense of unease. "Why do I feel like I've been here before?"

"You just said why," Kayla said tersely.

"No…not like that…."

Blue tried to help. "This room might have been lifted as-is from another building somewhere in the city. Maybe you've been to its original location."

"No." Kurt walked farther in, away from his companions, and crouched down on the floor. "I don't like this." When he stood up, there was a teleportation pad under his feet. He was preparing for tactical movement.

"I feel it, too. Oh, God." Kayla doubled over, with one hand in her hair. "It's him! He's here!"

"Where?" Blue looked all around the room. There was a dividing wall at its center, creating a wide, doorless entryway to the far side. Beyond that, on the back wall, was a closed lavender door. There were plenty of places for Eric to hide, but there was no movement and no sound from anywhere.

"I—I don't know!" Kayla staggered farther into the room, snapping her neck back and forth, eyes brimming with fear. "God, he's everywhere! I can feel him everywhere!"

"Kay, calm down!" Kurt called out.

But Kayla was unreachable. She continued toward the divide in the middle of the room, holding her head the whole way and swaying back and forth like a drunk. Blue started to jog toward her, ready to catch her if she fell, but she waved her arms above her head sharply and stopped him halfway.

"I can't do this, Blue! God, help me…!"

"Don't panic—stay with us! We need to stay together!" Blue said.

Then, Kurt felt something he'd never felt before. It was like being forced to exhale, except it was happening in front of him rather than from within. The air was acting like water being poured between two glasses, liquid rushing to fill the empty space.

Void!

Kurt understood too late. Kayla's stagger was interrupted by a pull like a vacuum, and even though she was leaning away from it, she was sucked across the room, screaming all the way.

"Aaaaaaaaaaaa!"

"Kayla!" exclaimed Blue and Kurt together. They ran to try and catch up with her, but she was already past the divide. Two heavy purple doors with round gold knockers glided into view from the other side and slammed shut over the entryway, splitting the room in half. Once they were closed and pressed together, a strange symbol flashed into being across them, drawn in deep violet.

Kayla's voice cut off.

"No!" Blue got there first, and pounded on the doors with both fists. "Kayla!"

"Stand back, Blue!" Kurt charged up his qi gun and fired to create an opening, just like he'd done outside. The ball of yellow energy hit the doors and broke apart with no effect. Kurt stared for a moment in horror, but then he dug in, recharged the gun, and started firing smaller shots at the doors and the surrounding wall, over and over again.

"Kurt!" Blue jumped aside to avoid one of the blasts. "Kurt! Kurt, stop!"

Kurt heard him and let up on the attacks. He was panting from his sudden exertion.

"It's not working…." Blue walked over and put his palms on the wall and doors. "We have to find another way to open them!"

"I doubt Eric left us a key." Kurt joined Blue at the doors and bent over with his hand rested on one of them, partly to inspect the bottom and partly because he needed a break.

"This isn't good!" Blue rapped his knuckles against first the right-hand door then the wall. "It feels totally solid…possibly for several feet!" He cupped his hands against the wall and shouted, "Kayla! Are you in there?!"

"The hell do you mean it's solid for several feet?" Kurt stood up. "There's a whole 'nother half of the room back there! We saw it!"

Kurt had recovered from his initial push, and now he charged his entire fist with qi. He leaned on one of the doors with his left hand and started punching the other repeatedly with his right. His energy dissipated over its surface and faded away.

The emblem above him remained unchanged, staring at him. It looked almost like a face: two flowery lines curved down through three broken lines, then stopped at three solid, V-shaped lines. Kurt swore he could hear it giving off a quiet hum in response to his attacks.

Blue tapped the wall with his ear pressed against it. There was an edge of panic to his investigation.

"Think about it, Kurt! You've been able to move through the void that exists in solid objects, but if it's Eric's dominant element, he might actually be able to reshape objects, by altering their empty space at the molecular level! This whole tower could change around us!"

"I don't buy that! We woulda felt it happening like when the tower went up!" Kurt felt himself getting tired again, so he backed off and glared at the mark on the door. "It's that thing that's doing it! It's some kinda qi trick…it's blocking my powers."

"It's a Seal of Broken Lightning."

The wall opened up noiselessly to Blue's right, revealing a tunnel that led through an ocean of solid, black rock. From this tunnel floated Eric. At first, his expression looked meditative, but once he was in the room and the tunnel had sealed shut behind him, he opened his eyes and smirked.

Blue stepped back. Kurt raised his rune and steeled himself.

"There's no point in trying to break through it. It's the strongest kind of qi shield a Linker can make, tied directly to my life force. Unless I take it down, that thing stays up as long as I'm alive. And now that I have my girlfriend back, as it should be—"

"What have you done with her?!" Blue demanded.

Eric's gaze was on him, and suddenly he was afraid. Kurt saw what was coming, and moved with the speed of qi. He prayed, in the space of an instantaneous thought, that his shield could block the power of the Siphon Stone.

The snaking white energy shot forth from Eric, and all Blue could think of to do was raise his arms over his face. He shut his eyes and prepared to find out what it felt like to have his original qi ripped out of his body. But he felt nothing. The beam bounced off and dissolved into the air. Blue looked at his arms and realized he was encased in a yellow glow.

Whew, thought Kurt.

"So you're Ciardi," said Eric, glancing at Kurt's rune. "You know, most Linkers can only put up one qi shield at a time. Protecting your buddy there leaves you defenseless."

"Guess I'll just have to be faster than you, kid," said Kurt.

"She...." Blue was talking again, weakly—Eric looked at him. "She was reluctant to fight you...in spite of all you've done, she refused to believe you were evil. She still cared for you, wanted to protect you...."

"Is that what she said? Ha!" Eric rolled his eyes. "She and I are gonna have a good, long talk after this. What the hell is her problem? The Earth itself picks me to be the alpha Linker, and she still won't believe me when I say I know what I'm doing! But what's new about that? No one's ever trusted me to be in charge of anything, not even my own Goddamn life!"

The tower shook with Eric's frustration. He ranted on, glaring at something past the ceiling, almost as if he'd forgotten Kurt and Blue entirely.

"Twenty years everyone's been telling me what to do! I never got to choose for myself, I never got to be the one in control! Can I be an artist, Dad? No. Can I take care of my own room, Mom? No. Everyone assumes I can't be trusted to make my own decisions. First it was my parents, then it was my teachers, and now my girlfriend!"

Eric dropped to the floor and pounded it with both feet; a ring of purple flew out from beneath him and went up the walls. "Hel-lo! How the hell am I supposed to prove I'm responsible when no one ever gives me a chance?! Well, guess what, Kayla—I don't care anymore! Nobody can tell me I'm not in charge this time, 'cause this time, it's my destiny! This is the shot I deserved all along!"

"So the first thing you do with your 'shot' is blow your cover by sticking a giant tower in the middle of New York. Way to make good decisions," said Kurt. He glanced over his shoulder—there was a lamp on the wall, lit and therefore wired to a power source, which he began to Link with. "The whole world's gonna be after you now, qi shield or no."

Eric shook his head and started floating again. He laughed. "Surprise, surprise, someone else who thinks that anything they don't understand is automatically a mistake. 'Blowing my cover' was the whole point—I'll just drain whoever they send! The more qi I put into the Siphon Stone, the farther its beam can reach. Pretty soon, I'll be able to drain people all around the world from right here. And then, once I have everyone's qi, the Linker Weapon will be finished, and the way the world ends will be up to me!"

"You're gonna drain everyone on Earth just 'cause you think you've got something to prove." Kurt spoke slowly, as if his mouth were filled with mucus. He clenched his fist to hide the rune as it flashed faster, preparing for action. "I don't believe in destiny. I'm gonna put you away because it'll make me feel good. And once you're dead, the Linker Weapon disappears, the balance is back in line, the seal's gone, and we've got Kayla back. That's what you said, isn't it—the seal's tied to your life?"

Hearing that was like a bucket of cold water thrown on Blue. Suddenly, instead of being focused on Kayla's loss, he remembered what she'd said and became her representative.

"Kurt…." he cautioned.

But Eric just laughed more. "And that, Kurt Ciardi, proves once and for all why I'm a better man for this job than you. You don't know anything! Do you honestly believe that the Linker Weapon caused the imbalance? I couldn't have even used the Siphon Stone if I wasn't already a Linker when I found it! Even if you could kill me and take the stone, it wouldn't stop the world from ending!"

Kurt's glare intensified, but on the inside he weakened. If what Eric was saying was true, it washed away everything he'd thought he understood. Kurt realized that he had no idea what the imbalance threatening the world was anymore, and that confronting Eric probably had nothing to do with fixing it.

"You're just too much of a coward to see the truth—*nothing* can stop the world from ending. The only thing Linkers can do is decide *how* it ends, and that job is mine. Who the hell are you to come in here and act like you're some kinda hero? The only reason you think I'm the bad guy is because I'm willing to work with something you can't accept! It's people like you, who see everything in black and white...."

Kurt tuned him out; his trepidation faded. There was still a reason for him to be here.

"The world needs to be fixed, not ended," he said, cutting Eric off. "I don't care what you think you know—as far as I'm concerned, you're just a selfish little brat!"

Eric grew quiet, seething, and floated back down to the floor.

"I could drain you right now, without your shield," he snarled, "but I won't. You've got a lotta nerve, actin' like you're better than me, stealin' my girlfriend—"

Kurt burst out laughing in spite of himself. "What the hell are you talking about? Don't worry, I got no interest in Kayla, but at least I'd still have a chance with her if I did!"

Making Eric angry and hoping he'd lose focus was a dangerous gamble, but so far, at least the angry part seemed to be working. Eric ground his teeth. His qi shield enveloped him, and purple energy evaporated off its surface, darkening as it spread.

"I heard the way she was talking at your house! 'Me and Kurt' this, 'two against one' that! You took the one person who ever gave me the benefit of the doubt and turned her against me!" Kurt felt the pull on his face again as Eric formed a void in his left hand. "I'll make you beg me to drain you! And maybe then I'll go back to where you came from and take your loved ones away and see how you like it!"

Kurt let out an angry howl and rushed Eric like a train. Eric did the same on his end.

Blue was hit by a wall of hot air as they flew into each other. He was safe, enclosed in Kurt's qi shield, but he still fell back to observe the fight from a distance, where he could keep an eye on both combatants at once. After colliding in midair, Kurt and Eric sailed almost all the way to the walls opposite where they'd started; on the way down, Kurt reached out and the light on the wall burst, releasing a jagged flow of raw electricity that surrounded him. As soon as his feet hit the floor, he spun around and used his whole body as an antenna, releasing bolts of lightning that arced toward Eric from all sides.

Eric quickly raised rectangular barriers out of the floor. Blue saw that he'd been right: Eric could use void to alter the matter of the tower. Kurt kept on pumping power from the wall, altering its angles of approach every second, but Eric moved the barriers with equal speed, then interrupted Kurt by creating a vacuum to pull him off his feet and bring him in closer.

Void wants to be filled, thought Kurt. He directed wind into the eye of the vortex, and with a bang like a popping balloon, he was blown back, free of the suction. Eric ripped chunks out of the floor to throw at him, but Kurt called the wind back to his side and sped up his dodging—without his qi shield, he couldn't afford taking too many hits. Soon, though, he was stopped when fire erupted in front of him, and the floor began changing shape in time with similar bursts of flame, using Kurt's dodges to force him back toward Eric. In seconds, Eric was able to reach out, grab his neck, and hoist him into the air.

He was stronger than he appeared. Kurt could feel the dark rune burning his skin.

What's he doing?! thought Blue. *Why isn't he fighting back?!*

Eric pulled the oddly willing Kurt so close their faces were almost touching.

"Your grandparents raised a moron," he said in a gravelly voice. "That's right—Rick and your qi told me everything. Maybe if you weren't so new to thinking for yourself, you would've been smart enough not to come here!"

And then Eric felt something nick his chin. A drop of blood flew up into his field of vision, dripping off a tiny barb of ice at the end of a thin strand of water.

Kurt's eyes flew open as he began pulling all the water from his trip across the river out of his still-damp clothes, fashioning it into similar, separate tendrils. Soon, there were dozens of them—they didn't have much range, but even once Eric let go of Kurt, he'd already brought him in too close. The ice barbs varied in size, growing and shrinking to Kurt's desire, arcing through the air and cutting Eric over and over. Eric staggered back, but Kurt ran with him, punching him while the ice storm continued its attack. Then he pulled all the water streams back at once, formed them into a ball, fashioned that into a spear, and rammed it directly into Eric's throat. The qi shield prevented severe physical damage, but the force catapulted Eric into the air backwards. Before he even came down, Kurt melted the ice back into water, covered him with it, and called back the lightning.

Eric avoided electrocution by setting himself on fire—he didn't seem to mind it. The water evaporated instantly, and then Eric threw the fire toward Kurt, who jumped aside but still got burned a little. Eric landed and ran to close the distance, sweeping a wave of flame from side to side in front of himself, trying to catch Kurt again.

Amid his ducks and jumps, Kurt searched for a spot on the floor between himself and Eric, found one, and kept his eyes there while he continued to dodge. Eric finally connected with his flame and ran even faster, hoping to keep it up, but Kurt grit his teeth and used the earth element to raise the largest bump he could in that spot. It wasn't big, but it was enough to trip up Eric, who never saw it coming. He fell almost right into Kurt's arms.

Kurt met him with a qi-charged fist in the gut. Similar punches followed, back and forth across Eric's face, wearing the Dark Linker down. Eric's shield seemed to be wavering: it flashed like a fluorescent light bulb going bad.

Blue looked at himself and found that Kurt's qi shield was shimmering at almost the same frequency.

They are *even*, he realized with surprise and relief. He looked at the doors, but the Seal of Broken Lightning was unchanged. *Good. Don't kill him, Kurt....*

Eric created small vortices around himself, trying to pull Kurt out of position, and when that didn't work, he ripped up more of the floor. Kurt grabbed Eric and yanked him along whenever he needed to move; the punches kept coming. Finally, Eric screamed and wrapped himself in flames again, but even with his left hand engulfed in fire, Kurt endured. He punched Eric twice more to unbalance him and then pulled him sharply forward, turning halfway around to change the pull into a throw. Eric hopped and stumbled, fighting to stay standing; he looked back and stared down the barrel of the qi gun.

Roaring from the effort, Kurt dumped most of his remaining qi into the largest burst he'd ever tried to form, and he worked so fast that he felt anemic. It was in his hands and then flying through the air in less than a second. The target was Eric's half-open mouth.

PSSSSHHHEEE!

There was a flash of white. Eric stopped moving.

The shot connected, but the qi ball burst into pieces like raindrops. Eric had frozen in place, stooped over with one foot off the ground, but despite this instability, the blast didn't push him back so much as a millimeter.

He spun around and floated back into the air with inhuman speed. Caught off-guard, Kurt forgot his drive and paused, raising the qi gun defensively in front of his face. He felt his adrenaline rush subsiding, and it became real to him that he'd already used up most of his strength, thinking Eric had done the same.

Eric stared down at him, lording over the room as he had upon entry, but all his smirks and grimaces were gone. His face was completely blank. He looked like he was about to start crying milk, irises partially obscured under a swirling white. The Siphon Stone glimmered and spewed small droplets of energy that faded into the air. Its power streaked across Eric's qi shield, now fully regenerated.

"Watch out, Kurt!" yelled Blue—certainly, Eric meant to drain him.

But then Eric spoke.

"Your understanding of your qi has increased manifold in such a short amount of time. But your understanding of our qi remains as limited as before."

"Blue!" shouted an exhausted Kurt. "What's going on?!"

"Uh!" Blue hadn't expected his services would be necessary during the fight. "I don't know—working on it!"

"We have unlocked the depth of our power," said Eric, his voice echoing as if overdubbed by a deadpan female, "but this knowledge will not save you."

Eric tore the wiring out of the floor—Kurt tried to fall back on lightning as well, knowing it was all he could rely on in his weakened state, but Eric's Link was too powerful to be overridden. Eric shot at Kurt from what seemed like ten directions, and for the first time in years, electric shocks pierced Kurt's seasoned hands. His sinuses emptied.

This time, Eric set Kurt on fire, before stamping out the blaze by ramming Kurt's body into the walls and ceiling repeatedly.

Blue concentrated harder than ever. He had to turn away from the sight of his best friend getting destroyed to have any prayer of completing a thought. But even looking in the other direction didn't free him from his anxiety—he could still see the qi shield around him flickering, straining, threatening to shatter with Kurt's defeat. He winced, clenched his teeth, and spun back around to face the problem as Kurt was facing it, with all the courage he had.

Something changed. Blue got the feeling that he was seeing something familiar, that phantom sensation he always had when he was one step away from a major breakthrough. His eyes boggled at Eric's visage, and information came rushing into and out of his head, facts trying to reach concert with one another.

Unless the Linker Weapon is done, Kurt and Eric are equal, but it isn't, but they aren't. Eric's almost the same as he once was when he doesn't speak as two. They unlocked the depth of their power. Hydrad trusted Eric to conquer the end of the world, not the world itself. How do you conquer a…concept…? Steal everyone's qi, redefine life and death…a weapon that can destroy but also create? What kind of—

Blue's head snapped up. "Oh, no!"

One more crash into the floor and Eric stopped, leaving Kurt prone before him. Kurt told himself to keep moving, grunted around the taste of blood in his mouth. He scrambled to a sitting position, but that was as far as he got before pain shot through his back and stalled him. He looked up at Eric, keeping disdain on his face regardless, but then did a double take to the left: Blue had come right up to them, walking as if in a trance.

"Blue! Get back!" Kurt called out. He knew he was one step away from passing out, and that if his qi shield broke, Blue could be drained.

But Blue didn't listen. Eric turned to look at him indifferently.

"Do not raise our ire. It will not be long before you are vulnerable."

"Blue!"

Blue had the fortitude of a man resigned to his own death as he addressed Eric, with a more controlled form of the anger he'd expressed over Kayla's capture.

"The Linker Weapon…." A gasp interrupted him. "We were expecting a bomb, or…maybe a gun—but there's only one thing I know of that can create just as well as it can destroy. The Siphon Stone, it just… funnels the qi it absorbs directly into your body!"

"Correct," said Eric. "We *are* the Linker Weapon."

Aw, hell. Kurt felt his stomach drop.

"But why a weapon? You…." Blue decided there was nothing to be lost, at this point, from being up-front. "You speak as if you want to have a profound effect on the structure of the world itself…you want to control the way it ends. How will turning yourself into a weapon help you achieve that? What is the Linker Weapon really intended to do?"

"The height of yin is the beginning of yang. The height of yang is the beginning of yin," said Eric.

Kurt was just barely able to struggle back to a stand.

"Life leads to death, and death leads back to life. The Linker Weapon will allow us to have control over both, and reveal to us the transition. As its power grows, the weapon, by its very existence, will put the end of the world in our hands, allowing us to shape it and gain what we desire most.

"You are inconsequential. Soon, you will be part of the Linker Weapon." Eric turned back to Kurt, who had positioned his hands for the qi gun again, but was straining to come up with ordinance. "You, however, have caused us a great deal of trouble, interfered much, and taken the one we love from our side."

Eric mimicked Kurt's technique, quickly charging up a purple bullet larger than any Kurt had ever attempted. Kurt prepared himself for the shootout, or what would be a shootout if only he could find a little qi to counterattack with. The creamy white in Eric's eyes began to fade, and his satisfied smile returned. When he spoke, the cocky college kid's voice was louder than the airy woman's.

"Now, die!"

PSSSSHHHEEE!

Kurt's body flew backwards through the purple glass window, which shattered along with the shield protecting Blue.

*   *   *

"Kurt!" Grandma leaped forward and reached for the TV screen.

"No!" Grandpa did the same. Cameras had been on the Darklight Tower all night, so someone was quick to zoom in when a person crashed out through one of the exterior walls and went into freefall. The TV screen showed a jerky picture that tried to catch up with Kurt and keep him centered.

Horror melted into a very uneasy calm soon enough. Kurt's fall slowed, then stopped. He remained hanging in midair, held by the power of wind.

"Oh, thank God! Thank God!" Grandma cried. She fell back into her seat.

Grandpa clutched her shoulder firmly.

"Get outta there, Kurt...!" he whispered.

Already, the info bar at the bottom of the screen had changed to say "Breaking News: Second Linker Appears at Darklight Tower." The cameras continued to probe the scene and the anchors continued to speculate. It wasn't long before someone took a closer look at the hole and saw more movement. Eric was floating down after Kurt.

*   *   *

Kurt knew he'd passed out for a moment. He didn't even feel the impact from Eric's attack, and he wasn't sure if he'd expended the last of his own power with an inconsequential counter-shot or just had it blown out of him. His state spared him the shock of falling through the window-wall of the tower and tumbling toward the street far below. Somehow, though, he was still aware of what was happening to him. Most of his thoughts were apologies to his grandparents.

And then he felt as if he were being held or wrapped in a warm hug.

And then he was aware again, startled, hanging in midair with a cushion of wind swirling beneath him. He had only fallen a few stories, and was still more than a quarter of the way up the Darklight Tower. He examined his rune and saw that it was active once more, though its flashing had slowed.

He looked around as his clarity returned. More helicopters were in the sky now, either from the army or the news, and though they kept their distance, they tried to get their searchlights to settle on him. The wind beat into his ears. He felt surreal, out of place, floating among dozens of dark buildings with hundreds of lit windows.

Then he looked up and found the hole he'd fallen through. Eric was levitating down to his position. He could just make out Blue standing at the edge of the hole, looking out.

Kurt grunted, came back to full consciousness, formed his qi gun, and fired two shots no bigger than real, lead bullets. Eric dodged both of them so fast he almost couldn't be seen while moving. That was all Kurt could manage: after the second shot, he felt the wind under him slipping, so he started trying to think of a better idea.

"It's over, Ciardi. You have to listen to me now," said Eric. "How does it feel to be proven wrong? I'm stronger than you at all the elements, Light and Dark!"

Kurt glared at him even harder to mask his desperate thinking.

"What's the matter? Nothing to say to me? Even now, you can't admit it? You'd rather just…stare at me with your wrinkly forehead and greasy hair? God, what are you, like, forty? And you tried to get with my girlfriend?! You're a pedophile, and you still think you can be in the right here?"

"I'm twenty-six," said Kurt. "Kayla ain't that much younger than me. Anything I'd do with her would be nice and legal."

"You'd better watch your mouth!"

The only point in provoking Eric now was making him think that Kurt was out of other tricks. It would work better, Kurt thought in frustration, if he could actually find something hidden up his sleeve; he kept searching.

"I could've drained you any time I wanted, but now I wanna hear you say you're sorry first! And if you don't…well, I don't *have* to drain you if you die, which you will if you run outta qi and fall down to the street. That's like a fifty-story drop, pal. So come on—what's it gonna be?"

The pad!

Kurt put his fingers to his forehead. He felt the sweat dripping from his hairline.

Eric snorted. "Really? Fine! Go ahead and kill yourself with one last attack—"

Sheeshoop!

Kurt's disappearance was just about the only thing that could have surprised him.

*   *   *

Blue knew where Kurt had gone as soon as he saw him vanish. He turned around, and found his friend standing on the pad across the room.

"Kurt!" he exclaimed. "Are you all right?"

"We gotta get outta here!" Kurt was disoriented after reappearing right side up on solid ground, but he ignored his headspins and ran stumblingly toward Blue. Blue glanced around, then started closing the gap between them from his side.

Eric didn't take long to sense that Kurt was back in the tower. He sped up the wind around him and took off toward the hole.

Please God, let this work, please let it work…! thought Kurt. He reached out his right hand for Blue; Blue returned the gesture.

Eric was just a few feet from the middle floor of the tower. He readied the Siphon Stone as Kurt and Blue came into his sights.

Kurt grabbed Blue's hand as soon as he could reach it. He didn't slow down even when they were about to crash into each other. He held on tight and squinted his eyes with concentration. He and Blue disappeared.

The Siphon Stone's beam hit the floor where they had been and broke apart.

ACT V

生与死

LIFE AND DEATH

Sheeshoop!

Kurt and Blue materialized in Kurt's living room; the first thing they did was finish up their head-on collision already in progress. They collapsed onto the rug in front of the couch, groaning from pain and exhaustion.

Back in Lowval, thought Kurt as soon as he opened his eyes. He was relieved to see Blue rolling away from him and sitting up. *Good, it worked —he teleported with me.*

"Kurt?!" Grandma was the first one into the room, running faster than Kurt had ever seen her run. He stood just in time to nearly get knocked down again by the force of her hug. Grandpa was right behind her, and he piled on as well.

"Thank God!" He pulled back and started examining Kurt's face. "Are you all right, Kurt?"

"Fine! Don't worry...I'm fine! Just...really tired," panted Kurt. "I used up almost all my qi...I think I did use it all, actually, I feel like I'm gonna faint—"

"Here, sit down." Grandma guided Kurt onto the couch behind him. Somehow, Kurt still found enough energy to feel disquiet.

"I couldn't do it, Grandpa," he said. "I used all my qi and I still couldn't stop him...."

"It's okay, Kurt. You did your best." Grandpa patted him on the back. "Remember what I told you—it isn't your responsibility any more than it was your mother's. Let someone else take care of it."

"Blue!" Kurt raised his head enough to look at his friend, who was leaning on the easy chair. "How're you holding up? Eric didn't hurt you while I was out, did he?"

"No, no, I'm all right…." Blue met his eyes; he looked small and scared. "Kurt…Kayla…."

Grandma became tense all over again. "Where is she?"

For a moment, the only sound was Kurt's heavy breathing.

"Eric took her," he said after a preparatory gasp.

"Kurt! We have to go back," said Blue, though he sounded like the idea terrified him.

"Are you nuts?" Kurt said. "I just got my ass handed to me!"

"But he'll drain her, or worse! God knows what Eric is doing to her, Kurt!"

"I…." Kurt became subdued. "I'm sorry, Blue. I can't save her. My Grandpa's right…someone else is gonna have to take care of things from now on. You saw it yourself. I'm no match for Eric."

Blue's face went through a long series of contortions, which eventually culminated in him looking down and away.

Kurt pitched forward and almost fell off the couch. He clutched at his ribs. "Damn…."

"Kurt!" Grandma reached out to catch him, but Grandpa put his arm around her.

"It's all right, Nana. We've seen this before, remember?" He put his other arm around Kurt and began coaxing him to stand. "C'mon, help me get him upstairs and in bed."

"Are you sure? Maybe we should take him to the hospital!"

"Think back to when Anna was training. Remember the few times when she really overdid it? She was just like this, but she said the qi grew back overnight and healed her up every time. He's just gotta sleep it off, that's all—that's what you feel like you wanna do, right, Kurt? Just pass out and sleep?"

"Yeah, I guess so," Kurt answered. The stairs were difficult, but with one grandparent on each arm, he was able to take them slowly. Still, he said, "You guys don't have to help me…."

"Oh yes we do!" Grandpa insisted. "We're just lucky we got you home safe and sound, Kurt!"

There was the sound of stomping from the living room below. Grandma looked around and saw Blue turning the knob on the front door.

"Where're you going, Blue?" she asked.

Blue pivoted in the doorway and shouted, "To find Laoshi!"

Ka-pumm!

*   *   *

Kurt saw some familiar things, and some new things. They were all out of order, displaced in time like years of photos shuffled like playing cards.

He stared down on the burning ships from somewhere in the sky. Their red, fiery sails bore a symbol he didn't recognize. But suddenly they were all intact again and heading back the other way. And then he returned to the harbor of Riktalash where it all began, except the island wasn't sinking this time. He saw crowds and crowds of people, all of them dressed differently yet the same, in pants, dresses, shirts, shoes, and hats of purple, gold, white, and brown. It was a slice of everyday life that predated anything else he'd seen, but somehow, the bad feeling wouldn't subside. Somehow, the city was still dying.

...been...Linkers...out of....

The people were indeed Linkers, almost every last one of them. Kurt didn't feel surprised. They seemed happy and comfortable with their ability to control the elements. Here, a man lifted another man into the air with wind, allowing him to light the street lamps with bursts of fire. There, a sidewalk vendor reshaped common rocks into sculptures with complex uses of void. Elsewhere, teams of warriors with lightning swirling around their hands surveyed the island and the sea beyond. They were the first to catch sight of the approaching fleet.

They...Empire...for....

Kurt moved inside, through the walls of the royal palace, to a room deep underground. A team of Linkers, both Light and Dark, trained their runes on a donut-shaped pool of water. Kurt dove in and swam deep enough to see that it led to the underside of the island, a rocky aquatic mountain rapidly becoming hollow as earth Linkers called pieces of it away for fire Linkers to refine. Up above, on the high shelves of the room, water cultivated strange plants, and higher still, void and more flames combined pots full of ingredients into a liquid whose color seemed to move between silver, green, and black. A long line of people came to drink from the pot, and once they'd had their turns, an emblem was painted in black ink on their foreheads.

Back at the crowd scene, Kurt saw that most of the citizens already had their marks.

Riktalash... island...Qin...father's...stuck...!

*   *   *

Kurt felt his conscious brain struggling to the surface, straining to find a context for those words, the first set that didn't seem to fit together. He was almost shaken from the dream, but he forced himself back in. The images were fading, the words becoming more desperate but harder to hear.

*   *   *

Everyone...shares...American...Drifter....

The ships pulled into the harbor. The king, a Dark Linker, and the queen, a Light Linker, came to greet them under heavy guard. The visitors were Asian—Kurt knew that much, though he still didn't know how to classify the people of the island city. As the leader of the expedition stepped onto the dock, the king extended his hand.

...Riktalash...asked...share...violent...afraid....

The captain was dragged off the street by warriors, along with a handful of his crewmembers. Everyone not captured was already dead on the ground—the air seemed to crackle with electricity, which mingled with smoke from recently lit fires.

The queen was back in her palace praying before an altar, sitting between symbols etched into the floor. Her dress obscured them, but with his dreamer's eye, Kurt could still see. It didn't matter—as with the other symbols, he had no idea what they meant.

...life, but not....

Pricking her finger with the tip of a seashell, the queen let a drop of her own blood fall onto a piece of green jade. The jade turned white and began to glow. Kurt saw her face from the stone's point of view, streaked with tears and twisted by competing sadness and rage. The man of smoke appeared behind her, distorting the walls around him into forests once again.

Death….

The king was dead. Kurt saw his body lying in state in the throne room, but there were no mourners, and the queen didn't linger there for long. Her face was like stone, devoid of all emotion save for determination. She waved to a guard and sent him down one flight of stairs, while she ascended another.

Kurt felt the images becoming hazier.

Listen…here…every…since!

The city was sinking; once more, Kurt saw it as if he were floating on the waves. He watched the red-sailed ships fleeing the destruction, pursued by warrior Linkers manipulating the water and throwing fire and lightning. All of them died when their qi ran out, plunging into the sea miles from a shore that was already submerged. By the time the last Linker went down, the ships were almost at a dead stop, clouding the sky with the black smoke of their demise.

…escape…wrong…dead…cursed…Drifter…bond…become… caused…!

Kurt saw a piece of flotsam and a dead body wash up on a rocky shore at the edge of an evergreen forest. Kurt recognized the corpse, but more urgently, he recognized the trees. He looked around, and there was the man of black smoke, standing over the body like a predator after the kill. Now the distortion behind him led back to Riktalash. Kurt saw the shadow-man bend down and remove the Siphon Stone from the body's stiffly clasped hand. Then the smoke shifted and the man became a red-eyed wolf; with a howl, he disappeared into the woods.

…succeeded, but…Eric…first…Project…revert….

He saw the queen back at the altar, using the seashell that had pricked her finger to trace the blood on the white jade into a symbol. This one Kurt had seen before.

…already…now…soon!

The queen was dead, her face blank. The captain of the red-sailed ships turned away from her and pocketed the Siphon Stone. A rune like Eric's flashed into view on his left palm.

…Broken Lightning…symbols…qi, but…no…yet!

Time skipped back one last time. Now the queen was in her throne room, staring blankly toward the balcony. Kurt couldn't see the man of black smoke anymore, but somehow, he was still there. The far door opened and the captain was thrown into the room. He regarded the queen with fear for a moment, but she didn't move or even look at him. Then he drew a knife and charged toward her.

...Bear...Stardust can...symbols...Drifter...Stardust!

The man of black smoke flew at Kurt and stopped between his eyes, hovered at the bridge of his nose like a mosquito. For the first time, Kurt could truly see him. He was the Drifter. He was Riktalash. He was Eric the Red.

*   *   *

Kurt sprang up and smacked his hand to his forehead. Heart beating near to explosion, he gasped and checked his surroundings. He was sitting in his bed. Birds were chirping. The sun was high and starting its afternoon descent. He looked at his hand—his rune was slightly active. He was healed and felt strong again.

He examined his room one more time, but there was nothing else to find. The images he had seen had been left behind in the dream.

He sighed and let his head fall into his hands.

*   *   *

Kurt plodded downstairs, sloppily dressed, and found his grandparents eating a late breakfast at the kitchen table. As far as appearances went, this was a perfectly normal day, like thousands of others before it.

"There you are, Kurt! It's almost one—I was getting worried," said Grandma. She got up to get another bowl. "Are you feeling any better?"

Kurt sat down and pulled the box of cereal across the table to himself.

"Yeah, I feel fine," he said. "Grandpa was right. The rune did its job."

"Well, you don't sound fine." Grandpa looked at Kurt, even though Kurt wouldn't meet his eyes. "Just 'cause your body's back in top shape doesn't mean your spirits are any higher, huh?"

Kurt didn't answer.

"Don't beat yourself up over it, Kurt. It wasn't your fault," said Grandpa.

"Yes, it was." Kurt pushed his breakfast aside and looked up. "Kayla was running away from Eric until I convinced her to help me. I got her all hopeful, and then I couldn't take him after all. Maybe beating Eric isn't my responsibility, but I *am* responsible for what happened to Kayla, because she wouldn't have even gone to that tower if I didn't talk her into it."

"Oh, Kurt…." Grandma didn't know how to comfort him.

"You're a good man for wanting to take responsibility, Kurt, just like your mother would have. But if there's one thing I would've changed about her, it was the way she tried to take responsibility for everything, even the stuff she couldn't do anything about," said Grandpa. He grimaced. "I hate the idea that Eric's got Kayla just as much as you do, but if he's as strong as he looks, we couldn't have saved her even if she'd stayed here. There's no use dwellin' on it. If you tried to help her now, Eric'd just get you, too. What good would that do Kayla?"

"Well, but…." Kurt was trying to sort out his idea even as he spoke. His thoughts were still murky, confused by his dreams. "I've been…maybe there's something I can still do, without fighting or putting myself in danger anymore. M—I mean, I, uh…."

"What, Kurt? Tell us," said Grandma, putting her hands on top of his.

Kurt held off for a few more seconds, and when he did begin to talk, he edited his words carefully. He wasn't sure how his grandparents would react if he told them who he thought was speaking to him through his dreams.

"Linkers get their powers when there's an imbalance in the world that needs to be fixed," he said. "When Kayla showed up here and told us about Eric, I thought that stone he was using must've been the imbalance. So I went down to New York thinking I was gonna fix the world and stop him from hurting people at the same time, except…it pisses me off, but Eric was right, and I was wrong. No matter how much of a bad person he is, if there wasn't already an imbalance, he wouldn't have his powers, either, and apparently, he couldn't have used the stone without them. So he's not the problem.

"But that means the real imbalance is still out there somewhere, and… maybe that's how I can help Kayla, by finding it and fixing it for good. I'm not strong enough to fight Eric, but if the Earth wasn't dying anymore, then wouldn't he and I both lose our powers? Then the police or Kayla or anyone could take him down."

"Oooooo!" said Grandma, looking back and forth between her husband and grandson with pride in her eyes. "That's a good idea!"

"Mmmmmf. I don't know, Kurt," said Grandpa. "I know you don't wanna give up, but at least we're safe here—you're safe here, in the house. Thank God you made it back once! I don't know if I want you going out again until this is all over."

"But we're not safe here, Grandpa," said Kurt. "Eric said that he's gonna drain whoever the army and the police send to try and stop him, and every time he drains someone, the Siphon Stone gets more reach. Eventually, he'll be able to drain anyone in the world without even leaving the tower!"

"Oh, my God…!" Grandma cupped her hands over her mouth. "They were sending more of the army down there this morning, weren't they, Papa?"

"Yeah." Grandpa shook his head; his face had become drawn.

"Don't worry, I'm sure it's gonna take him a while to get that much power," Kurt said, trying to head off his grandparents' fretting. "But he'll get it eventually—unless I find the real imbalance and take his powers away, that is. And let's not forget that the world is still ending. Even if someone else found a way to stop Eric, that wouldn't change."

"I still don't think it's a good idea, Kurt. With your Linking, maybe you could survive whatever's gonna happen, even if Eric's stone could reach here. And you're safer in the house than you would be if you went out God-knows-where to try and fix the world," said Grandpa. He put his arm around Grandma. "Don't worry about us. We're old…we've lived pretty good lives. It's most important to us that you make it through, Kurt."

"Yeah," said Grandma, nodding.

"Don't talk like that. At least let me run it past Blue. He knows everything—maybe we could figure out what the imbalance is from here, then decide if it's safe to go out after it." Kurt stood up and pushed his chair in, looking through the kitchen to the TV room door, which was closed. "Is he awake yet?"

"Blue didn't stay here last night. Were you too tired to notice? He left as soon as you got back and said he was gonna find Laoshi," said Grandma.

"Aw, crap. I dunno what he thinks that crazy old geezer is gonna tell him. He wouldn't even tell me anything!" Kurt turned to his grandparents and shrugged. "At least let me go bring him back. Laoshi's house is just on the other side of town, and I don't think he should be alone while all this is going on."

Grandpa thought for a moment.

"You're right, Kurt. He should be with us," he said. "Just be careful, all right? The keys to the Olds are on the hook."

"Thanks, Grandpa." As Kurt walked out of the kitchen, he muttered, "That's right, I gotta borrow their car 'cause I left the van down in the city. Boy, is that gonna be fun to explain to Mr. Garrison…."

*   *   *

Aaron Bluefield was on his knees, staring across the empty grass. He'd finally found a problem that his formidable brain couldn't solve, couldn't explain, couldn't even begin to understand. In trying, his head had become so crowded with chattering, competing thoughts that it was totally empty, the same way that all the colors mixed together made blank white. He was sitting in oblivion, and that was how Kurt found him.

"No way…!"

Kurt felt the same anxiety as Blue when he pulled his grandparents' Oldsmobile up to the curb behind Blue's Geo. He got out of the car and let it wash over him without subjecting it to critical inquiry, like his friend had. To him, it was as it was, and that was bad enough. This was Laoshi's address, complete with the familiar downward slope away from the road and the little stream winding its way through the property. But aside from these and other natural things like the rocks and trees, the lot was vacant.

"This is a nightmare!" Kurt said to himself as he stumbled down the hill, now devoid of a driveway. He saw his friend kneeling in the grass and called out, "Blue! Blue, what happened here?"

Blue said something, but Kurt couldn't hear it. "What?" he asked as he closed in and stopped, surveying the empty lawn again.

"I thought…last night, it could've just been all the stress from what happened in New York, my exhaustion from walking all the way here from your house, dehydration, a trick of the light and darkness…." Blue didn't move as he spoke. "I said to myself, 'go home and sleep—come back in the morning.' I'm not going to pretend I got a lot of sleep last night, but…."

"Blue, where is Laoshi's house?"

"It's still gone. I thought I was wrong…but it's gone."

Neither of them said anything else for a minute.

"You know what? Screw this!" Kurt shook his head. "He was never gonna help anyway. We haven't been back here in months. He coulda packed up shop and left town the day after we talked to him for all we know!"

"No, I…I came back here without telling you, about three weeks ago. I had tea with him. I thought maybe I could get him to tell me more, or at least give me some lead on where to find the papers he'd given away, or new copies of them, maybe. He wouldn't tell me anything…he just kept smiling and changing the subject."

"You went—" Kurt interrupted himself. "Never mind! Who cares what he knew or where he disappeared to? We have to go home now, Blue. There's nothing else to do here, and I need your help."

Blue didn't respond.

"You remember those dreams I've been having off and on since the first night I got my rune? I had the biggest one yet last night. There was stuff about forests, that same sinking island, this lady, a guy made of black smoke, and then there's a voice that's talking to me, but it's…it's like there's too much static, and I'm only getting part of the message. I can't explain it, but…I….." Kurt still had to struggle to believe what he was now saying out loud for the first time. "I think it's my mom. I think my mom is trying to tell me something."

"That's impossible," Blue said without turning around. "Your mother's dead."

"Yeah, but my Grandpa said I got some of her powers, and her memories! I felt it, when he was in the backyard training me the last couple days…I had all her technique already in me! So what if…like, the part of my brain that used to be her is talking to the rest of my brain? Like there's something my mom thought was important that my brain's trying to figure out, but so far, I can only get at those memories when I'm asleep?"

Again, no response.

Kurt groaned. "Come on! You're not safe out here, and I think there might still be something we can do. If we can figure out what the imbalance screwin' up the world is and fix it, then Eric's not a Linker anymore and the cops can handle him! I think maybe my dreams can help me figure it out, but I need your help, too! Okay?"

"What do you want my help for?" Blue lowered his chin. "I've already proven myself useless, and an utter failure…."

"Aw, dammit, Blue!" Kurt said. He knelt down beside his friend. "I'm the one who couldn't stop Eric! You're not even a Linker, for God's sake!"

"It isn't just that." Blue's face crumpled, and he turned farther away from Kurt. "All my life, I've been in a hurry for knowledge. It's all I know. Since I was a little boy, I accelerated my education, skipping through grades and classes. I paid more attention to my mind than my maturity, and now, here I am, a twenty-two-year-old professor who gets no respect whatsoever from his students and colleagues. I never learned how to carry the air of an adult. Even you've made fun of me from time to time about how I can't control my classes."

"Look, I—"

"Kayla was the only one who ever…I…and now she's gone. Linker or otherwise, I couldn't do a thing to calm her, prepare her, or help her. I'm not just a failure as a teacher and an adult, I'm a failure as a human being."

"I…huh…." Kurt seemed to understand now. "You really liked her, didn't you?"

"I don't know, I…." Blue sputtered, eventually managing to get out, "N-no, not like…the ramifications, she's a student, I'm a teacher—"

"Gimme a break! You're not even two years older than she is. And you just admitted you're a kid at heart, just like her!"

"But still! I have a—moral obligation, and…anyway, how do I even know? We were only together for three days, we…I…."

Kurt crossed his arms. "Blue. Listen to me, and answer yes or no. Did you think Kayla was attractive?"

"Well, I…certainly, I thought once or twice—"

"Yes or no!"

"Yes!" Blue paused, and for that moment, the muscles in his neck tensed visibly. "Yes, I did."

"And did you ever feel attracted to her? Like you wanted to…y'know, do whatever it is you do when you feel attracted to someone? Get to know her better, ask her out, throw a party at your house to get her to come over, anything?"

"Yes…."

"Then you like her. End of story." Kurt used Blue's shoulder to steady himself as he stood back up. "Geez, Blue, you weren't kidding that your brain's way ahead of the rest of you. Some things you just don't gotta think about so damn much!"

"I know. I should've learned that lesson years ago…but what does it matter? Kayla's gone, and we can't get her back."

"Are you listening to me?! I said there might be a way if we can fix whatever the real imbalance is!" Kurt said. "Kayla's got her qi shield to keep Eric from draining her, and I'm sure she'll hold out as long as she can, but we've still gotta get moving! Just come back to the house with me. Grandma and Grandpa want you back, too, and once we're there, we can start talking out my dreams!"

"What's the point, Kurt? There's no way we could rebuild any message your mother might have left you without some kind of reference, much less could we identify the imbalance in the world without more information regarding Linkers and their place, never mind natural imbalances in general. Ugh, if only…I came here hoping to plead with Laoshi one last time to at least give me the name of the former student who had his papers, but even if…I mean, after two and a half decades with no contact, who knows if we could—"

Blue stopped. As if energy and momentum had been building up inside him all along, he jumped to his feet, spun around, and seized Kurt by the shoulders. He looked into his friend's eyes with grasping urgency.

"Kurt," he asked slowly, "how old are you?"

"Twenty-six. Why?"

Slowly, Blue's mouth opened into a wide *O*, revealing some of his teeth. He was shaking.

"Follow me back to your house!" he called out—in the blink of an eye, before Kurt had taken so much as a step, Blue was already unlocking the door of his car.

*   *   *

"Grandma, Grandpa, I'm back! I found him!"

Kurt hadn't even finished his sentence when Blue rushed past him into the house. By the time Kurt closed and locked the door, Blue was completely out of sight, through the living room and down the back hallway.

"We'll be in the study!" he added. He heard the television playing and elected not to disturb his grandparents until they tested Blue's theory.

He walked to the study and found the door open. A cloud of dust had been stirred into the air, and the already messy room was becoming even more of a shambles as Blue clawed through the contents of the desk, the cabinet, and the bookshelf. Every few seconds, he'd switch from one to another.

"So…what do we do if you were wrong—"

"Don't worry—I'm right." Blue held up a handful of papers, typewritten but covered in longhand notation, then returned to his frantic digging. "Perhaps Laoshi was right to trust in the Way after all—the papers are in the hands of the one who needs them most. And there are months and months of your mother's own research in here…printouts from microfilm, journals, fully annotated books, personal notes…it's much more than I expected!"

Kurt ducked to his left when a piece of paper flew at his face, one of several Blue had tossed up in his mad dash. He ignored it.

"Then how come you don't look happy?" asked Kurt.

"Well, for one thing, Kayla's life is still at stake." Blue paused for just long enough to look Kurt in the eye while he said that, then kept going. "Also, this wealth of information would be fantastic for casual research, but we need to find something that'll help us in a hurry, like a way to pinpoint imbalances in nature or…proof that the Siphon Stone's effects can be reversed."

"Blue…."

"The point is," Blue grunted, lifting a bag full of old newspapers out from behind the desk and plopping it down, "sorting through all this could take weeks. We don't have that much time."

"Weeks?! I thought you said you could speed-read!"

"Speed-reading would be more effective in a situation like this if we knew what we were looking for. I could scan for specific words…so we already know Siphon Stone, imbalance…." Blue snapped his fingers. "Stay with me, Kurt, I'm formulating a theory. Let's say that your dreams are letting you receive your mother's knowledge. As far as we know, the dead can't gain any new knowledge, so perhaps the images and phrases you've been dreaming of represent some of the research we see here. Think of the words you heard—are there any that stood out?"

"Uh, okay…Riktalash, that's the name of the island I keep seeing… um…Drifter—oh, and Stardust! That came up at the end of the last dream."

"Drifter? Stardust? I was expecting more Eastern-sounding terminology. Even 'Riktalash' at least sounds vaguely Indian. Here, I'll start on this pile. You open up that standing cabinet," said Blue.

"Stardust I dunno, but I think the 'Drifter' is this guy made of black smoke. He...well, he looks like a person, but he never stays the same, you know? And then he turned into a wolf."

"Interesting...." Blue retrieved a volume from the nearby bookshelf, one of the only ones he could reach from where he sat, and dusted off its cover. "We should be circumspect about some of these details. A dream is still a dream—your subconscious imagination could have polluted the message in any number of ways."

"Maybe. But hey, if you want Chinese words, how about 'Qin'? I heard that at least once," said Kurt.

"'Cheen?'"

"No, Qin. Q-I-N." Kurt paused for a moment, surprised that he'd known the spelling so readily. He shook it off and continued pulling papers out of the cabinet.

"Qin, really...that's a funny coincidence...."

"Why?"

"Never mind. It's irrelevant—keep searching!" Blue was going through the pages so fast that he was almost reading two at a time. He stood up and walked over to the desk to retrieve the next batch.

"I think mosta the stuff over here is irrelevant, Blue. So far, all I'm seeing is a bunch of old stories copied out of library books. They don't even have notes on them."

"Anything can be relevant if your mother kept it! Don't assume!"

"Okay! Calm down." Kurt sucked in his stomach and spread his hands as far as they could go, grabbing one whole stack of papers from the cabinet at once and moving them onto the floor. Just as he was kneeling, a folder at the top of the pile slipped from his grasp and landed facedown, spewing its contents everywhere.

"Dammit!" He set the rest of the stack down and crawled around to recover the scattered papers. But as he stuffed them back into the folder, he paused. Something was written on the front flap in his mother's hand.

Blue noticed Kurt's hesitation. "What is it?"

"'The height of yin is the beginning of yang. The height of yang is the beginning of yin,'" Kurt read. He squinted at the folder. "That's what Eric said...."

"In the Daoist canon, that's actually a very common idea," said Blue. "I meant to tell you on the way from Wards Island to Manhattan—if we're following the Asian interpretation of nature, then your conceptualization of our mission is a little off. The Asian idea of balance is a wheel, not a scale. Balance is represented by even amounts of yin and yang turning in harmony, giving way to one another."

"Right, I remember the old fart saying that." Kurt continued to study his mother's writing. "But what does it mean for us? If Eric and my mom both said it—"

"It means give me that folder," Blue said, putting out his hand and receiving what he'd asked for. He dove in right away. "If your mother marked these papers with that saying, they could be exactly what we're looking for. It'd be great if she figured out and recorded whatever imbalance was plaguing the world in her time! But anything that describes an interruption of the wheel's turning would be an example of an imbalance we could compare against the current state of nature."

"Interruption?" Kurt's neck prickled. "You mean like the wheel got 'stuck'?"

"That's one way of putting it."

Kurt felt something straining to get out of his head.

"Hey, Blue—"

"Whoa! Hang on, hooold on." Blue came away from the folder holding something aloft. It was a story, photocopied out of some larger anthology.

"'Broken Lightning,'" he read.

"What?!" Kurt jumped up and ran into position to read over Blue's shoulder.

Han Chung lived in Xianyang. He had excelled as a scholar from childhood, and so it was not surprising that he rose to be in the employ of the emperor himself. Though he was strong of mind, his heart was weak and foolish, but the emperor saw Han Chung's potential in spite of his flaws, and so gave him a chance to prove his worth.

The emperor told Han Chung to journey to the islands of the immortals and bring back with him the elixir of long life, so that the emperor's kingdom might be eternal. He told Han Chung that he would have a fleet of nine small ships to fulfill his mission, plus men enough to crew them all. Han Chung fell to his knees and wept, saying "I am so honored, my emperor, that you would trust me with such an important task!", but the emperor told him to just rise and set sail as soon as possible.

So, Han Chung bid his tearful wife and his son goodbye, and he left the very next day for the coast. After three weeks of preparation and studying the ancient legends, Han Chung and his men set sail, and they traveled far to the east. He used his maps and the stars to guide the expedition where no man had sailed before, and for many days and nights the crews despaired, for all they saw was empty water.

But then, one night, Han Chung was awakened by Ming Zhou, who was keeping the watch. There were flashing lights on the horizon to the north, and when Han Chung came to the prow of his ship and looked as far as he could, he saw something tall in the distance. Surely, this must be a castle on one of the islands of the immortals, P'eng-lai, Fang-chang, and Ying-chou!

The wind was at their backs, so the men reached the island by morning, and then Han Chung could see the magnificent castles of the immortals. He told half of the ships to stay back while he and the rest pulled into the dock to determine the situation on the island. As soon as he arrived, Han Chung saw that the king and queen of the immortals had come to greet them, and they and all their people held broken lightning in their hands.

Han Chung knew that he had at last found what he'd been searching for....

"That's it!" Kurt cried.

"What?" asked Blue, startled. Kurt reached around him and pointed to an image that accompanied the story. It was a reproduction of a painting that showed small boats with dark sails approaching an island that seemed to glow, and which was filled with tall towers that looked like part of the natural landscape. Below the picture was its bibliographical information, including the title: "P'eng-lai."

"That's Riktalash, the city from my dreams!" Kurt ran his hands back through his hair. "It's not P'eng-lai, it's Riktalash! This really happened!"

"Hm! Well, even if it turns out to just be an old legend, your mother obviously thought something useful could be gained from reading this story." Blue started scanning over the rest of the text, and despite the dire situation, he smiled. "This is fascinating! 'The people of P'eng-lai were confused, and could not speak to the visitor, because he spoke a language that was different from their own. Even in writing they could not communicate, but Han Chung saw that they wrote with strange characters, and they read them from bottom to top, going toward heaven as immortals would…!'"

"Blue, look!" Kurt had been levering up one of the corners of the paper, trying to skip ahead while Blue meandered. Now he flipped the page and pointed to another picture with great urgency.

"Kurt, I was still reading that!" Blue complained. "What if we miss something critical?"

"Han Chung kills the king and queen and steals the Siphon Stone off her neck, we can get to that later! Look at this!"

Blue did look. It was a photograph of a stone tablet, found somewhere in the mountains of northeastern China, according to its caption. There were several "unknown symbols" etched into its surface. The caption explained that these pictographs might have been art or perhaps part of a lost tongue. Among them was the Seal of Broken Lightning.

"I don't believe it…!" Blue leaned in and stared harder; his glasses slid down his nose, and he pushed them back up. "But…your mother couldn't have…this symbol didn't become important to us until yesterday! How could she have known…I mean, unless she saw it someplace else, but still, how does Riktalash even figure into the scheme of things?"

"The Siphon Stone, I just said that! The Siphon Stone came from Riktalash," said Kurt.

"But as far as we know, your mother never even saw…and then there's the symbol of the seal! It can't be a coincidence that we're coming across it again. What does it…here, hold on."

Blue shoved the pages into Kurt's hands and bounded over to the bookshelf. He started scanning the titles; in moments, he was down to the third shelf out of five.

"What are you doing?" Kurt asked.

"Looking to see if your mother had a copy of the *I Ching*, the *Book of Change*! Read the caption under that picture! Whoever found the tablet hypothesizes that—ah ha!" Blue pulled a slim volume from the fourth shelf with a triumphant grin and opened it in his hands.

Kurt read the caption in full: *These symbols do not seem to belong to any known Asian language, contemporary or ancient, but they do have a common basis in solid and broken lines among them. Perhaps the artist was basing his creations on the hexagrams of the* I Ching. *Some scholars contend that this may be a representation of the lost language of the immortals, created from or perhaps informing the ancient divinations themselves.*

"The Seal of Broken Lightning has a flourish added to it, but I can see it now, too—it's basically three broken lines above three solid lines. Which makes it…*tai*, for 'peace'? That doesn't make sense…."

"Wait, I thought Riktalash people read bottom-up," said Kurt. He was only half-listening, because now he'd taken to thumbing through the rest of the "Broken Lightning" story himself.

"Good thinking, Kurt! Let's see…ah ha!" Blue shouted again. "Three solid lines followed by three broken lines—*pi*, 'obstruction'! That sounds much more accurate! So now we know that the Riktali language is based on the sixty-four ancient hexagrams!"

"Yeah, I'm sure that's really going to help," muttered Kurt. He kept on reading a sentence here or there out of the story: *But Han Chung was a coward, and he feared failing his emperor more than he feared the immortals and their broken lightning. So when the king would not let him hold the cup containing the long-life elixir, he reached for his knife and killed the king. The knife was made of pure jade and thus could slay an immortal, but as he died, the king flung the cup from his hands into the sea below, and so Han Chung was denied again….*

"Any of this could give us a clue to deciphering the imbalance! It certainly raises an interesting question—how did the Riktali find out about the hexagrams? The lines are ancient Chinese divination symbols, at least three thousand years old. Perhaps Riktalash had some interaction with the mainland long ago, and they picked it up then?" Blue said. "And while we're asking questions, what could it mean that these people were carrying 'broken lightning' in their hands? That's an intriguing description, and quite different from the context in which we heard the phrase 'broken lightning' used."

"They're all Linkers on this island. I saw it in the dream…ha! So that must mean their world was ending, too, even though they were immortal!" laughed Kurt. He read: *The queen of the immortals grieved terribly for her king, but she instructed her warriors not to kill Han Chung or any more of his men, but instead to imprison them in the royal palace. She knew of an ancient technique to bind one's life force in a small piece of jade by trading away her broken lightning. With this, she might be able to use Han Chung's life force to restore the life force of her king….*

"So perhaps 'broken lightning' was the phrase this storyteller used to describe Linking? Interesting…who wrote the story, Kurt?" asked Blue.

Kurt glanced back at the first page. "'Unknown,'" he said.

"Darn! But let's not get bogged down in those sorts of details. An island full of Linkers is an interesting enough discovery in itsel—" And then Blue staggered back and fell against the bookshelf. His eyes widened and his breathing hastened. "Holy…!"

"What?" Kurt was torn away from his reading.

"The ancient…!" Blue put his hand on his chest, and smiled in such a way that suggested he might be about to start laughing. "The *I Ching* and practically every scholar who's ever studied the hexagrams pinpointed their origin to heat-produced cracks in tortoise shells! But what if there was some other way, some more universal way, that the Riktali could have come by the same system of lines without traveling to China?"

Blue paused, trying to contain himself.

"I…my God, Kurt! If this…if it predates the tortoise-shell divinations, if it was perhaps a lost method of divining…this could stand the entire field on its head!" Blue came back over and knelt down next to his friend. "Light up your rune!"

Kurt made a perplexed face, but he raised his hand and complied.

"You haven't asked me to do that since day one," he remarked.

Blue wasn't listening. His mouth spread into an even wider smile, and then laughter overtook him. He fell off his knees onto his rear, giggling all the way.

"I was right! I was right!" he chanted. "Look at your rune, Kurt! I was right! Those intricacies that have been there all along—they're not just the creases of your palm illuminated! Hidden inside them is a hexagram!"

Kurt cranked his wrist around and brought his hand to his face. It was hard to tell—the lines only became visible when the two points of light tracing the outside of the rune came back to their starting positions at the symbol's top and bottom, causing it to flash. Since he wasn't actually Linking, they weren't moving very fast. After four or five cycles, he was just starting to see a pattern in some of the thicker lines.

"All broken…!" Blue was flipping through the *I Ching* again. "The receptive! The yin of the yin and yang! Kurt, this is fantastic! This is certainly part of what your mother would have wanted us to find!"

"Well, what does it mean?" asked Kurt impatiently.

"I don't know, but…here! Give me back the 'Broken Lightning' story!" Blue took it without waiting for himself to finish speaking. "There must be more we can glean from this, especially if it also explains the origin of the Siphon Stone!"

"I was reading—"

"I had it first!" Blue laughed. Kurt was about to argue, but he stopped himself. At least this seemed to be getting Blue's mind off his depression.

"You go over to the desk and start looking through the other drawers. See if there's anything I missed." While Kurt did that, Blue kicked his speed-reading skill into high gear: *As her man went to fetch the murderous visitor, the queen of the immortals hung the jade around her neck, and then tried to access its power by uttering the magic words. But the stone was too hungry, and by the time Han Chung was thrown into the room by the guard, the queen's life force had already been devoured. The guard had told Han Chung what fate awaited him, and now Han Chung saw his chance, for while he had been confined, the air of P'eng-lai had filled his lungs and placed broken lightning in his own hand as well.…*

"Listen to this, Kurt! It says the Siphon Stone drained the queen as soon as she put it on! And Han Chung became a Linker, too…Kurt, I'm starting to think all this really did happen!" said Blue. "The Siphon Stone's very existence, coupled with your mother's interest in this story, proves the existence of Riktalash! The only mystery is how the stone managed to get to Kline University and into Eric's hands after the island sank."

As Blue continued reading, he mumbled a second question: "I wonder why the stone didn't drain Eric when he touched it…or Han Chung, for that matter…."

Kurt opened the large, central drawer of the desk and found that Blue had already cleaned it out almost completely. The last few remaining pages were mostly copies of newspaper articles concerning Asian artifacts, plus two Native American tales. Especially since the articles were marked with large *X*s in his mother's handwriting, Kurt disregarded this batch almost immediately, tossing the papers onto the desk's surface.

He moved on to the three left drawers, which contained pens, pencils, ink, blank pages, and the like, but no more papers. Frustrated, Kurt switched sides and opened the right-hand drawers one by one. Only the first contained documents, but they were piled high—Kurt's heart jumped. These appeared to be more photocopies from library books, Daoist philosophy texts. He sorted through them quickly, setting aside any that mentioned the heights of yin and yang or the Way while leaving the rest in the drawer. By the time he was done, he had five more sets of papers to bring back to Blue.

But as he turned around and shut the drawer, something on the desk caught his eye. It was one of the Native American stories he'd found a few moments ago: "The Tale of Hiding Bear." He'd scanned right over it, but now, something in the title was making his brain itch again.

Bear…?

Meanwhile, Blue finished reading the "Broken Lightning" story: *As P'eng-lai sank into the ocean, never to be seen again, the secret of the long-life elixir was lost with it. The last of the immortals fled in all directions, some chasing Han Chung and his ships and setting them aflame, and some heading west toward where Han Chung had come from, in search of land and their salvation. As it turned out, Han Chung never made it back to his emperor, living the rest of his days adrift, and the survivors of P'eng-lai settled in the mountains far away, where they grieved for their fallen king and queen until the day they died, for with P'eng-lai destroyed, they were immortal no more.*

"This is so sad…." said Blue. Without looking up, he directed his voice toward Kurt, and continued, "The only unanswerable question is how accurate this account is. Was it written by one of the survivors from

Riktalash? Or from Han Chung's expedition? Or was the story passed on to someone who wasn't even there and recorded much later?"

Kurt didn't answer.

"Say...." But it didn't matter, because Blue kept going. "An expedition to find the long-life elixir, I wonder...." He flipped a few pages back in the "Broken Lightning" story and studied the painting of P'eng-lai.

"Ha! Here we go—the sails of those ships are marked with an old-style Chinese character! It says 'Qin'!" Blue exclaimed. He ran back to the bookshelf.

Kurt shook his head and looked up. "Huh? What about Qin?"

"When you first mentioned the word 'Qin' in connection with your dream, I thought of the Qin Project—the initiative to find the longevity treatment we've been hearing about recently. I thought it was just a case of your subconscious mixing details from your life with the memories you inherited from your mother. But now I see that your dream probably referred to the Qin empire of ancient China, particularly Qin Shi Huangdi, who—here we go!"

Blue pulled a book off the second shelf, this time volume one of Si-ma Qian's *Record of the Grand Historian*. He held it up for Kurt, who was already looking back at the Native American story and was therefore oblivious. Blue cracked open the book and kept talking anyway.

"Yes, here it is...mentioned several times, in fact. Shi Huangdi, the first emperor of Qin, hired scholars, magicians, alchemists, and adventurers to either create or discover the elixir of long life...now that I think about it, this is obviously what the Qin Project was named for! Ha! Hahaha, Kurt, it's incredible—there's even a record of Han Chung by name in here! He never returned from his expedition...no one knew what happened to him, but we do! I only wish I knew where he ended up after fleeing Riktalash."

"I think I might know."

Now Kurt had Blue's attention, and Blue realized that his friend was more absorbed in his reading that he had appeared. His blank expression was hiding what sounded like a great deal of tension. Blue put the book away and went over to him.

"What are you reading?" he asked.

"Here, I just finished." Kurt put the pages back in order and handed them to Blue.

Blue looked at the title, and said in a confused voice, "But…this is a Native American story. Everything we've seen so far points to Daoist or ancient Chinese—"

"Just! Just…read it, Blue," said Kurt. His hands were in his hair again, and this time it looked like they weren't coming out for a while. "That story…it's important, my mom was trying to tell me something, but I just don't know what."

"Okay…." Tense now himself, Blue started reading.

One day, the shaman's young son awoke and ran screaming from his home. The entire village came to the meeting area to see what was the matter, and the son, whose name was Bird Flies Far, cried that he had seen a ghost in his dreams. Soon, his father came, and would have taken him back home in shame to reprimand, but then he saw a curious mark on his son's right hand. He held it aloft and told the women to go forth and fetch their husbands back from the hunt, because the symbol meant that the end times were upon them.

Now, the tribe had been at war with one of the western tribes for years and years, so naturally everyone thought that the end times had come because the war had exhausted the earth and the spirits. The shaman brought his son back into the house to pray for signs, but in the meantime, he sent a scout named Deer Foot to spy on the other tribe and find out what was going on. The shaman's prayers could not attract the spirits' attention, and when he emerged from the tent, the village lookout was crying that Deer Foot had returned, but he was badly injured. The shaman ran to see Deer Foot, and before he died, he said that the western tribe had many wolves, so many that he could not see the ground, and he said these truly were the end times, for the Drifter had come. Then he died, and the shaman buried him and blessed his body.

The shaman knew this was grave news, for the Drifter was well-known among all peoples. Legend said that he was a man without a tribe who rose from the water beyond the setting sun, and that because he was without a tribe he could have many faces. His coming was a sign that meant the end. He was spoken of by the desert tribes of the far West, he was spoken of by the mountain tribes of the far North, he was spoken of by the plains tribes of the far South, and now he had come to the forest tribes of the far East. The shaman told the elder to gather the warriors and prepare to battle against the western tribe for the last time. The western tribe had been training and breeding wolves to fight with them, and so the shaman thought that it was because of this misuse of the animals that the spirits were angered, and the Drifter had come to announce the end. Perhaps if the western tribe could be defeated at last, things would turn out differently.

Now, there was one man in the tribe who was not a hunter or married, and who never did any work. This man, called Hiding Bear, lived in a house deeper in the trees than the rest, and he was rarely seen. Once, the village elder went to see Hiding Bear and asked him why he lived the way he did. Hiding Bear said that he was waiting for the world to come to him, instead of going to chase the world like his tribesmen. The elder thought he was very wise and so let him be, but the rest of the tribe scorned his laziness and wanted nothing to do with him.

On this day, while the preparations for war were underway, Hiding Bear made a visit to the village and asked the nearest person what was going on. "Oh, it's terrible! The Drifter has come to the western tribe, and the shaman's son bears the mark of the end times! Won't you help us march into battle? The enemy has trained many wolves to fight alongside them, and they will outnumber us easily." But Hiding Bear refused. He said, "Why should I rush off to battle when the world is already ending? The fighting will only anger the spirits even more. Do as you like, but I will await the counsel of the spirits before acting." So Hiding Bear left the village and went deep into the woods.

Soon, the elder led the villagers through the trees to a hilly clearing where their enemies were known to gather. There, they saw a sea of wolves, so many wolves that they filled the grass and forest as far as the eye could see. Then they saw the Drifter, as terrifying as the legends foretold, and he stepped atop the back of the largest wolf, then spoke for the entire western tribe. He promised death to our people, and to all people. The shaman told our warriors that it was time to fight and that they should be brave, but before long, many had been killed by the wolves and western tribesmen, and many others had been cursed with living death by the evil stone that hung from the Drifter's neck.

Blue looked up. "Kurt...!"

"I know," Kurt said. He looked like he was getting a migraine.

"This—" Blue stopped for a minute, searching for the words to express himself. "My immediate impulse is to think of the Anasazi, a cliff-dwelling tribe from the American Southwest who disappeared en masse for no apparent reason. I did some reading on them in college, and I searched for other tribes with similarly mysterious ends. I recall at least one in the Pacific Northwest, plus another in—"

Blue could barely pause to breathe. "Linkers manifest when the world is out of balance...but imbalances are also caused by humans...what if there were suddenly no more humans? I mean, we obviously don't want that to happen, but if we can learn from...according to Laoshi, the world has to be dying before Linkers will manifest, but it has to start dying from somewhere. We could be looking at a series of miniature Armageddons here, Kurt! Think about it! The story of Riktalash, and now this shaman who speaks of other tribes that disappeared when the Drifter came...if a gangrenous limb is killing the body, amputating it would save the rest! That's how Linkers have been able to appear several times without humanity ceasing to exist—these specific societies died, taking the source of the imbalance with them and making the world default back to a state of balance! Kurt! This helps—you and Eric were only about a hundred miles apart when you manifested! If what we're reading here is meant to tell us that Linking is regional, spreading out from the area containing the imbalance, then that means even if the whole world is dying, the center of it is somewhere nearby!"

"Blue—"

"Hang on, Kurt, I'm having another idea." Blue paced back and forth over the same four square feet of carpet, then stopped and said, "The 'Broken Lightning' story said Han Chung lived the rest of his days adrift, but it didn't say what direction he drifted in! Remember what Kayla told us —Eric believed that the Siphon Stone spoke to him. What if it would be more true to say that he sensed it? What if Han Chung, or Han Chung's body, washed aground in western America, and when a Linker from some Indian tribe became active, his rune led him to the stone the same way? That...my God, Kurt, that would explain the legend of a man who rose out of the sea with a cursed stone! Except there's not just one Drifter—he has 'many faces,' so perhaps whenever a Linker wears the Siphon Stone...!"

Blue felt his thoughts connect. "Kurt! That means Eric is the Drifter, too!"

The haze in Kurt's mind split momentarily.

"Yeah!" he exclaimed. "That's what my mom was trying to tell me! Part of it, anyway…." His unsettledness returned as he realized there was still something inside him that had yet to reveal itself.

"We have precedent in our hands now," said Blue. "This means that the Siphon Stone may have figured into several major appearances of Linking, which means several imbalances! If we can find more references to the Drifter, we may be able to discern a pattern in the imbalances to help us locate ours!"

"Finish reading that story first," said Kurt, sounding bitterly dejected. "I'm startin' to see a pattern, too…see if you still think it's a good one when you find out how the story ends."

Blue raised the pages again.

Now, Hiding Bear had gone north, to a cliff with a scar in the land below and all the stars of the sky above. There, he sat for three days and three nights while his brothers fought the wolves of the western tribe, and he prayed to the spirits for guidance. For a long time, they said nothing, but on the third night he had a dream in which he walked from the sea, to the desert, to the plains, to the forests. He looked up and saw it was still nighttime, and the great bird spirit had spread his wings across the sky and scraped dust from the stars. The dust rained on Hiding Bear, and when he looked down, he saw that his stone hunting knife now glowed like the stars.

The great spirit lit on the point of the precipice and spoke to him. "This is Stardust, the spirit knife," said the great spirit. "With this, you have my counsel, and you know what you must do." Hiding Bear wept and said, "Thank you spirit, for ending my long life of waiting. I know now that I must go and break the curse of the Drifter." Then he stood up, and it was daylight again.

Hiding Bear was one with the earth now, so when he ran, he reached the battle almost immediately. All of his brothers were either dead or cursed, but all of the western tribesmen had also fallen or been cursed by getting too close to the Drifter. Only the Drifter and the endless wolves remained. The wolves snarled at Hiding Bear, but he drew Stardust from his waist and split the earth with one cleaving. Now the wolves were scattered, and Hiding Bear ran past them before they could rise. The Drifter threw his evil light at Hiding Bear, but Hiding Bear raised Stardust and split the light, then he came forward and struck the Drifter. Once Stardust cut him, the Drifter fell in death, and his body shriveled up and blew away in the wind.

Hiding Bear looked around and saw his ruined tribe, and he became sad. He cut his hair, and from that day forth he traveled to the other tribes of the forest as Bear Who Remembers, so that his brothers could live on through his words. Eventually he married and had two sons, but he kept the evil stone on his belt for the rest of his days, then buried it before he died, so that no others would ever touch it and reawaken the curse.

"I…well, there's the 'Stardust' you mentioned, for one thing." Blue studied the last page—like "Broken Lightning," this story contained scattered pictures, mostly scanned photos of drawn-upon animal hides.

Blue winced. "I hesitate to…I almost want to suggest that this Stardust artifact could put you on even ground with the Siphon Stone. What's being described here is a blade capable of cutting qi—"

"Did you pay attention to the ending?!" Kurt snapped. "It's the same damn thing, Blue! First Riktalash died, then this tribe died, too, just like God knows how many of the other tribes you were talking about! And even stopping the Drifter didn't bring back the people the Siphon Stone drained!"

Blue cringed, thinking of Kayla again. He became a great deal quieter.

"Why would my mom want me to see this? Why mention Stardust to me at all? Even if it really existed, even if it still existed in a museum somewhere…."

"Um, well…." Blue turned back to the first page and said, "This story comes from the Pequopsee tribe. Their reservation, which includes a casino *and* a museum, isn't even as far from here as Kline University. Its proximity…maybe…."

"Forget it. I can't beat Eric. I couldn't even if I had Stardust. My mom wouldn't want me doing something that could get me killed—that's not the damn message!" Kurt shook his head, removing one hand from his hair but leaving the other. "Aaaaargh! I'm getting so much outta my head but I still feel like there's more, something big I'm missing! What was she trying to tell me?!"

"Don't give up!" Blue said, returning to the papers as much for his own benefit as Kurt's. "This was a wonderful find, but there's lots more to sift through! We have more to go on now—I have a feeling we're getting close to finally understanding your duties and possible choices as a Linker."

*   *   *

Hours passed. The search slowed down despite the enormity of Kurt and Blue's discoveries, either because the two friends were tiring out or because of the discouraging omen the legends had brought. At one point, Blue unearthed a folded printout from a microfilm reader, inserted into one of the books on the shelf to mark a page. It was an article about an amateur archaeologist who had found several Native American artifacts while digging the foundation for his backyard pool, artifacts that paid for the pool itself and then some once he sold them to the highest bidder. Among the grainy, black-and-white pictures was a close-up of the Siphon Stone, Riktali symbol and all, misclassified as a Native American charm and slated to be shipped around with a traveling collection. This explained how the stone had arrived at Kline University. Unfortunately, the article didn't yield much else, except for some notes from Kurt's mother, which Blue confirmed out of the *I Ching*: the Siphon Stone's symbol, appropriately, came from the hexagram meaning "to swallow."

*   *   *

The sun glared orange through the window. Blue turned on the desk lamp, then leaned back in his chair and sighed.

"Maybe we oughta take a break, Kurt," he said.

"In a second." Kurt was sitting in the armchair, reading from a tall, thick black book. Blue slung his jacket over one shoulder and went to join him.

"You were ready to stop two hours ago. What are you reading now that...oh." Blue sat on the windowsill beside the chair and looked at the pages while Kurt turned them. "I see. It's a photo album."

"And a scrapbook. There's all kinds of stuff in here...my birth certificate, my hospital bracelet from when I was born...." Kurt moved to close the book, but couldn't bring himself to do it. "I know, I know, I should be looking through the papers and books and stuff instead, Kayla's life is at stake...."

That last part made Blue flinch, but he shook his head and said, "I'm not going to tell you you can't look at your mother's scrapbook. If I did, I wouldn't be human anymore...then how could I save Kayla in good conscience?"

Kurt chuckled and cast one eye up at Blue. "You wanna be her knight in shining armor now? Oh, yeah. You like her."

"This is hardly the time for jokes, Kurt." Blue's face became flushed. "Let's just make sure we're *capable* of saving her. We need to go eat dinner and then come back to this with fresh eyes. Perhaps we missed something prior to finding what we did that will be clearer on the second pass."

"Just a sec. I'm almost done with this thing." Kurt turned past the current page of baby photos, and found two blank pages next. He kept flipping, first one by one and then handful by handful, making sure there was nothing else.

"Yeah, it's done. Let's go—" Kurt stopped. He saw a yellowed piece of newspaper sticking out of the back cover at an angle. He pulled it out, turning it over and over to find its relevance. When he did, his eyes widened, and he averted them with a groan.

"What?" Blue peered at the article, which was actually on two pages paper-clipped together. The second page was on top, so all he got was the shortened headline: "CAR ACCIDENT."

"Oh."

Kurt frowned into the corner of the room. Blue, unsure of what to do, patted his friend's shoulder and took the article from his hands.

"Maybe I should look first," he suggested.

"Why would my Grandpa save this? He must have done it!" Kurt said, not denying Blue's request. "Why keep around a reminder of his daughter's death? Why put it in her scrapbook of my family and me?"

"Don't overthink it, Kurt. We both know that everything your grandparents do for you is out of love," said Blue. "How about this—if you'd never manifested as a Linker, or if you'd never shown them you were a Linker, they might have passed on themselves without ever telling you what happened to your mother and father. You were going to sort through this room eventually. Maybe this was your grandfather's way of leaving some of your legacy for you to find, just in case he never got to be the one to tell you."

Kurt turned back around, looking thoughtful. "Yeah, maybe that's it…."

"Whoa!"

"Yah! What?!" After settling into somber reflection, Kurt was nearly jarred out of his skin by Blue's cry.

"Except this article isn't about your mother at all! Well, not mainly, at any rate. Listen to this—it's the front-page headline." Blue read, "'Prominent scientist dead in tragic accident.' Subheadline, 'Qin Project co-head William Galant killed in watery car crash!'"

"William…Bill, that's my dad! Right, my grandpa told me about him, but not too much…." Kurt stopped. "Wait a minute, did you say the Qin Project? Isn't that the—"

"Yes! The immunization that makes you live forever, the immortality treatment!" Blue's eyes were glued to the page; in less than a minute, he'd read the entire article. "I mean, the reporting doesn't go into specifics, because the Qin Project's aims were mostly secret until just a few years ago. Apparently, your father was one of the original front-runners of the initiative. One of the other researchers says here that his loss was felt as both a friend and a scientist...he predicts that your father's death will set back research and development by at least a decade! If the Qin Project is only just being made commercially available now, then he was right. Kurt, your father must have been an extraordinarily intelligent man!"

"Grandpa didn't tell me any of this...." Kurt crossed his arms and thought for a moment, twisting his mouth this way and that. Finally, he asked, "Does the article say anything about the guy who...the Dark Linker?"

"Not much. His name was Andrew Lemas, a total unknown... apparently, he was something of a loner. Your grandfather must have either inferred most of the situation, or else maybe when he held you at the site of the accident, your mother was able to impart knowledge to him in the same way that she left her memories to you. In any case, this report doesn't characterize the accident as a murder, just as the result of reckless driving on Lemas's part."

"He was the Dark Linker that matched my mom," Kurt said icily. "I can feel it...it must be part of the memory I got from her. Grandpa was right about that, and he told me he felt it at the time, like you said. It *was* a murder! He went after my mom 'cause he wanted the world to end before she could fix the balance, just like Eric!"

"Never mind what I said," Blue interjected; while Kurt spoke, he'd gone back over the article. "Near the end, there is some speculation of foul play, but not because anyone knew anything about Linking or your mother's fight with Lemas. According to a Professor Frederick, your father had actually been working from within to slow down the Qin Project during the last months of his life, 'citing the need to reevaluate its possible impact on society before moving toward commercial release.'"

Kurt's posture straightened, and his eyes narrowed. His head was starting to hurt again. He thought back to the legends he and Blue had been reading earlier.

"Frederick had intended to put the project on hold for at least a few months while making a formal inquiry among the rest of the scientists and politicians involved. I guess he thought someone might have hired Lemas to kill your father and stop his moral objections. This is really your father's article, Kurt—the fact that his wife and child were also in the car is only mentioned in passing."

"What about the runes?" Kurt asked, in a tone that suggested he was leading to something. "Wouldn't someone have noticed the symbols on my mom's hand and her killer's? Didn't they at least guess that it mighta been gang related or something?"

"Mmmm…." Blue scanned over the pages again. "If anyone noticed the runes during the autopsies, they didn't mention them or else didn't draw a connection. Maybe…well, maybe when a Linker dies, his or her rune vanishes."

"Just like it would if the imbalance got fixed." Kurt was staring straight ahead with his mouth half open. "I know what it is, Blue."

"What?" asked Blue. Kurt had spoken with such quiet intensity that it made him shudder.

"Remember what the old fart told us the first day—me and Eric wouldn't be the only *qi ren* for long. The Earth makes more Linkers as the imbalance gets worse. Eric said the same thing when he was talkin' to the city from the top of the tower. In those stories we read, all those tribes and that island had a buncha Linkers—that means their worlds were just about to end. You said it was like cutting off a bad limb, that once the whole societies died, they took their imbalances with them. But the only reason that worked was because everybody dying was still an option."

His words flowed out with a deadpan tone, but they had the speed of a flooded river. Blue was hard-pressed to interrupt until Kurt paused.

"What do you mean, Kurt?"

"The world kept going for twenty-five years after my mom and that Lemas guy died, and then Laoshi said me an' Eric were the first Linkers to manifest. If we were first and not them, that means our imbalance is different from theirs—we've just been assuming that without thinking about it! But what that means is…if no more Linkers showed up after my mom died, but the world didn't end, either, her imbalance musta gone away at some point, except this time, something stopped it without everything crashin' down around everyone. And now, we find out that the cops never found her rune or her killer's, and everyone else just thinks the guy was hired to kill my dad! What are the odds that both runes disappear and Linkers stop manifesting right after the accident?!"

Blue jerked his chin forward. "Kurt, are you suggesting—"

"What if Lemas *was* going after my dad?" Kurt couldn't have slowed down his speech if he tried. It was a geyser, his mother's memories and his own thoughts gushing from his mouth together. "What if my mom and him lost their powers as soon as my dad…think about it, Blue! The only things everyone has to do are live and then die. People are born, and then they die, and then more people are born, like a wheel. Except now, we have the Qin Project shot that makes people live forever, and if my dad were still alive, we woulda had it a lot sooner. If people never die, then maybe it breaks the cycle…like, the wheel is stuck on life!"

While Kurt leaned forward into his hands, Blue fell back against the window. His eyes dried out from not blinking. He looked back and forth between the article and Kurt.

"So your father's death temporarily resolved the imbalance by stalling out the Qin Project, causing your mother and Lemas to lose their powers?" Blue wiped his hand across his mouth and cheeks. "And the imbalance has been the Qin Project all along, because it alters the natural processes of life and death? Kurt, you may just be right about this…."

"I am right!" Kurt looked up. "Riktalash, Blue! They had the damn eternal-life elixir, and because of that, practically everyone on the island was a Linker! I saw it in my dream—with all of 'em living forever, the streets were crowded as hell, and they hadda mine the rocks under the island practically hollow just to keep making stuff! Why do you think it sank when that Chinese guy started blasting his way out? That's why my mom showed me Riktalash in my dreams. I dunno about all those Indians, but Riktalash's imbalance was the same as ours!"

"But, does that mean…?" Blue held up his palms. "Now, Kurt, don't take this the wrong way, but…um…if Lemas…that is, if he…."

Kurt saw where Blue was heading. His face became darker, angrier than Blue had ever seen it, so much so that Blue found he had to turn away. Both of them fell silent, but the elephant had already entered the room, and it wasn't going to leave.

"He killed my parents," snarled Kurt after a few minutes.

"I know, but—"

"There's no 'but'! He was a murderer! That makes him a bad person no matter what!" Kurt grunted and punched down on the arm of the chair. "Just 'cause life is the imbalance doesn't mean death is the answer. My mom was good enough to understand that! Why else would she have left me memories that would lead me to here? Hell, I bet she was the one who convinced my dad to slow down the Qin Project, because she figured out it was causing the imbalance!"

Kurt stood up. "Look at the article again, Blue. Where's the Qin Project's office?"

"Um…." Blue flipped back to page one. "Northern New Jersey, the Sidney Grant Research Facility…just across the river from New York, actually. Huh, certainly sounds nearby enough to be the center of the current—"

"Listen up—this is how we take Eric's powers away, stop what he's doing, and hopefully do what the Indians couldn't and reverse the Siphon Stone," said Kurt. "We drive down to Jersey, bust our way into the Qin Project, and level the Goddamn place. Destroy every copy of the recipe and all the shots they already made. Make it so they couldn't get it back even if they worked for another hundred years! That's how you fix the world the good-guy way—without killing anyone."

"Except for the millions and millions of people who would have bought the treatment," said Blue. His features became drawn. "I really urge you to think this decision over, Kurt. No matter how you rationalize it, very few people are going to celebrate you as a hero if you take away their chance at eternal life."

"Ha! Anybody who wants to live forever is just too stupid to see that it'd be hell further down the road. And besides," Kurt scoffed, "they've got other things to worry about. What good is a body that lives forever if your qi's trapped in the damn Siphon Stone?! I'm doing the world a favor—even a short life is better than forever as part of Eric's weapon!"

"Mmmmm." Blue clicked his tongue and inhaled through his teeth. "I still don't know. We're talking about committing multiple crimes… breaking and entering, vandalism, mass homicide in one sense. Regardless of the moral basis of our actions—"

"Fine! Lemme go run it past my grandpa," said Kurt. He stalked out the door and called over his shoulder, "I'm sure he thinks this immortality thing is as stupid as I do!"

Blue listened to Kurt's footsteps thumping away to the other side of the house. He sighed and knelt down to gather up the most important papers they'd discovered. After a moment's thought, he elected to leave the scrapbook intact, article and all, and he copied the general location of the Sidney Grant Research Facility onto a small piece of paper in his wallet. He would worry about the exact street address once he and Kurt reached the town; there was little doubt in his mind that they were going, no matter how ambivalent he felt.

Once he had "Broken Lightning," "Hiding Bear," the *I Ching*, and several other photocopies from Daoist texts under his left arm, Blue edged out the door and went to join the Ciardis in the kitchen—he figured Grandma would have dinner on by now. But as soon as he came out of the back hallway and into the living room, he saw that the kitchen lights weren't on. He couldn't smell any food being prepared, nor could he detect humidity in the air from boiling water or even the dry heat the old gas stove would have produced.

"Kurt?" he called out. When there was no immediate answer, he focused his hearing, and after a few moments, he was able to make out irregular bass vibrations moving through the walls. It was the familiar sound of a TV set whose volume had been turned up too high. Blue put the papers down on the living room coffee table and headed for the other end of the house.

When he turned the corner around the stairs, he found Kurt in the doorway of the TV room right away, but something was wrong. Another few steps, and he saw that Kurt wasn't leaning into the room like he might to speak with his grandparents, but was leaning back against the door, which was closed. One more step, and he was at the proper angle to see an odd shaft of light that illuminated Kurt's hand over his face. One more, and he could hear Kurt crying.

"Kurt?" Blue closed the distance by jogging. "Kurt, what is it? What happened? Kurt!"

Blue felt light reflecting into his eyes off the backs of his glasses. He tried to avoid it at first, but then turned around to find out where it was coming from: not from the kitchen, but from above him, where an angled hole in the ceiling continued through a tunnel cut in the wall, down into the TV room. Blue looked up through it and saw the second floor, and beyond that, the sky.

Kurt opened his mouth, but only sounds came out, not words. He didn't uncover his eyes. He choked and sobbed, seeming on the edge of a breakdown, and leaned abruptly back against the door, practically striking his head on the wood. For the first time, Blue grasped how much taller than him Kurt was, because he'd never seen Kurt look so small.

"I...." Blue stammered. "I...."

"Leave me alone," Kurt said.

Nearly catatonic, Blue walked through the kitchen, opened the back door, crossed the backyard, and sat down under the singed and broken maple.

Kurt slid his back along the door and collapsed. His cries faded into the empty house.

*   *   *

Blue sat outside for more than an hour, racking his brain. He probed practically every day of his life up until that point, but found no precedent to tell him what to do next. As the late afternoon sun hit him straight in the eyes, he sneezed and hit his head on the tree trunk; he lost his train of thought. That was when he remembered something Kurt had said to him earlier that day.

Some things you just don't gotta think about so damn much!

That was hard for Blue, so he elected to focus on one thought, one choice, and with that, defeat all others. He decided to get up and get moving, then keep moving so fast that there'd be no time for any thoughts beyond the notion that he must continue. He crossed the yard and reentered the Ciardis' home.

The TV room door was still closed, undisturbed. Blue looked right and saw the silverware drawer in the kitchen ripped out from its place below the counter, overturned on the linoleum with its contents strewn everywhere. He looked left into the living room, and then he saw Kurt sitting on the couch, bent over the coffee table and surrounded by giant, black-handled knives. His palm was faceup on the tabletop, rune dimly active. Whatever he'd been trying to do to it had thankfully failed.

Blue didn't stop walking; in fact, he increased his speed. By the time Kurt looked up, all he could see was Blue's chest as his friend threw his arms around him.

"Blue, what the hell! Stop it! Stop that! Get off, leave…leave me alone…."

At first, Kurt resisted and pushed Blue away, but Blue hung on. In seconds, Kurt's words dissolved into more crying, and he surrendered. It was awkward for Blue, and even more so because he'd gotten himself stuck in a position leaning down on Kurt, with one leg bent and one extended farther back. But he forced himself to stay until Kurt had poured it all out of him, until his sobs faded to quiet sniffles. Blue wasn't sure how long it took, but by the time he pulled away and sat on the edge of the coffee table, both his thighs were asleep.

"I'm so sorry, Kurt," Blue said. "I'm here for you now."

He paused to let Kurt release more of his grief. Not once did Kurt look up at him. Blue waited and waited for him to, but even when Kurt finally grew silent, his face remained down.

"Kurt," said Blue, "look up. Look at me."

Kurt slowly responded. His eyes were burned out, dead. Blue made sure he had Kurt's attention locked in before he spoke again.

"They're fine, Kurt. They're going to be fine."

"How?!" Kurt's gaze retreated, first to the side and then back to the floor. "How do you know that, how can you know that?! All the stories said the same damn thing, Blue! Even the one time someone could beat the Drifter...!"

Blue waited again. Kurt sobbed for a few minutes, then sniffled.

"I know it because of you, Kurt. I know it because I stopped thinking about it so damn much." Blue braced his elbows on his knees and rested his face in his hands, staring straight into Kurt. "Every person is different. Every situation is different. Your faith and your perseverance will find a way to bring them back. You've taken all you can from your mother's ideas, and you've even gone beyond them to discover what nobody else in all these papers and all these times before you could. You're willing to see this through for the people you love, no matter how hard it is, and that's why you're going to succeed, Kurt. You're the bravest person I've ever known."

He paused.

"And I know you're brave enough to understand what I'm going to say, even if it might sound...well...here it is. Kurt, I...you're only human. You feel horrible about what happened here today, and...but, Kurt, you need to stop mourning for people who aren't dead, so you can get moving again." Kayla's face flashed across his mind. "And so do I."

Kurt looked up, this time of his own volition. He seemed confused, and maybe angry, but more than anything, the look in his eyes was vulnerable. Waiting.

"You can't afford to mourn them now, when you're the only one who can reverse this before it turns from hollow life into true death...before there's no more world for them to come back to." Blue stood up and grabbed his papers with trembling hands. "It's time to get them back, Kurt.

Before Eric can reach any farther, before he decides he can just drain you and reach his goals unopposed."

Kurt shifted across the couch, grabbed its arm, and fell back down the first time tried to get up. The second time, he couldn't even pool the necessary strength to brace himself. Third time was the charm, though, and then he was on his feet and facing Blue.

"What if…." He shook his head, clenched his rune-adorned fist for strength but found only emptiness. "Dammit! I'm…what if…dammit, Blue! What if we get to Jersey and destroy the Qin Project, and it doesn't bring them back? What if all the shots aren't even there, and destroying this one lab isn't enough? What if I was wrong, and that's not the imbalance at all?"

"You were right. I believe you were right because it makes sense and because I trust your perceptions of your dreams and your feelings," said Blue. "But we're not going to New Jersey yet, Kurt. For one thing, if Lowval is in Eric's range now, then New Jersey certainly is, too. If he was able to figure out that the Qin Project is the source of the imbalance, meaning that his power is dependent on its continued existence, I doubt he's going to let you go there without a fight. Second…I know it's a scary thought, but robbing Eric of his powers might not restore the qi trapped in the Siphon Stone to its rightful owners. We may have to try something nobody we read about has tried—breaking the stone open. Both that and a possible confrontation with Eric will require more power than you have right now, and I think a weapon that can cut qi might do the trick."

Blue held up "The Tale of Hiding Bear." "The Pequopsee reservation is only two hours north of here. We should at least see if they know anything about Stardust. If we're lucky, they'll have it in their museum waiting for us."

"But—the longer we take…if we waste time trying to find Stardust, Eric's just gonna get more reach and drain more people! I don't know if I can…." Kurt couldn't finish.

Blue thought of Kayla again and became newly numb.

"Why should it matter to us? Everyone we really care about is already in Eric's hands somehow or other," he said. "It makes little difference how quickly we act at this point. And it makes little difference how much more powerful he gets…he was already too powerful for you to defeat the last time. Theories and tactics are our only advantages now…we should try to be as prepared as possible. We'll only have one more chance to save them."

Kurt mulled it over.

"Okay," he said. He turned toward the hallway. "Go outside and warm up my...go warm up the car. The keys are on the...wait, here...."

Kurt tossed him the keys out of his pocket and walked away. Blue headed for the front door—for a moment, he hesitated, a strange impulse to listen taking hold of him. But he forced his respect for Kurt over morbid curiosity. He left the doorframe, and let Kurt's voice fade away behind the engine.

"Hey, Grandpa, Grandma...heh, it's me, Kurt. I'm sorry, but...I'm gonna have to break my promise to you...."

ACT VI

幽灵剑

A PHANTOM SWORD

Kurt only spoke twice during the trip. Most of the time, he just stared at the blurry trees and guardrails out the passenger side window, while Blue guided the car along the highway in silence. He thought of his grandparents, the things Hydrad had said, Kayla, Eric, his mother and father. He felt his palm buzzing the whole time, as if his rune had activated of its own accord and was telling him to release all his qi at once in a burst of anguished rage, catharsis. The elements and his ability to use them never crossed his mind—all that was secondary now.

What Kurt said first was, "I keep hearing this thing in my head."

Blue had gotten used to the silence, so it took him a moment to process, understand, and finally respond.

"You mean a voice, like the one in your dreams?" he asked.

"No. Least I don't think so...it's more like when you get a song stuck in your head, except it's just one sentence. The thing is, I can't tell if it's an idea I had, or if it's something my mom told me in one of the dreams that I don't get yet...or if it's...like, in between."

"What's the sentence?"

"'There is only one Drifter.'"

"Huh." Blue glanced over at Kurt quickly; his friend was leaning his face against the window glass. "How interesting. It's not even true. The Pequopsee legend implied the exact opposite, that there were several incarnations of the Drifter. Even if I'm wrong, and it was a single Linker migrating from tribe to tribe, Eric would still be the second Drifter incarnation."

"Maybe…but it's comin' from inside me. It feels like I've thought it for a long time, but I didn't realize it until now. Like I said, I don't know."

Nearly an hour after that, when the two of them were less than thirty minutes from their destination, Kurt spoke again. This time, he sounded more troubled, and before he said anything, Blue heard him fall forward in his seat and start to moan. He looked and saw that Kurt was holding his head.

"What's wrong?" he asked.

"I feel…." Kurt groaned, interrupting himself. "It's like I'm getting… stabbed by a million different knives in my head all at once, from everywhere! Except…only half of 'em hurt me, the rest…they feel kinda really…they feel good!"

"That's…." Blue felt panic rising through his stomach as he started to imagine things like heart attack, stroke, and seizure. "Well…well, what do you think—"

"Linkers." Kurt froze with an expression of wide-eyed clarity. He slowly put his hands back in his lap and sat up straight. The premonitions, now that he understood them, bothered him no more.

"That's what it is," he said. "More Linkers are manifesting, some Light and some Dark. A bunch of 'em are really far away, but some are closer— there! There was one in that car over there, on the other side of the highway! God, he's…she's, whoever, they're going down to the city, to Eric! They believe him when he says he's king of the Linkers, that he's the only one who knows what's gotta be done. Some of 'em feel like they're staying put, for now anyway, but there's so many of them, and there's more coming…they keep coming…."

Kurt turned to Blue, wearing a pained expression.

"Blue, we're runnin' outta time. The Earth is dying."

"But how can that be?" Blue's disbelief quelled his fear somewhat. "The immortality treatment existed already, and somehow I doubt…well, maybe more people would be making appointments to get the shot, what with Eric's doomsday rhetoric, but there's only so fast the patients could be processed. And I don't think it's available outside of Qin Project headquarters yet! How could the Earth's death be accelerating to produce Linkers at a quicker rate?"

"I don't know. But I know what I feel, and I can feel them. There're Linkers popping up all over the place now…."

Those were the last words he said until the trip was over.

*   *   *

With the world ending, New York in a state of emergency, and Eric's reach able to extend at least a hundred miles outside the city, Blue was surprised at the painlessness of the drive. Perhaps, he thought at one point, the draining kept more people hunkered down in their basements than it spurred to evacuation. Either that, or everyone who was fleeing was heading west, or maybe nobody yet knew they needed to flee this far from the center of the crisis. And then there was the explanation he didn't want to believe: that Eric had already drained everyone for miles around. Judging by the holes in the roofs of other houses, which Kurt had done his best to ignore by looking down at his knees on the way out of town, it had seemed as though the two of them were the only ones left in Lowval.

The silence gave Blue a lot of time for these kinds of thoughts. He was troubled to think that Kurt's rune should have been like a homing beacon to Eric, and yet Eric hadn't even attempted to drain him. All the other Linkers manifesting might have been enough to disrupt his reception, but in his heart of hearts, Blue knew it was more than that. Linking wasn't a mechanical process—it was one tied to the person's will, and it had clearly been Eric's will to target Kurt's grandparents, not to mention everyone else in town. Blue knew that the only reason he and Kurt had been spared was because Eric still planned to descend on them in person at some point, and finish Kurt off with his bare hands.

*   *   *

The residential parts of the Pequopsee Reservation were far off the road, hidden deep in the pine and maple forest. That left the large, white rectangle of the casino building to greet Blue when he pulled into the parking lot; its windows flashed from black to white as they reflected the streetlamps' glow.

Blue had no trouble finding a space: the lot was deserted, except for a few cars near the front that probably belonged to the Pequopsee tribesmen themselves. He could see the museum peeking out from behind the casino, a smaller and squatter version of its brother structure. Both buildings were as dark as the sky—Blue hoped the tribe hadn't shut things down in anticipation of the apocalypse.

"Are you tellin' me this place is gonna be closed?" groused Kurt as he stepped out of the car, voicing Blue's concern.

"I'm…not sure. It could just be that there are no visitors…no one wants to leave their homes, with all that's transpiring. Also, it's getting pretty late." Blue had the thought that Eric's power might have beaten them here, but he decided to leave it unsaid. He searched his mind for thoughts to reinforce his hopes—for one thing, he hadn't seen any Siphon Stone beams streaking across the sky during the trip.

"And anyway," he said, "this is a reservation. The Pequopsee live here. We can just walk into the actual village and get someone to open the doors for us if we need—"

"Screw that. We're already gonna burn down a science lab later tonight." Kurt clenched his fist as little wisps of qi escaped his rune. "What's a couple more doors?"

"Um…I suppose." Blue covered up his anxiety by starting to cross the parking lot; Kurt walked beside him. "Luckily, it's already dark. We'll be done here and down in New Jersey well before morning. That means fewer people inside the Qin Project that we'll have to worry about evacuating."

Kurt and Blue followed the sidewalk to the front doors of the museum, which were unlocked. But inside, the place was dark and deserted. A lifelike diorama leered at them from off to the right, a Native American warrior thrusting his spear down on a giant, hairy creature. The lights from the parking lot, filtering through the glass doors and windows, revealed the shadows of many similar statues and artifact cases lining the walls farther in, but nothing more.

"Hello!" Blue called—he heard his voice bounce along the corridor and back to him. "Hello! Is there anybody here?"

"Yes." Kurt and Blue both heard the crack of the speaker's heels against the floor tiles now, but it still seemed like he had come out of nowhere. He was a middle-aged man whose long, black hair was streaked with gray. He wore a charcoal suit and tie, but there was an animal-skin vest draped over him, and several strings of blue and red beads hung from his neck. He also wore a headband from which a single feather protruded, going back behind his left ear. From the looks of things, he'd been doing just as Kurt and Blue intended to do: raiding the exhibits.

"I'm surprised to see any visitors, with the world in such dire straits," the man said. "I'm sorry, but I'm going to have to turn you away. The museum is closed."

"Yes, well…we're not here as tourists, sir. We're looking for—"

"The doors were open," interrupted Kurt. His tone was impatient.

"A number of my tribesmen and I came here to put on the old ceremonial garments, and to join our last tribal elder in prayer down below, at a replica of the spirit cave," said the man. "It's not as good as the true spirit cave, which was destroyed when the highway was built, but our sentiment should be all that matters. In any case, that's why the doors were open."

"I thought you Indians didn't do that sorta stuff anymore," said Kurt.

"Normally, most of us don't, though we do try to keep the lore and heritage of our people alive. But in this case…." The man held up his right hand—a rune like Kurt's flashed to activity, throwing shadows over the exhibits. "The omen of the end times has appeared on many of us. We are all descended from halfblood…the Pequopsee are already dead, destroyed long ago in the battle foretold by this same omen. This is enough to make us believe."

"Yeah, I guess the end of the world would make a lotta people find religion," Kurt said. He lifted and activated his own rune. "In any case, you and me are in the same boat."

The man was startled. He recoiled, and stammered, "I…I shouldn't be surprised, I suppose, but—"

"We've come here following 'The Tale of Hiding Bear.' I believe he's the one you mean when you speak of a common descent from halfblood. He would've been the last pure Pequopsee tribesman," said Blue. "In the story, we read about an artifact called Stardust which enabled Hiding Bear to defeat the Drifter. We've come to see if you have it, or know how we could find it."

"Stardust…yes, we thought back to Hiding Bear as well, when the news of the disaster in New York came to us," said the man. "We believe that this young man who claims to be directing the end times is the Drifter born again, with the cursed stone of legend around his neck. Our stories speak of the Drifter in many places at many times, as if he were a man of smoke, able to shift his appearance and identity, but always retaining the stone to mark his presence. The appearance of the Drifter has always led to the end of the tribe...he is said to turn the strength of the tribesmen back upon them, fighting as if all are one within him.

"The world is a great deal smaller now than it was in the time of my forebears. Some would say that we are all one tribe now, and the fact that you and I both bear the omen seems to mean that is indeed the case. This calamity will be far-reaching, and this Drifter more powerful than any previously known."

"If it weren't for that damn rock, I'd be as powerful as him!" Kurt felt his qi pulsing out from his body, as if trying to prove his point—he glowed in a way similar to how he would glow with his shield activated. "Linkers...people who have the omen come in pairs, and any two that get their powers at the same time match each other strength-wise. Me an' Eric were a pair."

"I...." The man closed his eyes and held out his rune in Kurt's direction. "My tribesmen and I could feel each other's hearts as we came to bear the omen, because we are connected in this...but now, I can feel that you *are* stronger than any of us. You may be correct to say that you are the equal of the Drifter. There is...."

The man's eyes opened wide, then seemed to cloud over.

"There's so much sadness in you. I'm very sorry...you must have experienced a great deal of hardship, Mr...."

"Ciardi." Kurt looked away and deactivated the rune. "My name's Kurt Ciardi."

"Aaron Bluefield," offered Blue.

"I'm Kieran," said the man. He gestured slowly with his arm, and began walking down a curving hall to the right. "Come with me—Stardust will do us little good once the world has ended. If you can light the same glow within the blade as Hiding Bear once did, you're welcome to take it with you."

The museum was labyrinthine, composed of winding, interconnecting hallways, stairs, and blacklit tunnels that contained faithful reproductions of cave art. It was obvious that the exhibits were meant to be traversed in a specific way, one that told the story of the Pequopsee from prehistory to present through lovingly re-created statue scenes and preserved artifacts.

"Fascinating...and magnificent," Blue whispered. "I would love to come back here someday, and study this place as it was meant to be studied...."

Kurt said nothing.

Kieran led them down a short flight of stairs, and the museum opened up before them into a long, tall room, filled with fake trees through which fake Pequopsee hunted their fake prey, human and animal. Many small, mazelike paths crisscrossed the forest, but they all intersected at a gray dome of rock in the center. Kieran passed it for the moment; Kurt and Blue saw several other tribesmen inside the dome, huddled around a bent-over, white-haired man dressed only in ceremonial skins. They were trying to light a fire with wood brought from outside.

"Here." Kieran walked a few steps ahead and stopped at a glass case, turning on its interior lights with a switch on the side. Blue noticed an outcropping of rock in the forest beyond the guide ropes—it jutted out over a trough of land meant to represent a ravine.

"This is where Hiding Bear meditated and spoke with the great spirit," he realized.

"Yes," said Kieran. "The true place no longer exists, like the spirit cave, but this is what you came here for. Take it."

Kieran reached into his pants pocket and took out a key, then unlocked and opened the top of the display case. Kurt and Blue stepped forward. There were three shelves, containing arrowheads, broken knife points, a few tiny hide pouches, and a plateful of shriveled herbs. Prominently displayed on a stand, in the center of the top shelf, was a gray stone knife about a foot in length. It looked charred by fire; its handle was continuous from the blade and still had a matte look from being held many times.

Slowly, Kurt reached into the case and took the knife. It was heavier than a kitchen cleaver of similar size. It felt unwieldy.

"This is it?" Kurt said. He spun around and looked at Blue, then Kieran, then Blue again. He shook the knife angrily in front of him. "This is the same 'Stardust' that can cut qi? Hiding Bear used this thing to…dah!" He scraped the blade across his skin fiercely; nothing happened. "It's not even sharp!"

"Here, let me take a look at it," said Blue. But Kurt charged his hand with qi, drawing electricity up from the wires in the floor, intending to destroy the knife. All he got for his trouble was a snapping noise and a bad shock. He jumped back and dropped Stardust, clutching his hand; Blue waited a moment before picking up the artifact.

"Gah!" Kurt grunted. A handful of cracks had formed in the stone knife, but Kurt was still the worse for his actions.

"Stupid piece of...." Kurt paced around to the side of the display case, rubbing his hand and forearm. "Damn earth-rock reflected my lightning qi!"

"I'm sorry you didn't find what you were looking for," said Kieran.

"Don't be so sure!" Blue's excitement drew Kurt's attention, and made him forget about his arm for the moment. Blue held up Stardust—some of the cracks on its side were still glowing from the heat of Kurt's attack.

"I think you may have just performed your first divination, Kurt!" Blue said. "When you heated up the stone, lines appeared...there's a hexagram in here!"

"Really?! Well, write it down before it disappears!" Kurt took off back down the path. "I'll run out to the car and get—"

"I brought it!" called Blue, stopping Kurt. He reached into his jacket and took out the papers, then separated the *I Ching* from them. "I figured it was best to be prepared. Now, let's see...."

Blue flipped through the *I Ching*, searching for the hexagram that matched the cracks in the ancient knife. One solid line, then two broken ones, then solid, then two more broken. It was more than halfway through the list, so Kurt and Kieran were left waiting for several minutes.

"Got it!" Blue said at last. He turned to Kieran and asked, "Does the concept or phrase 'The Keeping Still' mean anything to you? Or perhaps 'Bound?'"

Kieran looked surprised again. He took the knife back from Blue and studied it closely.

"Stardust told you this?" he asked. Blue nodded.

"There is an old meditation technique," Kieran said. "In your language, its name would roughly translate to 'The Stillness.' It is an intense process, a spiritual journey in which the Pequopsee warrior looks deep within himself and faces his personal truth. The warrior sits and contemplates a campfire until he is on the verge of sleep, and then he uses special herbs that turn the fire white. The smoke from this fire reflects his truth by guiding him in dreams, bringing him to speak before the spirits. It is said that this journey can be long and winding, but if the warrior is able to return to the waking world, he will bring with him the knowledge he needs to reach his destiny."

Kieran laid the knife back into the case, almost dropping it as he tried to set it back on its stand.

"This is the technique Hiding Bear is said to have used to commune with the great spirit."

"Ha *ha*!" Blue clapped his hands. "Kurt, that's it! Your rune knew what to do, and through your frustration, it communicated with us! Imagine what powers you could still discover if you learn to use it to its fullest potential, beyond the seven Linking elements…you could even tap into the secrets of the Earth itself!

"Kieran, can you still create this white fire?" Blue asked.

"Yes, but we don't have enough of the herbs left to make more than one or two attempts—the recipe to blend the herbs has been lost since the generation of Hiding Bear. It is said that many attempts could be necessary to reach The Stillness, even for the most experienced Pequopsee." Kieran went back into the display case and removed the plate of dried plant matter. "You can try, however. If you came to know of The Stillness through the connection between your mark and Stardust, then this is your destiny."

"Ha! I don't do destiny," Kurt snorted. "Everyone keeps talking about destiny! The way I see it, the Earth wants me to save it, so it gave me my powers, period. It's about damn time it told me what to do with them!"

"In any case," said Kieran, walking with care so as not to spill the herbs, "follow me. The rest of my tribesmen are already lighting a fire in the spirit cave, and though it is only a reproduction, the spirit cave is still the best place for you to meditate. We'd be glad to lend you our fire as well —we'll light another and continue to pray for salvation in our own way elsewhere."

They'd walked farther into the fake forest than Kurt had realized; even moving as fast as they were, it took almost five minutes to get back to the spirit cave. Kurt felt apprehensive, and the sensation only increased when Kieran told him and Blue to wait while he ran ahead and began talking to the rest of the Pequopsee in a fast-moving tongue. Kieran's tribesmen seemed half amazed and half skeptical, although the elder jumped to his feet and started pointing at Kurt right away, abandoning his attempts to get the fire lit. Kurt averted his eyes to avoid seeing what parts of the elder's wrinkled body weren't covered by the sparse animal hides.

"Are you sure about this?" he whispered to Blue.

"Aren't you?" Blue asked, surprised.

"It was sounding good until he started talking about an 'intense spiritual journey' that could be 'long and winding.' We don't exactly have time on our side here."

"'Long and winding' could just be a figure of speech. And remember what we talked about back in Lowval," Blue said. "Stardust led us here, and according to the legend, its original owner used it to cut qi. This could be the key to reversing the effects of the Siphon Stone. If so, it'll be well worth any amount of time we spend on it."

"But what if...." Kurt hated to think it. "What if I can't reverse the effects of the stone, no matter what? Eric's...got everyone I love, *we* love, but what about all the other people he's still gonna drain? The longer I wait to take care of the Qin Project, the more people I let him get to...and it'll be on my shoulders. I just...I dunno if I can let...just 'cause I wanna get everyone I care about back doesn't mean I should abandon everyone else, or the world! What if the world ends while we're sitting in some cave, Blue?! I mean, if it's what my rune is telling me to do...but what if that's different from the reason the Earth gave me the rune in the first place? I betcha Eric's rune never told him to go out and drain people!"

"Kayla said something similar on our way up the Darklight Tower. She was worried that her emotions would cause her to make selfish choices, even in the face of her duty to the entire world. Kurt, I know you. You'll make the right decision when the time comes, just like she would. Besides," Blue continued, "think back to what Eric said—as long as there's a single person left alive and undrained, the Linker Weapon can't perform the way he wants it to. The world won't end until Eric drains you, which he'll have a harder time doing if you can come away from this any stronger at all. If you ask me, you *are* fulfilling your responsibility to the Earth by attempting the spirit journey."

"All right, all right." Kurt stepped forward—Kieran was waving to him. "Looks like we're up. Let's get this over with."

The spirit cave had mostly cleared out when Kurt and Blue approached. Only Kieran and the hobbling elder remained. Although he was following his tribesmen, the elder made a point of stopping to turn and look at Kurt—he took Kurt's right hand and examined the rune. He followed up by shaking Kurt's hand furiously, smiling and saying something in his own language.

"Uh...thanks." Kurt understood the general idea. "I'll do my best, I promise."

"Here you are, Mr. Ciardi." Kieran handed Kurt the plate of herbs. "Throw half of these onto the fire just as you begin to feel yourself falling asleep. If you are still awake when the fire turns orange again, you can use the other half for a second try, but after that, there's no more."

"Two shots, got it." Kurt nodded. "You guys gonna be somewhere close by if we need you for something?"

"We'll be at our reservation town, in the forest. Follow the footpath from the parking lot." Kieran patted Kurt on the shoulder. "Good luck. You hold the hope of the entire world in your hands."

Kurt looked into the cave. Blue had already taken a seat next to the pile of firewood. He picked up the stones the tribal elder had been striking, held them out, and got some sparks going on the first try. The wood was ideally prepared—in seconds, the flames were climbing high.

"I got it lit!" Blue called to Kurt. He shrugged, smiled, and added, "I was a Boy Scout for about six months—lighting campfires turned out to be my sole physical forte. We can get started right away!"

"Great," Kurt muttered.

*   *   *

The Pequopsee had hauled real rocks into the museum to re-create their spirit cave, so sitting in it felt authentic. Kurt and Blue were surrounded by paintings and carvings from walls to ceiling. These depicted animals, humans, maps of the stars, and sometimes combinations of the three interacting. Presumably, they were based on the décor of the original spirit cave. The drawings seemed to dance in the crackling light from the fire.

Blue started dozing almost immediately, feeling his long night of worry and walking catch up to him at last. Kurt, however, wished that he'd set his alarm that morning—sleeping in had allowed his qi to recover, but now it seemed as if it would be hours before he'd feel tired again. Even the emotional drain of losing his grandparents had been converted into a kind of nervous energy dedicated to getting them back. Sleeping felt like an annoying interruption to him.

He almost opened his mouth to speak to Blue at one point, but not only was he hesitant to disturb his friend, he didn't have much to say. He considered throwing the first of the herbs into the fire when Blue began to fall asleep, as if he could search for the truth and enlighten Kurt when he woke up, but Kurt knew that he probably had to do it himself.

Two hours passed.

Mr. Garrison's gonna fire me, Kurt thought. *Not that it'll matter if the world ends. And if I saved it, he'd be an asshole not to hire me back.*

Still, Kurt felt some anxiety over his job at Lowval Electric. He started moving his hands back and forth like he did when he was tossing electricity between them with the help of his rune. For the first time, he realized how much he missed working with wires and circuits.

Another hour.

Kurt tried to tire his eyes out by examining all the artwork in the cave. It was boring him, so he kept at it, reasoning that that seemed like a step in the right direction. Bored people often fell asleep. The bottom dropped out of that plan, though, when he found something interesting that all the human figures had in common—their torsos were drawn as Linkers' runes, some like his and some like Eric's.

I wonder what that means, he thought. *Did Linking turn into the whole way these people saw themselves? But how was there time for that, if Linkers only started manifesting just before they all died? Maybe the news got passed around by a bunch of different Indian tribes over the years, like the legend of the Drifter....*

Kurt forced himself to stop thinking. It was keeping him awake. He squinted his eyes shut, leaned back against the cave wall, and let his right hand fall near the plate of herbs. He felt petulant. He wanted to be ready.

More hours crept by.

Finally, Kurt started to feel fatigued. If he'd thought about it a little harder, he'd have realized that fatigue wasn't enough, and that he was still far from falling asleep. But he was trying not to think too hard. He opened one eye halfway, giving himself just enough sight to count out half the herbs, and then he threw them into the fire.

The flames turned white instantly, and the fire surged in size and heat. The cave filled with a bluish-gray smoke. Even if Kurt truly had been ready to nod off, that would've shaken him wide awake. For the three seconds before he started coughing uncontrollably, he stared at the fire in awe.

Guess that's why the Indians needed a lotta time to get this spirit quest thing done, Kurt thought, wiping tears filled with ash from his eyes. *It must take forever to get used to this kinda fire, and I've only got one more chance!*

Kurt tried to close his eyes again, but they were too irritated. He reasoned that if he were really tired, it wouldn't matter whether or not he tried to stay awake, so he gave in and studied the white fire. It had a gray-black core down near the base, where the flames licked at the wood, and it remained bigger than the normal, orange fire that had been its previous incarnation. Eventually, Kurt stopped coughing, but he didn't feel any more ready to sleep. At least he hadn't managed to wake Blue with any of the heat, smoke, or noise he'd generated. He strained and stared, but all he saw was the fire's slow transition back to orange. The smoke above him cleared.

Time lost all meaning.

Kurt settled into a state suspended just above the sleep that would never come. Now he genuinely was tired, but rest still eluded him, along with any answers his dreams might bring. He felt as if he was going to stay this way for the rest of his life.

Giving up, Kurt threw in the rest of the herbs and watched the fire turn white again. At least it was entertaining. The smoke enveloped him, filling the whole cave somehow without obscuring the art on the walls, but Kurt was prepared for it and didn't cough this time. He let it invade his eyes and his nostrils, keeping focused on the dancing white all the while.

After he didn't know how long, clarity suddenly cut through, and Kurt's exhaustion disappeared. It was replaced by frustration.

God dammit! he cursed to himself. *This was stupid...God knows how many more people Eric drained while I wasted the night in here!*

Kurt stood up and walked out of the spirit cave; he needed some fresh air, or at least he needed whatever passed for fresh air in the lower floors of a museum. At first, he was confused, thinking he'd stepped outside, but then he remembered that the fake spirit cave was surrounded by a fake forest, and he shook his head at his own stupidity. He strolled through the plastic trees, running his hands across their bark, looking for a suitable one to lean against while he stretched his legs and pondered his next course of action. He walked for a long time.

And then, with no warning whatsoever, Kurt stepped through some thick bushes, and found that he had to cover his eyes against powerful sunlight. He squinted around two of his fingers, but he didn't believe what he saw, so he pushed through the pain and looked directly. He was standing in the Painted Desert, sand under his feet and a mesa in the far distance, the angry sun beating down on him and making his jacket hang heavy upon his shoulders.

It felt familiar somehow.

"Blue?" said Kurt, alarmed. He turned back, but the forest he'd come from was gone, and so was the spirit cave. There was only an endless plane of driftless sand, with an occasional rock or cactus to interrupt the monotony.

Kurt spun all around, but couldn't even find the tracks he might have left walking to his current position.

"Aw, hell," he muttered.

And then there was a voice behind him.

"Ah! So, your search for the Way has led you here. None arrive in this place except through their own means and in their own time, but finding these things is a virtue in itself."

No matter how long he went without hearing it, Kurt could never have forgotten that voice. He slowly turned around, and by the time he laid eyes on the old man, half his body was clenched.

"You," he spat.

"Are you surprised that you see me here, or are you surprised that exploring the legends and rituals of the Pequopsee has led you back to the same true and constant Way the Daoists speak of?" wondered Laoshi. He stood floating in the air, looking down at Kurt.

"Actually, I was thinking it's time you gave me some straight answers." Kurt positioned his hands for the qi gun, but when he tried to create the bullet, he found that he felt nothing. Bewildered, he unclasped and reclasped his hands, then tried again. Still nothing. Finally, he turned his palm to his face—his rune was completely inert, and no matter how hard he focused, it stayed that way.

"What the hell?!" He immediately laid blame on Laoshi. "What'd you do? Did you take my powers away? How do I get them back? Tell me!"

"I would not know what happened to your powers, nor do I have any way of taking them from you," Laoshi said. "This is your dream. Everything here follows your will, not mine."

Kurt sputtered and pointed, trying to come up with a rebuttal, but he couldn't get much further than the words "I" and "you." He looked away and back several times, and the distracting fact that he still wasn't sure how he got into the middle of this vast desert helped to mute his anger.

Eventually, Kurt settled into simply glaring at Laoshi, whose mysterious smile never faded.

"Please listen to me, Kurt—I only wish to congratulate you. When I first met you, you were a man who let the world ebb and flow around you without knowing your place in it. It has been half a year since then, and in that short amount of time, you have discovered much about yourself and your surroundings, and have seen the rock in the stream for what it truly is. Having thus accepted your place, you need only make one final leap to become a true sage—this is the leap back to where you began, the 'holding fast to the mother' described by the great teacher Lao-tzu.

"As before, however, these are simply the facts I have learned from my years of study. How you interpret and use them is up to you. There is only one truth that will satisfy you, and for the sage who knows his place, this truth is easily seen."

Kurt frowned at Laoshi harder and harder while he spoke, but as soon as he got to the part about Lao-tzu, Kurt lost his nerve and looked away. When he opened his mouth again, his voice, though still resentful, had become little more than a murmur.

"You could've told me, you know."

"What could I have told you?" Laoshi asked.

"About my mother! That you knew her, that she had your papers, which means I have your papers! About how Eric couldn't be the imbalance, about how Light and Dark aren't just good and bad all the time, about the Drifter, about Riktalash and the Siphon Stone and…."

Kurt's voice trailed off. He still hadn't looked back at Laoshi.

"When I praise you for finding your place, I praise you for carving your own path in life," Laoshi said, "and when I speak of the sage, I speak of a person who has the courage to let the path carve itself when it must. You and I are not men who believe in destiny, but we do believe in cause and effect. Your mother's research was her path, and I taught her no more than I taught you. To guide her would have been to assign her causes, which would have made the effects not entirely her own. This would have misled her on the way to discovering her place.

"The same holds true for you. I did not know if you knew anything of your mother before we met—it was something you came to discover on your path as *qi ren*, but I did not know your path would go in that direction, nor would I have presumed to direct it. As you have discovered by following the Pequopsee's path back to the Way, there are many avenues to reach your truth. You could have learned of your mother in many ways, none of them necessarily connected with your journey as *qi ren*, and you could have discovered a path as *qi ren* that never intersected hers."

"But this isn't about me!" Kurt exploded. "It's not about what I want, or how I feel—it's about saving the world! It's about me being really good at this Linking crap for some reason, and me being the one the Earth asked for help because of that! That's my 'place,' isn't it? You…why did you leave it to chance?! If I knew what the imbalance was right away…dammit! Did you want the world to end if I didn't figure it out in time?! Was it that important to you that I turn into a 'sage' along the way?"

"Your potential to be a sage, your innate awareness and your nearness to your place, is what made you a strong Linker. It is why the Earth was able to reach out to you, and so maturing in this capacity has helped you in your journey. But I myself wanted nothing from you, or from the world," said Laoshi. "Change is the Way of things. The Earth has always been changing, and the intervention of the *qi ren* in the imbalance will only determine the nature and magnitude of the current change. The mere presence of *qi ren* guarantees an eventual return to balance. As the strongest Light Linker, you are able to play a large part. You desire to see the world return to harmony without the loss of all you are familiar with, but this is only one among many ways that *qi ren* can influence the imbalance and the end of the world, and whether or not it is the truest for you has always been your decision. No one, not even the Earth, can make that choice for you."

Kurt's posture fell. "So Eric was right…."

"He does what he must, what is true for him," said Laoshi. "You and he are much alike in this respect—why else would you have manifested at the same time?"

"Okay, that's it!" Kurt gnashed his teeth. Even with his rune inactive, he could still raise his fists. "I don't care what you say about this being in my hands and you not wanting anything, you've got a lotta nerve calling yourself my 'Laoshi' when you haven't done any teaching since day one. Even then, all you did was back up what Blue and I already figured out! You wanna be my Laoshi? Then why the hell don't you teach me something I can use?!"

"Ah! But as you have discovered your place, forged your path, you have come to know it far better than I ever could. Furthermore, neither you nor I can predict the future, and therefore we cannot know what will be useful until the time of use arrives. Still, you are merely asking that I inhabit my place as I have presented it to you, and this is a natural, reasonable request. So, as your Laoshi, I will teach you the most important lesson you have already learned."

"What?!"

And then Laoshi was gone. Kurt blinked—he hadn't taken his eyes off the old man for even an instant, but suddenly, he wasn't there anymore. Kurt looked around again, but as before, all he saw was the endless desert.

He threw back his head.

"I HATE YOU!" he screamed. The horizon swallowed his voice without returning an echo.

"You know that?!" Kurt added, just as angry but less loud—his throat was burning. "I hate you. Man, as soon as I get my powers back, I'm gonna kick your ass…!"

And then, Kurt felt something. There was a pull leading him back and to the left, but it wasn't coming from his still-inactive rune. It was coming from somewhere else, someplace he couldn't identify, as if his qi were buzzing inside him without gathering in any single place. He hesitated, but then turned around, and all of a sudden, he wasn't alone anymore.

"Blue?"

"Fascinating…." Blue seemed to look at the desert from every possible angle, except for the angle that would have caused him to face Kurt.

"Yeah, I don't get it either," Kurt grumbled. "Help me out here, Blue. Where do you think we are? How did we get here—how come you got here so long after me? And hey—you just missed the old fart! He disappeared, but he was here, too! How—"

"Do you know what you're looking for here, Kurt?" As he asked the question, Blue slowly pivoted and met Kurt's eyes. He was so expressionless that he was completely unreadable.

"What?" Kurt, however, was unmistakably baffled.

"Do you know what you're looking for here, Kurt?"

"No! How the hell would I—" Kurt felt something in his head, like a distant memory or a dream within a dream. His palm ached with intangible desire. "I…the Stardust we saw…it wasn't the real Stardust. I'm here to find Stardust."

"And how are you going to do that?" asked Blue.

"I dunno. My rune isn't even working, I…well, it's sort of working, it's like…." Kurt felt something else; he was starting to become dimly aware of a connection between his chest, his head, and his palm, like a wire inside him. "You have an idea, don't you?"

"Of course. I always have ideas," said Blue. "You know how Eric could sense the Siphon Stone once he became a Linker? Maybe you can sense Stardust the same way."

"Hey, that's a great idea! Thanks, Blue…but wait a minute, I'm still not sure how the Linker's sense works. Well, I mean…I guess I could try…." Kurt held up his palm and scanned it across the horizon in front of his face, trying to feel any reaction at all. "There's nothing. It's not even lighting up."

"You aren't doing it right," said Blue.

"Come on, Blue! You're not helping at all!" Kurt paused—he didn't want to be mad at his friend. Far more than anger, he could feel affection for Blue running through him, tracing the course of the wire that he imagined was connecting the various parts of himself. Now, though, he could also feel the wire receiving some kind of signal from Blue, reinforcing that very affection. Was that how he'd realized Blue was standing there before seeing him?

It's not the powers you sense, it's the person, Kurt thought. He concentrated harder and went back to scanning the desert, but with a new tactic. His brain shouted, *Is anyone else out there?*

"Kayla!" Kurt stopped and held his arm out almost due west, so that he was staring straight into the half-sunken sun. The light didn't bother him anymore.

"Come on, Blue! Kayla's here, too—this way!"

Following his arm and the pull from within, Kurt started walking across the hard sand. Blue stayed a step behind him on the left, exactly where he'd first appeared to Kurt, and said nothing. The passing of cacti and rocks was the only clue that they were making progress: the horizon, the distant mesa, and the sun all seemed to stay in exactly the same place.

And then Kurt was standing at the base of a large rock, tall and jagged, with a stone arm and stone fist protruding at an angle from the top. Kayla was clasped inside the fist, struggling to break free.

"Hold still, Kayla! I'll get you out!" Kurt clasped his hands together, charged up the qi gun, and fired. The blast broke the stone fist without harming Kayla, and she started to fall.

Kurt looked at Blue. "Hey! Aren't you gonna catch her?"

"Oh, right!" Blue ran forward and caught Kayla sideways in his arms —he got there just in time. Once he had her, he lowered her onto her own feet and let her go, but she turned and wrapped her arms around him. He returned the gesture, and all of a sudden, they were holding each other. They stayed like that for a while.

Kurt looked at his rune while he waited for them to finish. He'd been relieved to feel it working a moment ago, and in fact, it had seemed so natural that he'd almost forgotten it had failed to activate earlier. But now, the symbol was dark again—when he thought about it, he hadn't even seen it light up when he'd fired the qi gun. Something was still different. He tried to reactivate it, but couldn't get any further than that strange, connective sensation of the wire.

Kurt decided he'd waited long enough and walked over to Blue and Kayla. They broke apart and faced him just as he got there.

"Hey, Kayla. You all right?" he asked.

Kayla whispered something in Blue's ear.

"She's fine," Blue told Kurt. "She says thank you."

"Good. We need your help again, Kay. We're looking for Stardust—it's somewhere in this desert. Have you seen it? Do you have any idea where it would be?"

More whispering.

"She says she's sorry…she doesn't know," said Blue. "But she thinks you should ask your grandparents. They're so nice, and they knew more than you thought they did before."

"My grandparents…?"

Kurt shut his eyes and redoubled his focus—he raised his palm to the desert once again. This time, he made almost a full circle before he stopped and opened his eyes. He was facing back the other way now.

"Come on!" he cried. He took off running, not looking back at Blue and Kayla but certain they were keeping step with him. Kayla was slightly behind him on his right, and Blue was back in his original position, slightly behind and to his left.

As he ran, Kurt became aware that he wasn't casting a shadow. In fact, he felt like a silhouette of himself against the backdrop of the sun, which now seemed to be getting closer. The mesa was as far away as ever.

Kurt squinted ahead, and for a long time, he saw nothing. But then, there was his house, rising in the distance. Soon he was only a few hundred yards away, and he could see how the sand and dry air had cracked the paint, but it didn't matter, because he was home. He got even closer, and he saw Grandpa coming out the front door to meet him, with Grandma right behind.

"Grandpa!" Kurt plowed into him and felt himself being spun around in a joyful hug. "Grandma! Grandpa!"

"Kurt! You're safe!" Grandma said. She joined in the hug, too, and Kurt felt like he was released at last. Years and years of emotion poured out of him, filling his chest and mind and hands. He felt the connections within him expanding, completing, and becoming stronger, and his whole body filled up with warmth.

"I was so worried about you," Kurt said.

"You don't have to worry, Kurt. We're fine," said Grandpa.

"Thank God!" Kurt ducked his head into Grandpa's shoulder again. "You're all I have! I thought I lost you…!"

"You'll never lose us, Kurt," Grandma said. "And we're not all you have. You have them, now, too." She pointed at Blue and Kayla, who were standing off to the side. They came closer and smiled at the reunited Ciardi family.

"I know." Kurt nodded to his friends, but then went back into the hug. "But you're…I love you! You're my family! I can't…I'm just so glad you're okay…."

Grandpa lightly pushed him far enough away that he could look into his grandson's eyes. He smiled.

"Kurt," he said, "you have a job to do."

"I…." Kurt let go of his grandfather and smiled back. "I know. That's why I'm here. I'm looking for the real Stardust. Do you know where it is?"

"Don't you?" asked Grandpa.

Kurt became confused at first, but then he searched the feeling within himself, following the wire all the way through and back to where he started. He looked left and saw the tower of rock looming in the distance.

"Of course I do." He laughed. "There's only one place it could be!"

"Then you know what you have to do." Grandpa patted Kurt's arm. "Yer a good boy, Kurt. Go get it. We know you can!"

"Come with me. All of you!" Kurt spun around the circle of his loved ones, looking at each in turn. "Please, everyone come with me. I need you."

"Of course we'll come, Kurt," said Grandma. She took her place alongside her grandson and reached up to ruffle his hair. "Lead the way."

Kurt started walking, and the others followed, their steps perfectly synchronized. A few times, Kurt looked back at his house, happy to have it there even as it wore away in the hot desert winds. He never seemed to be getting any farther from it, though, and the mesa never seemed to be getting any closer.

Watched pot never boils, reasoned Kurt—he decided to focus on the rock tower exclusively. Before he knew it, it was twice as near, and right after that, he was there, staring upward from its base, unable to see the top anymore. There was a cavern opening in front of him, like black paint on the red and brown rocks. He kept walking, leading everyone inside.

The cavern tunnels were numerous and mazelike, but they all went slightly uphill. Kurt didn't hesitate anymore—he knew which paths to take, where to turn. Once he reached the center of the rock tower, halfway up, he would find what he'd been looking for.

The path stopped splitting, becoming a single, curved corridor. Around the last bend, Kurt saw two doors hewn into the rock. One led left, into a large, circular room. The other was directly in front of him, and he could see a medieval-looking sword glowing silver, bathed in a shaft of sunlight coming in through a hole in the ceiling. The sword was stuck halfway into a flat-bottomed boulder, and its handle bore a sideways, kite-shaped impression that would fit the rune in Kurt's hand when he held it.

"You go on, Kurt," said Grandpa. Kurt turned around, feeling everyone move to his left, out of place. They now stood on the threshold of the empty room.

"We have to go this way," Blue explained.

Kurt nodded. "Okay. I'll be right there, just let me grab the sword."

Kurt started advancing into the other chamber, his arm out and his hand open in anticipation. But he didn't feel excited. In fact, the farther he walked from his family and friends, the more he felt like he was doing something wrong. The sight of the glowing blade in front of him turned his stomach; he slowed to a stop.

The cavern began to quake, and its ceiling began to crumble. Kurt spun around, and he saw that there were large rocks falling down all around the empty room.

"No!" Kurt instinctively ran to his loved ones' aid.

"Kurt!" But Grandpa's voice stopped him. "Go get the sword! We'll be fine!"

"But…no, I need it to save the world," Kurt told himself. He turned back, and saw that rocks were piling up in the doorway. Soon, the sword would be blocked off and crushed. He started to run, but he stopped again —each step forward still made him feel sick inside. He looked over his shoulder, and saw that the door to his family's room was sealing up just as fast as the door to the sword chamber, if not faster.

Kurt's face twisted in determination. He screamed and ran back to the left room, diving through the waterfall of earth. He felt rocks hit him on his back, legs, and arms, but it didn't hurt enough to stop him. From his flying leap, he went into a somersault that brought him onto his knees, jerked his head down, and thrust his hands outward. A moment later, he'd created the largest qi shield he'd ever attempted, a yellow dome that covered almost the entire room. His eyes squinted shut in concentration; his teeth ground with the effort.

"Kurt, go!" shouted Grandpa. "Don't worry about us! The whole world is more important, you're more important!"

"No it's not, no I'm not!" Kurt's voice cracked as he struggled to be heard over the avalanche. "Don't you understand? I need you! Who am I if I'm all alone? Why am I fighting to save everything if not for you? What good is balance in an empty world?"

Kurt never looked up, but somehow he knew. The doorways had both sealed, and the sword was gone.

Slowly, the avalanche stopped, and the room became quiet. Kurt turned off his shield and fell forward, palms down against the rock. His rune was glowing again, almost burning through the floor.

He spoke quietly. "I don't care what the Earth wants. Who knows if the Earth can even want anything? All I know is what I want, what feels right to me, and all I know is you. Even if the whole world died and there was no balance left to fix, if we were all still together…somehow, it'd be okay. I don't care if it is selfish! Screw the world if I can't save you!"

Kurt didn't get up for a long time. If he'd thought he'd found the depths of his soul before, drained them of emotion, he'd been wrong. He didn't feel clearheaded enough to move until his hands had worn an impression into the ground, and the sand beneath him was saturated. Yet somehow, when he stood, he didn't feel sad. The wire inside him was still there, still strong, and he knew he'd made the right decision.

When he looked up, he saw Grandma, Grandpa, Blue, and Kayla standing together. They were all smiling. They held their hands out, and between them, they supported the sword.

"You helped us, so we decided to help you. We got the sword for you," said Blue.

"You still need it to do what you have to do," said Grandma.

"Nobody wants to see you upset. We all love you, Kurt, and we trust you, too," said Grandpa.

Kurt laughed. "Thank you, thank you all!" He walked toward them to claim the blade. "I couldn't have done it without you!"

"Ah!"

Kurt whirled around, and there was Laoshi, levitating a few feet off the ground just like before. His head was only a few inches shy of the ceiling. Kurt bent his neck down and ran his hand back through his hair.

"You gotta quit sneakin' up on me like that," he said. But all his malice toward the old man was gone. Even while he looked nonplussed, he was still smiling, and when he met Laoshi's eyes again, that didn't change.

"Do you still want me to teach you?" Laoshi asked.

Kurt thought for a moment, and answered, "Yeah…but only the way you want to. I already know what lesson you were talking about when you said it was the most important, and that I already learned it. Well, actually, I guess it learned me, so I had it all along, but…it's like that rock in the stream thing, y'know? Where I just hadda look and see what I was doing to understand what I hadda keep doing?"

Laoshi nodded.

"You don't have to tell me if what I think would be right for you," said Kurt. "I already know it's right for me. Just gimme the facts for now."

There was a pause; Laoshi gestured toward the walls and floor.

"The Earth has qi, just as you and I do," he said. "It expresses its qi through the elements, just as you express yours with your hands and feet. You are *qi ren* because of your ability to give some of your qi to the Earth, and receive some of its qi in return. This allows you to borrow the use of the Earth's elements, and it allows the Earth to borrow the use of your heart. In this way, the Link is completed, and its purpose fulfilled—the Earth and *qi ren* each receive from it what they would not have on their own."

"I get it." Kurt smiled even wider. "It's not like the Earth has something it wants, it just…goes toward balance on its own, right? Making

Linkers is just a part of that, isn't it? Like, if only people can cause or fix imbalances, and the Earth has to get back in balance, then it has to work with people to do it by trading qi with them! I can't...not let my feelings tell me what to do, because even if what I tried to do instead was figure out exactly what the Earth needed to get back in balance, if I got rid of my feelings, I wouldn't be human anymore. What would the Earth have to gain from Linking with me after that?"

"If this is your truth as you have come to it," said Laoshi, "then you have succeeded, no matter what path this truth guides you down, or what end it leads to."

Kurt looked toward the corner of the room. His loved ones were gone, and the sword was stuck back into a boulder, just as it had first appeared to him. He didn't feel worry for his grandparents, or Blue and Kayla, because somehow, the connection was still there—they were still there. The warmth still pervaded his body.

"Yeah, I succeeded," he said. He smirked at Laoshi one last time. "You know how I know that? 'Cause I'm not afraid anymore."

Laoshi closed his eyes and bowed. Kurt returned the gesture.

Then he spun on his heel and walked over to the sword. This time, he was eager to feel it in his hand. He stopped when he reached the base of the rock, planted his right foot against it, swung his right arm out and around, and smacked his palm down on the sword's hilt. Immediately, he felt his rune grow hotter and more active, and the sword seemed to become a part of him, an extension of his arm, his rune, his mind, his heart, and all of it through that mysterious wire. He felt his qi flowing up and down the blade, away from him and back to him, pulling him out of himself and simultaneously drawing the sword in. Kurt braced himself, inhaled, and pulled with all his might.

*   *   *

There was a sound like electricity echoing through hollow steel.

"Guh!" Kurt snapped out of the deepest sleep he'd ever known and jerked backwards into the wall of the spirit cave. He groaned, went to rub his back where it had collided with a sharp irregularity in the rock, but then he realized his right hand was already occupied. He brought it around and gazed upon the true Stardust.

It looked different than it had in his dream. It was a giant, elongated kite in the shape of his rune, a shimmering construct of yellow energy. It pulsed throughout with glowing fibers, brighter yellow like shots from the qi gun. Kurt cranked his hand around at the wrist—the sword felt solid, exactly the right weight, and its sides looked sharp.

He laid his left hand on the center of the blade, and confirmed that it was indeed a physical object made from his own qi. When he took his hand away, still amazed, he noticed that he'd been covering another hexagram that sat between the upper corners of the sword. It was in constant flux, sometimes totally opaque and sometimes nearly invisible, rendered in a darker shade of yellow that was almost black. After a moment's worth of staring, Kurt discerned its pattern: one broken line on top of two solid lines, then three more broken lines.

Blue had begun to stir as soon as Kurt moved. Now he slowly turned his head and peeked around his eyelids to see what was going on. It didn't even register with him that the fire had gone out, and he was just turning back around to settle in when something clicked inside him. He scrambled to his knees and almost slammed his nose into the sword.

"Kurt…!" he whispered, his grogginess already gone.

"It's…here, I think I can—" At a thought from Kurt, the sword vanished with the same hollow, metallic sound that had marked its appearance. He twisted his hand around to look at the rune, now back to normal, then waved it for a few seconds. After that, he clenched his fist and reformed the sword. He grinned.

"I was right. It is a technique, just like the qi gun," he said, proud of himself. "I had it in me all along…I just didn't know where I hadda look for it."

He dematerialized and rematerialized the sword several more times, laughing to himself. Blue just shook his head at first, eyes wide open, but then, he came to his senses and held up his hands.

"Wait, wait, wait! Keep it there for a minute, hold it out so I can see…." Blue examined the blade, then reached into his coat and pulled out the *I Ching* again. He flipped through the hexagrams; this one didn't take long to identify.

"Number forty-five…'clustering'…'Gathering Together.'" Blue looked at Kurt, and his mouth burst open with happiness. "Kurt, you did it!"

"Yeah, well…I guess I couldn't have done it without you. Thanks for helping." Kurt stood up, chuckled, and put the sword away before Blue could ask him to explain what he meant. "Come on—we got what we came here for. It's time to go pay a visit to the Qin Project!"

ACT VII

THE HEIGHT

Kurt stamped out the fire's embers while
Blue gathered his papers and stretched out his aching muscles. Sleeping
sitting up against hard rock hadn't been good for him; Kurt, surprisingly,
felt no pain. He wouldn't truly be in high spirits until the Siphon Stone was
broken and the apocalypse was averted, but he led Blue back through the
halls of the museum with energetic confidence.

The first thing that gave him pause was passing underneath a skylight.
It was bright white—there was a cloud cover outside, but it was obvious
that the sun had been up for some time.

"Crap!" Kurt looked at Blue. "We were in here all night?"

"And most of the day, from the looks of things," said Blue. He pulled
out his cell phone and flipped it open. "Yes, it's late afternoon, all right.
Three-forty-four, to be exact...oh, my God!"

"Somethin' wrong?"

"It's the...!" Blue stopped and looked at Kurt with panicky eyes.
"Kurt, according to this, we were in the spirit cave for three days!"

"What?!" Kurt became as alarmed as his friend now.

There was a pause.

"I...guess that explains why I feel so hungry," Blue said.

"We'll raid the museum cafeteria on our way out," said Kurt. He
started walking again; he growled softly at first, but then got louder. "I
knew this 'Keeping Still' crap was gonna take too long. Least I got the damn
sword."

"That reminds me, I wanted to ask what you saw in the dream, Kurt," said Blue. "I mean, I'm sure some of it was very private, but I'm still curious—"

"No point in keeping secrets this late in the day. I'll tell you all about it in the car. It's gonna take a while," said Kurt. "In the meantime, I wanna know if you dreamed about anything. You were asleep in the cave, too."

"Yes, but I fell asleep long before you did. At least, that's how it seemed things were going when I started to feel drowsy. I didn't even get to see the fire turn white, which I assume you were able to do." Blue thought for a moment. "And yet...I do feel like I dreamed of something, I just...can't remember any of it, really. My head feels hazy when I think about it. It's like...all I can remember is feeling like I was half in, half out of the dream...almost as if I were a fleeting presence in somebody else's dream...."

"Huh. I wonder," said Kurt.

"What do you...oh, hello! Kieran!" They were nearing the front doors now; Blue saw the old Pequopsee standing in the lobby, apparently looking at one of the exhibits.

Blue jogged up to him. "Kieran, we did it! Kurt was able to accomplish The Stillness, and he found the true...oh, no!"

Kurt knew before he got there, but he still had to turn away—he would never feel comfortable with the vacant stare of the drained. Before he averted his eyes, though, Kurt noticed something. He reached out and ran his index finger across Kieran's shoulder. It came away dusty. A glance right confirmed Kurt's suspicions: the rest of the tribesmen he'd seen at the spirit cave were all frozen as well, in mid-walk, just outside the front doors.

"They never even made it back to the reservation," Kurt muttered angrily. "Eric must've drained them right after we sat down!"

"This is awful!" Blue exclaimed.

"Yeah, and you know what's even worse? Suddenly, I'm feeling pretty damn alone." Kurt raised his rune and turned toward the door. "Remember all those Linkers I told you I felt on the drive up, how they were manifesting everywhere? Well, now I don't feel any of 'em anymore, and somehow I don't think that means the imbalance got fixed while we were napping."

"Well, what *does* it mean?" asked Blue.

"I don't know for sure yet, but I've got a bad feeling...." Kurt waved for Blue to follow him. "C'mon, we're gonna have to break into the cafeteria and take what we can to eat in the car. The faster we get down to the Qin Project, the better."

"No problem," said Blue with a final look at Kieran. "I've lost my appetite."

*   *   *

Blue didn't expect slow going on the highway—with three days lost and the crisis growing all the time, no one in their right mind would be heading toward New York. But even before he got all the way up the on-ramp, he and Kurt knew that something was wrong. Plumes of black smoke were rising from near and far, filling the sky. There were dozens of them.

"Oh, my God…." As soon as the car climbed onto the actual highway, Blue could see what looked like total gridlock at a glance but was really a catastrophic pileup. Apparently, there'd been a mass exodus northward at some point, which Blue had been anticipating all along, except Eric had sent beams to drain those who tried to escape. The traffic had been too dense to move fast, so most of the cars were just pressed up against one another, idling until they ran out of gas, but it looked like a few feet had fallen onto accelerators after the draining. These were the sources of the fires—vehicles plowed into one another on the shoulders, overturned in drainage ditches, exploding from trying to speed through a solid wall of cars but finding too much resistance to move even the ones against their front bumpers. The northbound highway was full as far as the eye could see, over hills and valleys, and the smoke signals marked the path back to New York.

Southbound, the interstate had been relatively empty, but that meant its accidents were worse. Blue was so shocked, staring at the horror across the divide, that he almost smashed into an overturned Jetta in the center lane. There were several more like it up ahead, on the shoulders and roadway alike, some in gnarled, inextricable pairs.

"Should…." Blue choked and forced himself to look ahead. "We should help them, Kurt."

"I got it. You just keep driving, fast as you can…don't hit anybody," said Kurt. "The best way we can help them is to stop Eric. This has gone on long enough."

He still sounded confident, self-assured in the course that he'd chosen, but nevertheless, there was guilt in his voice. The sight of the cars was too much for him, so he kept his eyes focused on the crank while he rolled down the window and stuck his right hand out. He lit up his rune, and seconds later, thunder rumbled. Raindrops started to mingle with the wind pushing against his palm.

The rain cloud spread out as far as Kurt could make it, and it followed him and Blue down the highway, extinguishing the worst of the fires.

*   *   *

It really is the end of the world, thought Kurt.

The destruction kept getting worse as he and Blue finally entered New Jersey, by which time the sun had already set again. Not that Kurt had seen the sun at all—as the forests surrounding the highway had turned to suburbs and then commercial strips, the fires had become bigger and more numerous, and the sky had only gotten blacker. Once Manhattan came into view in the distance, there was the Darklight Tower again, seemingly glowing with Eric's qi, and above it, the sky wasn't just black, it was stormy and pulsing red.

Many of the New Jersey industrial parks were leveled, some still erupting into blasts as flames reached gas tanks that hadn't yet ignited. Kurt shut off his rune and let the rain stop—it was futile.

He looked across the ruins, able to see much since the factories and refineries had been built over flat marshlands. He saw the wreckage of several dozen U.S. Air Force fighters, part of a more concentrated assault against Eric. Some of the damage in New York, and, indeed, in some of the smaller towns Kurt and Blue had passed through on the way down, appeared to have been caused by crashes or errant bombs. The city skyline looked like a set of broken, hollow, black teeth. Kurt wondered if the government hadn't written off New York as a lost cause at some point, then hit Eric with everything they had left before finally losing to the Siphon Stone.

Millions of people gotta be dead, not just drained, Kurt realized. His face puckered. *All those people who weren't stuck in traffic, the people living in those buildings, the army...aw hell, anyone in the air....*

Kurt jerked his head up and away from the hand he'd been resting it on. The car was sliding to a stop in the middle of the highway, a jarring sensation even though the empty lanes permitted it.

"Why are we stopping here?" Kurt asked.

"We're…." Blue looked left across the guardrail, toward some empty land. He paused. "This can't be right…."

He opened the door and hopped over the rail; Kurt followed. The dirt was wet and squishy with a rainbow-streaked mixture of fluids, and his nostrils burned from the chemical vapors and toxic smoke in the air. He glanced from side to side, taking everything in once more. Black, orange, and red seemed to be the only colors left in the world.

"Careful!"

Blue stopped Kurt just in time. They were at the edge of a massive, circular crater that looked like it was on loan from the moon. The dirt down below was charred, and a latticework of tiny embers sent some last wisps of smoke steadily into the air, but by and large, this place wasn't getting any more destroyed.

"Here, Kurt. Look at this," said Blue. He'd been searching the ground with his feet, kicking the dirt around, and even now that he'd found what he'd been looking for, he was still loathe to use his hands. He waved Kurt over and tapped with his toe.

Pang pang. It was metal.

Kurt looked down and saw an ash-covered sign, half-buried in the tainted soil. He could just make out the words "SIDNEY GRANT" in big, black lettering. There was more, plus an address on a line below, but it was all damaged beyond recognition.

"What does it mean?" asked Kurt.

"It means we drove all the way down here for nothing." Blue pointed to the crater. "This was the Qin Project, Kurt. Emphasis on *was*. I don't know about you, but I couldn't even isolate a shard of glass at the bottom of that hole, let alone any of the long-life formula or any copies of the recipe."

"So Eric's big firefight with the army did it for us? Ha!" But then, Kurt looked at his palm. The rune was still there.

"No," said Blue. "We've seen a consistently high level of destruction since we left the reservation, but I'm sure you'll agree that this is exceptional. This place was targeted specifically, and ferociously."

"You think someone down in D.C. figured out that Linkers get their powers 'cause of an imbalance in nature, then found out what it was and tried to get rid of it?"

"That would be pretty far-fetched, wouldn't it? Besides, look at the perfection of the crater, almost as if it were carved out by hand to be a perfect half sphere. Look at how evenly its floor is burned. No kind of bomb would give the user that sort of precision control…it would require direct mental engagement."

"What, you think Eric did this?!" Kurt exclaimed.

Blue nodded. "It's certainly the explanation that fits best, as far as I can tell."

"No it doesn't! I mean…okay, I guess it looks like it was done by a Linker, and Eric's right here and he's powerful enough, but how did he even figure out what the imbalance was? And let's not forget, he didn't wanna fix the world—he wanted to make it end on his terms! Why would he destroy the Qin Project if doing that would take his powers away?" Kurt looked at his palm again, then shoved it toward Blue in frustration. "Except it *didn't* take his powers away, 'cause otherwise I wouldn't still have *my* powers! Was I wrong about this, too? I swear to God, Blue, every time I think I've got something figured out…!"

Blue's gears were turning, as always. His brow furrowed.

"Think about the Daoist conception of balance, the wheel," he said. "Balance requires even quantities of yin and yang, turning together in harmony and giving way to one another. The Qin Project disrupted the balance because it created the potential for there to be more life than death in the world. If life were to completely eclipse death, covering the entire wheel, it couldn't spin at all anymore, and the world would truly end, just like when Riktalash became hollow and sank. Logically, the same should be true in the other direction, and it's even easier for us to conceive of the apocalypse that way—the world would also end if death were to completely eclipse life."

Blue turned and looked across the burning marshes as he spoke, compelling Kurt to do the same.

"Clearly, if there's still an imbalance in nature, and the imbalance is measured in life and death, there must still be more of one in the world than the other. Just based on what you see here, which would you say there's too much of—life or death?"

"Eric turned it around?!"

"As if he grabbed the wheel and wrenched it backwards," said Blue in disgust; he mimed the motion with his hands. "We're 'stuck' on death now. You, myself, Eric, and Kayla may well be the only people left on Earth right now…of course, Kurt! This is what he meant when he said that the Linker Weapon would allow him to take control of the end of the world! He wasn't the imbalance before, but now he is, because he's drained so many
people—separated their original qi and their body qi! That's…!"

Blue paused. He took off his glasses and pressed his thumb between his eyes.

"There's precedent for this…I had done some reading on the subject even before all this started, actually. Daoists believe that every person has two souls—the *hun* soul, which goes to the afterlife, and the *po* soul, which stays in the Earth. I've been taking these two souls as analogous to the two types of qi, original and body, which is why I was sure you could never exhaust your body qi. Your original qi, your *hun* soul, would never have been touched by anything you could do on Earth, so, in theory, it could always recharge your *po* soul. But here's the important thing, Kurt—the two souls are joined together in life and separated in death, and if I'm remembering right, they separate slowly. By ripping peoples' original qi out and storing it in the Siphon Stone, Eric has effectively created a new kind of death, one that's simultaneously natural and unnatural. This explains why you felt so many more Linkers manifesting at such an increased rate on our way to the reservation! With Eric directing this kind of an imbalance, one that gets dramatically worse every time he drains someone, the wheel moved toward being completely dominated by one side much faster than it would have if the Qin Project's treatment had been allowed to slowly spread across the world!"

Blue put his glasses back on and tried to compose himself.

"Of course, that still doesn't answer the question of why Eric would bother to destroy the Qin Project at all, unless it was just to spite you. That begs the question of how he knew you'd figured it out, let alone how *he* figured it out. He didn't seem to care very much about the source of the imbalance when we confronted him, and even if he'd gone looking for it to protect his powers…well, clearly that's not what he did."

"Huh…."

Blue knew that tone of voice well, though he was used to hearing it on his own lips rather than Kurt's. It was the tone of familiarity blended with novelty that came when the knowledge in a person's head aligned, forming a new idea. Blue glanced at his friend and saw that he was smiling.

"What is it, Kurt?" he asked.

"I think I mighta finally figured something out that's not gonna change before I get to see if I was right or not," Kurt said. He saw Blue twisting his head at him curiously, and added, "Ohhh, no! I'm holdin' back on this one 'til the time comes, just to be sure. I'm tired of being wrong—you'll find out the truth when I do."

"Very well," said Blue, shrugging. "I'm not going to play guessing games with you while the world is crumbling around us."

"Either way," said Kurt, "we've only got one more stop to make. No use putting it off any longer."

"Right...."

They stood there for a few minutes, regarding the Darklight Tower standing across the water from them like a boxer in the other corner of the ring. The monolith stared down on them, looking angry, and for the first time, Kurt found that he could sense Eric's rage permeating the air all around him. He'd definitely been here, definitely destroyed the Qin Project, and whether or not Kurt's speculation proved correct, he'd definitely done so with an incredible amount of anger.

Thunder rumbled in the distance. Soon the black and red clouds would unleash a deluge of acid rain fueled by the burning world below.

"Don't even think about leaving me behind," said Blue.

"Don't worry. I know it's not gonna be safe in there...I mean, no place would be, but...look, even though...." Kurt sighed. "I really need ya on this one, Blue. Even if all you can do is stand off to the side and cheer me on. You're all I got left now...I don't wanna forget why I'm doin' this."

"I—" Blue didn't know what to say, except, "Certainly, Kurt. Anytime. You can count on me."

Kurt flashed him a thumbs-up sign. "Good."

"Well, we'd better get driving!" Blue broke away and started power walking back to the car. "Depending on the amount of rubble and such blocking the roads, it could take a lot more than the standard half-hour to reach Manhattan from here."

"Leave the car. We don't need it." Kurt shut his eyes and focused for a minute. "My pad's still up there, in the tower. Eric didn't touch it...guess he knew I'd be coming back sooner or later. Just grab whatever papers you think we're gonna need and come put your hand on my shoulder."

*   *   *

Sheeshoop!

Kurt and Blue appeared on the checkerboard floor. The window-wall Kurt had broken, as well as the other sections of the room that had been torn up during his fight with Eric, were fully repaired. Even the light fixture was back where it belonged, with a new bulb, or perhaps the same one reconstructed by the power of void. The tall purple doors and the Seal of Broken Lightning glowered at them, just like before. If anything, the symbol seemed darker.

"W-we're back…." Blue became nervous at first, clutching himself, but then he shook his head. It was silly to be afraid at this point. "Now what, Kurt? Should we wait for Eric to come down and greet us like last time? He can certainly sense us here, if he couldn't sense us from much farther away. There wouldn't have been any interference from other people, after all, since he drained…Kurt, be prepared. He must be unimaginably powerful now."

"Don't worry, I got it. But that's a damn good reason not to let him sneak up on us—we'll sneak up on him!" Kurt started walking toward the seal. He thrust his right arm outward and opened his hand; Stardust shimmered and stretched into existence.

"This sucker's supposed to cut qi. Let's see if it lives up to its promise!"

With a long grunt, Kurt segued from walking to running, and he raised the sword back above his right shoulder with both hands. Somehow, he knew how to wield it, even though the closest instrument he'd ever held before was a screwdriver. He turned his wrists so that the blade's edge pointed to the doors, and when he got close enough, he brought the sword down with all his strength. He cut a line from top to bottom, right to left diagonally through the obstinate Riktali symbol.

There was a sound like a digital scratch.

Pwoiyao!

Kurt straightened up, lowered the sword, and stepped back.

At first, there was no change. Then Blue started to hear another sound, like the sound a person's feet made while walking across the frozen surface of a shallow puddle. Seconds later, he started to see bright lavender cracks spreading across the emblem, growing out of a single, arcing crack that matched Kurt's strike path exactly. The formation of the cracks sped up until both doors were completely covered by jagged, connecting lines. And then, with a crisp shattering noise, the shards flew away from the door and vanished, doing no damage but taking the Seal of Broken Lightning into oblivion with them.

"Hmf!" Kurt grinned. He stepped forward again, drew the sword back into his rune, and placed his palms on the doors. He grunted one more time, leaned with his full weight, and creaked the doors open. The other side of the room was just as Kurt remembered it: empty with only one lavender door on the far wall. The feet and feet of black rock Eric had put there had disappeared along with the seal.

"You did it!" Blue clapped excitedly. He ran up and looked through the entryway, astonished. "That sword must focus your qi—it really is powerful enough to cut through Eric's strongest shield!"

"All I did was break the connection between his qi and the doors. No Link, no seal." Kurt started leading Blue across to the other exit.

"So you interposed your own qi to interrupt his Link, I see." Blue sounded oddly uninterested all of a sudden; he was looking all around the back half of the room. Once he'd made two complete spins, he turned back to Kurt and said, "Kayla's not here...."

"'Course she's not. Eric's probably got her right with him, and I'll bet he lives up at the top. That's where he's gotta be to make sure the stone can reach as far as it can, right? 'Sides, so far the top half of this thing looks a lot more finished than the bottom half did—makes sense if this is the part he lives in." Kurt came up to the lavender door. He reached out for the knob, opened it, and found a flight of stairs beyond, leading up and around to the next floor.

"We're only halfway there right now," he reminded Blue. "Let's get climbing."

Kurt and Blue walked up the stairs, which were wooden and obviously taken out of a different building than the room that preceded them. They turned 180 degrees in the middle, so that the exit from the stairwell faced back into the next room. It was very similar to the one below it, with the same purple walls and gold trim near the ceiling, but this was more of a parlor than a reception area, with bookshelves, couches, and a red carpet; a lamp on a desk and another in a corner provided soft light. The walls were still transparent at the sides, showing what was left of the darkened city. This room was much smaller than the last one, which meant that Eric must have padded out its walls with more asphalt to keep the tower uniform looking from the outside. Kurt confirmed this when he opened the next stairwell door and found a brief hallway before the actual stairs.

Many of the next rooms were redundant, exact copies of the ones below them. Kurt refused to believe that so many purple-and-gold waiting rooms with white-and-black floors existed in New York. Perhaps Eric had manipulated the paint and materials at the molecular level to make everything match. That would make sense, Kurt thought, as he kept expanding his theory on Eric's motivation. He smiled to himself, knowing now why the room halfway up had seemed so oddly familiar to him the first time he'd seen it, and why it made sense for Eric to want it that way.

Kurt and Blue never tired. They quickened their pace as the path up the tower dragged on, charging through the seemingly endless progression of rooms and stairs. At one point, they traveled down a long, narrow hallway that took up an entire floor. Its walls were translucent on both sides, and though they were much thicker than the window-walls on lower floors, some optical illusion kept them from seeming that way. The tops of what buildings still stood around the Darklight Tower were much nearer to Kurt and Blue's level on this floor than they had been the last time the intruders had passed a window; the devastation outside gave them a moment's pause.

They bolted through an expensive-looking kitchen, with a center island and a stainless-steel fridge and oven. One flight after that, they reached an elaborate bedroom, the bed dressed in a red canopy and purple sheets and standing on golden feet. All four walls were opaque except for a rectangle to the right of the nightstand, no larger than a normal window. From here, New York was far below them. Kurt, gasping, wiped the sweat from his brow, but he knew they were getting close and he refused to slow down. He practically fell through the plain wood door next to the dresser.

The final flight of stairs was narrow, and it spun around and around by taking a hard right turn every seven steps. There was a black-painted metal railing, but Kurt didn't bother using it. He looked up and saw the light of the sky above him, tinted purple by the glass of the tower's roof. Four more turnarounds and he was there, with Blue right behind. They emerged from a hole in the floor directly into the penthouse.

This last room looked to have been made from scratch, unique except for the ubiquitous checkered floor pattern. It had no padding on the sides, so it was one of the widest spaces in the upper half of the tower, and it was decidedly the tallest, its ceilings bending up and away to form the obelisk's point in the center. Kurt and Blue couldn't see that point yet, because there was a wall several yards ahead of them, separating their small portion of the penthouse from the rest. There were two purple doors in the center of the wall, closed, identical to the ones in the room halfway up, except taller and with no seal. Twin comets of energy hovered at the point where the doors met, in place of handles; they chased one another in a circle.

On either side of the entryway, there were two gigantic symbols, each one dominating half of the wall. The one on the right looked like a wave rising from the ocean, consisting of two arcs moving toward each other as they got taller, connected by six unbroken lines. The one on the left looked like a hole in the ground, a circle intersected by twelve smaller lines that cut from outside to inside, suggesting movement inward or down. Kurt realized that these symbols were familiar to him as well, and now he had a pretty good idea of what they meant.

He looked back at Blue, who was a step behind him and to the left. This felt to Kurt like it was the proper place for him. Despite the amount of vertical running they'd just done, neither Kurt nor Blue was panting anymore. Blue looked at Kurt with lowered eyebrows that seemed extra thick, severe, and expressive.

"You ready?" Kurt asked.

Blue nodded. He stuttered for a moment, then reached into his coat, took out the *I Ching* and held it over his heart, as if it would protect him.

"Yes," he said.

Kurt took one more moment to look up through the ceiling at the sky. He could see the swirling clouds, still red but stained to brown by the purple glass. He could feel the electricity contained there, yearning to crash down to Earth. He brought up his palm and made sure his rune was active, ready to call on that power and set it free. Slowly, he leveled his gaze back on the door.

He inhaled through his nose and started moving.

This set of doors was heavier than the last. Blue had to push against the left door while Kurt took the right. Both of them together managed to get the doors moving, after which they kept going on their own until they were fully open.

Kurt stepped inside ahead of Blue and found exactly what he'd expected: a throne room. The point of the obelisk was visible now, a corner in the sky where all four sides of the ceiling converged. The far wall was solid black, and twin tapestries hung there, probably taken apart and restitched with the use of void, bearing symbols identical to the ones above the entrance. There was a dais against the wall, also black and looking as though it had been dropped into the floor from above. In the center of this platform was a gigantic red and black throne speckled with gold trim. This, too, Kurt was able to recognize, albeit vaguely.

And there was Eric, sitting on the throne, looking just as Kurt and Blue had left him, except with wilder, dirtier hair. His black pants, black shirt, and red tie were still the same, as was the Siphon Stone hanging from his neck. It pulsed and sparked with power even though it didn't appear to be turned on at the moment. It seemed almost filled to capacity.

Eric didn't stay sitting for long. He jumped up and approached his two guests with an accusing finger in the lead and a quaking fist bringing up the rear.

"It *is* you!" he shouted. "How the hell did you get up here?!"

"You mean how'd I break through your seal downstairs?" Kurt regarded Eric indifferently. "You'll see. How'd it feel to you when I did that, anyway? Could you feel me doing it?"

"What, do you wanna know if it hurt me?!" Eric snapped. "Oh, you are some kinda bastard!"

"Kayla!"

Kurt was so focused on Eric that it was Blue who first noticed there were two more people in the room. Kayla and Hydrad each stood to one side of the throne, Kayla on the right and Hydrad on the left. Both of their faces bore the same vacant expression.

"You monster!" Blue started running across the room toward the throne.

Kurt and Eric thrust out their runes at exactly the same time, looking like synchronized swimmers who'd spent weeks practicing the maneuver. Fortunately, Kurt's qi shield appeared around Blue immediately, while the Siphon Stone's beam still had to travel. Once again, Blue was saved from being drained. He froze halfway to the dais and examined the glow around his body that had now rescued him twice.

This time, he said something about it.

"No, Kurt! You can't afford to protect me! You need your qi shield to stop him!"

"Don't worry, Blue! I'm sure this time—this is the right thing for me to be doing." Kurt turned back to Eric. "'Sides, you don't wanna drain me right away, do ya? Which means I don't need my qi shield at all if I think I can beat you without taking any hits."

"You are so—!" Eric checked himself. "Listen. It's already obvious that I was right...take a look around and tell me the world isn't about to end. The three of us are all that's left—once I have your qi, the Linker Weapon is done! The only reason I haven't taken it yet is because I'm still waiting for my apology."

"What about Kayla? How did you...?" Blue was still in shock, and he switched back and forth between staring at her zombified body and Eric. Only when he glanced at Kurt's qi shield again did he start to get mad.

"How did you drain her if she was an active Linker? Did you just...did you attack her until her shield broke?!"

"Of course not! I love Kayla!" said Eric with a disdainful look in Kurt's direction. "She was the only one who ever gave me a chance before I was a Linker, the one person who loved and accepted me for who I was. Some people might've tried to take that away from me, but in the end, she chose my side! Even if there was no other reason for me to see this through, I'd still do it because of her—to show her that she did the right thing by having faith in me!"

"You...you got her to trust you...and then as soon as she let her guard down, you drained her! You...I...." Blue gasped and sobbed, then turned away. He raised his hand as if to block the sight of Eric further. It seemed like he might be about to fall to his knees.

"Hang on, Blue!" Kurt called to him. "I told ya, I got this. I'll take care of it—trust me."

Kurt's composure never broke once. He looked Eric in the eye again and crossed his arms, his posture firm enough to speak with authority, but too casual to suggest that he was about to start throwing punches.

"Y'know something, kid? I was thinking on the way here, and I realized that I don't really know you too well. I don't know that much about you. I mean, sure, you're an angry guy, and you keep saying it's 'cause people told you what to do your whole life. Nobody ever treated you like a grown-up, or even like a smart kid...you never got a chance to make it on your own. Maybe you won't believe me when I say this, but I understand.

"You and me had the same kinda life, except I *let* my grandparents and my teachers and my bosses tell me what to do, 'cause I was okay with it. I get that having it forced on you made you mad, and I get that you hate people like me who make it seem like it's not a big deal…just like I used to hate college kids like you, back when I thought you were all a buncha rich know-it-alls taking handouts from Mommy and Daddy without really knowing what you had. So yeah, I get that you're angry, and I get why."

Eric stood glaring at him, trembling from the very rage Kurt described, but hidden in the back of his gaze was genuine surprise. He didn't move yet.

"But that's really all I know about you," Kurt continued. "I could judge you just based on that and the shit you've done since we met, but you know what else? I trust the people I care about. That includes Kayla…she said that no matter what you did, you weren't really evil. Which means, maybe the anger's yours, and maybe I understand that…but this—"

Kurt gestured around the room and out at the destroyed city below with both arms, pivoting side to side at his hip.

"This I don't understand. But that's okay, because according to Kayla, this isn't you. Which means you're not the one I gotta talk to."

Kurt cupped his left hand around his mouth, leaving his rune free. He shouted straight at Eric's face, but it seemed like he was calling out to someone much farther away.

"Yo, Riktalash! Front an' center!"

Eric screwed up his mouth and drew back.

"Kurt?" Blue snapped out of his daze, and despite a glance in Kayla's direction, he moved back toward Kurt and Eric with newly rapt attention.

"'There is only one Drifter,' except there were a buncha Drifters," Kurt said. "The only thing they had in common was that they all had the Siphon Stone to help 'em do whatever they were doing. How can there have been a buncha Drifters *and* only one, unless all of them were also you, Riktalash. You've been in the Siphon Stone since the first time you put it on, haven't you? I don't think you planned it that way—I think you meant to trap Han Chung in there instead, but maybe you didn't really know what you were doing. It's your voice I hear when Eric's talkin' like he's two people, isn't it? It sure as hell sounds like there's a woman talkin' outta his mouth those times. He was the first one you drained, so you could take over his body and reach outta the stone through him. That's why the only part of Eric I'm getting' to meet is the part that's a whiny asshole, which I guess makes sense. Linking is qi trading, so you wouldn't need to trade for something you already have, and let's face it, you've gotta have a pretty big chip on your own shoulder to do what you're doin' to the world."

Blue's mind was racing—he was overwhelmed, unable to find fault in Kurt's assessment of the situation and blown away by the reality it described. Eric face was still the picture of anger, but he hadn't moved since Kurt started talking, as if he were unsure what to do next.

And then, the stone lit up, Eric's eyes went white, and he began to levitate about two inches off the floor. Kurt jerked his chin at him and smiled.

"There we go," he said. "Once I figured you out, I finally understood why there were so many Drifters. Ever since Han Chung killed your husband, the king, you've been trying to figure out a way to bring back the dead. Not even your immortality treatment could do that. First, you tried the Siphon Stone, and you got stuck inside it for a couple thousand years for your trouble. But you didn't give up, didja? You thought you could use the end of the world, and the Linkers that come with it, to figure out the secret of changing life and death around. Every time you felt a Linker manifest somewhere nearby, you called out to him and got him to put on your stone. Then you drained him, controlled him, tried to make him and yourself into the source of the imbalance, so you could control that, too. Eric is the Linker Weapon—your weapon, your way to create so much death that it turns back into life with you there to watch it, except you've never quite gotten it to work out that way, have you? You tried a buncha times with the Indians and it didn't work, but this time, I bet you feel like you're coming pretty close, huh? Eric must've been a hell of a catch for you. After all these years, here we are, back at the same damn imbalance that destroyed Riktalash, and you've found a guy who wants everything his way just as bad as you do."

Eric said nothing. As soon as the stone had activated, his expression had gone blank, as though all the nerves in his face were dead. He kept floating there silently, so Kurt kept on prodding.

"I shoulda made the damn connection between this place and Riktalash the second I got into that room where you had Eric put the seal. Purple and gold, same colors. And I really shoulda figured it out when I was reading the stuff my mom left behind for me, 'cause that was when I found out that the Seal of Broken Lightning was a symbol from your language, just like the one in the stone and those other two on the fancy blankets back there. No way would Eric have known how to write Riktali without you telling him. But I didn't really get it until Blue and me got down to the Qin Project, which you blew up, even though you risked having Eric lose his powers when you did it." Kurt smirked. "What'sa matter? Pissed off that some 'commoner' got his hands on your royal recipe for eternal life?"

"We destroyed the Qin Project because it was a mockery. Named for the nation that sent those men to destroy our kingdom, based on sciences that raped the land we revered, mixed from ingredients made through unnatural means—our methods and our motives were pure." Somehow, there was just as much anger in the voice as before, even though the tone was deadpan and Eric's face still showed no emotion. "But we were already certain that the imbalance had been shifted. The Linker Weapon may not yet be complete, but the world is ours now. Only you remain in our way… and you cannot turn the wheel back on your own."

He's conversing with a spirit thousands of years old…! Blue was speechless.

"You should help me put things right…let go of everyone inside the Siphon Stone. After that, I'd be willing to break it and set you free, too," said Kurt. He pointed out at the city again. "What do you think you're gonna get outta this? If you're looking for revenge, you're on the wrong continent, and the guy that sent Han Chung after you is long dead. You've just gotta face facts. Even if you did figure out how to make life from death, your island sank a long time ago and took everything with it, including your husband. There's nothing to bring back…you have to let it go. Look, I know it's hard. I know how hard it is to lose someone you love." Kurt scowled. "Believe me, I know, thanks to you."

"As do I!" Blue called out.

"Life leads to death, and death leads back to life," said Eric. "By bringing the world to the point of total death, we, who are human and yet not human, will witness the beginning made from the end, and learn how qi can be re-created where none exists. Once we know the method, we will heal the world by repairing the qis of our choosing from within the stone." The voice became louder. "You are wrong. The integrity of the body is meaningless. The spirit endures, and the power of the *qi ren* has no limits beyond our will. Our world ended because of Han Chung's intrusion—you outsiders have been the true imbalance all along. Our efforts will purify this world and restore the holy oceans to their glory as providers and protectors. Riktalash will be reborn, perfect and unending, and you who have tainted the Way will be erased forevermore."

Kurt hardened. He took two steps back and brought out Stardust, leveling the point at Eric's face.

"Well, then," he said, "it looks like I've got one more kid to save. It's time for you to get outta Eric, Riktalash!"

Kurt breathed in, and started running toward Eric like he'd run for the seal downstairs, blade at the ready. Eric dropped back onto the ground, but otherwise made no move to dodge or block the coming attack.

"We have the qi of all the world within us," he said. "We are not frightened of—"

Pwoiyao!

Eric's eyelids flew up, and the white swirling over his pupils winked out. Both his hands jumped to his head as he let loose with the loudest scream either Kurt or Blue had ever heard. At first, Eric's voice and the voice of Riktalash expressed their pain together, but almost immediately, Riktalash vanished from the equation. Kurt had hit the Siphon Stone dead on, and now, tendrils of yellow energy were dancing across its surface. Kurt followed through and swung again—the tendrils shot up in size for a second when they made contact with the sword, and a small crack appeared over the symbol within the stone.

"Aaaaaaaaaaaa!"

Kurt hesitated, his first set of motions now complete.

They're bonded pretty deep, he realized. He glanced at Blue, who looked back at him in horror. Kurt remained still for a moment, but then he made himself frown, turned back to Eric, and lifted the sword again. Eric cried out and raised his arms over his face, but the Siphon Stone was still vulnerable.

"I know this hurts now—"

Pwoiyao!

"But you'll thank—"

Pwoiyao!

"Me—"

Pwoiyao!

"Later!"

Pwoiyao!

Eric cranked his arms upward; the floor followed his direction and enclosed his whole body in a black-and-white box.

"Shit!" Kurt started slashing at the bunker. Stardust dissolved Eric's Link with the material from the floor, making it crumble away like loose dirt, but it was too late. Kurt found emptiness inside, and Eric reappeared yards away, coming up through a hole in the floor. He'd turned on his purple qi shield and was levitating again, but the Siphon Stone was still dim, chained by residual energy from Kurt's sword. The cracks were slowly sealing up.

There was a pause, and the air felt saturated with potential energy. Kurt held his position. Eric glowered at him; Kurt was used to seeing him mad, but this time, it was a different, more desperate kind of anger.

Kurt took the offensive again.

"Stay away from me!" shouted Eric; Kurt heard a whooshing sound. Before he was halfway to Eric, twin jets of water burst through the purple glass windows and divided the room, creating a two-foot-thick wall of ice. Blue dove out of the way and wound up on Eric's side of the split after a hard landing against the spine of the *I Ching*. But Eric barely had time to admire his handiwork before part of the wall began to glow red, and Kurt burst through with his sword on fire. Stardust could also channel the elements like an extension of his rune; necessity was the mother of invention.

Kurt made a wind-assisted jump onto and off a piece of ice in midair, soaring up to Eric's level. He swung the sword and sent an arcing bolt of lightning a few inches ahead of his body. Eric dodged but left himself open —the next slash passed his defenses and hit the Siphon Stone. His shield lessened the effects of Kurt's qi, but still he screamed again, and his rage deepened. He grabbed hold of Kurt's wrists and dragged him toward the floor.

Lightning struck a hole in the ceiling, fell harmlessly through Kurt's chest, and hit Eric's, barely missing the stone. Eric cried out and dug his nails into Kurt harder—Kurt struggled to keep Eric below him so he would hit the floor first. He switched between eye contact with his adversary and glances at the rapidly approaching tiles.

They both hit bottom and bounced, Eric's backside in the lead. Eric's shield protected him, but Kurt had the wind knocked out of his lungs. The floor opened up at a thought from Eric, and by the time their bounce crested, there was another, farther drop below them. Kurt looked down, past Eric's shoulder, and saw the levels that he and Blue had climbed through on their way to the penthouse melting into the walls like the end of a cartoon in reverse. The furniture from the studies and bedrooms started to fall as the tower hollowed out.

Eric spun Kurt around and threw him off, so that Kurt was now falling faster. Kurt twirled out of control for a moment, but then he used the power of wind to right himself and slow down. He looked up and saw Eric coming after him, darting from point to point with sudden movements. With the Siphon Stone damaged, wind was Eric's weakest element, so he had to use small, powerful vacuums to pull himself along—Kurt could also a feel a larger void somewhere below him, helping gravity drag him toward the ground. Eric closed in, charged his left fist with qi, and geared up for a punch, but Kurt swung Stardust in front of himself and made Eric jump back.

"Stop it!" Eric shouted. Kurt could see, now, that he was crying.

They caught up to some of the free-falling furniture as the last of the lower floors melted away, turning the tower into a long, vertical tunnel. Kurt strengthened the wind around himself and managed to get footing on the side of a couch, but he'd be hitting bottom soon, and without his shield, it would probably kill him even if he let the couch take the brunt. Eric grinned, happy to let that happen—he even raised some spikes out of the floor in the basement to help things along.

What happened next only took three heartbeats; Kurt knew because his blood was pumping loud in his ears.

One. He saw Eric slow to a stop in midair and cross his arms, still smiling.

Two. He pushed the wind to its limit but felt himself losing the battle against Eric's void.

Three. He called for two lightning bolts, one to strike his body and one to strike the couch. With a little prayer, he tried something he'd never tried before—altering the magnetic charge of the electricity.

KAAAKKKKK!

The couch hit the ground and split into hundreds of pieces against the spikes, but Kurt was already on his way back up, propelled by repulsing poles. He barely processed the stomachache he got from reversing directions so fast. A third bolt of lightning struck the left wall of the tower, and this time, Kurt gave it the charge opposite his own, so that it would draw him in. Once his feet were on the wall, he reversed his charge and kicked off, sailing ten stories into the air and toward the opposite wall. Another bolt struck where he landed, ready to receive him, and he repeated the process.

Meanwhile, Eric was pulling himself back toward the top floor with more localized vacuums. There'd be a snapping noise and a burst of upward momentum, and whenever he started slowing down, he'd make a new void above his head to replenish his speed. But when he saw the lightning strikes, he looked down, flinched, and messed up his timing, allowing Kurt to gain ground while he faltered. He began trying to stall Kurt and keep moving at the same time—he started reforming the tower's floors to cut Kurt off.

Kurt refined his technique with every jump, and was already quick enough to stay ahead of the barriers; Eric only slowed himself down more by dividing his attention. The gap between them continued to close. Eric gave up on re-creating the floors and formed an even larger vacuum above himself, which hurled him toward the penthouse. Kurt saw it and timed his next jump carefully—he called down a lightning bolt with a charge opposite his own, directing it into the hole he and Eric had fallen through. As the lightning struck, Kurt jumped into it, using its magnetic pull like an ethereal track leading straight up. He made eye contact with Blue, who was peering down from the edge of the abyss.

Just as Eric snapped through the hole, Kurt came up fast and tackled him from below, propelling them both higher. Blue cried out and fell over backwards.

Eric was at the mercy of Kurt's momentum now; he heard Stardust flash back into being, felt Kurt raising it to strike the Siphon Stone. Frantic, Eric created an extra charge of qi in front of his chest, and when Kurt connected, there was an explosion that blew both combatants to opposite sides of the room. Eric hit so hard that his rear end carved a trough into the floor. Kurt came down slower, but crashed into the wall, left arm first.

Wa-chk! went the crisp sound of breaking bone.

Blue cringed; he felt like throwing up. *Eric's taking more hits, but Kurt's still losing! They may be even offensively now…!*

"Kurt, will you forget about me?!" Blue was surprised to hear himself yelling with such stern authority. "Put your shield on!"

If Kurt heard him, he ignored it. He got up and started back toward Eric, left arm hanging limply at his side. Eric was already on his feet, and a little bit of the Siphon Stone's glowing, spewing energy was starting to break through. He laughed when he saw that Kurt was injured, then raised his palm, calling individual tiles up from the floor and setting them in spin. He made them fly at Kurt from various angles, one by one in rapid succession. Kurt couldn't dodge them all, and before long, one hit him in the left temple and destroyed his concentration.

Dammit, Kurt! Blue knew what he had to do. He dropped the *I Ching* and ran for the dais.

The floor crackled with electricity as Kurt pulled whatever he could from the lower tower, struggling to find every last ohm left over from his magnetic jumps. Everything but instinct was beaten out of him now—he pulled the charge into Stardust, drew in his left leg, kicked with his right, and started spinning. With help from the wind and the sword, he became a human top that generated an electrical field for protection.

Eric's anger was palpable to Kurt, invading his body through his rune, and with his Linker's sense, he tried to use that anger to guide his spin in the right direction. But Eric changed his attack pattern, made dozens of tiles rise all at once and surround Kurt, then close in together. Kurt could feel it happening; he brought his right hand down to meet his left at his stomach, switched from Stardust to the qi gun. He charged and fired. The blast cut through the tile ring and hit Eric, catching him off-guard, but the kickback made Kurt's broken arm roar with pain, and he fell, too, pummeled by the remaining tiles as his spinning stuttered.

It didn't matter. Kurt could only think of the ending world outside. This was all-or-nothing time. He brought Stardust back and rushed Eric with his head down, only glancing up so Eric couldn't blindside him somehow.

But then he stopped. Eric wasn't fighting anymore—he was standing still, looking to his left with his mouth hanging open. Kurt turned as well, and soon his face mirrored Eric's.

Blue had Kayla in his arms, dipping her like he would during a slow dance. They were kissing; Blue's eyes were closed from the intensity, and though Kayla's were still open, frozen as she was, somehow, she seemed affected, too. Blue pulled back, then straightened up and drew Kayla in close. He scowled at Eric, but his posture trumped his disdain, making it all the more evident that his true feelings were protective, not scornful.

When he whispered to her, never taking his eyes off of Eric, it seemed as if he truly believed she could hear him.

"Don't worry," he said. "It's all right...Kurt will fix everything."

Eric's breathing started getting louder, more rapid and shallow. His arms tensed up, his fists balled, and his whole body began to shake.

Kurt shouted, "You bastard, stop!" He ran as fast as he could.

"If the Siphon Stone's effects can be reversed, this won't even matter," said Blue.

Eric shot ten yards into the air; he swept his left arm backwards and tore up an entire section of the floor, knocking Kurt off his feet. The Siphon Stone shed the last of Kurt's qi and enveloped Eric in a white glare.

"If they can't, then we've already lost."

Eric screamed and arched his back, and a white-and-black-speckled beam larger than his whole body poured out of the Siphon Stone, burying the dais. The power discharge gave off an emotionally suffocating force that kept Kurt down—it was the purest form of Eric's anger yet released. And yet, somehow, Kurt felt a bit of relief hit his chest then, as if a fraction of his pain had suddenly been cured. But he was too busy trying to force himself to stand to think about it much.

The blast lasted for a full minute, and when it finally faded and Eric glided back down to the ground, Blue was as empty-eyed as Kayla, petrified with his arms still around her. Despite its ferocity, the beam hadn't moved them an inch. With an aching heart, Kurt understood what he'd felt moments ago. Eric had marshaled enough force to blow the qi shield right off of Blue, hurling that part of Kurt's qi back to him.

Reality seemed to go on vacation. The next thing Kurt knew, he was up and watching Eric streak over to the dais, grab Blue and wrench him apart from Kayla. Eric punched Blue over and over across the face, then flung him high into the air, almost through the point of the ceiling.

"Leave him alone!" Kurt ran to the dais, but Eric was already on the move, flying after Blue. Kurt skidded to a stop and followed Eric with his eyes, staring in helpless horror as Eric dashed back and forth through Blue like a bullet, keeping him suspended with repeated hits. Kurt felt the corners of his eyes burning as he formed the qi gun at his waist again, preparing to dump everything he had left into a lethal blast. But Eric saw him—he took hold of Blue and threw his limp form at Kurt. Kurt fumbled, tried to raise his one good arm, but Blue came down too quickly to be caught and plowed Kurt back into the edge of the dais, twisting his left arm underneath him.

Kurt stayed on the floor for what felt like an eternity, lost in despair and pain. He only looked up when he heard Eric projecting laughter at him from the center of the room, where he was still floating.

"You think—!" Eric laughed even more; the white in his eyes flashed as he and the queen vied for control. "You think I didn't want this?!"

Riktalash chose me, the world chose us. Shaping the new balance is our right, I've earned it, and I am not gonna let a pair of arrogant, controlling, girlfriend-stealing bastards deny me when I'm this close! So great is your hubris that you would even presume to tell us we are not entitled to our betrothed. It's not right! She belongs by our side. WE WON'T LET YOU TAKE THE ONE I LOVE!"

Kurt felt a vacuum tug at his face, and he saw chunks of the ruined floor being drawn toward Eric as he prepared his finishing blow. This wasn't just void—the density and the size of the qi blast forming between his hands was creating a gravity well.

Kurt!

Kurt knew he was looking at the end of his life. The purple energy in Eric's hands expanded to fill his outstretched arms, turning so dark that the Siphon Stone was lost inside it.

Kurt! Your shield! Put up your shield!

Right! Kurt came to his senses. He reached deep inside himself and raised a yellow dome of qi big enough to cover his whole body, plus a few feet in either direction. He drew Blue and Kayla in as best he could, forcing even his broken arm to clutch them against himself. He closed his eyes, grit his teeth, held his breath.

*   *   *

Outside the city, a murder took off for the clouds cawing and screeching, shaking a few leaves from the tree they left behind. They had a perfect view of an explosion that rivaled a hydrogen bomb and, in its darkness, made the cloudy sky seem perfect white for a split second. The blast spread out in the shape of a ring, its bottom level with the pinnacle of the Darklight Tower, its height extending almost to the stratosphere. The energy would spread for miles before showing any signs of slowdown.

The crows weren't alone: a great wave of birds went up from the suburbs as the explosion's wind came closer. Some escaped, some didn't.

*   *   *

Hydrad! thought Kurt dazedly. He looked right, then left, then right again, and finally, he saw the college student's body falling backwards and headfirst toward the ground more than a hundred stories below.

"Mmmf!" Kurt winced, but managed to extend his left arm enough to hang on to Blue and Kayla, freeing up his right hand to create a cushion of air around Hydrad. The best he could do was deposit the boy onto the roof of a nearby building—after that, he needed the wind to save himself and his friends.

It wasn't enough. They were gliding down faster and faster, between the buildings, above the naked streets of Manhattan. Kurt was able to straighten out so he looked like Superman carrying two passengers, but he was helpless to slow their descent, and even if he managed to coast down onto the sidewalk, the friction would tear Blue and Kayla apart. He couldn't seem to make his qi shield hold the shape of a dome while moving, so at the moment, only he was protected.

Just before they hit bottom, Kurt mustered up a final gust to flip himself over, and he held on as hard as he could to keep his friends from blowing away. His invulnerable back absorbed the grinding impact from a slide that went on for an entire city block. Finally, he felt himself stop, exhaled, let Blue and Kayla roll off him, and dropped his arms to his sides. He grunted again from moving the broken one too abruptly, but it didn't seem to hurt as much this time. The qi shield was either bracing it or starting to heal it.

But Kurt forgot the pain as wonderment seized him. He swung around into a crouch, leaned over Blue, and stared hard into his languid eyes.

"Blue?"

Kurt?

"Blue!" Kurt smiled wide and started laughing—he didn't think he needed to understand. "Blue! I can still talk to you! And you saved my ass up there!"

You could hear me? Astounding! It was as if Blue's thoughts were being funneled directly into Kurt's head. As far as Kurt's perception went, it was barely different from chatting with him over a sandwich on his lunch break. He was elated.

"Kayla!" Kurt turned to his left. "Kayla, can you hear me, too? Say something!"

No response.

"Kayla?" He turned back. "Blue, why can't I do this with Kayla?"

I-I'm not sure! I can hear her just fine! I've been able to since just before I was drained…incidentally, I'm glad Eric did that before he started attacking me. Despite what you might think, none of what he was doing actually hurt. Even though Blue's face was expressionless, Kurt could tell that he was thinking as hard as ever. *We must've hit the nail on the head, saying that Eric breaks the connection between body and soul by draining original qi. I can't move or feel anything, but I'm still here! My po soul was untouched!*

"You mean *you* hit the nail on the head," Kurt said. "You're the smart one."

But that still doesn't answer the question of why we can communicate. And why you can't hear Kayla, even though I can.... Blue paused. *Say... do you think...I apologize if this sounds awkward, but we have a fairly strong friendship at this point, wouldn't you say?*

"Hell yeah!" Kurt tapped his shoulder. "You're my best friend, Blue! You're one of the only real friends I've ever had!"

But you don't have that sort of a connection with Kayla. She and I, however, got to speak in private several times, especially while you trained with your grandfather, and besides that, I...honestly, Kurt, this is great! I almost don't mind being drained, because in those last few seconds, I could feel her accepting my affection for her, and it was right after that that I started to hear her again! As if I opened myself up to her, causing her to do the same! I have an understanding with her just as I do with you, even if it is a different kind of understanding!

"Ha!" Kurt hopped to his feet and clenched his fist. "'There's more than one type of Link that can be forged!' No damn kidding, old man!"

You think this is what he meant?

"Yeah! And if I'm right...!" Kurt closed his eyes. "Grandma? Grandpa?"

We're here, Kurt. We're fine.

That was Grandpa's voice. Kurt opened his eyes and a few tears rolled out.

You just tell us what you need us to do, and we'll do it. We're all with you, Kurt!

Kurt held out his hand and formed Stardust once more. He stared at the hexagram embedded in the blade, and his smile returned brighter than ever.

"'Gathering Together....'" he remembered. He said, "All you need for Linking is an even trade of qi. Maybe when people have these kinds of connections or...understandings, maybe they have a Link, too! Everyone is a Linker, even if they can't Link with the Earth! My grandparents can trade qi, and so can you, Blue—we all traded qi with each other without even thinkin' about it, because we're connected!"

Then why couldn't you hear us back at home, Kurt? We tried to tell you we were okay! said Grandma.

Kurt thought for a moment.

"My dream!" he said. "I didn't know everything I could do until I had that dream! It's not like I learned anything new, it's more like I…like I opened myself up the same way you did, Blue! Like I found out what was true for me all along—that was the lesson I already learned! That's what Stardust is really for!

"And now," said Kurt with a laugh, "I know why I keep losing to Eric. Man, am I a moron. It's so damn obvious!"

What? asked Blue.

"While we were in the spirit cave, I was thinking about how I miss my job, and it's not just 'cause I want everything back to normal. It's 'cause it's who I am—I'm an electrician, God dammit! It's what I know best, it's how I think, but I keep going at this Eric thing like some kinda ninja! The hell do I know about fighting? The hell do I know about balancing out nature? As of right now, I am officially done trying to figure out all this philosophical crap. I'm only even a lightning Linker because I know power—if being an electrician made me into a Linker, then that's what oughta show me how to *be* a Linker!"

Attaboy, Kurt! said Grandpa.

"Yeah! And as an electrician," Kurt said, shaking his head at himself, "I know there's only one way to crack that stone."

Which is? asked Blue eagerly.

Kurt laughed. "You'll see! But here's what I need you guys to do. If I traded some of my qi to you, then I should still have a Link with your bodies even though you don't." Kurt groped around for the feeling from his dream, the one like a wire within him, and found it now with ease—he knew he was right. "But you can trade qi with more than one person, so even if you're not connected to your own bodies anymore, you're connected to someone's, and I'm connected to them, too, through you! Grandma, Grandpa, look for anyone else you might have traded qi to! Distance shouldn't matter—try and talk to them! Blue, you do it, too, and tell Kayla. Then all of you tell whoever you can reach to do the same thing with anyone they can reach, and tell them to tell whoever they can reach…!"

Kurt ran out of breath, but it was all right. Even if they hadn't understood his words, his loved ones could see directly into his heart now. They were on the job long before he finished speaking.

And you say I'm the smart one, joked Blue. *So, how do you visualize this in electrical terms?*

"Think about it this way—the Siphon Stone lets Eric take people's original qi, right? Blue, you said original qi was like a generator, and body qi was like the power that the generator makes. That means a body is like a battery! When Eric, or maybe I should say Riktalash, takes original qi, all he's really doin' is makin' his generator bigger—that's why he's so much stronger than me, 'cause his body qi gets put back faster. But if he can connect himself to a buncha generators, then why shouldn't I be able to connect myself to a buncha batteries? You've all still got your body qi…I think maybe if I can get everyone in the world all Linked up, I can tap into that power and use the sword to patch it into myself!"

Kurt raised Stardust like a lightning rod, like the conductor it was meant to be.

"Who cares if Eric's got a big generator? We're gonna be a whole grid!"

*   *   *

Eric stood in the last section of clean floor, a pristine circle in an ocean of tar dust. The checkerboard tiles of the penthouse were now the roof of the Darklight Tower: the point of the obelisk, the walls that supported it, and even the dais had all been pulverized to grains by Eric's last attack. Eric himself was unaffected, apart from even messier hair that stood on end in its own grease. His face was still consumed by anger, but his eyes were closed. He was concentrating, holding his rune out in front of his chest like a divining rod.

For a few minutes, he barely moved. And then, his eyelids flew up—he felt wind on his face.

Slowly, Kurt rose over the side of the tower, smiling and pumping his newly healed left arm. He stood on a platform of air, glowed with the light of his qi, held Stardust at his side. He stepped onto the roof and came forward to face Eric.

"You will not be able to break our Link again," Eric said. The queen's voice and diction had almost completely taken over, yet the meaning behind the words still seemed to fade in and out. "We have traded nearly all of our qi…the memories and power of Riktalash are part of us now. There were many Drifters, but now there is only Eric the Red."

"We really are alike, then," said Kurt. He felt warmth wash through his chest. "I think my silent partner's better, though."

"The height is at hand," said Eric. "Riktalash will be reborn with or without your cooperation."

The city below began to fill with columns of white light, spaced erratically apart and shooting into the sky. Their appearance was the last motion of a long wave that had begun on the other side of the world. One by one, the still forms of the drained were lighting up as their body qi ignited.

"You will believe, little man," said Eric. "We have labored long and hard to bring the world to a place where life can replace death. Once we learn this final secret, we will repopulate New Riktalash by returning the qi of the worthy from the Siphon Stone. You would have done well to trust us and perhaps earn a place among the chosen."

"You don't trust *yourself*. You don't know what you want," said Kurt. "Maybe you'll figure it out once I separate you and Riktalash for good. But if either of you was really sure about what you're doing here, you wouldn't have to keep yappin' to me about it."

"SILENCE."

Eric leaped higher than ever before.

Kurt felt the pull of void again. The dust at his feet rose in a cloud and engulfed Eric. It formed a sphere that covered him completely, then shot off into five branches, one heading straight up, two breaking horizontally, and two more plunging straight down until they hit and shattered the checkerboard tiles, by which time they had coalesced into legs with rounded feet. The horizontal branches became arms with hands, and the vertical one became a neck and a head. Eric was now a monstrous man of black smoke, with red eyes like dying coals. The Siphon Stone, which still hung around the giant's neck, stood out as a single dot of white—Eric's qi had deepened from purple to pure black.

Kurt snorted and rolled his eyes.

"So you're still a little kid after all, huh?" he muttered with a chuckle. "I wonder what this is compensating for…."

"Our tolerance for your smug attitude has reached its end," Eric thundered. His voice sounded deeper through his giant shell, as though he were shouting into a wide pipe.

"Why do you still battle us? Why do you find it so easy to scorn and ignore our words? Why do you assume that it is your place to intercede and disrupt our views, our choices, our relationships, as though only you and your culture know right from wrong?" The giant's head seemed to glare down on Kurt. "Is it because you believe that life is always good and death always bad? Do you seek to avenge your friend, your grandparents, the others whose sacrifices were necessary to reshape the world? Or are you simply scared of the enormity of that which you cannot control?"

The last of the people in New York Linked up—the columns of light now stretched as far as the eye could see, their glow contrasting with the dark sky and ashen ground. Kurt held up Stardust and smirked at Eric. His qi lightened from yellow to pure white.

"Why does there have to be a difference?" he asked.

Eric punched the ground, but Kurt jumped to the side and swung his sword at the giant's wrist. He expected that at least the tip would connect, but instead, it felt like he was hacking at emptiness. Stardust went right through Eric, even though his cloudy form had been solid enough to crack the floor mere seconds ago.

He changed the empty space! Kurt realized.

Eric swept his hand across the tiles toward Kurt; Kurt traded Stardust for the qi gun and aimed for the Siphon Stone, but Eric hit him before he could fire, knocking him into the air. Kurt tried to turn himself around by summoning the wind, but Eric raised his other hand and swatted him down along the side of the tower. There was an explosion as Kurt hit the ground.

And immediately, there was another one as he emerged from his crater. He was running sideways up the exterior wall of the tower, Stardust held behind him and purple glass shattering under his feet. Somewhere in his grid, there were Linkers who augmented his control over earth, allowing him to drag two big concrete slabs up with him, one on each side. He sent these at Eric's face to cover himself while he jumped, righted himself, and scraped Stardust across the Siphon Stone with all the force of his forward momentum.

Eric swung with both arms, but Kurt used bursts of wind to keep himself in flight while dodging. Frustrated, Eric howled and called snaking streams of water up from the mains in the former road below. He cooled their tips and prepared to freeze Kurt on contact, but Kurt protected himself with a ring of fire, waved into existence by a circular hand motion. As soon as most of the water had been diverted past him, Kurt hurled the flames at Eric, hitting him in the chest and melting some of the tar dust. Kurt moved in and landed in the gooey asphalt before Eric could take the foothold away.

Kurt struck the Siphon Stone again and again, sweeping his sword back and forth. Each hit cracked the stone more. But Eric drew him into his body and spat him out his shoulder blades before he could do more than superficial damage. Kurt brushed against something on his way through the giant—shirt fabric. The true Eric was still in there somewhere, the heart of the Drifter.

Kurt had barely hit the ground before he saw a foot coming down on him.

Eric stomped twice, then realized that he was trying to crush a newly laid teleportation pad. Kurt was off to the left, laying another. He glanced up just as Eric turned, and gave the giant a nodding sneer to goad him into coming closer. At the same time, he squinted at Eric's chest and examined the Siphon Stone—it was already repaired.

Screaming, Eric pivoted and stomped again, but Kurt wind-dashed through his legs and laid a third pad behind him. He felt like he could keep going, so he darted away again and laid a fourth. The previous three stayed. Kurt continued.

Kurt, you need to put constant pressure on the stone! These glancing blows won't do it! said Blue. *I thought you had a different plan this time!*

I do! replied Kurt in mid-run. *I just don't want Eric to know that!*

Kurt had now laid twelve pads. He stopped on the last one and stood smirking at Eric. He put the sword away again and charged his qi gun.

'Sides, this is actually kinda fun now that we're even!

Eric raised his foot to try squashing him again, but Kurt disappeared.

There was a constant, quiet whine as Kurt teleported between the pads at random, seeming to exist translucently on all of them at once. Eric picked one and kicked at it, but hit nothing: Kurt was moving too fast. Undaunted, Eric put his foot down on the pad and left it there, but Kurt just took it out of his rotation. Eric whipped his head back and forth, disorienting himself.

Then Kurt opened fire. Eric wasn't fast enough to see which direction the qi gun shot came from, let alone block it. A new crack cleaved into the stone and started to heal right away, but Kurt recharged and fired another shot from a different angle, renewing and widening the original fissure.

Eric grunted, waved his arms around, and finally roared. Kurt was raining white qi bullets into his chest now. Finally, Eric let out his frustration by Linking with the entire island of Manhattan, creating a powerful tremor that tore down even more of the city.

Kurt stumbled as the floor shook and lost his focus for a moment. He threw out his arms for balance, and thus lost the qi gun as well. Eric didn't waste any time: he kicked Kurt to the opposite edge of the roof, then called up a twelve-way qi blast that blew the pads away and hurled debris high into the air. Eric grabbed it all, pressed it together with fire, and hurled the resulting meteor at Kurt with escape velocity.

Fun? said Blue as Kurt jumped, reformed Stardust, and used it to slice the meteor in half. *Are you insane? The entire world is on the line here, Kurt!*

Kurt jumped to the edge of the roof opposite Eric and raised his palm to the heavens. The clouds began to rumble and flash. He visualized Eric as the old maple tree in his backyard.

KRAKOOOOOM!

Lightning bolts cascaded from the sky, striking Eric and the tower beneath him on all sides. At first, Eric floundered, but then he, too, fell back on his dominant element. He created a massive black hole in front of himself, crouched as if to hold it in his hands, and tried to pull Kurt in. Kurt ran away at first, but then he got a wild idea, turned around, and pointed Stardust into the void.

Stretch! he told it.

The sword split in half from its point to its hilt—pushed by Kurt and pulled by Eric, the two qi strands wove a double-helix pattern that carried them forward. Kurt used earthen shackles to nail his feet to the floor as the sword strained at his arm, stretching all the way through Eric's vortex and up to the Siphon Stone. The stone was pinned between the two strands as they tried to cross one another; for a few moments, Kurt achieved constant pressure, and the stone began to crack again.

Eric abandoned the void and tossed up the ground under Kurt, knocking the sword away from his chest. Kurt shrank Stardust back to its normal size and started running circles around Eric, snaking from side to side to avoid chunks of the floor that rose and attacked him. He made a point of going slow enough that some of the smaller ones connected.

What are you doing, Kurt? asked Blue. *What is your plan?!*

Oh, all right. See, if you're an electrician, you know how generators break. Only way I see to do that on purpose here is to OOOF! Kurt took another hit. But, as before, even though his thoughts were interrupted, Blue's connection with him allowed understanding.

But that's giving Riktalash what she wants! he protested. *What if you cause Eric's version of the apocalypse?*

Riktalash and my mom said the same thing! I know my mom wouldn't want it Eric's way, said Kurt. *And what did I tell ya? I'm through tryin' to figure out this 'wheel' crap! I'm in this to save you guys, period, and the only way I know how to put constant pressure on a generator is by overloading it!*

Eric lost the last lingering thread of his temper. He began throwing his whole massive body at Kurt, flailing his arms and legs. His gesticulations almost had the appearance of break dancing. Kurt couldn't avoid being hit much longer.

It's too late to argue. Do what you think is best, Kurt, said Grandpa.

He's right, Blue agreed. *I'm sorry for my doubts. We all trust you.*

Kurt slowed down even more and let himself get hit by one of Eric's feet. He let himself fly across the roof and skid to a stop on the tiles. He let himself stay down.

Eric turned, looked at him, and paused. The wind faded, leaving the air still.

Don't apologize. I'm glad you make me think, but I'm sure about this, said Kurt. *No matter what else happens, I know I can put everyone's qi back this way. If doing that happens to put the world back in balance at the same time….*

Kurt struggled to his feet, leaning over and clutching his right arm.

Then the old fart was right again, he finished. He couldn't help a quick smile; Eric missed it. *Well, I guess he'd say I was right…all he really did was get me to come up with the idea.*

"Do you surrender?" shouted Eric; Kurt staggered, feeling like the Drifter's voice had fists of its own.

Kurt took a shaky step forward, then cried out and fell to one knee. His qi shield shattered. His chest heaved from exhaustion, and he stuck

Stardust's point into the ground to steady himself. When he looked up, his awed expression was the only genuine thing about him.

"It's not about fighting…it never was," he gasped. "Maybe you were right after all, Eric…heh…how about that…?"

The giant Eric regarded him stoically, his inhuman eyes vacant.

"As much as we would like to gloat," he said, the Siphon Stone lighting up, "we have a job to do."

Kurt jumped back up and raised the sword. The draining beam fired.

Okay, Mom, this is it! Help me find my way back!

The sharp crackle of energy came and then faded. A hollow, irregular thumping echoed through New York—the columns of light had gone out, and the bodies projecting them had fallen. Only Kurt remained standing, but although Stardust was still in his hand, his original qi was gone.

*   *   *

"That…that's it…." said Eric in a voice barely above a whisper. "I did it…."

He thrust his enormous, smoky arms into the air.

"I did it!" he yelled, laughing at the empty city. "I did it! I brought the imbalance to its height! I'm one with the Earth now—in your face, everyone who didn't believe me! The joke's on you, 'cause I'm still here!"

"No, you aren't."

The voice seemed to speak directly into Eric's ears. He spun around—there was a man floating in the air behind him, higher than where the point of the Darklight Tower had been. He stood on nothing at an improbable angle, his face bent down toward Eric as if his feet were planted on an incline.

"You only think you are," he said.

"Who are you?!" Eric demanded. He fired a beam of black qi that passed right through the man without so much as disrupting his robe.

"You are only able to express a fraction of your true self because your Link with the Siphon Stone, with the ghost that dwells there, is different than anyone else's," said the man. "There is more than one type of Link that can be forged. All that is required is an even trade of qi. This is true, but the more qi is traded, the more what you are doing ceases to be Linking and becomes a simple exchange of positions. You are Eric the Red—you are the anger and cruelty of an embittered young man, but the soul, mind, and ambition of a very old and impertinent spirit. Neither of you knew your places alone, nor did you seek your places once you came together. Instead, you multiplied each other's stubbornness, and your qi became entangled with the spirit's such that you could only exist when your ideas and feelings found an accord with hers. In this sense, you are no more whole than the other drained."

Eric's red eyes lit up with a low humming noise. He didn't notice that the Siphon Stone was beginning to crack again.

"You're wrong!" he said. "Riktalash didn't drain me—we made each other better! She taught me how to use my powers, how to get people to listen to me, and in return, I did the one thing she never could. I took control of the imbalance! I made myself into the embodiment of death and ended the world the right way! And now that it's all over, I'll turn into the embodiment of life and remake a balanced world, one that'll never end again! Don't you understand? I'm the only one who can save everybody!"

The man smiled and shook his head.

"Heaven, Earth, and humans are the three powers of the universe, the three ultimates which sustain and structure all we know," he said. "In one sense, exchanging positions with the spirit was good for you. It has brought you and the spirit closer to your own places than ever before, by focusing your actions and clearing your minds. Your places knew you all along, and now they have found you, but still you do not know them. This is because you have not looked at yourselves and seen where you stand, but have instead become concerned with reaching beyond the place of any human.

"Neither man nor Earth can control life and death—that is the domain of Heaven alone. It is the Way of man to experience these things, and the Way of the Earth to witness them. And just as it is the Way of man to do things that will alter the Earth for good or for ill, toward balance or away from it, so it is the Way of the Earth to exist through all man does and find its own place, its path back to harmony. Whether he knows his place or not, no man can work in the domains of Heaven and Earth, because although he may try, he is in fact still working in the domain of man. Thus, only one thing remains—to teach you the lesson you have already learned."

Cik. Cak.

"The height of yin is the beginning of yang."

Kakk!

Eric looked down at the Siphon Stone. It was riddled with fissures.

"The height of yang is the beginning of yin."

Kakk! Cik! Ka-kakk!

"Life leads to death…."

Eric gasped and tried to contain the stone first with his giant hands, then with his human hands. His monstrous body of black smoke was dissolving.

"And death leads back to life."

Kakk kakk kakk!

Tiny grains flew off the Siphon Stone. Bent shafts of white light began to pour out of it. Eric screamed.

"It is only frightening when you do not know it, though it may still seem overwhelming until you accept it," said the man. "The sage who knows his place concerns himself with the Way of man, and lets the Ways of Heaven and Earth be. He lets the world ebb and flow around him, and thus finds that his choices are already made."

The symbol within the stone split as the largest crack yet formed over it. A beam of light, tipped with a sparkling bead like a pearl, shot through Eric's grasp. The bead flew into Kurt's chest, and with a gasp, he spun around and dropped to his knees.

He looked back over his shoulder at Eric and grinned.

"Gotcha!"

Eric glanced at him, then returned to the stone with even wider eyes. His mouth hung open. He shakily opened his hands and let the stone go, keeping his gaze fixed to it as it rose slowly into the air. The rope binding it to his neck had snapped. He looked at himself, at his body, at his hands. The dark rune faded, and then it was gone.

*   *   *

The Siphon Stone shattered. Its glimmering particles drifted down like fine snow. In place of the stone, a throbbing point of light appeared, like a tiny star with a human pulse.

The Darklight Tower flashed, turning first from purple to black and then from black to white. After that, it crumbled into the rooms and boxes and chunks of asphalt it had once been, and toppled into the street.

The pulsing light split into innumerable beads that streaked away on trails of white. Some of them went nearly straight down. Millions more flew far, curving over the horizon to reach the other side of the world. A few drifted upward and faded to nothing, clearing away the clouds as they went.

Afterword

Broken Lightning is an old story. The idea of a "Linker" first entered my head when I was about fourteen, and the basic framework of the struggle between Kurt, Eric, and Riktalash began to take shape around the year 2000, when I was sixteen. My worldview was much more limited then, and the world I was viewing was quite different: the Twin Towers hadn't fallen yet, the Internet was mere background noise instead of a lifestyle, and there was nothing more real to me than sitting in the back seat of my various friends' cars, feeling gusts of summer night wind hit me through the open window while the endless lawns of suburbia passed us by. Westwood, New Jersey was the whole of my universe.

Perhaps, then, it wasn't surprising that the first official draft of *Broken Lightning* came out looking a lot like my other nascent writing project of the time: *School Kids SG*. I was unsatisfied with this. Though I wouldn't have had the words or even the concepts to express it, I could feel on some level that high school wasn't a versatile enough setting to contain both worlds without making one feel redundant. Bored and frustrated, I knew there was more to *Broken Lightning* than the framework I was trying to fit it into, and because I couldn't see it—because high school and suburbia were all I knew, the only settings toward which my mind naturally drifted —I also knew that I wasn't ready. I put the draft aside half-finished and let my image of Linkers stay largely unexamined, having faith that I'd know when the time was right to approach *Broken Lightning* again.

More than a year later, in the last, cold days of 2001, I received word that I'd been accepted to Bard College, and when I toured the campus in the spring of 2002, I did so as a young man who was beginning to strain against the boundaries of his universe. I wanted to leave behind the life I'd known and find the life I imagined. It was during my first visit as a prospective student, sitting with a group of other eighteen-year-olds in a wood-paneled room on the top floor of the admissions cottage, that I first heard about Bard's senior project. As a Bard student, I'd be required to write a book-length paper (or, if I preferred, a book) to form the capstone of my education. Right away, I thought of *Broken Lightning*. *School Kids SG* was developing well enough on its own by then, and I was wary of formalizing even a small slice of it as an academic assignment. I'd need a story for which I knew the general outline but had no concrete direction, no grand vision I'd be scared to compromise—a story I'd be willing to discover as I went but still cared enough about to commit to the journey. I entered Bard the following fall with senior year already on my mind; I was confident that, by then, I'd have found what I needed to give *Broken Lightning* its voice.

It didn't take long. My very first semester, I took a course in Chinese fiction on a whim. Something happened there: the principles of Daoism, the aesthetics of the fantastic tales by writers like Pu Song-ling, the deep concepts, like family and belonging, that were favored over formulaic Hollywood romance, and the philosophy embodied by the opposing yet complementary forces of yin and yang meshed effortlessly with the way I thought as a writer. Discovering Daoism was an instant boon for *SKSG*, but more than that, I sensed that the Chinese ideas of duality, their interpretation of the elements and nature, and even their unique literary theory were, together, a natural fit for *Broken Lightning*. I could see the story I'd been reaching for in my textbooks, waiting for me between the lines. By the time I was a sophomore, I'd made Asian Studies my official major, and as I continued gathering interests and information, I eagerly awaited the moment when I could tie it all together and try to draw out something new that still felt like it had always been there.

This book was the culmination of four very provocative and surprising years of study, but I didn't approach it as an academic. I made it a creative project first and foremost, revisiting the parts of the original story I'd held onto in my head and perceiving them all over again through the lens Bard had given me. My professors encouraged me to write this way and graded me based on the story's ideas and execution, asking only that I give a nod to the usual senior project requirements by writing a brief, scholarly paper to serve as an afterword. This is that paper, altered only so much as to be understandable to a non-academic audience, and to take into account edits made to *Broken Lightning* after my graduation.

*   *   *

The first and foremost way that my studies influenced the story was through Kurt. It was an immutable fact for me coming in that Kurt was going to be a hard man to know, distant and detached from everyone except his grandparents. He is, in fact, named for his disposition. Although he eventually becomes close with Blue, Grandma and Grandpa Ciardi are the Kurt's only family, and he has an instinctive motivation to protect them, which he does in a novel way—by allowing *them* to protect *him*, granting them control over his life so they will be less inclined to exhaust themselves worrying about what he does when they aren't present. In this way, Kurt can be seen as the embodiment of *wu wei*, "inaction" or "non-action" in English, a principle described by Laoshi as letting the world ebb and flow around oneself.

This concept appears often in the writings of the Chinese philosopher Chuang Tzu. In the chapter titled "Free and Easy Wandering," Chuang Tzu speaks of a man named Sung Jung-tzu: "The whole world could praise Sung Jung-tzu and it wouldn't make him exert himself; the whole world could condemn him and it wouldn't make him mope" (Watson 31). Chuang Tzu often expresses his ideas through anecdotes like this one, leaving his work open to widely-varied interpretation. This isn't surprising, since Chuang Tzu was known for being distrustful of language in general: "'Words exist because of meaning; once you've gotten the meaning, you can forget the words. Where can I find a man who has forgotten the words so I can have a word with him?'" (Watson 302). He seems to suggest instead that people learn best through hands-on experience: "'When [you] chisel a wheel…you can get it in your hand and feel it in your mind. You can't put it into words, and yet there's a knack to it somehow.'" (Watson 152-153).

Burton Watson offers his perceived definition of *wu wei* in the introduction to his translation of the *Chuang Tzu*: "…this term [does not mean] a forced quietude, but a course of action that is not founded upon any purposeful motives of gain or striving…[i]n such a state, all human actions become as spontaneous and mindless of those of the natural world. Man…merges himself with Tao, or the Way." (Watson 6). In *Broken Lightning*, I chose to interpret "spontaneous and mindless" *as* "naturally occurring." This is why, by the end, Kurt's choices are as "made for him" as they were when he was letting his grandparents make them, but in the sense that there's only one choice natural to Kurt, and that choice can be seen as long as he isn't explicitly striving for anything else.

This recognition of one true path, in which all his choices are obvious, is something Kurt earns over the course of the story. As soon as Kurt becomes a Linker, he is forced to start making choices on his own, and thus the end of the story represents a willful return to the state of inaction he had once stumbled upon by accident. The idea of this circle comes from Lao-tzu's *Tao te Ching*, which puts it this way: "When you know the mother, go on to know the child, after you have known the child, go back to holding fast to the mother." (Lao-tzu 59).

Besides providing a map for Kurt's developmental arc, Lao-tzu's circle of the mother also tracks with Kurt's evolving conceptualization of what does and should motivate him. He starts out protecting his loved ones, then, when he believes he's been given a greater responsibility, he resolves to protect the entire world. However, once he realizes that the welfare of those closest to him never stopped being the most important thing in his heart, he returns to acting on their behalf directly. Having come to "know the child," which in this case is his quest to restore balance to the world, Kurt is confident that going back to his original focus will allow him to succeed, because by defending his loved ones, he also defends the Earth, and may even find a more effective way to do so from that vantage point.

And then there's the more literal cycle of Kurt's relationship with his actual mother, Anna. Kurt starts by learning the truth about her, and then those revelations lead him through a sequence of events during which he comes to know himself (the child) better. In the final scenes, Kurt takes this heightened understanding of himself and his place and applies it back to his mother's ideas, and in doing so, he discovers what only he can do to repair the imbalance that threatens the Earth.

But Kurt does more than gaze inward over the course of the story: he also makes judgments and forms opinions of the people and things around him, such as the Qin Project's immortality treatment. He is skeptical of the long-life elixir's effectiveness and, in any case, he sees eternal life as something that would be a burden. To explore these feelings, I turned once again to the writing of Chuang Tzu, particularly a chapter titled "Autumn Floods." In an anecdote recorded there, Chuang Tzu speaks with two officials representing the king of Ch'u, who wishes Chuang Tzu to become administrator of the kingdom. Chuang Tzu responds to this invitation by telling the officials that he has heard of a 3,000 year-old tortoise that is kept in a box in an ancestral temple; he asks them if they think the tortoise would rather have eternal honor in death, or be alive and dragging its tail in the mud. When the officials respond that it would probably prefer the latter, Chuang Tzu says, "'Go away! I'll drag my tail in the mud!'" (Watson 188).

On the surface of this, it seems like Chuang Tzu might advocate the use of the Qin Project immunization. But as Kurt points out in Act IV, wanting a lifetime isn't the same thing as wanting immortality, and in the case of the turtle, being "immortalized" as sacred is presented as the opposite of being free to seek pleasure. Therefore, I see Kurt and Chuang Tzu as being in agreement: they both argue that it's better to live a normal, worry-free life than to strive for something which may seem better, but which would be troublesome in reality.

*   *   *

For the most part, the functions and limitations of Linking power remain unchanged from the first draft of *Broken Lightning* I started and abandoned in high school. Still, I looked to several Chinese texts and traditions as I began my first serious and in-depth exploration of the rules that govern the *qi ren.*

The tradition of the Chinese fantastic tale, in particular the writing of Pu Song-ling, was a major source of aesthetic inspiration for me. One of Pu Song-ling's most famous works is *Liao-zhai's Record of Wonders*, a collection of stories involving encounters between humans, spirits, and immortals, each of which ends with commentary added by the "recorder," as though someone actually witnessed these events. One of these stories, "Blue Maid," tells of a man named Huo Huan who married an immortal woman. In order to retrieve her from the immortal realm, which exists inside a mountain behind walls of solid rock, Huo Huan must use a magic trowel given to him by a Daoist, which could "cut into the stone of the garden wall, which, at every motion of [the Daoist's] hand, fell away as if it were decomposed." (Owen 1120). I thought of this object more than once while visualizing Kurt's weapon, Stardust. Additionally, the tone and style of "Blue Maid" and the other stories in the *Record of Wonders* helped me write the "Broken Lightning" legend Blue finds in Anna's study.

It is explained in *Broken Lightning* that the power of Linkers comes from body qi, which is constantly regenerated by the Linker's original qi. There are many Daoist texts that speak of original qi as separate from other qi—it's described as a small amount of energy that makes a person who they are, present from birth until death. By reading Livia Kohn's analyses of Daoist religion and culture, I also learned that Daoists believe in, "two essential souls…[which] form the nucleus of primordial *qi* and make up the living person; the *hun* or spirit soul of celestial origin, and the *po* or material soul that belongs to earth…," and that "[a] newly-buried person was still thought to be present [for several generations after death]…the two souls [would just be] starting to separate, [and] *qi* would still be active in the body…." (Kohn 56). With a little poetic license, I fused the idea of two kinds of qi together with this idea of two souls, and came up not just with a basic "soul map" (Figure 1) to hint at the way life and death work in Kurt's world, but also with the operating principle of the Siphon Stone.

Eric is able to use the stone to steal original qi from living bodies, deconstructing and disrupting the *hun* soul but leaving the *po* soul and the body qi surrounding it intact. Therefore, the person is still present in their body even though part of them is inside the Siphon Stone, generating body qi for Eric to use. Kurt uses Stardust to create a bridge between himself and the drained via mutual understanding, which allows him to access their *po* souls and their remaining body qi. Blue says in Act VII that Eric created "a new kind of death," but depending on how you look at it, Eric and Kurt may have also created new kinds of collective life, both of which depend on the Daoist idea that death grants people the ability to be in two places at once.

The other major component of Linking besides qi is, of course, the set of elements on which a Linker can draw. The actual Chinese language had the biggest influence on this part of *Broken Lightning*'s mythology, but it didn't help me

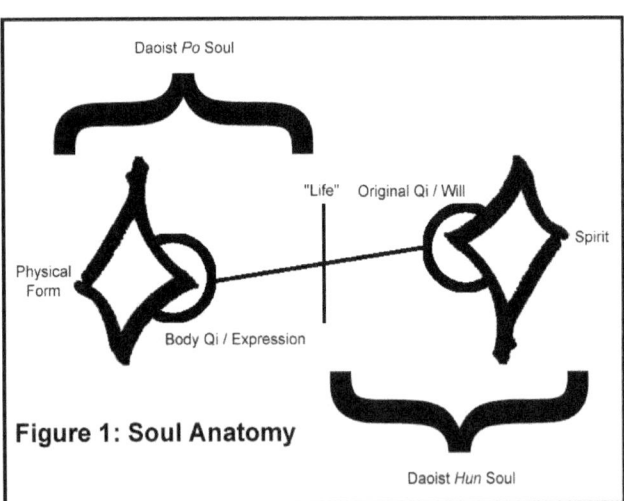

Figure 1: Soul Anatomy

Daoist *Po* Soul

"Life"   Original Qi / Will

Spirit

Physical Form

Body Qi / Expression

Daoist *Hun* Soul

decide which elements to choose so much as how many. In Chinese, the number four is considered unlucky because it is a homophone for the word "death" (both are pronounced *si*). Three, therefore, is a lucky number because it stops short of four—this is why many ancient Chinese poems have three stanzas (*e.g.*, "Dew on the Way," circa 600 BC, according to Stephen Owen's *An Anthology of Chinese Literature*), and why the line patterns used by the *I Ching* to perform divinations appear as trigrams and hexagrams, multiples of three. With all this precedent in place, it seemed fitting to set up the Linking elements in a way consistent with the reverence of the number three, *i.e.*, organized primarily into three pairs; I even carried threes over into other aspects of Linking, such as the limit on the number of warping pads Kurt can place.

Besides examining the mechanics of Linking, I also relied on my studies to explain how people would make the leap from being normal to being a Linker, and suggest the methods by which Linkers might come to hone their elemental skills. Lama Thubten Yeshe, a master of Tantric Buddhism, says, "Instead of viewing pleasure and desire as something to be avoided at all costs, tantra recognizes the powerful energy aroused by our desires to be an indispensable resource for the spiritual path. […] [B]ecause our present life is so inseparably linked with desire…we must make use of desire's tremendous energy if we wish to transform our life into something transcendental." (Yeshe 19-21). It made sense to me that Kurt would be scared by the unfamiliarity of his powers at first, yet still remain curious as to why it felt good to use them. With this as my foundation, and with Laoshi acting as a guide, I imagined Kurt overcoming his fear by giving into and then exploring his desire. The good feeling associated with Linking became his reason to continue practicing and refining his control, as well as an indicator of whether he was discovering something new and useful or pushing himself too hard. Using Kurt as a case study, I essentially proposed that the training of a Linker is similar to the path of Tantric enlightenment.

Then there is the matter of the runes themselves—in particular, the way that they tie into Kurt's and Eric's identities, and the way that Kurt's rune sometimes seems to communicate ideas or directions to him. Beyond the idea of inverted light and dark symbols, I approached the design and nature of the runes by way of the *I Ching*. A "primary manual of divination…consulted for an oracle message by following a process of manipulating yarrow sticks, [which] to a great extent it is still used in this way today" (Yao 57-58), the *I Ching* describes all eight possible trigrams (sets of three solid or broken lines) and the sixty-four hexagrams which can be made by combining them into pairs. When spontaneously formed and recognized during certain rituals, these patterns and their assigned meanings form the building blocks of ancient Chinese fortune-telling. Incorporating this branch of Asian Studies into *Broken Lightning* was one of the last decisions I made before I started writing, and by putting the *I Ching* in Blue's hands, I was able to employ hexagrams to enrich the runes (and some of the constructs and phenomena that extend from them) in ways that helped me develop plot, character, and subtext.

Hexagram number two, *k'un*, the Passive Principle, is comprised of six broken or Yin lines, which "symbolize the qualities of the Yin principle—earthly, passive, negative, female, dark and so forth." (Blofield 49). It may seem incorrect to have assigned this hexagram to Kurt's rune rather than Eric's, but I did so for several reasons. First,

Figure 2: The Yin and Yang Wheel

the classic diagram of the yin and yang wheel (Figure 2) shows that each half contains a small circle of the other, implying that Kurt should possess some attribute that would normally be associated with Eric. (Although we never see Eric's rune up close during the story, it contains hexagram number one, *ch'ien*, the Creative principle, comprised of six unbroken lines.) Second, the cause of the imbalance in nature is reversed in Act VII, making light and dark exchange places entirely. In other words, the positions of the two sides of the wheel are both mixed and malleable. Finally, according to the Wikipedia aggregate of translations from several times and sources, *k'un* can also be interpreted to describe the Receptive principle—that which gives in without giving up, going with the flow. That would seem to fit Kurt's personality, his beliefs, and his ultimate actions perfectly.

Kurt's rune produces two more hexagrams in addition to the one it bears. The first, created through "accidental divination" when Kurt causes cracks to form on the blade of the original Stardust, is number fifty-two, *kên*, meaning Desisting, Stilling, or "The Keeping Still." ("I Ching"). Blofield writes, "When it is time to stop, then stop; when the time comes for action, then act! By choosing activity and stillness, each at the proper time, a man achieves glorious progress. The stillness imaged by this hexagram means stillness in its proper place." (Blofield 187). This seemed like the perfect hexagram to tell Kurt and Blue what to do at the Pequopsee Reservation, and it also implies, once again, that Kurt's final decision will be one of *wu wei*. The second extra hexagram is number forty-five, *ts'ui*, which means Gathering Together or Assembling according to Blofield. It appears within the blade of the true Stardust—an extension of Kurt's rune —once Kurt learns how to form it. Again, Blofield adds color: "Persistence in a righteous course brings reward…[t]his hexagram implies assembling. Willing acceptance is conjoined with joy. A firm line (the fifth) occupies the central position (in the upper trigram) and wins response from the other lines…(our actions will) accord with the will of heaven." (Blofield 174). This description corresponds to both the true purpose of Stardust and the plan Kurt devises at the end of Act VII. By using Stardust to assemble all the people of the world into a grid, Kurt is able to equal Eric's power, and in using the grid to accomplish his personal goal of restoring his loved ones' qi to their bodies (as opposed to focusing on his cosmological goal of restoring balance to the world), he willingly accepts his own truth, and from that starting point, he ends up saving the world after all. His actions do, therefore, "accord with the will of heaven."

Having examined the types and behavior of qi, the ways a Linker might train, and the nature of a Linker's rune, I at last considered the mental aspects of Kurt's powers, which not only help him unlock the final secrets of Linking, but are also integral to his periodic dreams. There is a famous passage in the *Chuang Tzu* in which Chuang Tzu describes a time when Chuang Chou dreamed he was a butterfly, unaware that he was Chuang Chou. He then awoke, but "he didn't know if he was Chuang Chou who had dreamt he was a butterfly, or a butterfly [now] dreaming he was Chuang Chou. Between Chuang Chou and a butterfly there must be *some* distinction! This is called the Transformation of Things." (Watson 49). Kurt's final dream and the acquisition of Stardust reflect some of my thoughts on this relativism and the search for "distinction." Did the sword form in Kurt's hand as he meditated, thus causing it to be present in the dream? Or did the sword only appear in the waking world after Kurt dreamt about it? Where did the details of the dream really come from? How were Laoshi, Blue, Kayla, Grandma, and Grandpa present in the dream, and what might the nature of their presence say about the boundaries not just between dreaming and waking, but between Kurt's mind and any of theirs? In this case, I didn't so much borrow Daoist themes for *Broken Lightning* as allow Daoist questions, the very essence of philosophy, to guide me in conjuring thought-exercise scenarios and asking questions of my own within the story—questions that aren't necessarily intended to have fixed answers.

There are several other instances of crossover between Kurt's dreams and reality, such as the initial appearance of his rune, the nagging familiarity he senses about the rooms in the Darklight Tower, and, of course, the transfer of knowledge to him from Anna. All of these are based on the musing at the heart of the Transformation of Things—the idea that the borders which define reality as we know it start to seem less concrete as you consider a plurality of perspectives—and I think that resonates in a story that defines the apocalypse in terms of nonmoralistic change. Linking, in this context, is the act of breaking down distinctions in the service of an overall balance, and because the questions that led me to it were Daoist in origin, this answer, and many other possible answers, are themselves inherently steeped in Daoism.

*   *   *

Riktalash first appears less than ten pages into the story, and although its name, history, and relevance are only revealed gradually, the island kingdom and its monarch are two of *Broken Lightning*'s key ingredients. One of the most enjoyable and unexpected parts of approaching this project through the lens of Asian Studies was the imperative to draw on a variety of new influences and unlock a better understanding of Riktalash, both for the purpose of defining clear details to enrich the text and to add new dimensions and perspectives to plot and character.

As a world close to ending, Riktalash was an island full of Linkers, meaning that their society was both governed and populated by people bearing either a light or dark rune. Duality, then, was embedded in their lives, and although an isolated society couldn't have literally been "Daoist," it seemed plausible to say that a similar way of thinking could have grown out of their situation. Therefore, I first imagined the Riktali as a people that perceived the world in terms of complementary opposites, and given that their whole world consisted of an island and the ocean, the interplay between land and sea became one of the primal truths guiding the queen and lending shape to her goals. Despite New York's proximity to Eric and its suitability for his plan to lure the military, I don't believe it's a coincidence that the queen and her host sought another island city to serve as their base.

Since the ocean and shore, as basic forces of the world, are constantly touching and interacting, it would seem to make sense for the Riktali to instinctively look for that tension elsewhere in the world and amongst themselves, being ever conscious of the thin dividing line between yin and yang. This is where the name and concept of the "Darklight Tower" came from. I pictured Eric's tower as a reproduction of a Riktali ceremonial site (formerly one of the palace spires), designed as a meeting place for the two halves of the world in all their forms, where struggles between them could be resolved. Rituals of great importance were observed and took place there, including the creation of the Siphon Stone by Queen Riktalash, as seen in Kurt's dream. I believe that the similarities in décor between Eric's tower and the original are telling—although reimagined with modern aesthetics, the nature and meaning of the place remain the same.

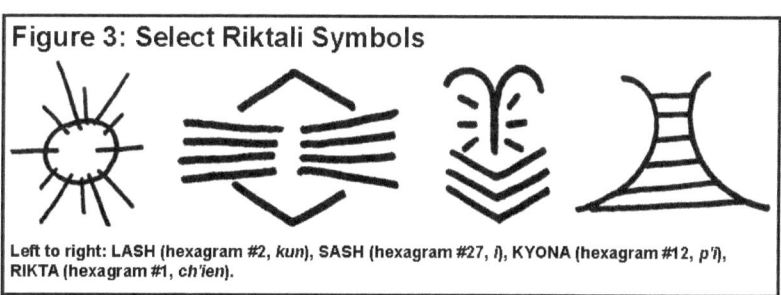

Figure 3: Select Riktali Symbols

Left to right: LASH (hexagram #2, *kun*), SASH (hexagram #27, *i*), KYONA (hexagram #12, *p'i*), RIKTA (hexagram #1, *ch'ien*).

To delve even further into the Riktali way of thinking, I decided to create a handful of characters in their language. Having already built the hexagrams of the *I Ching* into the runes, starting from those line patterns and then embellishing them made sense. This began as a primarily artistic undertaking—I wanted to know what the symbols looked like so that I could better describe them in the story. However, thinking about what the Riktali might have added to the hexagrams also helped me imagine what

Riktalash was like as a society, which added depth to both the dream sequences and the ethereally-present Queen Riktalash.

I went back to *ch'ien* and *k'un* to create the first pair of Riktali symbols, one for the Creative and one for the Receptive (Figure 3). These symbols prompted me to do the most thinking about Riktalash's unique viewpoint—while deciding how to stylize the hexagrams into characters that would carry the spirit of yin and yang, I focused on the Riktali perception of the sea as the creative source of life, and the natural tide pools on the shore as receivers. This led me to design one symbol as a wave and the other as a sinkhole, and from there, I extrapolated an entire artistic sensibility for Riktalash based on the immutable and ever-present building blocks of nature, chiefly the flowing of water and the stationary aspect of rock. These ideas helped me form the approach I used for the art of other Riktali symbols, and they gave me the vision of a city carved from the landscape that I tried to impart through Kurt's dreams and the "Broken Lightning" fantastic tale. Although the Riktali didn't necessarily exist in harmony with the natural world, its presence loomed large in their lives, both because they had to look to nature for their means of survival and because they were able to engage with the Earth directly, through Linking.

Two more important Riktali symbols came from hexagrams twelve and twenty-seven (*p'i*, obstruction and *i*, swallowing, respectively). Hexagram number twelve refers to, "Stagnation (obstruction) caused by evil-doers…heaven and earth cut off from each other. To conserve his stock of virtues, the Superior Man withdraws into himself and thus escapes from the evil influences around him" (Blofield 112), and number twenty-seven refers to, "Nourishing…[w]atch people nourishing others and observe what manner of things they seek to nourish themselves… [p]ersistence brings good fortune to those who nourish themselves on what is fitting" (Blofield 140). *P'i* became the Seal of Broken Lightning, because it describes the nature of the seal as well as the method Kurt discovers to break it. Conversely, I used a somewhat twisted interpretation of *i*'s meaning to create the emblem of the Siphon Stone, casting Eric and Queen Riktalash as anti-sages who would nourish themselves on what is improper and thus eventually have ill fortune.

But leaving all language, philosophy, and detail aside, Riktalash was primarily inspired by Chinese ideas of immortality. The islands and other lands of the immortals are often spoken of in fantastic tales, but it was the appearance of immortality elixirs and the quest for long life in actual

Chinese history that caught my attention the most. In *The Grand Scribe's Records*, Si-ma Qian speaks of Shih Huangdi, the first ruler of the short-lived Qin empire, and his quest to become immortal:

> "Hsu-fu of Ch'i and others memorialized, saying that there were three islands of immortals in the sea, called P'eng-lai, Fang-chang, and Ying-chou, where the immortals lived… The Emperor [Qin Shi Huangdi] thus had Han Chung, Master Hou, and Scholar Shih seek for the long life elixirs of the immortals…the First Emperor…was enraged, "I have…recruited…the practitioners of [magic] methods, to seek wondrous drugs by means of alchemy. Now I have heard that <u>Han Chung has never reported back after he left</u>, and Hsu Fu and his associates have spent cash countable only in myriads, but the elixir is yet to be found." (Ch'ien 142-150, emphasis mine)

Following from this passage, I imagined an end to the life and adventures of Han Chung, both to explore the identities of Riktalash and its queen through conflict, and to explain how the Siphon Stone could have made it from Riktalash to America.

*   *   *

By far, the most prevalent way I fused Asian Studies with my story was to build a Daoist cosmological structure into Kurt's world: the entire *Broken Lightning* universe is predicated on an unending cycle, as illustrated by the yin and yang wheel. By viewing this cycle in terms of the forces which can bring stress upon it—for example, man intruding upon nature—I was able to explore and find new applications for some key philosophical concepts, examining them in the contexts of free will, the human mind, and morality, among others. *Broken Lightning*, here, was my vehicle for exploration, and an opportunity to perform case studies in my personal understanding and interpretation of Daoism.

To begin with, *Broken Lightning* suggests two ways the yin and yang cycle might be rendered imperfect: the wheel could stop turning, becoming "stuck" on either side, or one half of the wheel could grow larger than the other, threatening to dominate the entire wheel. These interpretations are not mutually exclusive—as Blue notes in Act VII, a wheel dominated by only death would be "stuck" by default, as no alternate (life) side would exist to turn and trade places with it. But no matter what terms are used to describe it, an imbalance in the wheel essentially means that one half has gained outsize strength at the expense of the other. Lao-tzu tells us that the height of yin is the beginning of yang and vice versa, through lines such as, "[t]he heavy is the root of the light" (Lao-tzu 31), and "[t]urning back is how the way moves" (Lao-tzu 47). Visually speaking, this means the fattest portion of either half of the wheel is where that half is strongest, but it is also where the other half's tail begins. In a scenario where the two parts of the wheel aren't the same size anymore, this progression is no longer as clear-cut. Thus, the world ceases to function correctly.

Kurt would have liked to nurture the weaker side of the imbalance by bringing an end to the Qin Project, but once that became impossible, he came up with an alternate method—he nurtured the strong side of the imbalance and waited for the weak side to resurge on its own. Kurt may not have been thinking in such cosmic terms (he saw his plan as a simple act of overloading the Siphon Stone), but nevertheless, the fact that this approach could work at all assumes a second yin and yang wheel that supersedes the wheel of life and death on Earth. To use Laoshi's demarcations from the end of the story, this second wheel would have to exist in the domain of Heaven. From the point of view of the larger wheel, imbalance itself is just the complementary opposite of balance, and would start to give way after reaching its height. To my mind, this suggests that even an out-of-control imbalance in nature should begin resolving itself at the very moment it takes complete hold. As suggested by Laoshi, getting to that tipping point one way or another is the whole reason the Earth creates Linkers. This might appear to render the entire conflict of *Broken Lightning* moot, but remember that allowing Eric to reach full power in order to bring about his downfall was not the optimal sequence of events, as far as Kurt was concerned. More of the world Kurt knew would have been preserved if the original imbalance (the Qin Project) could have simply been removed.

To take a more humanistic look at Daoism, I turned once more to the *Chuang Tzu*. Watson refers to this passage from Chuang Tzu's "Discussion on Making All Things Equal" as "fiendish" and translates it as follows:

"Everything has its "that," everything has its "this." From the point of view of "that" you cannot see it, but through understanding you can know it. So I say, "that" comes out of "this" and "this" depends on "that"—which is to say "this" and "that" give birth to each other. […] [T]he sage does not proceed in such a way, but illuminates all in the light of Heaven. He too recognizes a "this," but a "this" which is also "that," a "that" which is also "this." […] A state in which "this" and "that" no longer find their opposites is called the hinge of the Way. […] [The man of far-reaching vision] relies upon [the constant] alone, relies upon it and does not know he is doing so. This is called the Way." (Watson 39-40)

I think what's being suggested here is that there are actually three parts to the yin and yang wheel, not two. In the story, Laoshi calls them the yin, the yang, and the "other," that last part being the yin and yang turning in harmony, or, to put it another way, the completed wheel taken as an entity in itself. By giving the unified state of the yin and yang its own name, "the hinge of the Way," and stating that from this perspective, the natures of the wheel's two halves change (they no longer "give birth" to each other but instead simply exist together), Chuang Tzu is saying that the completed wheel is more than the sum of its components. It is a unique, third thing that can and should be examined separately.

Laoshi draws a connection between the yin and yang and the id and superego of human (Freudian) psychology. Just as the yin and yang turn together to create the other, the id and superego combine to form the ego, the functioning person. Kurt is never more of a complete man than when he finds the one place where his desires and duties intersect—using his powers on behalf of the people he cares about. In addition to being a new application for Daoism, this way of thinking provides another explanation for how Kurt fulfills his ultimate purpose as a Linker, because as Laoshi said, a Linker who has reached his full potential both contains and embodies the other, or in this case, the ego. As is revealed in Act VI, only a human conscious of and following his heart has something to offer the Earth in the trade of Linking, and if ego is synonymous with personhood, then only a man who has achieved the proper balance of id and superego can even be called fully human. While this may not definitively put the question of fate vs. free will to rest, the importance of the individual self in this equation is a powerful argument in favor of Kurt's point of view, at least in his world.

The idea of the yin and yang as complements, not simply opposites, is key to the formation of *Broken Lightning*'s complex and, at times, relativistic morality. At the beginning, Kurt sees the world in simple terms —his job is to "save" the Earth from the imbalance, which he assumes must be caused by some malevolent force. Therefore, Eric becomes the "bad guy" while Kurt is the "good guy." Extending that logic further, Kurt believes that Light Linkers are inherently good and Dark Linkers are inherently bad; because Eric and Hydrad were cruel to her, Kayla comes to this conclusion as well, and Kurt's superficial impressions of those two Dark Linkers provide him with no reason to adjust his attitude or expectations. Only at the end of Act V, when Blue implies that the man who killed Kurt's parents might have had good intentions, do the lines start to blur. From that point on, Kurt moves steadily toward the position of the moral "other," one who can see past his immediate judgments of peoples' actions and goals to the framework that explains them, and to their position within a broader context. That mentality allows him to see himself and Eric as two halves of the same whole, each with their own desires but both part of a system that has no intrinsic tendency toward good or evil. At that point, Kurt becomes a sage or Superior Man, and from his new perspective, he is able to conceive of and accept the only remaining solution to the imbalance, which a less-developed version of himself might have dismissed as "letting Eric win."

The final ways in which *Broken Lightning* expresses its Daoist cosmology are mechanical and cosmetic. Including these details was my way of showing that Asian Studies had influenced every part of this book, from its thematic fundamentals to its literal presentation; it was also fun to think about how the mundane aspects of Kurt's world might call back to its deeper nature. The most obvious examples of visible Daoism are the many pairs of complementary opposites in the story; to begin with, there are two Light Linkers and two Dark Linkers, and both members of each pair have names that sound vaguely alike (Kurt and Kayla, Rick and Eric). Also, though they come to possess it differently, Kurt and Eric eventually obtain equal amounts of qi, for use in combat or otherwise (they are evenly powered at the point their purple and yellow auras turn to black and white, evoking the image of the yin and yang wheel). Kurt and Eric also each have the spirit of a dead woman inside them, augmenting their powers and acting as silent guides and guardians. It is through Anna and Riktalash that they come to two very different interpretations of nature, which turn out to be the same after all.

Even the setup of the elements themselves shows an opposite-complement structure. There are three each of the Light and Dark elements, and each one has a counterpart force in the other group. These Light and Dark element pairings are complementary as well as opposing because, taken together, they form the whole of nature, and because one doesn't so much cancel out the other as transform it (for example, combining water with fire would yield steam). Qi, as the "seventh element," represents the "other" in exactly the way Laoshi describes—it exists at the meeting places of man and Earth, of Earth and element, of soul and body, and thus both represents and enables a variety of connections that result in distinct wholes. Together, the elements map out the entirety of Kurt's world, a microcosm of the larger forces at play as well as the tool set that helps define them. In the literal as well as the metaphorical sense, the elements are everything.

*   *   *

Broken Lightning is more than just the final version of that old high-school story—it is my undergraduate thesis. In this project, and at Bard overall, I learned to enjoy my education again and to see how much good studying all kinds of different topics could do for my writing. I discovered new sources of inspiration, started asking new layers of questions, and found new drive to carry me into my adult life and writing career. I owe it all to the teachers who worked with me, to the friends and family who supported me, and to you, who read me.

Works Cited or Consulted

Blofield, John. I Ching (The Book of Change). New York: E.P. Dutton & Co, Inc, 1968.

Ch'ien, Ssu-Ma, William H. Nienhauser, Jr. (ed), Tsai-fa Cheng et. al. (translators). The Grand Scribe's Records, Volume I: The Basic Annals of Pre-Han China. Indianapolis, ID: Indiana University Press, 1994.

Grinnell, George Bird. "Adventures of Bull Turns Round." Access Genealogy. June 17th, 2004. April 23rd, 2006. <http://www.accessgenealogy.com/scripts/data/database.cgi? file=Data&report=SingleArticle&ArticleID=0024683>.

"I Ching." Wikipedia: The Free Encyclopedia. Various. March 30th, 2006. April 5th, 2006 <http://en.wikipedia.org/wiki/Book_of_changes>.

Kohn, Livia, ed. Daoism and Chinese Culture. Cambridge, MA: Three Pines Press, 2001.

Lao tzu. Tao te Ching. London: Penguin Books, 1963.

Learn Chinese Characters. April 23rd, 2006. <http://www.zhongwen.com>.

Owen, Stephen ed. An Anthology of Chinese Literature. New York, NY: W.W. Norton & Company, 1996.

Shan, Jun. "Chinese Name and English Name." About.com. The New York Times Company. April 12th, 2006 <http://chineseculture.about.com/library/name/blname.htm >.

Watson, Burton. The Complete Works of Chuang Tzu. New York, NY: Columbia University Press, 1968.

Yao, Xinzhong. An Introduction to Confucianism. Cambridge, UK: Cambridge University Press, 2000.

Yeshe, Lama Thubten, Jonathan Landaw (ed). Introduction to Tantra: A Vision of Totality. Boston, MA: Wisdom Publications, 1987.

About the Author

Jonathan V. Cann was born in Manhattan, raised in suburban New Jersey, and educated in upstate New York. He holds a degree in Asian Studies from Bard College, and has written novels, memoirs, video games, and comics. He lives in Queens.

www.ingramcontent.com/pod-product-compliance
Lightning Source LLC
Chambersburg PA
CBHW070905180626
46817CB00003B/923

*9 7 8 0 9 8 9 4 8 5 2 3 4 *